THE GIRL SHE LEFT BEHIND

JO BARTLETT

Boldwood

First published in 2024 in Great Britain by Boldwood Books Ltd.

Cover Design by Head Design Ltd

Cover Photography: Shutterstock

A CIP catalogue record for this book is available from the British Library.

Paperback ISBN 978-1-83533-650-2

Large Print ISBN 978-1-83533-651-9

Hardback ISBN 978-1-83533-649-6

Ebook ISBN 978-1-83533-652-6

Kindle ISBN 978-1-83533-653-3

Audio CD ISBN 978-1-83533-644-1

MP3 CD ISBN 978-1-83533-645-8

Digital audio download ISBN 978-1-83533-648-9

Boldwood Books Ltd
23 Bowerdean Street
London SW6 3TN
www.boldwoodbooks.com

For L, who couldn't stay, with much love xx

AUTHOR'S NOTE

Dear Reader,

Writing this novel has been a labour of love. It tackles perhaps the most emotive of subjects: suicide. I have family members and close friends who have been affected by suicide, attempted suicide, and severe mental health challenges, which I could never hope to do justice to in a work of fiction. It's an incredibly complex and painful subject, and no one person's experiences of these issues will be the same as another's. I hope with all my heart that nothing in this novel causes anyone whose life has been touched by this kind of tragedy to feel any additional pain, and I have spoken to therapists and social workers, reviewed police procedures, and had the support of three brilliant editors in trying to tell Phoebe's and Lucy's stories in the most sensitive of ways, because I believe what they go through is an incredibly important story to tell. The legacy of childhood trauma is often devastating, but again it can affect people so differently and lead to such diverse outcomes, and I wanted the sisters' stories to represent this.

If you have been affected by any of the themes in this novel, please reach out for support at one of the sources below:

www.samaritans.org

www.mind.org.uk

www.thecalmzone.net

www.childline.org.uk

www.missingpeople.org.uk

www.womensaid.org.uk

Take care and much love to you all.

Jo xx

1
_____

I'm still not sure if I can do this. Even as I sit here on the sand, watching the boats chug out to sea and disappear from view, I'm asking myself if I can possibly disappear too. I've been here for hours, scribbling in my sketchbook, as Mum always puts it, and weighing up whether or not to leave.

I thought it would be easy – when I was at the kitchen table, writing you that note and trying to explain why I was leaving behind all the things that were supposed to give me a reason to live. But sitting on this beach, the grey waves crashing over each other as they race towards the shore, I'm starting to lose my nerve.

In some ways, it would be so much easier to climb back up the path and head home, as if the intention to disappear had never crossed my mind. The bus back to Appleberry runs every half an hour and I could be home before anyone even knows I've gone. That way, you'll never have to get the call telling you about my note. But, deep down, I know I can't do that.

A dog walker strolled past me and held his hand up in greeting; it was all so normal. Everyone else's lives are carrying on, but mine has unravelled like a dropped cotton reel and, as hard as I try, I can still only think of one way out. It will hurt a handful of people, but they'll get over it and I won't have to be around to watch the fall-out. But if I stay, it will be much worse, because there's a good chance, if I do, that a monster will get her own way – the same monster I've drawn in my sketchbooks from the moment I could hold a pencil. She wouldn't recognise herself, because she doesn't see a monster when she looks in the mirror. But you'd know it was her instantly. I wish I could leave you this last drawing, and the explanation I've written here, but I'm taking this sketchbook with me. If I don't hold it in my arms when I go, there's an even greater chance I'll turn back. I need to feel her with me, in the pages of this book, pressed up against my chest. She's the reason I'm doing this and, when I'm gone, the world might finally listen to why I had no choice. There's no other way, deep inside I know that, but it's still not easy to leave.

I'm going now, before I change my mind. I'm as ready as I'll ever be and the note I wrote is here, inside the pocket of my coat, the envelope crumpled into a ball long before I put it there. You see, just this morning, I was so close to changing my mind that I threw it away, only to fish it out of the wastepaper bin and stuff it into my pocket – decision made. Probably.

I'm asking a lot of you, I know that. But you can't mess things up any more than I have, and I really believe you'll get this right for Darcy, in a way I never could. That's why I need to stop writing now, stand up and drop my coat onto the rocks behind me, before I take my first step towards the sea. It's time to go.

2

'Can you see it? That's the outline, just there.' The doctor jabbed his finger in the direction of what looked to Phoebe exactly like the rest of the grey blobs on the screen.

'So it hasn't grown?' Brushing the tips of her fingers across the part of her neck where the lump sat, she shivered. He probably made hundreds of life-changing diagnoses, but at least she wouldn't be one of them.

'No, the follow-up tests and biopsy show it's definitely benign and there's been no change in the last three months. I think we can safely say it's stable.' He turned away from the screen that was displaying the results of her latest ultrasound. 'In fact, it's probably been there for years.'

'It wouldn't surprise me.' Phoebe muttered the words under her breath; the last thing anyone wanted to hear was her sorry tale. 'Do you think I should do something about it?'

'There are a couple of options. I can put you on the list to have it removed or you can just leave it in there, if there aren't any sudden changes.'

'I don't think I'll bother having it taken out if it's not dangerous. I've been swallowing golf balls for so long it would probably just come back anyway.' The doctor's eyebrows almost disappeared into his receding hairline. 'Not literally swallowing them, I mean *emotionally*.' Phoebe was already wishing she'd kept her big mouth shut. Even saying a word like 'emotionally' out loud made her want to disappear up her own behind.

'Ah.' The doctor clearly hadn't been expecting that sort of admission either and he probably didn't want to open up a can of worms that were well outside his remit. He was an ear, nose and throat specialist, dealing with a benign thyroid tumour, not the kind of psychotherapy expert Phoebe probably should have opened up to. 'So you feel the effects of the tumour more when you're stressed?'

'I guess. That's when I feel like something's physically lodged in my throat and it makes it hard to swallow. But they told me last time it's all just psychosomatic.'

'And do you get stressed a lot?' Maybe he fancied a change from examining ear canals after all.

'Not really.' Out of the corner of her eye, Phoebe caught a glimpse of the countryside scene on the consultant's wall and for a moment her thoughts drifted to Appleberry. 'Not since I moved to London anyway.'

'Really? Most people find it far more stressful living here.'

'I know.' Phoebe didn't add the words that were burning in her throat – at the very place where the tumour quietly sat – *but most people haven't grown up with a mother like mine.*

* * *

Phoebe scrabbled around in the bottomless bag, which had seemed such a good idea when she wanted to fit her MacBook or a pile of paperwork in it. But when she needed to find her keys in a hurry, it was a nightmare. Just as she finally hooked the keys out of the dark recesses of the bag, she dropped them straight onto the floor. Standing up after she'd retrieved them, all the blood seemed to rush down to her feet. That must have been why she thought she could see something that couldn't possibly be there – a pheasant perched on the roof of her car, his yellow-rimmed eyes boring right into her soul. It was like spotting a refrigerator wedged between the barriers on the central reservation of a motorway, it was so out of place. But it was definitely there and it was staring at her too.

'What the hell are you doing here?' She hated the way it just kept looking at her, its unblinking eyes fixed onto hers. It didn't make any sense. The nearest stretch of open countryside was miles away and the only birds she ever saw these days were pigeons. The pheasant seemed far less fazed and it was showing absolutely no sign of moving. She'd always hated being in close proximity to birds, ever since being chased down a farm track in Appleberry by an angry goose. Their beaks seemed specifically designed to attack and the squawking was like someone raking their fingernails down a blackboard. She didn't even like the bird-song that everyone else raved about, especially not the four o'clock morning chorus outside her bedroom window when she'd still lived in Appleberry. Give her London any day, and city pigeons who knew how to stay out of their fellow Londoners' way, exactly like the humans who lived alongside them.

'I don't care if you're here on a day trip to see the King, you can sod off now because I need to get to a meeting.' Phoebe waved her arms in the air and got onto her tiptoes, sure she'd seen something in a documentary about making yourself look as big as possible to scare off animals. It might have been a documentary about bears, but surely the same principle had to apply. Apparently, the pheasant didn't think so, because its only response was to peck the roof of her car.

'Oh for God's sake.' She was having a Mexican stand-off with a bloody bird. She had a meeting scheduled with the director of digital marketing at her firm's biggest client, the sort of contract that would prove she'd finally made it to the top level of the business. But she couldn't even outwit a pheasant.

Pulling her phone out of her bag, she clicked on the screen. There had to be an article on Google about how to chase off birds. Failing that, she could throw the phone at the pheasant, but some do-gooder who'd never fallen into a bank of stinging nettles trying to outrun a goose, would probably jump out from behind a tree and perform a citizen's arrest.

When the phone suddenly burst into life, it very nearly followed her keys onto the tarmac. Her dad's number flashed up on the screen and for a moment she debated whether to answer it. She could always tell him later that she had still been in with the consultant when he rang, and put off hearing about her mother's latest drama until she had a glass of wine in her hand. But that wasn't fair on him. He had to live with her mother day in and day out. God only knew how he wasn't permanently attached to a bottle of something alcoholic. He was either a saint or a masochist, and Phoebe could never quite make up her mind which.

'Dad.' She got the word out somehow, despite how hard she was gritting her teeth.

'Oh thank God, I thought you might be in a meeting and not be able to answer your phone!' He was breathless, and she was so sure she knew what was coming that his next sentence literally took her breath away. 'It's Lucy; she's gone missing.'

'What do you mean, *missing*?' Despite the pheasant still fixing her with his beady eyes, she had to lean against the car to stop herself from sliding down it. Her sister had every reason to want to *leave* Appleberry, to tell their mother where she could stick her opinions, and never look back. But the word *missing* had very different connotations, and Phoebe was suddenly aware of her own heartbeat as it seemed to double in pace.

'No one's heard from her for two days.' Her father paused for a moment. 'They found her coat at Craggy Head, but nothing else… At least not yet.'

'What was she doing at Craggy Head?' Phoebe's mind was racing ahead, to a place she didn't want it to go. Craggy Head was more than twenty miles from Appleberry and it was famous for all the wrong reasons: as a suicide blackspot. But there had to be another explanation, any other explanation. Lucy would never willingly leave her young daughter, Darcy, behind.

'I've got no idea.' Her father sounded exhausted, as though he'd been up all night worrying about his youngest child. Even if he had, it was far too little, too late. 'She had a row with your mother and we hadn't seen her in over a week. I thought she was just keeping out of the way until things calmed down a bit.'

'Is Darcy with you?' Phoebe might have been the sort of hands-off aunt whose contact with her niece consisted mainly of extravagant gifts, rather than regular visits, but she couldn't bear the thought of the little girl being left with her grandparents while her mother was missing. Darcy certainly wouldn't get any comfort from her grandmother. Her father might try, but anything nice he did for anyone other than his wife had to be done covertly. Otherwise, there'd be hell to pay. That was the way it had always been and most of the time it seemed it was easier for him not to bother doing anything at all.

'Darcy's staying with one of Lucy's friends. Your sister made up some story about us all going to a family wedding where children weren't invited. It was her friend who raised the alarm when she didn't arrive to pick Darcy up. Then someone found her coat lying across the rocks at Craggy Head.' He sounded as if he couldn't believe his own words.

'Just her coat?' That didn't necessarily mean anything; it was only a coat. Maybe someone else had taken the coat from Lucy or she'd been mugged and was sitting in a hospital somewhere, confused and with no ID to help the medics work out who she was. If Phoebe was clutching at straws, she couldn't help it. Guilt at their last conversation was already tightening the lump in her throat, making her more aware of it than she'd ever been. But fear had hooked its claws into her too, and it wasn't letting go. Whatever reasons she tried to come up with, something like this was completely out of character for her sister, and it pointed to the one thing Phoebe couldn't bear to consider.

'The police said there was a note in the coat pocket, but they haven't let us see it yet.' The shuddering sigh her father emitted barely needed a mobile connection for her to hear it in London. 'All we know is that she wants you to come home and look after Darcy and your mum's gone into meltdown as a result.'

'There was a note?' Phoebe's stomach contracted and for a moment she thought she might actually be sick. She barely even registered the comment about her mother's meltdown; she wouldn't have expected anything else. But a note left in a location like Craggy Head made the obvious conclusion seem all the more likely, except she still couldn't process it. Not Lucy – despite everything she'd been through, she just wouldn't do that to Darcy. Phoebe was sure of it. *Almost.*

'Your mother can't believe she'd do this to her. Asking someone other than her to take care of Darcy. What are people going to think?'

'You've got to be joking; you can't seriously tell me that's what you're worrying about. You're unbelievable. The pair of you.' Phoebe's face had gone hot, and she was struggling not to shout at her father. He'd been weak, when he should have been strong, and had danced to his wife's tune for his daughters' entire lives. But her father was like a marionette, with about the same amount of backbone. Everything was controlled by Phoebe's mother, and the vast majority of her anger was reserved for the puppet master. 'That's a new low even for Mum, isn't it? She's never able to think about anyone but herself.'

'Phebes, don't, she's upset.'

'For all the wrong reasons.' Her mother could take a running jump. Surely even she couldn't make Lucy's disappearance all about her? But their mother wasn't the only one in the family who'd let Lucy down. The last conversation Phoebe had had with her younger sister was still running through her head, like a sinister soundtrack on a continuous loop. Those *couldn't* be the last words they'd ever exchange. They just couldn't.

'When can you get here?' Her father's voice was trembling; at least he was having a normal reaction to his daughter being missing, even if her mother never would. He'd have to hide those emotions in front of his wife, if he wanted to live to tell the tale.

'I'm already on my way. I'll be there within a couple of hours.' Cutting off the call, she turned to face the pheasant, who was still staring in her direction.

'Just drop dead, will you!' Maybe the bird was a Londoner after all, because it finally took flight, along with a flock of pigeons who'd been scavenging in the bushes at the edge of the car park.

This was it. She was going back to Appleberry; her mother would be there and her sister had gone missing, quite possibly forever.

3

'I've phoned the nanny and she's going to pick Norma up and keep her until I know what's going on.' Phoebe tried to keep her voice level as she joined the coast road that marked the last leg of the journey to Appleberry and prayed the signal would hold out until she'd finished talking to Adam.

'I wish you'd stop calling her a nanny. She's a dog walker.'

'That's not what it says on her website.' Phoebe didn't want to get into another argument with Adam about her beloved dog. She was already well aware he thought it was ridiculous she paid someone to take Norma out twice a day while she was at work and that she kept an eye on what the dog was doing via a state-of-the-art pet-cam. But she'd just told him that Lucy was missing and now wasn't the time to get into another debate about *that bloody dog*, as he was so fond of saying. 'I just want Norma taken care of while I'm away and it's one less thing for either of us to worry about.'

'Fair enough.' Adam's voice lost its edge. 'I'm sure everything's going to be okay, you know. Lucy probably just needed a break from your mum. You can hardly blame her; after all, you started running and didn't stop until you made it all the way to London.'

'She wouldn't leave Darcy.' Phoebe squeezed her eyes shut for a split second, holding back the threatened tears, but they burnt at the back of her eyes instead, making it hard to re-focus on the road.

'Sometimes people act out of character.' Adam was doing his best to reassure her, but he didn't really understand. He barely knew Lucy. It wasn't like they were a proper couple. They were flatmates who sometimes had sex. Friends with benefits, apparently, but neither of them had ever even entertained the L word. Phoebe wasn't even sure she would have believed in the concept, if she hadn't already met the love of her life: a squashed-faced little pug called Norma.

'I hope to God you're right.' She might actually have offered up a prayer, if she bought into all of that. Although at that point she'd happily have shaken a tambourine for Jesus – or anyone else – if she thought it would bring Lucy back safely.

'Stay in touch, okay? And if you need me to pick Norma up from the dog walker, then just let me know?' Adam sounded like he meant it and for a second she considered asking him to come down to Appleberry, so she could lean on him, the way you were supposed to lean on a friend when the proverbial hit the fan. No one but the two of them seemed to understand their relationship, though, and it would just complicate things, even if he was willing to come. Thank God her best friend, Scarlett, had moved back to Appleberry the year before. Although Scarlett had more than enough on her plate. Phoebe couldn't rely on anyone when it came down to it. It was up to her to find out what had happened to Lucy, even if the possibility terrified her.

'I'll ring you.' She made the promise and disconnected the call, just as her car reached the brow of the hill. The church that clung to the hillside above Appleberry suddenly came into view. She was home.

* * *

'Thank goodness you're here!' Her father flew out of the front door almost before Phoebe had a chance to engage the handbrake. Roger Spencer was probably best described as beige. He'd had rust-coloured hair, once upon a time, and his favourite anecdote was recounting the time he'd been mistaken for Robert Redford by a checkout girl in the Canterbury branch of Sainsbury's, which he took as a great compliment despite being twenty-five years younger than his idol. These days, even his rust-coloured hair had faded to a light sandy brown, liberally sprinkled with grey, and his baggy cords and V-necked jumper, worn over a light brown polo shirt, all had the same washed-out appearance. He was a poster boy for the downtrodden and, as soon as she saw him, Phoebe experienced the familiar sensation of wanting to hug him and shake him all at the same time.

'I can't believe she's really done it, can you?' In the end, Phoebe let herself be folded into her father's arms, despite her determination to try and have a sensible conversation with him before she saw her mother. Once he was in front of his wife, he'd moderate his every word. Phoebe had seen it a million times before.

'I don't want to believe it, but the police seem to think that if we haven't heard anything by the end of the first two weeks...' He couldn't finish the sentence and Phoebe swallowed hard. *Two weeks*. There was plenty of time for Lucy to make a reappearance before it came to that.

'Is Darcy still with Lucy's friend?'

'Yes, the police asked for your details and said they wouldn't be able to hand Lucy over until they'd run some basic checks on the three of us.'

'Do you know anything about this *friend*?' Phoebe's chest tightened. Surely it had to be better for the little girl to be with family, rather than with someone none of them knew. Although maybe not, especially if that family came in the shape of Darcy's grandmother.

'Not really, just that his name's Jamie and he runs the forest school that's linked to Darcy's nursery. He's got police checks coming out of his ears already, apparently, so they said the logical thing was to leave her with him, until they can check us out. Although why any grown man would want to work with kids has to raise a few eyebrows if you ask me.'

'That's Mum talking, isn't it?' Phoebe pulled away from her father, half-expecting to see her mother working his strings from all the way inside the house.

'You have to admit she's got a point.'

'I'm sorry, Dad, but I don't.'

'Let's not argue about it.' Her father seemed to have lost his ability to defend his point of view altogether, but when he squeezed her shoulder, it said far more than his words ever could. Hidden deep inside him was the father he could have been, Phoebe was convinced of it, but it was just one more thing her mother had taken from them.

'We'd best get inside anyway, or your mother will get even more upset. Have you got any bags?' He was always searching for things to do, as if looking busy would keep him out of trouble. But it was never that easy.

'Just one. I grabbed a few things, made some calls to rearrange work, and then headed straight down.' For a second she wondered if the frantic call she'd made to her company's biggest client was going to lose her the job she loved. But, even if it did, it was a price she'd have to pay. She wasn't going to end up like her mother; all that mattered now was getting Lucy safely home to Darcy – she was the only one in the family capable of caring for her daughter for any length of time. 'Shall we face the music, then?'

'If you're ready. This has hit her hard, though.' Her father furrowed his brow and Phoebe wished for the hundredth time that it was her mother who'd disappeared. But life didn't play fair like that.

* * *

'Can you believe she's done this to me?' Janet Spencer barely even glanced up to acknowledge her daughter's arrival, her face so twisted that her eyes looked like black slits. 'Doesn't she realise this makes it look like I'm a failure as a mother?'

'I don't suppose that was at the forefront of her mind.' Phoebe wanted to scream into her mother's face that *of course it bloody well reflected on her*, because she'd been the worst type of mother it was possible to be. But she didn't. It would be pointless; her mother wouldn't hear the words and, even if she did, it would only make things worse. It was like they'd all taken a vow of defeat over the years and her father wasn't the only one who'd given up trying to reason with a woman who thought everything that happened in the world revolved directly around her. Her mother had even stopped speaking to their neighbour, Mrs Wolowitz, when she'd mentioned that the man who ran the post office had mistaken her for Janet. Phoebe's mother hadn't stopped ranting for the best part of a fortnight that Mrs Wolowitz looked nothing like her – she was 'far too plain', apparently. Then Janet had started to accuse Mrs Wolowitz of copying the way she dressed, and flirting with Phoebe's father. The poor woman was doing nothing of the sort, but none of the family even tried to argue with Janet. As long as the idea existed in her head, it was a fact as far as she was concerned.

'If that wasn't bad enough, Lucy wants Darcy to stay with *you* and the police told Dad they'll follow her wishes as long as everything checks out. What are people going to think about me then? That I'm not even good enough to look after my own granddaughter? How could she be so selfish?'

'I didn't think you'd want Darcy staying with you.'

'That's not the point.' Her mother pushed her white-blonde hair away from her forehead. 'When she gets back, I'm going to give her a piece of my mind.'

'What if she doesn't come back?' Phoebe forced the words out, trying not to think about what might happen to Darcy then.

'Don't be stupid; she's just attention-seeking, the way the pair of you always have.'

'Janet, don't.' Her father laid a hand on her mother's shoulder, for once daring to raise his head above the parapet, but his wife instantly shrugged him off.

'Don't *you* start, Roger. I've got enough to worry about without you adding to it.'

'No one's even asked me if I'm okay to look after Darcy.' Phoebe looked straight at her father. It wasn't the sort of conversation she could have with her mother, given that it required the application of empathy – something Janet Spencer didn't appear to possess a single shred of.

'And *are* you okay to have her?' Her father's eyes seemed to get more deeply set every time she looked at him, as though even they were cowering from his wife's temper.

'Yes.' The word came out without Phoebe meaning it to. She might not think she was the right person to look after her niece, or even that she was capable of it, but less than five minutes in the company of her mother had convinced her that the alternative would be a million times worse. The narcissistic personality disorder Janet refused to believe she had, and wouldn't seek treatment for, had taken hold of her mother years before. If anything, its grip seemed to be tightening. Phoebe might have absolutely no idea how to care for Darcy, but, whatever happened, she couldn't let her mother ruin another childhood.

'Do you think I should talk to the police?' Phoebe looked at her father again.

'It can't hurt; maybe you could speed the process along a bit, too, so that all the gossip that's stressing your mum out dies down a bit quicker.' Her father's eyes darted towards her mother, then back to Phoebe. 'The family liaison officer left me his number; maybe you could give him a call?'

'I'll take the number with me and go for a walk. I'm going to try to speak to some of Lucy's friends too. There might be something they can tell us that helps us find out where she's gone.'

'I think that's for the best; your mum needs a break from all the stress.' Her father was already fussing around his wife and turning his back on his daughter. Some things never changed. As long as she was back in Appleberry, she was going to have to contend with her parents' behaviour, and the idea made her depressed and exhausted, all at the same time.

4

The phone call to the family liaison officer, PC Bradley Harrison, had done very little to reassure Phoebe. His matter-of-fact announcement that over nine hundred people went missing in the UK every day, but that most of them turned up sooner or later, made it feel like Lucy was anything but a priority.

Stupidly she'd pushed him, asked if he thought Lucy would be one of those people, and he'd answered more honestly than she was ready to hear. It seemed the location of the coat and the fact she'd left a note suggested there was a good chance there'd be another outcome. The police were clearly aware of Lucy's medical history, and the battles she'd faced with her mental health. Phoebe should probably have been encouraged by that, but not if it meant they'd already made their mind up about the reasons for her disappearance and were disregarding other possibilities as a result. The prospect of them giving up on finding Lucy made it hard for Phoebe to breathe. She couldn't allow them to write her sister off, because she definitely wasn't ready to.

PC Harrison had also informed her that a small boat had been stolen from its mooring at Craggy Head on the day of Lucy's disappearance and had later turned up abandoned and floating out at sea. It wasn't a good sign, but he promised that until they had more concrete evidence, the investigations would run their course. She just wasn't sure she believed him.

If Phoebe had expected helicopters to circle everywhere from Appleberry to Craggy Head until Lucy was located, she'd have been sadly disappointed. According to her father, the police had already searched Lucy's address and taken away some evidence for review. They'd also asked if Lucy had a passport, but as far as Phoebe knew her sister had barely left the village where they'd grown up, let alone the country.

PC Harrison had requested some photos of Lucy, so that they could be uploaded to the police system to check against CCTV and be used in any media campaigns they might run. It didn't come as any surprise that her parents hadn't been able to provide any recent ones. Janet had never been the sort of person to have photographs of her daughters or granddaughter around the house. She knew her father kept one of her and Lucy hidden inside his wallet, behind a membership card for a long-defunct video store. His wife's photo was the one inside the clear plastic slot at the front, for the whole world to see, because she wouldn't have it any other way.

Lucy's decision to stay in Appleberry didn't seem to have made her any closer to their parents and, if she wanted to be a part of their lives, it still meant dancing to their mother's tune. According to Lucy, Janet had only wanted her and Darcy there when the occasion was about her. Woe betide anyone who didn't make a fuss on her birthday, or Mother's Day. Phoebe had spent over three hours, the week before the most recent Mother's Day, searching for a card that said as little as possible. She didn't want hearts and flowers, or sentimental odes to 'the world's greatest' mother, because it was all bullshit. The trouble was, the card industry didn't seem to have cottoned on to the fact that not everyone thought their mother was 'simply the best'.

Lucy's life had looked sad from the outside. She was the same little girl she'd always been, still desperate to be loved by someone who never would. But if Phoebe could have taken back her words when she'd said that to her sister, she'd have done it in a heartbeat. And, despite her lack of surprise, it still broke her heart that her parents didn't have a recent photograph of Lucy to give to the police.

PC Harrison had questioned whether Phoebe was planning to share Lucy's disappearance on social media and had said that could sometimes create useful leads. Although he'd warned her that it could also generate red herrings and weirdos who got something unfathomable out of pretending to be the missing person. More than anything she wanted to read Lucy's note for herself, and he'd promised to bring it to her parents' house the next day, when they brought Darcy home, assuming that all of Phoebe's checks were clear. She managed to resist the urge to tell him that he was wasting his time running unnecessary checks on her, when he could be helping to find Lucy, but it hadn't been easy. He was just doing his job and he didn't realise yet how dysfunctional Lucy's background was. Give him a few more visits to the Spencer household, and he'd understand.

* * *

Phoebe forced herself to head back towards the house she'd grown up in, but with every step the desire to turn around and walk away as fast as possible was getting stronger. She couldn't stay there. Not even for a night. Being around her mother made it almost impossible to shake off the dread about what Lucy's disappearance might mean. Phoebe could understand exactly how her sister might have been driven to the point of ending her life. Years of their mother's abuse would have driven anyone to the edge, but Phoebe couldn't bear to think of Lucy feeling that desperate. She wasn't ready to face it, and it was yet another reason why she didn't want to be anywhere near her mother. Phoebe had just passed the newly built village hall, completely lost in her thoughts, and it took her a moment to realise that someone was calling her name.

'Phebes, is that really you? Why didn't you tell me you were coming down!' Scarlett West had been her best friend since they'd started at Oaktree Forstal primary school together. Now Scarlett was a teacher there, and she'd finally found happiness after being put through the mill by her nightmare ex-husband. They hadn't lived in each other's pockets, especially during the years that Scarlett had spent in Cornwall, and Phoebe had been in London, but they'd always shared the big things. At least until now. It was clear from the expression on Scarlett's face that she had no idea about Lucy's disappearance. Maybe the gossip wasn't as widespread as Phoebe's father had feared.

'I wasn't planning on coming down, otherwise I'd have let you know, but when I heard Lucy had disappeared, I just had to get here as soon as I could.' Guilt stabbed at Phoebe's gut for lying. The truth was, she hadn't called Scarlett because she'd had no intention of telling her what had happened, even though her fingers were itching to dial her number the moment she'd heard the news. If she'd told Scarlett, she'd have had to talk about the possible reasons for Lucy's disappearance and she wasn't ready for that. Her best friend would also have found a way of getting her to confess the thing she feared most: that all of this was her fault.

'What do you mean Lucy has disappeared?'

'She's left Darcy with a babysitter and no one has heard from her in days.' Phoebe hadn't expected her voice to crack, but seeing a friendly face had been too much.

'I can't believe she'd leave Darcy.' Scarlett furrowed her brow and Phoebe wanted to cry, because neither could she. None of it made sense; Lucy adored her daughter, and her sole purpose in life had appeared to be giving the little girl a vastly different childhood to the one they'd had.

'They found her coat at Craggy Head and she'd left a note...' Phoebe couldn't bring herself to admit the implications that had, but the unspoken meaning hung between them.

'Oh God, I'm so sorry, Phebes, but it might not be what it sounds like.' All the colour had drained from Scarlett's face, and she seemed to be struggling to find the words that Phoebe had been repeating in her own head, ever since she'd heard the news. If it was impossible for her best friend to even acknowledge the prospect of suicide, then it couldn't be true. After all, she'd known Lucy all her life too.

'But what if it is?' The words tumbled out of her mouth before she could stop them, which seemed to be becoming a habit. Something about seeing Scarlett had opened up the floodgates. Her best friend had always been the one person who could get away with hugging her, never fearing that she might get the brush-off, if she thought a hug was what Phoebe needed. Scarlett clearly thought so now, and if Phoebe had been anyone else, she would finally have given in to the tears that seemed to have burnt away the inside of her throat in her attempt to keep them in. When you'd learnt as a child that crying didn't do any good, it stopped being the release it was for other people.

'I thought it would be all over the village by now, people talking about it being no surprise that one of the Spencer girls would do something like that.'

'No one would think that, and anyone who'd take pleasure in

this would have me to answer to.' Scarlett's jaw was set in a firm line as she pulled away, and Phoebe had seen that look before: when a group of older girls had cornered her in the playground, just after the two of them had started secondary school together and had chanted that Phoebe's mum was a psycho. It was the usually mild-mannered Scarlett who'd suddenly launched herself at the ringleader, fists flying like it was fight night in Vegas. It was at that point that Phoebe had started to grow a harder shell and, over the years, it had got tougher and tougher, until she'd stopped letting people in altogether. Everyone who'd spent any time with Janet knew that her mother could be difficult, but Scarlett was the only person other than Lucy who really understood what their mother had put them through – what she was still putting them through, whenever they gave her the chance. Phoebe had run from Appleberry as soon as she could, but for some reason Lucy had stayed, and now she might have paid the ultimate price.

'I'm glad people aren't saying that about Lucy, but I can't help worrying it means no one even knows she's missing. The police say they're following procedure, but I've got a horrible feeling they've already convinced themselves she's dead. So they're not going to prioritise looking for her, are they? The family liaison officer admitted to me that resources are limited.' Phoebe's throat felt like it had closed up altogether now. Maybe if she tried forcing herself to cry it would happen and she'd feel better. At the very least she might remember how to swallow again.

'Did the police actually say they thought she was dead?' Scarlett reached out and touched her arm and suddenly Phoebe wished she was the kind of person who could ask for another hug.

'The guy I spoke to this morning said that sometimes the obvious explanation was the right one. But not always.' It was what she was holding on to.

'What about the note? Could that give us any clues? If there's anything I can do to help, you know I'll be here for you.' Scarlett's eyes were round with concern, and even if Phoebe might not be able to ask for another hug, it felt as if her best friend had wrapped her arms around her again. The very fact that she'd said *us* meant that Phoebe didn't feel completely alone any more.

'Thank you, and I'm so glad you're here.' Phoebe touched Scarlett's hand briefly, which was about as touchy-feely as she was ever going to get. 'I haven't seen the note yet, but the police liaison officer is going to bring it over. Apparently it's all very vague.'

'Maybe you'll see something in the note that they don't. After all, no one knows her better than you.' Scarlett was talking about Lucy in the present tense and that meant more to Phoebe than she'd ever be able to explain. But the truth was, she didn't know Lucy nearly as well as she should have done. Both of them had spent so long trying to be the daughters they thought their mother wanted that they'd hidden parts of themselves even from each other. And now it might be too late.

'I really hope there's something in the note that makes sense. I can't believe she's done anything drastic; leaving Darcy is completely out of character.' Phoebe shook her head. 'Could you imagine ever leaving Ava?'

'No, but it's not always that easy to explain why people do the things they do. Sometimes we all get desperate, but it doesn't mean she loves Darcy any less.' Scarlett had been through her fair share of having to try to understand the irrational actions of others. Her now ex-husband had walked out on her and their little girl, Ava, without an explanation or any warning, and she'd been left to raise her daughter alone and sort out the debts he'd left behind. He'd turned up eventually and pushed for a reconciliation, which Scarlett was long past considering, even before she discovered that he'd made another woman pregnant. So, if anyone understood that things weren't always what they seemed, it was Scarlett.

'I know, it's just...' Phoebe couldn't even finish the sentence. Until they knew for certain what Lucy had done, she couldn't even start to make sense of it. 'I don't want to drag up bad memories for you about Luke's disappearance.'

'I don't even want you to think about that; this is nothing like it. I just want you to promise me that you won't try to get through all of this by yourself, whatever happens. Because I know what you're like.'

'Okay, I promise.' Phoebe wouldn't admit it to herself, let alone Scarlett, but she needed her old friend more than ever. It was like being backed into that corner of the playground again, without being able to see any way out, and all she wanted was for someone to step in and fix it. But that wasn't going to happen. The Phoebe Spencer that most of the world knew was a tough cookie who took no prisoners and didn't seem to have any tangible emotions, and she was going to have to maintain that façade to get through this. But knowing she could let her guard down with Scarlett felt like a life-raft in the midst of a storm.

'Where are you staying? Not with your mum and dad?' Scarlett looked horrified at the thought, and Phoebe shook her head.

'I can't stay there. I've decided to go to Lucy's and, as soon as the police and social services clear me, I'm going to be looking after Darcy. So it makes sense to do it in her own home. Hopefully that will help a little bit.' Nausea swirled in Phoebe's stomach as she spoke. She had no idea how to take care of a child, let alone a little girl who'd been abandoned by the one person she trusted most.

'You might not think so, but you'll be fine, I promise, and I'm five minutes away.' Scarlett glanced at her watch. 'I'm really sorry, but I've got to grab Ava from her dance class, otherwise I'd come to

Lucy's with you. But just call me any time, okay? Even if it's in the middle of the night. And if you're okay with me letting Cam know what's going on, he can cover for me with Ava if needed.'

'Yes, tell Cam. I might need both of you to help me to spread the news locally anyway. The police said that a social media campaign might help.' Phoebe swallowed hard. The thought of Lucy's face being plastered everywhere online made her feel sick again, but she didn't have a choice. She had to get her sister home whatever the cost. 'Give Ava a kiss from her rubbish Auntie Phoebe; I still owe her and Darcy a trip to the toy shop. As soon as things calm down a bit, I'm going to start stepping up. I promise.'

'You're not rubbish and you don't owe the girls anything – they're both going to love having you around and so am I. Even if the circumstances are terrible. I know you hate me saying this, but I love you and there's nothing you can say or do to change that.'

'You too.' Phoebe pulled a face; it was as much as she could say. The L word definitely didn't trip off her tongue, and she wasn't even sure she could define what it meant. But Scarlett was in the top five people she cared about in the world – six if she counted Norma, which she definitely did – and that was as close as she could come to defining it. 'See you later and I'll call you tonight.'

As Scarlett disappeared, breaking into a jog in her determination not to be late for Ava, the nausea swirling in the pit of Phoebe's stomach threatened to overwhelm her. This was what real motherhood looked like up close: selfless and stressful, with one eye constantly on the clock, and guilt about even the tiniest mistakes you might make. Phoebe hadn't been around enough to understand how her sister did things, and their own mother's example was no measure of good parenting. Could she really do this: take care of Darcy and just get on with things, while the little girl's mother was out there somewhere, missing? Lucy would be back, she was sure of it, she had to be, but even a few weeks of being a stand-in parent felt impossible. There was her job, her life in London. Adam and Norma. Her only hope was to track down Lucy as soon as possible, and the best chance of doing that would be to go to her place and look for clues. If she could just piece those together with what Lucy had said in the letter, she was sure she could work it out. The alternative didn't even bear thinking about.

5

Lucy might have done something completely out of character, but whatever turmoil she'd been going through, some things remained unchanged. She still had the wellington boot plant pot that Phoebe had bought her when she'd first moved into her own place. There was a groove between the heel and toe where Lucy had always kept her spare key, and Phoebe felt her spirits lift a bit as her fingers found the reassuring outline of the metal.

The cottage was even smaller than Phoebe remembered from the handful of times she'd visited. The hallway that led off from the front door was cluttered with toys, and a pedal bike was almost completely blocking the entrance into the sunny kitchen, which Lucy had said made her fall in love with the place. Stepping over the pedal bike, Phoebe let out a breath, the resulting sigh filling the silence in the kitchen. It all looked so normal. There was half a loaf of uncut bread still sitting on the side and a coffee cup upturned on the drainer, right next to a matching plastic bowl and cutlery set adorned with a cartoon character that even Phoebe recognised as Peppa Pig. It didn't look anything like the kitchen of someone who was planning to head out to sea and never come back.

There was no sign of the computer in the kitchen, but Phoebe knew it would be around somewhere, and there was a good chance it might hold the key to finding out where Lucy was. The police hadn't said anything about removing it; the only things PC Harrison had mentioned taking were some paperwork, so they could look into whether Lucy had accessed her bank account since her disappearance, and a hairbrush. Phoebe had been hit hard at the mention of that, because she'd known the only reason they needed it was for Lucy's DNA. She was terrified that the police were giving up on finding her sister before they'd even started, and had already assumed she was dead. As long as they put enough effort in, they'd find her, because Lucy wasn't dead. If she had been, Phoebe would have known; she'd be able to sense it somehow. Life wouldn't just go on as before. Her sister was still here, in every corner of the cottage. It was waiting for her to walk back in, and all the police needed was to do their job properly. The sensation of a hand clawing at her throat every time Phoebe thought about Lucy wasn't a sign she was gone. It was fear that the authorities weren't doing all they could, and of what the letter might reveal about why she'd left. Guilt prickled at Phoebe's scalp as she looked around the kitchen, at all the things her sister had walked away from. Some of Darcy's drawings were attached to the fridge with a magnet. Lucy wouldn't have left her daughter. She just wouldn't – she had to come back.

Lucy made a living making and selling personalised gifts and the back of the kitchen had been turned into a makeshift workshop, with a long wooden table covered in small pots of paint, and jars of brushes in various states of cleanliness. There was a row of wooden Russian dolls, half-painted with the faces of a family who must have commissioned Lucy to produce them. She sold everything she made through an online shop, so her computer was as important to Lucy in keeping a roof over hers and Darcy's heads as anything else in her workshop.

Walking into the living room, it was as if someone had punched Phoebe in the stomach, knocking all of the air out of her body, and she shivered even though sunlight poured through the window. *Someone's walked over my grave.* It was an expression their father had always used when a sudden shiver had caught him by surprise, and she remembered Lucy asking him for an explanation of what it meant. The three of them had been at Lake Pippin, without Janet, and it had been one of those rare and wonderful days when Roger had been able to be the kind of father they wanted. They'd been allowed to paddle in the shallows, and he'd tried to teach them to skim stones. Nothing special to anyone else, but it had seemed magical to them, and just having the chance to ask him questions without being scrutinised by Janet had been so precious. He'd explained to Lucy that it was just a silly saying, an old superstition, but after that she'd said it every time she shivered. And, for a moment, Phoebe was convinced she heard her sister again, saying those very words out loud, but the only sound was the tick-tock of the clock on the wall.

Phoebe was having to fight a really strong urge to turn and leave; just being in the room made her feel hollow inside and that was something she'd battled against for so long. But Lucy's disappearance had brought all those feelings back. Normal people were filled with love but being raised by Janet had hollowed Phoebe out. She didn't have the certainty of knowing she was loved by her family, the way most people did. She struggled to show her sister and father the love she had for them, too, because Janet had stamped on any sign of that she saw.

It was weird; an emptiness inside shouldn't feel like anything, but the truth was it ached so much it was almost unbearable. Over the years, Phoebe had tried to fill the gap with other things. Her friendship with Scarlett had been a big part of that, but even the way Phoebe interacted with her wouldn't look *normal* to someone observing from the outside, and showing her emotions felt completely alien. She had to be guarded in every relationship, because when the person who was meant to love you most in the world didn't, how the hell were you supposed to trust that anyone else ever really would? Instead, she'd filled her life with things that were much more easily measured, success at work being the biggest part of that, and the unconditional love of her little dog.

It had all helped the pain of that emptiness recede just enough to bear. But, with Lucy missing, it was back, and the ache was worse than ever as she stood in Lucy's cottage, evidence of the family life her sister had built all around her. There were pictures covering almost every inch of wall space. They were mostly photographs of Darcy, but also some of the little girl's artwork and even a few of Lucy's own paintings. It looked like Phoebe's niece was destined to take after her mother, given the prolific number of finger paintings and potato prints around the house. Phoebe sighed; she'd have no idea how to keep Darcy occupied. Maybe she should let her stay on with Jamie after all. That would be the easiest option and Darcy might well prefer that. It wouldn't be for long, anyway. There was no way Lucy could stay away from the things she used to fill her own emptiness, otherwise the ache would become unbearable again.

Phoebe wanted to be angry with her sister, the way they had been with one another so many times over the years, because it was easier than admitting how sad they were, and how much they needed each other. But now, standing in her living room, Phoebe's throat was burning again with the force of pent-up sorrow. She understood exactly what had driven Lucy to try and escape, and she should have been there for her sister. Anger had always been easier to acknowledge than pain, but they should never have been anything but allies, and Phoebe couldn't accept it was too late to change that. She'd never accept it, unless she had irrefutable proof that Lucy was really dead.

'Who the hell are you?' A man's voice from behind Phoebe made her turn round so fast that she caught her knee against the corner of the coffee table and fell backwards onto one of Lucy's armchairs, sending a row of books on the shelf behind her tumbling to the ground. This was it: Lucy was missing and now she was about to be murdered by a burglar in her sister's front room. The Spencer sisters had been dealt a poor hand from day one, but even she hadn't expected it to end like this.

Suddenly fight or flight kicked in; she couldn't leave Darcy to her mother's mercy, and, mustering a courage she didn't know she had, she reached down and picked up a book, hurling it at the intruder's head.

'Do you seriously think that's going to help the situation?' He caught the book in one hand and narrowed his eyes. 'Hold on, I've seen your face before – you're Phoebe, right?'

'I might be.' She wasn't going to give him any more information than she had to, but she had to admit he was suddenly looking less like a burglar who might be into a bit of murdering on the side. But then she'd seen enough crime documentaries to know you never could tell. For some reason she'd always found those sorts of programmes weirdly comforting, probably because it was reminder that there was always someone who was worse off than her. But right now she had bigger things to worry about. About six feet two inches of bigger things looming directly above her. Maybe he was a police officer, but he wasn't wearing a uniform and PC Harrison had told her they'd be in contact first if they wanted to search the cottage again.

'I've seen your photos in Lucy's kitchen; she talks about you a lot.' The man smiled for the first time, and she couldn't help noticing how warm his voice sounded. If he was a murderer, it was going to surprise everyone, especially as his blue eyes crinkled in the corners, as if smiling was the default position for his face. But there was still no way she was letting her guard down when it mattered most.

'I can't say the same about you.'

'Well, I'm happy to fill you in, as long as you don't hurl that copy of *Harry Potter and the Deathly Hallows* at my head.' As he spoke, she released her grip on the second book that her fingers had been curling around.

'It's a deal.'

'I'm Jamie Callaghan.' He held out his hand. 'Lucy's friend. I live next door and I've got Darcy staying with me.'

'Where is she?' Phoebe got to her feet.

'At nursery at the moment. I wanted to come over and pick up a few things while she wasn't about. I thought if I brought her over later and she could see all her mum's stuff lying around, but that she still wasn't here, it might make things more difficult for her. Especially as I wasn't sure how the police had left the place.' Jamie's brow creased and Phoebe could see why Lucy had trusted him with Darcy. There was something so open about his face when he looked at her and putting the little girl first obviously came naturally to him. 'Then when I realised Lucy's key wasn't there and I saw you rummaging around in the lounge... it sounds stupid now, but I thought you might be in here robbing her.'

'Well, I won't take offence if you don't, seeing as I had you pegged as an axe murderer. You and Lucy must be close, if she told you the secret about the key, not to mention trusting you with Darcy.' Phoebe fixed her gaze on his face, waiting for a hint of something that might suggest he knew more than he'd told the police about Lucy's disappearance. Maybe there was a chance he was an axe murderer after all, although the more she looked at him, the less likely it seemed.

'We're pretty good friends.' The smile suddenly slid off his face. 'At least I thought we were. I guess she wanted Darcy to stay with someone she knows, and I run the forest school she comes to a couple of times a week, so I suppose I was the obvious choice. I still can't believe it, though. She'd been a bit down and I told the police that, but she loves Darcy so much.'

'That's exactly what I thought.' Either Jamie was a very good actor or he was as shocked by Lucy's disappearance as she was. It wasn't a surprise to hear that Lucy had been low, because there'd been a pattern of that their whole lives, mostly linked to when their mother was at her worst. For some reason Lucy had always chosen to stay, but maybe this time had been more significant. If Phoebe was going to stand a chance of finding out what had been going through Lucy's mind when she disappeared, she needed to ask the right questions. 'Have you got time for a cup of tea or coffee? There are some things I'd like to ask you.'

'Of course, let's straighten things up in here and then maybe I can try and help you find what you were looking for.'

'It was Lucy's computer; I thought I might be able to find out if there are any clues to where she might be or...' She still couldn't bring herself to finish the sentence.

'The police took it.' The openness of Jamie's face when he looked at her this time was heartbreaking. Neither of them needed to say the words out loud; it was obvious what the police were looking for – evidence that her disappearance had been planned. 'They obviously had the same idea.'

'I spoke to the family liaison officer this morning and he didn't even seem to know that. What the hell hope have they got of finding her and bringing her home, if they don't even share information with each other properly?'

'Maybe it's part of their strategy. I suppose they have to rule out anyone Lucy knows who might have been involved in her disappearance in some way. They might deliberately be keeping things to themselves. I only know about the computer because I saw one of the officers carrying it out when I was being interviewed by her colleague. They seemed fixated on whether she might have met someone online and gone off with them, and that maybe this new boyfriend didn't want her to bring Darcy. They seemed to think it's the most likely explanation if she's still...' Jamie stopped and shook his head. 'But she'd never do that. Lucy was pretty guarded and she took a long time to trust people. So the idea of her starting a new life with someone she'd just got into a relationship with makes no sense.'

'Is that what you wanted, a relationship with Lucy?' Phoebe hadn't meant to be so blunt, but she needed to know if there'd been an agenda to Jamie's friendship with her sister.

'No, there was never anything like that between us.' Jamie looked at her again, and somehow, beyond any doubt, she knew he was telling her the truth.

'Right. Let's get this place straightened up a bit, then, shall we, and see if we can find anything the police might have missed. But I'll put the kettle on first.' The words sounded ridiculous, as if that simple act might somehow make everything okay. Swallowing hard, she wondered for the hundredth time how so much could change in such a short time. Less than ten hours ago all she'd had to worry about was the benign lump in her throat and now her whole life felt like it had been chucked into a blender. It was as if the earth had started shifting beneath her feet and it wouldn't stop until they got Lucy home. Jamie might be a virtual stranger, but he might also be the best shot she had of making that happen.

Filling up the kettle, Phoebe stood on tiptoes to peer out of the kitchen window at the highest point she could. There it was, the view of the church spire opposite the village green that Lucy had always wanted to have, but which you could only spot if you got yourself into a position that a contortionist would be proud of. For some reason Lucy had always been drawn to the church, even though Phoebe would never have described her sister as religious. Phoebe had found her hiding out there quite a few times over the years, when she'd needed to escape from their mother, and she'd told Phoebe that she found the atmosphere calming. Although anywhere out of earshot of their mother had been calm in comparison.

'Lucy loves this cottage too; she can't just have upped and left.' Phoebe spoke as she heard Jamie come into the room, but she didn't turn and look at him. She couldn't drag her eyes away from the path, still hoping Lucy might suddenly appear, hurrying down it to get home to Darcy.

'It doesn't make any sense. Like I said, she'd had one of her low phases, but in the days before she left it seemed like she was coming out of it, and she had all sorts of plans for growing the business. I was really hoping she might have found the right help to keep things on more of an even keel. Last year, she hit a really rough patch and I was genuinely worried then that she might do something... *drastic*. But this was nothing like that. Nothing.' Jamie pulled out a chair, which scraped across the slate kitchen floor, as Phoebe finally turned to look at him.

'Was she still taking her medication?' The muscles in her jaw clenched at the thought that Lucy might have been struggling again and that she hadn't felt able to reach out to Phoebe for help. Since they were teenagers, they'd both been on pills prescribed by the doctor, to cope with the fallout of living with a mother like theirs. Phoebe had managed to completely wean herself off the anti-anxiety medication three years after leaving Appleberry, but Lucy had never seen the need to try. 'If the pills help, I'd be an idiot not to take them' had been her mantra, and Phoebe had figured she was right. Even if Lucy had chosen to leave the village where they'd grown up, the legacy of being raised by Janet Spencer would have followed her, and she might still have needed a combination of therapy and medication as a result. There'd never been any judgement on Phoebe's part for that and there never would be. The people who got on their high horse about it didn't understand anxiety and depression, and they had no idea what damage a traumatic childhood could cause. Sometimes it was damage that just couldn't be undone.

'I know the doctors had adjusted her medication and she also told me she was seeing a new therapist, which I really thought was helping. She seemed so much more positive, but now I'm wondering whether it was because she was making plans to leave.'

'Without Darcy? You said yourself that she'd never leave her to go off with someone.'

'She wouldn't, but sometimes Lucy worried that she wasn't doing the best job as a mum, even though she was devoted to Darcy. I think it was because...' Jamie sighed, clearly not sure how to finish the sentence, but he didn't have to.

'Because she was scared of turning out like our mother? Or that by choosing to stay around, she was allowing our mother to play a part in Darcy's life?' Despite having known Lucy's fears, the fact she'd shared them with Jamie was like another punch in the gut. The last words Phoebe had said to her sister layered on the paralysing terror that Lucy's disappearance was all Phoebe's fault. 'But if she was planning it and putting on such a convincing act... that doesn't sound like someone who'd do something desperate, does it?'

If Phoebe was clutching at straws, she couldn't help it, and Jamie shook his head. 'I don't know and I'm really sorry, but I'm not going to be able to tell you anything useful about the day she disappeared. You're right, though. If she had all this planned when she dropped Darcy off, then she missed her vocation as a professional poker player because her face didn't give anything away.'

'I just want to know what she said. In case there was something you didn't pick up on.' She didn't miss the face he pulled in response; it probably sounded like an accusation, but she didn't have time to tread on eggshells. She needed to know everything, and she needed to know it now.

'She asked me if I could have Darcy while you all went to a family wedding; she said that no kids were allowed and that Darcy's father had been due to have her for the weekend, but that he'd let her down at the last minute.' Jamie ran a hand through his hair. 'I guess looking back it should have rung alarm bells. Darcy's dad has hardly had a mention in the whole time I've known Lucy and I'd certainly never seen him at the house, but she just seemed so... normal.'

'How long ago did she ask you if you could look after Darcy?'

'Not until the night before she left. Lucy said she wanted Darcy to go somewhere she wouldn't miss her mum too much and she loves being outside with the dogs and chickens at my place. God, looking back, even comments like not missing Lucy too much seem a lot more significant. I just didn't think anything of it at the time.'

'There's no reason you should have done.' Phoebe handed Jamie a cup of tea and sat down opposite him, a tiny bit of the tension leaving her spine. Maybe it really was something to do with Darcy's dad. He wasn't the nicest of people and none of them had heard from him in years. But, if he'd come back on the scene and started harassing her, she wouldn't want Darcy to get caught up in that. Scarlett had gone through a similar thing with her ex, even receiving anonymous calls and texts making veiled threats, and Phoebe knew how much it had spooked her. She hated the thought that Lucy might have been through the same with Darcy's deadbeat dad and hadn't told Phoebe about it because they weren't speaking properly. She knew she hadn't always been the best of sisters, but she hoped to God she hadn't been as awful as that.

'Do you think there's any chance Lucy's got *involved* with Darcy's father again?' As Jamie spoke, Phoebe tried to read his expression. Despite his earlier insistence that there'd only ever been a friendship between him and Lucy, and Phoebe's certainty that he was telling the truth, there was a clouded look in his eyes, as if the thought of Lucy and another man might bother him more than it should. Suddenly there were goosebumps covering her skin. She didn't even know this man and she could be making the worst decision of her life by trusting him. This whole situation was making her question everything, but whatever the real story between Jamie and Lucy, building a relationship with him had to help. If he did know more than he was saying, it might make him let his guard down. And, if he didn't, she had a feeling she was going to need to call on his advice to make sure Darcy got through all of this as unscathed as possible.

'I very much doubt she'd ever get involved with Callum again, not after all the pain he caused her. She finally realised what a loser he was after Darcy was born and he disappeared to spend the summer in Ibiza, hanging out in clubs and sleeping on the beach. He wouldn't do anything to hurt Lucy physically; he's just one of those people who'll never grow up.' Phoebe gripped the handle of her mug much harder than she needed to. Janet had done her best to come between Lucy and Callum, and she had a feeling that might have been part of what had driven him away. It had certainly worked with Phoebe's former fiancé. Maybe Callum had decided that he wanted a relationship with his daughter after all, but she still couldn't see that happening. One thing she was sure of was that Janet had succeeded in putting both her daughters off starting serious relationships, unless they could be certain they could completely trust the other person. And as far as Phoebe was concerned, that kind of certainty was an impossibility. 'And, from everything she told me, I'm as sure as I can be that there hasn't been anyone significant since Callum left.'

'At least we can rule that out, then.' There was no doubting the look of relief on Jamie's face. 'The police said she left a letter?'

'I haven't seen it yet, but there's got to be some clue to where she's gone, some sort of subtle reference that the police wouldn't understand. I'm going to find her, whatever it takes, and bring her home to Darcy.'

'If there's anything I can do?' Jamie looked so earnest, but she shook her head. It was up to her to find Lucy; it was the least she could do.

'You've done more than enough already. By having Darcy, I mean.'

'Do you want to come to the nursery with me, to pick her up? I'm sure she'd be really happy to see you.'

'I've got to wait for the police and social services to okay everything before she can come and stay with me. It seems crazy, but we've got to go through all of the proper channels.' Phoebe just hoped her niece would at least remember her enough to be willing to stay with her until Lucy came home. She obviously knew Jamie far better than she knew her only aunt – another failing on Phoebe's part. 'Would you be all right to keep her until they agree for me to take her? I was going to stay here, but it seems so weird without Lucy. I think getting Darcy back to my place and away from all the reminders, until her mum gets back, might be the best thing I can do for her. But I might still need to bombard you with questions, because I've never done anything like this before.'

'You're going to take her to London?' Jamie's face was doing its thing of giving far too much away again; he clearly didn't think it was a good idea, even if he was desperately trying not to say as much.

'I thought I could get a childminder or something, as I'll need to go back to work, at least for some of the time.'

'I thought finding Lucy was your priority?' Jamie sounded like he was making an accusation and he obviously realised it. 'Sorry, I didn't mean it to come out like that, it's just that Darcy is confused enough about her mum not being around and if she's suddenly uprooted to a strange place and away from everything and everyone else she knows, I think it might be even more distressing for her.'

'She'll be with me.' The words were half-hearted, because in truth Phoebe was little more than a stranger to her niece and it seemed Jamie was well aware of the fact. 'And I can chase things up with the police and get a social media campaign up and running just as well from London as I can here.'

'Whatever you think is best.' He drained his tea and stood up. He might not have told her how wrong he thought she was, but his newly clipped tone said it all. 'My mobile number is pinned to Lucy's noticeboard; give me a call when you're ready to come and get Darcy.'

'I will and thanks again.' Her certainty that Jamie wasn't a threat, and that he hadn't orchestrated this whole thing so he could hide Lucy's body in the woods, was back. Whatever his relationship with Lucy was – or had been – it couldn't have been more obvious that he just wanted what was best for Darcy. Phoebe did too, but that didn't mean she had to stay in Appleberry. She felt as uncomfortable being back in the village as she always had done, and she wasn't sure she could hang around for more than a couple of days. Not even for Lucy.

6

'Miss Spencer?' The police officer at the door removed his hat as Phoebe nodded in response. 'I'm Constable Harrison – Bradley – we spoke yesterday?'

'Yes, come in.' She stood aside and let him cross the threshold of her parents' house, a huge crow behind him squawking as if she might throw it some scraps. There was even less chance of that than of her mother not embarrassing them all in the next half an hour. Staying at her mum and dad's house the night before had seemed the lesser of two evils – after the silence of Lucy's cottage had made her disappearance all the more real – but only just. 'My parents are in the lounge.'

'Is there any news?' Her father got to his feet as soon as Bradley entered the room, but her mother didn't even move.

'I'm sorry, Mr Spencer, there's nothing further yet. We've spoken to some of Lucy's friends and there are one or two potential areas we want to investigate further, but we don't have anything concrete at this stage. We'll be looking at Lucy's online presence too, but all these things take time. For now, I just wanted to come and let you know that the checks on your other daughter are clear.' He turned to look at Phoebe. 'So if you're willing to have your niece stay with you, until we can find out what's happened to your sister, we can get that sorted as soon as you're ready.'

'That was quick.' Phoebe wasn't sure how to react. The reality that she was about to become a stand-in parent was terrifying, but if it was really what Lucy wanted, she was going to give it her all.

'In emergencies, the authorities have the ability to return checks within twenty-four hours of the request. At least that's one less thing for you to worry about.'

'Thank you, Bradley.' She gestured towards the sofa; if her parents weren't going to ask the poor man to sit down, then she'd have to do it. After a night in her parents' place her attitude to what she'd perceived as police incompetence had softened. None of this was their fault and falling out with their family liaison officer was more her mother's style than Phoebe's. Just like building a relationship with Jamie was in Darcy's best interests, building a good relationship with the police had to be in Lucy's. 'Please, take a seat. Can I get you a coffee, or tea?'

'No, thank you.' Bradley sat on the sofa at the opposite end to her mother, who finally turned to look in his direction. He acknowledged her with an awkward half-smile and Phoebe found herself wondering how many times he'd done this before. Even if he'd been through this process a hundred times, she very much doubted Bradley had ever encountered anyone quite like her mother. He pressed on all the same. 'I also wanted to reassure you that we're doing everything we can to find Lucy. We're working with the coastguard and the local police at Craggy Head are continuing their investigations there too.'

'The coastguard?' Phoebe knew what that meant. They weren't looking for Lucy; they were looking for her body.

'We're just covering all bases.' Bradley's face didn't seem to know what to do with itself and it was stuck between attempting a reassuring smile, and a grimace. 'And I promise you'll be the first to know if we hear anything. Anything at all.'

'It won't be in the papers, will it?' Janet Spencer spoke up for the first time.

'I suspect it will and, to be honest, as I told Phoebe yesterday, it might be the best chance we have of tracking Lucy down if the coastguard don't find any clues.'

'I want to know what they're going to write about me before they print it.' Phoebe's mother had the tone she recognised so well. It was narcissism at its finest. Phoebe might have seen and heard it far too many times before, but it still had the power to take her breath away.

'I don't think that's what they'll focus on.' Bradley reached out a hand to comfort Janet, obviously misinterpreting her reaction as shock. Why else would any mother react the way she had? 'Try not to worry about things like that; the important thing is that we find Lucy.'

'Of course it is.' Phoebe's father stepped in before his wife had the chance to speak again and reveal to the poor policemen that in Janet's world there was nothing that didn't revolve around her. It might have become the uncomfortable norm for them as a family over the years, but Phoebe still hated seeing the look on other people's faces when her mother really got going.

'What about the letter?' She couldn't get through another day without reading what her sister had said and knowing whether she'd mentioned the final conversation they'd had. Maybe making this about her made Phoebe more like her mother than she ever wanted to admit. But even if it did, she couldn't help it. She had to know if Lucy's disappearance was because of her.

'Yes, sorry, of course. It's only a copy, I'm afraid; we need to hold on to the original for now, just until Lucy is found.'

'Was it in an envelope?'

Bradley nodded.

'Was there anything written on that?'

'Just that the letter should be passed to you, and only you, in the event of someone finding it. The person who found her coat on the beach went straight to the nearest police station with it. They'd opened the letter, thinking it might be some kind of prank, but when they read the contents they realised how serious it could be.' He held out a folded piece of paper for Phoebe to take.

'What's she said about me?' Janet made to grab for the letter, but Phoebe was too quick for her.

'I want to read it on my own, Mum. I'll let you know if there's anything you need to see.' Stuffing the copy of the letter into the pocket of her jeans, she turned back to the young police officer. 'Is there anything else we could be doing to find Lucy, do you think? Would it help if I went up to Craggy Head and spoke to the police there?'

'I don't think that's necessary at this stage but, as I said yesterday, sharing the missing person alerts on social media can be really helpful. The most important thing is that you stay easily contactable so that Lucy can get in touch if she decides that's what she wants to do, or if there's any other news.'

'Her friend, Jamie, said you'd taken her computer. Has anything shown up on it?' Half of Phoebe wanted the police to find the answer and the other half didn't want Lucy's secrets being pawed over by a bunch of strangers, judging her for private messages and even the things she'd bought. Worse than that was that it might reveal that Lucy had been so desperately unhappy that she'd rather die than stick around and keep fighting. It was like the letter was burning a hole in her pocket; she was desperate to tear it open and dreading it all at the same time.

'The computer's still with the lab at the moment and, as I said, these things take time. I do know that a lot of the history had been cleared off, but they've got ways of finding out what's been deleted. But like I promised, you will be the first to hear if we've got anything to tell you.'

'Thank you, shall I see you out?' Phoebe could sense her mum almost twitching in the corner of the room, looking as if she was ready to explode at any moment and Bradley didn't deserve to be in the firing line when she did.

'That's fine, I can see myself out. I'll be in touch.' He stood up and Phoebe nodded in response, holding her breath until she heard the front door close behind him.

'You've *got* to keep this out of the papers, Roger.' Janet's eyes were so wide the whites were showing all the way around, and the vein in her neck was looking much more prominent than it should. 'They'll be after stories about me, trying to find people who'll say bad stuff and blame all of this on me. They love that sort of thing.'

'For God's sake, Mum, this isn't about you!' Phoebe was only too well aware that arguing with her mother was pointless, but she couldn't help it. If the journalists really did want people to say bad stuff about Janet Spencer, they wouldn't have to look very far. 'If an article in the sodding local paper helps us find Lucy, I don't care what they print.'

'Well, you've never cared about me, have you?' Her mother spat the words out. 'I suppose you're jealous because of the way that policeman was looking at me? You've always been jealous of the way men look at me, but it's not my fault you're still on your own.'

'One thing I can honestly say, Mother, is that I've never once in my life been jealous of you. Frightened of you, yes. I've also been terrified by what you'd do next, envious of the relationship that my friends had with their mothers, and horrified by some of the things you've done. But being jealous of you would mean I wanted to be like you, and I'd rather be dead.' Inside Phoebe's head she was screaming, but the words that came out were strangely calm, as if she'd rehearsed them. The truth was, she had.

Ever since her mother had managed to obliterate any chance she might have had of maintaining a functioning adult relationship by ruining things with Eddie, Phoebe's ex-fiancé, she'd had a thousand imaginary conversations when she'd spelt out exactly what she thought of the woman who'd given birth to her. Phoebe had tried to say all those things, back when her relationship with Eddie had imploded, but her mother had twisted and manipulated the situation over and over again, until Phoebe had started to doubt her own sanity. But the words had been waiting there, burnt into her heart, and Lucy's disappearance had finally been enough to bring them to the fore. She might have hidden it most of the time, but her love for her little sister had turned out to be far fiercer than anything she'd felt for her ex-fiancé.

Despite Phoebe's calm delivery, her mother's hand flew to her mouth, and her father immediately crossed the room, taking his wife in his arms and enabling her behaviour yet again. Even in the midst of Lucy's disappearance, he couldn't find it in himself to openly support his daughters. Part of Phoebe suspected it was a misguided attempt to protect them all, by trying not to provoke even greater wrath from Janet. But maybe if he'd been honest about what he thought of her behaviour, even once, her mother would finally have accepted she needed help. But he always just folded, like a badly made deckchair that was more likely to crush your fingers and make you cry out in pain than support your weight. It still hurt every time, but it was never a surprise.

Desperate to leave, Phoebe turned and walked out. She might not have regretted the words, but their meaning suddenly hit her. What if Lucy had felt the same? What if she really would rather be dead than risk being anything like their mother? For the first time the prospect that Lucy might actually have taken her life hit Phoebe even harder and her legs were threatening to give way. All she could do was half-run, half-stumble, clutching Lucy's letter in the curled-up fingers of her fist, desperately hoping she'd be clear of the road where her parents lived before her legs finally gave way. Yet somehow she kept going, all the way to her sister's cottage, her lungs burning like they might actually be on fire. But she couldn't outrun the truth, no matter how hard she tried.

Phoebe was breathless as she leant against the kitchen door in her sister's cottage, having put as much distance between herself and her parents as she could, as quickly as possible. There'd be recriminations from her father at some point, a gentle but firm reminder that she needed to bear her mother's feelings in mind above everything else. It was safer that way, was what he'd always told the girls. When the three of them had talked about Janet's behaviour out of her earshot, Roger had freely admitted how wrong it was. But he'd been even more certain there was nothing to be done about it, and he'd told his daughters they'd just have to learn to live with it, and to always try their best not to provoke their mother, exactly as he had done. But there were some things it was impossible to learn to live with, and that only left one option.

Even the view out of the window to the woodland beyond couldn't do anything to lighten the darkness inside her. It was a beautiful summer's afternoon, drifting into evening, and birds were flying above the canopy of the trees, darting in and out exactly as they pleased. Phoebe envied their freedom and a memory suddenly came back to her as she watched them from a safe distance, still putting off the moment when she read her sister's words.

Lucy had been about twelve at the time. She'd loved art since she was tiny, and that day she'd drawn a superhero and pinned the picture to her bedroom wall. Phoebe had teased her for doing something so childish, as older sisters so often did, but Lucy had been defiant. She'd told Phoebe that the superhero was who she wanted to be, because superheroes could fly, and if she learnt to do that, she could escape their mother whenever she wanted. It might have been ridiculous, at her age, for Lucy to believe that could happen. But, at almost fifteen, Phoebe found herself longing to believe it too. If they could just learn to fly, they'd be free. Sixteen years later, she had to believe Lucy had finally learnt how to fly. There might be no way she could have taken flight under her own steam, and she probably couldn't even have got on a plane without the police being able to trace it, but maybe she'd jumped on a train, or a bus. Anything that would finally allow her the freedom she'd craved for so long. When she was settled, she'd send for Darcy. That had to be Lucy's plan.

The first thing Phoebe was going to do in the morning was call Bradley and ask when the police would complete the check on Lucy's bank account. That could give her the hope she so badly needed that her sister was okay, but for now all she had was the letter and the prospect that it might reveal something she would never be ready to read.

'All right, I'm going to open it.' Phoebe said the words out loud to the empty room and edged towards the kitchen table. Pulling out one of the chairs, she sat down, slowly unfolding the crumpled paper. It was typed, but with her name and two haphazard kisses handwritten in Lucy's distinctive style at the bottom. Her sister was artistic, but had always had the most horrendous handwriting, like a hungover spider had crawled across the page, and she'd clearly wanted Phoebe to be able to read every word.

Dear Phoebe,

I know you're probably raging at me right now, asking how I could be so stupid, so selfish as to up and leave you and Darcy behind. But I also know that, deep down, you'll understand the reasons why.

I just can't do it any more. I wake up wanting to go back to sleep. I just want the world to stop because I can't be what people expect me to be. Darcy deserves more and the thought that I might end up giving her the same sort of childhood we had breaks my heart every day. We've talked about it often enough. I've never had the strength to break free from Mum like you did, and I know now that this is the only way I'll ever do it.

The one chance I have to protect Darcy is by making sure I never allow Mum to be a part of her life. So, whatever happens, just promise me you'll make sure she never gets her claws into Darcy. For a long time, I held on to the hope that I could make Mum love me, or at least love her only grandchild. Except all I did was put my daughter in harm's way. Despite that realisation, I knew I'd never really be able to stop trying to change who our mother is, and I couldn't do that to Darcy. If I have to sacrifice my life to keep her safe, it's a price I'm more than willing to pay. The only other option was to take her with me, and that's the one thing I'm not prepared to do.

Darcy deserves a happy life and that's why I want you to be the one to take care of her. I'd like her to stay in Appleberry if you can bear it. She loves forest school and she'd happily spend all day in the woods, but I know that's probably too big an ask. Appleberry means Mum and we both know that isn't an option for you. You're much stronger than me and, whatever you decide, I know you'll do the right thing for Darcy in the end.

I'm sorry, Phebes, but I just can't stay. I love you, always have, even when we were so busy competing for something we'd never win that we sort of lost each other. I love Darcy too, like that old cliché, more than life itself. Stay strong and be the mum to Darcy that I never could.

    Lucy xx

It took three attempts to read the letter all the way through, the tears that she'd thought she'd forgotten how to cry finally blurring Phoebe's vision. Seeing Lucy's agony reflected in her letter was breaking her heart and she was terrified it might be too late to try and help her, but Phoebe had no idea if her sister was saying she was running away, or that she'd gone for good. If she'd done that, it wasn't just the fault of the woman living a mile away, on the other side of the village. Some of the blame lay at Phoebe's door too, because the last time they'd spoken, it had been her who'd told Lucy she was in danger of forcing Darcy to relive their childhood. They'd been words said in anger, ones she hadn't for a moment truly meant, but she couldn't take them back. How the hell was she supposed to take care of her niece, when it was her fault that Darcy's mother wasn't around to do it herself?

7

Phoebe had barely been able to function for the first couple of hours after reading Lucy's letter. She'd sat in a chair, staring into the space in front of her, trying to process the possibility that her sister might actually be dead. But no matter how hard she tried to make sense of it, she just couldn't believe it. How could Lucy ending her life, and leaving Darcy with someone who had absolutely zero experience of caring for a child, be even remotely plausible?

If Lucy had wanted to keep Darcy away from Janet and Roger, she could have gone to stay in Phoebe's flat in London, at least until she figured out where to make a fresh start. Escaping Appleberry was the only chance of escaping the legacy of being one of the Spencer girls too. Plenty of people who'd crossed their mother's path had been left in no doubt that she was a narcissist. But she was also a skilled manipulator who had an uncanny knack for preying on the naïve and vulnerable, and Janet was capable of convincing some people of whatever she wanted. In that narrative, she was the innocent victim who'd done her absolute best to raise two troubled and ungrateful daughters.

Their mother was so adept at it, she even managed to get her 'recruits' to do some of her dirty work for her. Phoebe knew that to her own cost, having received emails at work from one of her mother's 'friends', accusing her of being cruel and breaking 'poor Janet's heart'. Phoebe had laughed at first; anyone who was under the impression that her mother even possessed a heart was sadly mistaken. But then she'd been called in to see her boss, who'd told her that he and some of her colleagues had received the same email. Phoebe had been asked to explain the situation, but she'd never been 100 per cent sure he believed her. Even if he had, there was a chance that some of her colleagues had been hoodwinked into believing that she'd somehow mistreated her mother. After all, there were plenty of people who believed there was no smoke without fire, and there'd been times when it had caused Phoebe so much pain, she couldn't think of a way forward. In the end she'd distanced herself from everyone who reminded her of her mother's existence, including her sister.

It was why one of the comments in Lucy's letter had made Phoebe's stomach drop. *'I've never had the strength to break free from Mum like you did, and I know now that this is the only way I'll ever do it.'*

It would sound ridiculous, to anyone who hadn't lived their life, that Lucy was willing to die in order to finally be free of their mother. But the scariest part was that Phoebe understood why Lucy might feel that way. Only someone who had been pushed to the edge as often as they had, could ever comprehend that level of despair.

Yet she still refused to believe the letter was a suicide note. It didn't spell out that her sister was going to kill herself and all she could do was pray that Lucy had found another way of being free of their mother, one that didn't end with her death. Janet Spencer wasn't worth dying for, she wasn't worth anything. Deep down, Lucy had to have known that too, it was what Phoebe was holding on to, and she desperately wanted proof she was right. It was why, when she finally stopped staring into the space in front of her, she started to search through the cottage again. There had to be something, somewhere, that provided evidence of Lucy making another choice. A booking for a flight or a hotel, an advert for a live-in job offer somewhere that she might have applied for. Anything to give Phoebe something to cling on to.

Almost an hour later she was still searching. She picked up one of Lucy's sketchbooks, putting it down again, before searching through a drawer for the third time. But something about the sketchbook seemed to be calling to her. It wasn't going to contain the evidence she so desperately needed of Lucy still being alive, but it would be a way of connecting with her sister, of looking at artwork she had created, and that was something Phoebe badly needed too.

All the sketches inside were beautifully done, and she stared at each of them for a long time, taking in the tiny details Lucy had so beautifully captured. But it was the drawing on the fourth page that caught her breath, even before she noticed the words written opposite. It was a sketch of two young girls paddling in the water, and she instantly knew it was her and Lucy. They were smiling, and it was a perfect representation of one of the days they'd spent down at Lake Pippin with their father, when Janet Spencer had been nowhere in sight. Phoebe knew it for certain, even before she read the words.

Lake Pippin was our special place. It was where we got a taste of what could have been. Dad was never allowed to take photographs, in case Mum found them. But this is what I remember, this is what it felt like – me and my big sister, having fun. They were carefree days, so few and far between, but even in the midst of those snippets of happiness, we always knew time was running out fast. When we got back home, it would only ever be a little while before our mother lashed out again. It was usually Phoebe who suffered, and it took me a long time to realise that she often deliberately provoked Mum, as a way of protecting me. If only Dad had been as strong as Phoebe, we might have had a whole childhood filled with carefree days. But he wasn't. And the problem is, I'm far more like Dad than Phoebe ever was. Which is why, if I want Darcy to have a carefree childhood, I'm going to need my big sister to step in one more time.

The words were swimming in front of Phoebe's eyes, and it had nothing to do with the fact that her sister's handwriting was so difficult to read. She'd never known that Lucy had been aware of how often she'd deliberately acted out when she'd thought their mother might be about to pick on her little sister. And she'd had no idea that Lucy was so scared of not being able to protect Darcy, the way their father had never truly been able to protect them, despite the tiny slivers of happiness he'd managed to provide. There was a physical pain in her chest as she looked at the picture again, and she wished with all her heart she could turn back time to the moment that Lucy had so exquisitely captured. Except it was gone forever, and possibly Lucy was too. But Phoebe had no idea how she'd live with that, if it turned out to be true.

8

It was still early enough for the makeshift beach on the edge of Lake Pippin to be completely empty. The man-made lake was hidden half a mile's trek into the woods behind the back of Jamie's house, and his biceps felt like they'd had a good workout pulling Darcy down the path in her wagon and trying to avoid all the bumps in the track. Looking after the little girl for the past few days might have got Jamie up even earlier than he was used to, but having the lake to themselves was worth losing sleep over any day. Darcy was happy pottering about with a bucket, picking up a random collection of stones, and marching through the shallows in her pink glittery wellies like a pro.

Fisher, Jamie's poodle terrier cross, was living up to his name and following hot on Darcy's heels, plunging his face into water and occasionally emerging with something to crunch on. At that moment he was proudly carrying a mouthful of pondweed around with him, like a highly prized trophy, his tail wagging. He'd have to have a bath before Jamie took him up to The Pines care home later. The pet therapy scheme might be a hit with the residents so far, but taking in a wet, muddy dog who smelt of stagnant pond-water might not go down quite as well.

Darcy and Fisher were still taking the lead when they reached the part of the lake that was known locally as the Lovers' Shore. There was a large heart-shaped rock there, which local legend claimed a farmhand had made 150 years before, when the river that ran through Appleberry was dammed, to provide more water for the tannery that had once been sited just outside the village. The story was that he did it to try and win the hand of the landowner's daughter. There was no evidence of it being true, but it was a romantic notion and the name had taken hold.

Jamie was so busy watching Darcy trotting over towards the rock that he didn't see the other person on the beach at first, her dark long-sleeved T-shirt and black jeans almost making her blend into the crop of smaller rocks that surrounded the Lovers' Shore. The woman's head was bowed and, when she finally looked up, she seemed to stare straight in his direction without seeing him.

'Everything okay?' He was almost level with Phoebe by the time he spoke, and when she nodded it wasn't entirely convincing.

'Sorry, I was miles away.' Phoebe was nothing like her sister. Lucy had short brown hair and hazel eyes, and spent most of her life in dungarees. Even in jeans and a T-shirt Phoebe looked polished, as if the casual clothing had been tailored to fit. Her hair was longer and much darker than Lucy's, almost black. The day before, Jamie would have sworn her eyes were grey, but in the sunlight they seemed more like violet. She looked striking and sad in equal measure.

'I could tell.' He took a seat on the rock next to her. There was a good chance she didn't want his company, but after everything that had happened with Lucy he wasn't taking any chances. He might have had the training that was supposed to equip him to deal with a vulnerable person, but when you were facing it in real life, it wasn't quite so simple. Thankfully Darcy was still engrossed in filling her bucket and she hadn't even noticed that her aunt was there. Phoebe seemed to read his thoughts.

'Should I talk to her now, do you think?' She looked over to where her niece was busy examining her latest find, her eyes widening as she watched the little girl. 'She's changed so much since I last saw her.'

'They do that really quickly at Darcy's age.' Jamie gave her what he hoped was a reassuring smile. 'She's happy playing at the moment; why don't you wait until she comes over? It might feel less intense for you both that way.'

'Good idea. God, I'm going to be so hopeless at all of this.' Phoebe let go of a long breath. 'It's why I was out here in the first place, trying to work out how on earth Lucy thought it was a good idea to trust me with this much responsibility.'

'Have you been here long?'

'I stayed at my parents' place again last night, but I couldn't sleep. I've only been there two days, but I already know I can't do another night. I got up about four this morning in the end.' She shook her head. 'I suppose Lucy told you what it was like for us growing up?'

'I know you didn't have it easy.'

'We used to dream about how different things would be when we grew up and how happy that would make us, because we'd understand how lucky we were to finally be free.' She sighed. 'Except somewhere along the line we started competing with each other to try and be the one who finally made Mum love them. Lucy did it by staying close, always trying to be around for our parents. I decided I had to get out altogether, and that I'd finally prove myself to Mum and make her proud – earning her love – by having a successful career. But both of us were on to a loser from the start.'

'Lucy said your mum had a diagnosis, but she wasn't interested in getting help?' He didn't want to push Phoebe and he was surprised by how much she'd opened up already; she seemed like a different person to the one he'd met two days before. But if she wanted to talk, the least he could do was to listen.

'She doesn't think she needs help, and she didn't believe anything the doctor told her. Dad only persuaded her to see the GP because they were called in for a health MOT when they got to forty. She definitely wasn't expecting a diagnosis of narcissistic personality disorder, and that was almost twenty years ago now. But as far as she's concerned, she's acting in a perfectly rational way.' Phoebe tugged at the hem of her sleeve. 'Dad has always been someone who would do anything for a quiet life, and he lets her think it's okay. So why should she bother getting help? I don't think he could stand up to her if his life depended on it. Or if mine and Lucy's did.'

'That must have been really hard, but at least you had each other.'

'I've been a terrible sister.' Phoebe's voice was steady, but there was a tiny pulse throbbing in the corner of her eye. 'My niece is thirty feet away and I might as well be a stranger. The poor little thing will probably scream the place down and cling to your leg, begging you to let her stay. That's not right by anyone's standards, is it? She and Lucy are the only family I've really got.'

'Just because you don't live in each other's pockets, it doesn't mean you've been a bad sister.' He wanted to tell her she was wrong about Darcy, but there was no way of knowing how she'd react. Children of her age didn't have a huge capacity for remembering people they didn't see very often, and the last thing Phoebe needed was for her niece to have a screaming tantrum and refuse to go with her. Not to mention what that would do to the little girl who was already confused and missing her mum. A gradual approach might work better for both of them, but he had no idea if that was something Phoebe would agree to. In the meantime, he wanted to give her whatever crumbs of comfort he could. 'Lucy always spoke about you with real affection, and she must have thought you were the best person to look after Darcy.'

'My parents are hardly great competition, are they? And I don't suppose she thought it would be fair to leave Darcy with you indefinitely, although that might well have been for the best. I wish I knew what she was really thinking when she decided to disappear.'

'I take it the letter didn't help?' He'd been desperate to ask since the moment he'd seen her, wondering if Lucy had said anything that might give them more clues about where she'd gone. He'd told the police what he could, but there were things he'd promised not to share with anyone else. That was easier said than done, with Lucy's devastated sister sitting by his side. He was hoping that the letter would reveal the things he knew, but he had a horrible feeling it wouldn't. And the guilt about keeping that from Phoebe weighed him down more and more every time they spoke.

'It did in some ways. I got the sense that she just wanted to get away, at any cost, and I understand why. But I still don't know if that means she's gone for good or not...' They fell silent for a moment as Jamie searched for something to say, when nothing he was able to offer could help. The urge to blurt out what he knew was almost overwhelming, but it could cost him everything. Without warning, a streak of toffee-coloured fur hurtled towards them, leaping onto Phoebe's lap and then off again, straight into a huge puddle beside her, sending up a splash of water in all directions.

'Fisher, for God's sake!' Jamie got to his feet, but the dog was already fifteen feet away by now, chasing a mallard that kept letting him get just close enough and then shooting up into the air and flying another twenty feet or so away and landing with a lopsided descent, as if one of its wings was a bit out of kilter with the other one. 'I'm so sorry. He's got absolutely no manners!'

'Don't be, he's lovely.' Phoebe smiled for the first time, and he could suddenly see the resemblance with Darcy. The little girl might have her mother's colouring, but all three of them had the same disarming smile. Although neither of the sisters displayed it as often as they should.

'He's a pain in the arse some of the time! He can be as good as gold when he puts his mind to it, but at times like this he doesn't do my credibility as an animal behavioural therapist a lot of good.'

'I thought you ran the forest school?'

'I do but I do some other stuff too, including therapy of both the human and animal kind. Judging from what you've just seen, you might say it makes me a jack-of-all-trades and a master of none! I do some counselling; run the forest school two or three days a week, depending on the time of year; run a pet therapy scheme, and I do some behavioural therapy with pets gone bad.' He laughed at the expression on her face. 'Sorry, I know that makes it sound like a bad documentary on an obscure satellite channel.'

'It does a bit, but it also sounds like an interesting way to earn a living.'

'I love it, the variety and the work I do. I originally trained as a therapist and did that full time, but I've cut down the number of clients I had by almost three quarters. I prefer applying what I've learnt out in the forest, or by helping people realise the therapeutic benefits animals can provide. I wanted to be a zookeeper when I was a kid and maybe this is just my way of getting the next best thing.'

'So you're in the business of fixing people's problems? Should I be worried that you're working out how to try to fix mine?' She gave him a suspicious look and he couldn't help laughing.

'I promise not to offer to fix any of your problems, unless you've got a dog who won't eat its food from a bowl, or you want to know why it will only sleep behind the dresser.'

'Actually, I've got a pug called Norma, who could probably do with your help.' Phoebe pulled a face. 'I think it's my fault she's the way she is, because I've treated her more like a baby than a dog. At least that's what Adam says.'

'Adam?' Jamie glanced across at Fisher, who was still stalking the mallard he had absolutely no chance of catching, and tried to ignore the tightening of his scalp as he waited for Phoebe to respond. Of course she had someone waiting at home for her to come back as soon as she could, and with Lucy missing he should have much bigger things on his mind than her sister's relationship status.

'Adam's my... I don't know what to call him. Let's just say we live together and he laughs at the fact that I use a dog nanny service to take care of Norma while I'm at work, and I watch her on a webcam from the office whenever I get the chance.' She gave him a quizzical look, as if daring him to laugh too.

'It's not uncommon for people to treat their dogs the way you do, especially the ones who don't have children. It's not necessarily wrong, but you might find there's a bit of readjustment when you take Darcy back to London. Not just for you, Darcy and Adam, but for Norma too.' Jamie fought the urge to ask more about Adam – this man she lived with, who didn't have a *label*.

'I've decided I'm not going back.' Phoebe picked up a pebble and tossed it into the water in front of her. 'At least not straight away. Lucy asked me in her letter not to uproot Darcy and there's no point in me causing her all that stress, if her mum's going to be back soon. So until we know otherwise, I'm going to work out a way of staying down here.'

A tiny part of Jamie recognised that the relief flooding his body wasn't just because he thought that was the right thing for Darcy, but he didn't want to acknowledge it right now. 'How does Adam feel about that?'

'I haven't told him yet and I'm more worried what I'm going to do about work. I've been wondering how I can make things work for everyone.'

'And did you come up with a solution?'

'Not yet.'

'Jamie!' Darcy was not far from turning four, and over the years that she and Lucy had been his neighbours, he'd grown really fond of them both. He might have let her mother down by not spotting the signs of her desperation, but he was determined not to let Darcy or her aunt down.

'Yes, sweetheart?'

'I got lots of pretty stones!' She thrust the bucket towards him and shot Phoebe a shy look from under her lashes.

'You have, and some lovely smooth pebbles. We could take some of these home and paint them.' He looked from Darcy to Phoebe and back again. Maybe a stone-painting session would help the two of them reconnect, without the pressure of the little girl knowing she'd be moving in with her aunt. 'Do you know who this is?'

Darcy nodded and then shot another look in Phoebe's direction.

'Who is it, sweetheart?'

'Mummy's sister.' Despite recognising her aunt, Darcy was still squirming, as if she couldn't quite believe that the woman in front of her was a close relation.

'That's right, it's your auntie Phoebe.' Jamie put his hand on Darcy's shoulder, letting her know that he was still there and that she was safe. He desperately wanted this first meeting to go right, for both of their sakes, but so much hung on how Phoebe handled it.

'Hi, Darcy. Can I have a look in your bucket?' Phoebe addressed her niece, who did a sort of sideways walk in her direction, taking the bucket back from Jamie.

'My stones.' The little girl twisted a strand of light brown hair between her fingers as she passed the bucket over.

'They're beautiful.' Phoebe took out a large grey stone and turned it over in her hand. 'Oh my goodness, you're so clever, you've found a fossil! It must have been in the river before it was dammed.'

'What's a fossil?' Darcy frowned, taking a step forward to peer at the stone in her aunt's hand.

'It's where the imprint of an animal who was here thousands of years ago is left behind in a stone. Can you see the shape here? That's part of the tail of a fish.'

'I can!' Darcy was almost dancing on the spot. 'Can we look for more? You can help me!'

The little girl had already grabbed hold of her aunt's wrist, not even waiting for the answer, but both of them were smiling as Darcy dragged her to the edge of the water. Phoebe might have her doubts, but Lucy had been right, she was more than capable of looking after her niece. Jamie just had to help her realise it.

* * *

Despite Phoebe's almost pathological inability to cry, when Darcy had asked whether she could come shopping with her and Jamie, tears had welled up in Phoebe's eyes and she'd had to blink them back. She'd always felt like an alien from another planet when Scarlett or Lucy had said they'd been moved to tears by something their little one had said or done, but in that instant, she got it. She understood for the first time how a tiny little person like Darcy could make you feel like the centre of her world, and make you want to put her at the centre of yours. She wasn't naïve enough to think that parenting was all sunshine and roses, but there was just a tiny glimmer of hope that it might not be completely beyond her capabilities either. She couldn't get too carried away, though. They were only an hour into this getting-to-know-you lark, and being at the little girl's beck and call twenty-four-seven was going to be a whole different thing.

By the time they were halfway up the village high street, Darcy had slipped her hand into Phoebe's. Their progress was slow and the three of them were now spanning the width of the pavement, like an especially unwieldy version of the three-legged race at a school sports day. Jamie had one hand hooked through Fisher's lead and the other holding Darcy's left hand, while Phoebe held her right one. They had to stop for a while outside The Toy Box, where a replica wooden Ferris wheel filled the window of the shop, with dolls and teddy bears sitting in the swinging chairs to enjoy their ride around and around the window. Darcy's little eyes were wide with wonder, and Phoebe had to fight the urge to take her into the shop and just buy every toy Darcy liked the look of. She was going to have to find a way of doing the everyday, ordinary stuff with her niece, until Lucy came home, and starting off by spending a fortune in the first toy shop they passed wasn't the way to go about it. Phoebe might know next to nothing about looking after children, but even she could work that one out.

'Shall we go home and paint these stones, before I have to go to work?' Jamie crouched down to speak to Darcy, after he'd picked up the supplies he needed from the pet shop.

'Can we go to the swings? Mummy always takes me there and I want to show Auntie Phoebe.'

'Well, sweetheart, if you want to help me feed the chickens and collect the eggs before you go to nursery, we're not going to have time. But maybe we can all go to the park together another day.'

'Okay.' Darcy wrinkled her little nose, not looking as though she was entirely sure she'd made the right decision in choosing chickens over the swings.

'Let me know if you get tired and I'll give you a piggyback.' They'd dropped Darcy's trailer at the back gate of Jamie's house on the way past, but he clearly knew enough about looking after pre-schoolers to realise that a nearly four-year-old might not be able to make it all the way down to the centre of the village and back again. It wouldn't even have occurred to Phoebe, and it was another reminder of just how much she had to learn.

'So have you and Adam been together long?' Jamie's question took her by surprise, as they headed up towards the church, which clung on to the side of the hill at Appleberry's highest point. The primary school where Darcy was due to start in September was almost opposite the church and the village green just beyond that. It was the sort of idyllic picture-postcard English village that could have easily featured on the front of a biscuit tin, but things weren't always what they seemed, much like Phoebe's relationship with Adam. She'd surprised herself at how much she'd already opened up to Jamie, but she'd been deliberately vague about the set-up with Adam. Lucy had never really understood it, so she could hardly expect a man whose life had been thrown together with hers to get his head around it.

On the rare occasions she'd tried to quantify her relationship with Adam, people either didn't believe that one of them wasn't secretly in love with the other, or they judged them for what they clearly saw as a sordid arrangement. Not that Phoebe cared; it suited the two of them and they were both grown-ups, with minds of their own, so what anyone else thought was their problem. Except it suddenly mattered more than it should what Jamie might think, not least because he was going to need to trust her enough to hand Darcy over to her care. It was easier to let people assume whatever they wanted to about her and Adam, and keeping any explanation hazy was a well-rehearsed approach. She'd only had one romantic relationship that had fitted into other people's idea of what that should look like, but the way things had ended with Eddie shouldn't have been anyone's idea of normal. Even now it was almost impossible to believe any of that had happened, especially after her mother's attempts to twist the truth. So, if what she had with Adam bothered anyone, she couldn't care less. Usually.

'We've lived together for three years. On and off.' It wasn't actually a lie, more of an omission of the whole story. She and Adam had first got together three years before, but the on-and-off nature was the whole premise of the relationship, not the make-up and break-up stuff 'normal' couples went through.

'But you're happy together now?' He was pushing it, and he seemed to realise that as he watched the expression that must have crossed her face. 'I'm sorry, it's just Lucy said once that neither of you had been very lucky in love.'

'I suppose that depends on how you define luck and what you're looking for in a relationship. Lucy's always been far more traditional than me in that respect, but I don't really buy into the whole love thing.' As soon as the words were out of her mouth, she wished she hadn't said them. She had a horrible feeling he might be about to ask her what she meant, or to try to persuade her to offer up her definition of love.

Any attempts to psycho-analyse her just caused Phoebe to shut down. Therapy was a route she'd been offered more times than she could remember, but after the first couple of attempts she always resisted, and she certainly wasn't open to an improvised version, in the middle of Appleberry, with her inquisitive niece hanging on every word. Maybe it was time to put Jamie on the spot instead.

'What about you, is there someone waiting for you at home?'

'Just me, Fisher and the three girls in my life.' He laughed as she turned to look at him. 'It's all right, they're all chickens – Betty, Hetty and Petula.'

'Petula?'

'Yes, after the singer. I inherited all the chickens. Betty and Hetty were rescued from a battery farm, and someone found Petula wandering around the bottom of the High Street and asked me if I would take her in. She was found downtown, you know, like the Petula Clark song? I just had to name her that.'

'Sometimes the names pick themselves, don't they? When I went to pick out which pug puppy I wanted, Norma was much paler than her siblings. Her face was jet black like the others, but her coat was almost peroxide blonde whereas the rest were sandy, so I decided I had to name her after Norma Jeane, you know, Marilyn Monroe's real name.' The only trouble with talking about Norma was that it made Phoebe miss her all the more. The dog never minded when she held her too close, if she'd had another abrasive text from her mother. She was the outlet for Phoebe's affections, and she never expected anything in return. Phoebe's relationship with Adam might not be perfect, but she seriously doubted there were many men who'd be as tolerant of the pug who slept on the end of her bed and snored louder than a navvy. Although if it had come to a choice between him and the dog, it would have been no contest. Norma had taught her what unconditional love was, and now she just had to try and replicate that with Darcy.

'It's a good job neither of us have ever been trusted to name a baby!' Jamie grinned. 'Do you want to come back to my place to paint the stones with Darcy, or would you rather go back to Lucy's? I've got everything set up on the kitchen table. It's been like an art studio since Darcy came to stay; it's her favourite thing to do after nursery. She's a chip off the old block in that respect.'

'If you're sure I won't be in the way, that would be great, thank you.' Phoebe was in no hurry to get back to Lucy's place, where she'd have to look at those half-finished Russian dolls on the side again. It was too stark a reminder that her sister had got up and gone right in the middle of things. If she'd just needed a break from everything, Phoebe could understand that, but she'd have planned it better. Having to stop halfway through a project would have driven Lucy mad, and the fact she'd done so smacked of desperation. Which was scary. 'Who has Darcy when you're at work?'

'She comes with me to the forest school, and I've booked her into some extra sessions at the nursery the rest of the time. Thankfully they've been great, but I've been juggling things around where I can. I've got to go up to The Pines care home with Fisher this afternoon, though, and I'm not sure if the nursery can squeeze Darcy in. I'd normally make my excuses, but we've just set up a pet therapy programme there and I don't want to start cancelling sessions before it gets properly established, if I can help it.'

'That sounds fantastic.' Aware of how much Norma had done to save Phoebe from her own demons, she understood what a programme like that could do. She still hadn't admitted to Jamie that the police checks were back, but she didn't think he'd want things to move too fast for her niece, any more than she did. And if the police had already told him about the checks, he'd clearly decided not to mention it. But baby steps couldn't hurt, and this might be the ideal opportunity. 'I can take Darcy this afternoon, if you think she'll be okay with it?'

'What do you think, Darcy?' He spoke directly to the little girl, who was humming an unrecognisable tune, still clutching their hands. 'Would you like to spend the afternoon with Auntie Phoebe? Maybe you could do some more fossil hunting.'

'When's Mummy coming home?' The innocence of Darcy's question made Phoebe forget how to breathe for a moment, and she couldn't have come up with an answer if her life had depended on it. Thank God Jamie was a million times better at this than she was.

'We don't know yet, darling.' Jamie dropped down onto his haunches, looking Darcy directly in the eyes. 'But there are lots of fun things we can do until she does, and I bet Auntie Phoebe has got loads of photos of her dog, Norma, on her phone. She's even cuter than Fisher by the sounds of it.'

'I love dogs!' Darcy's face instantly transformed at the prospect of scrolling through a camera roll full of cute photos of Norma, and Phoebe let go of the breath she'd been holding. If she'd managed to speak at all, she had a horrible feeling she'd have said the wrong thing, or promised something she had no way of knowing she could deliver. She had no idea how she was supposed to suddenly pick all of this up overnight. It was terrifying just how badly she might handle caring for her niece, and what the consequences of that might be for Darcy.

'Do you think she'll be able to cope with going back to Lucy's?' Phoebe whispered the words as Jamie stood up again and they continued towards the lane where his farm and Lucy's cottage sat side by side.

'I think so. She won't attach any significance to the things that you do when you're in there; all she knows is that her mum's gone away for a while. I think we just need to take it day by day and not say anything we might have to go back on. If she thinks we've lied to her, she won't be able to trust us. But there's no need for us to tell her more than she needs to know before we get any further news either.' Jamie kept his voice low so Darcy couldn't hear him, but she was already humming another tuneless melody, her mind on other things for now.

'Okay. I just need to make a few phone calls about work and Norma, then I think the best thing to do would be for me to move into Lucy's place. Just until she comes home.' Phoebe bent down to pat Fisher as they finally reached the gateway to Jamie's farm. The dog's ears were crisp with dried-on pondweed, nothing like the velvety softness of Norma's. 'Darcy seems to love dogs, so maybe bringing Norma down here will be a good thing.'

'I'm sure it will. For both of you.' Jamie opened the gate into his driveway. It was like another world from the cottages that were dotted around most of the village. His house looked as though it was several hundred years old, but it was much bigger than Lucy's and set a long way back from the road, on a large plot, which backed onto the dense woodland that hid Lake Pippin in its depths.

'This is lovely.' Phoebe followed Jamie down the pathway at the side of the house, Darcy already rushing ahead of them. Her niece picked up a basket at the edge of the driveway without any prompting, almost running down towards the chicken house about a hundred feet away. 'She seems to know her way around.'

'She loves being outside. Some of the kids at the nursery struggle to adjust to the forest school, although most of them come to love it in the end, but Darcy took to it from day one.'

'I can see why Lucy chose to leave Darcy with you; I just wish she didn't feel she had to.' Phoebe touched his hand briefly, surprising herself with the powerful urge she had to do it, and his eyes clouded for a moment.

'Me too. And I can't help thinking I should have done more to help her, that I should have noticed how close to the edge she'd got and not put it down to another low patch.' She recognised the expression of guilt on his face, because it was the same expression that stared back at her every time she looked in the mirror. Maybe it was true, and neither of them had done enough to help stop Lucy's desperation spiralling out of control, but it was no good blaming themselves or each other. They had Darcy to look after now, and she and Jamie were going to need to be a team.

9

_____

Two days after they'd found the fossil, Darcy had moved in with her aunt. Phoebe wouldn't have survived the first full week of looking after her niece without Jamie's support. Normally Scarlett would have stepped up to help too, but she was committed to accompanying a Year Six class on a week-long activity holiday to celebrate their upcoming transition from primary to secondary school. She'd told Phoebe she felt terrible about it, but it had probably been for the best in some ways, and it meant there was no choice but for Phoebe to step up to the plate when Jamie was at work. As well as the pictures that Lucy had of her and Phoebe pinned to the corkboard in the kitchen, she'd found a stack more in a box file on one of the bookshelves, and she and Darcy had looked through them together. There were only a few from when they were young, mostly official school photos that Janet had no doubt felt obliged to buy in an attempt to pretend she cared. Their mother probably couldn't wait to offload them, which explained why they were now in a box file and not on display in her parents' home. Telling her niece stories about growing up with Lucy had been another way of them bonding, but she'd been careful to give a Disney version of their childhood, picking out only the very best bits to share with the little girl.

Parenthood – albeit by proxy – was a revelation. Everything took ages. Getting Darcy out of the door for nursery was like a military operation and, for the first time, Phoebe understood why working mothers sometimes gave their children biscuits for breakfast or went to work with more Weetabix in their hair than they'd managed to get their children to eat. After a few difficult conversations with her boss, they'd come to a temporary arrangement for her to keep working while she was in Appleberry. She'd be doing the sort of work the company normally contracted out to freelancers, designing analytics systems for less high-profile clients.

The huge deal she'd been working on had gone to someone else in the team, and she had a feeling the position she'd spent years establishing in the company had disappeared along with Lucy. But she couldn't worry about any of that now, despite the fact her career had been the most important thing in her life for as long as she could remember. In an instant, it just hadn't seemed to matter so much any more. Once upon a time, her motivation came from getting feedback from a client telling her they loved her work or securing a new contract for her firm. But now, it was finding a way to make Darcy smile. It had become almost her entire focus, and she'd never have expected, a couple of weeks before, that she'd be willing to hop around the kitchen like a frog, just to make her niece giggle. Darcy was mostly okay when Phoebe gave her yet another vague answer about when her mother was coming home, but sometimes the little girl's lip would start wobble, and in those moments, Phoebe knew she'd be willing to do anything to take her niece's pain away. And hopping around like a frog seemed a tiny price to pay.

Caring for Darcy had helped distract from her own pain too, and she didn't have as much time to dwell on everything. But when Darcy went to bed, Phoebe went straight back to searching. She'd trawled through all of the parts of Lucy's social media she could access, and she was working her way through everything else. Phoebe had a whole new appreciation for her sister's talent as an artist, and she wished she'd told Lucy more often how proud of her she was. She longed to tell her sister the funny things Darcy said, and every morning she prayed it would be the day when her sister would finally come home. Life had changed so much, so quickly. But they were the only things that mattered now – making Darcy as happy as possible, and bringing her mother home. Everything else felt like a waste of time.

When Bradley rang to confirm that Lucy's bank account hadn't been touched since her disappearance, Phoebe's world had shifted beneath her feet for a second time, and she'd been forced to face up to the very real prospect that her sister might never come back. The young policeman had tried to be reassuring and had told her that it didn't necessarily mean anything, that maybe Lucy was staying somewhere she didn't need money, because someone else was providing it for her, or that she'd set some funds aside before disappearing. Phoebe wanted to believe it, more than she'd ever wanted to believe anything, but every day it was getting harder. Bradley had definitely seemed more empathetic since meeting her mother, and open to the idea that Lucy's disappearance might not be as final as it first appeared. He must have realised Janet was capable of making anyone want to run away. But despite his increased optimism, for Phoebe, hope seemed to be disappearing with every passing day. There'd been nothing for her to hold on to, no glimmer that Lucy was still out there somewhere, despite an article on the front page of the local paper appealing for anyone who had news on her disappearance to come forward, along with a widespread social media campaign that had already been shared all over the country, and beyond.

Her father had called regularly that first week, but only to ask when Phoebe was going to go round and apologise to her mother. He barely asked after his only grandchild, let alone how Phoebe was coping, and, in the end, she'd started screening his calls. It was killing her not knowing where Lucy was, and whether or not she was okay, and she found it impossible to believe that her father wasn't hurting too. But he was doing it again, putting her mother's feelings above everybody else's – including his own – because it was easier that way. It shouldn't have been a surprise and it shouldn't have hurt so much; after all, it was what he'd always done. But it made Phoebe feel even more alone, and it wasn't just her mother and herself she was angry with any more. Her father had to take some of the blame of Lucy's disappearance too. He'd let her down so many times, and he was still doing it now.

Jamie, on the other hand, texted her all the time to check how things were. He was there to reassure her when she thought Darcy might be running a temperature, even though it was the middle of the night. He'd taken Darcy to some of her nursery sessions and to the forest school with him, even on the days she wasn't scheduled to go, so that Phoebe could get some work done. Trying to write complicated data analysis programmes with a three-year-old begging to play another game of hide and seek, or with CBeebies blaring out in the background, was a challenge Phoebe definitely wasn't up to just yet and one she'd never thought she'd have to face.

Something else she didn't want to accept was that there was a very good chance Lucy might not be home for Darcy's upcoming fourth birthday. The idea that the little girl wouldn't have her mum there was already making Phoebe wake up in a cold sweat in the early hours of the morning. It was enough of a struggle to get to sleep in the first place, but when her deepest fears crept into the darkness of the bedroom and shook her awake, getting back to sleep was completely impossible.

Having Norma there might have helped, but she was still with the dog-nannying service. Adam had insisted he couldn't get away to bring her down the first weekend she'd spent back in Appleberry. Part of the reason why the arrangement between them had worked for so long was because he resolutely lived the life he wanted – they both had, up until now – so she couldn't really complain when he wasn't willing to change his plans for her benefit. But being without Norma was a physical ache. She needed the comfort that only lying with Norma curled up on her lap seemed able to provide. She was sure it would help strengthen her bond with Darcy too. The little girl was still desperately missing her mum and she seemed to want Jamie more than Phoebe, despite the early promise their relationship had shown. Realistically, she knew she was expecting too much, too soon, but any sign that Darcy might be unhappy staying with Phoebe made it feel like she was failing at the most important job she'd ever been given.

She tried telling herself it was only natural that Darcy had such a strong attachment to Jamie; after all, he'd been far more present in Darcy's life than her aunt had. But she couldn't help thinking that having Norma at the house might help Darcy too. It was blatantly obvious that part of the draw with Jamie was his dog, Fisher, not to mention the chickens. Maybe having the pug in the house would give them both the comfort they needed while they waited for news. Adam had promised to bring her down on her second weekend back in Appleberry. If he didn't, she'd already decided she and Darcy would be taking a road trip of their own to collect the little dog.

Pick-up and drop-offs at Darcy's nursery were another revelation. At thirty years old, Phoebe had thought she'd left all that playground stuff behind her. She might have developed a hard shell after her first term at secondary school, but she could still remember the pain she'd never let anyone see, not even her best friend. The physical bullying had stopped, but the sly looks and comments hadn't. Phoebe had perfected a look of perfect nonchalance, like it was all water off a duck's back, but being told that your mother was a nutter and that you must be too, over and over again, would get to anyone in the end. Unfortunately, Janet had got involved with run-ins with other parents, and even some of the teachers, too many times for Phoebe to ever be able to fly under the radar. So finding herself on the receiving end of judgement at Darcy's nursery, even if it was of a very different kind, was an unwelcome shock.

'How old is your little girl? Henry only started last month and I'm still struggling to work out which children are in his age group. They all seem to be at such different stage, *developmentally speaking*.' On the surface, it was a friendly enquiry. The super-glamorous woman who struck up a conversation with Phoebe outside the gates of the Little Monkeys nursery school was pushing a buggy that probably cost as much as a small car. She looked like she'd stepped out of the pages of a glossy magazine and Phoebe was more conscious than ever that the clothes she'd borrowed from Lucy's bedroom were a terrible fit and that scraping her hair back into a ponytail might have kept the Weetabix out of it that morning, but that was about the best she could say. The way the woman was looking her up and down made it obvious Phoebe wasn't the only one who thought so.

'She'll be four next month.' Phoebe decided not to explain that Darcy wasn't hers. It was a long story and not one she was particularly keen to get into, especially as her niece was already pulling at her arm for them to get moving.

'I wanna go to the park!' She had quite the grip for someone who was just over three feet tall.

'In a minute. I'm just talking to this lady.' Phoebe forced a smile, despite the fact that she was every bit as desperate to get going as Darcy.

'Really? Well, I suppose not everyone Henry's age, or even the older ones like your daughter, are able to focus on activities the way he can.' The woman raised an eyebrow. 'Henry's just turned three and he rode in his first gymkhana last weekend.'

Phoebe didn't speak for a moment, waiting for the punchline, only it didn't come.

'Wow...' She searched the recesses of her brain for the right words, all the time fighting not to say that she couldn't give a damn about Henry's equine talents and that his mother personified everything that terrified Phoebe most about parenting. The sort of competitive parenting that forced children to live up to unrealistic expectations was exactly why she'd decided she never wanted kids. Janet had only ever wanted her daughters to reflect well on her, caring far less about their happiness than she did about laying claim to their achievements in public, while belittling their efforts in private. But Phoebe didn't want Darcy to suffer for any outburst she might make, so she added a distinctly half-hearted, 'That's amazing.'

'Yes, his instructor says he has excellent balance and of course we were very fortunate to identify his talent at such a young age. Some people never discover theirs.' The woman glanced down at Darcy, who was clutching a very abstract painting in the hand that wasn't still desperately trying to pull her aunt away from the conversation. Seeing this stranger curl her lip slightly, as she compared Darcy to her amazing son, Phoebe suddenly had the urge to yank off the woman's expensive-looking wooden beads and shove them down her throat. How dare she look at Darcy like she was inferior. The kid was bloody amazing. Her mum had disappeared overnight and been replaced by a virtual stranger. Yet, despite clearly missing Lucy, Darcy still spent most of her time singing. And her first smiles in the mornings were worth a million gymkhana rosettes.

'Darcy's very artistic.' She didn't want to explain to this woman that her niece was a whole lot more than that, but the urge to stick up for Darcy, and the accompanying anger bubbling up inside her, took over. Rationally, she couldn't have explained why it mattered so much. But it did.

'Colouring and playing are all well and good, but since we decided to send Henry here I've been pressing the nursery to think about developing a gifted and talented register.' Henry's mother ran a hand through her hair and there wasn't a trace of Weetabix on show.

'But the oldest kids here are four, aren't they?'

'You can never start cultivating your child's talents too early.' Henry's mother fixed Phoebe with a serious expression. 'Do you work?'

'Well yes, I—' Before she could explain, the other woman cut her off.

'And do you use that as an excuse? Because if you do, *don't*. So many working mothers say that they don't have time to spend fully developing their children's potential, but trust me, it's the most important thing you'll ever do. My life is super busy, but I still fit in lots of coaching with Henry and his older sister, as well as running them to all their activities.'

Phoebe opened her mouth and then closed it again. There was nothing she could say. This woman seemed determined to share her unwanted parenting advice with anyone she could corner. A couple of other parents, standing just behind her, were rolling their eyes. So, there was a good chance Henry's mother launched into her almost evangelical wittering on a daily basis. The more experienced parents had clearly heard it all before and learnt to stay out of her way. Maybe getting through a conversation with Henry's mother was some sort of initiation test, to see if she could spot a disastrous approach to parenting when she saw one, and steer clear of anyone spouting that sort of nonsense in the future. But Phoebe had already seen enough disastrous approaches to parenting first-hand to last her a lifetime.

* * *

When Jamie called round early on Friday evening, just after Darcy had gone up to bed, she was still caught between dismissing Henry's mother as a neurotic nightmare and wondering if there was a tiny grain of truth in her accusation that Phoebe might not be doing enough to stimulate Darcy. Especially when it felt like she was using the TV as a babysitter, while she tried to shoehorn her old life in around this new one she'd unexpectedly found herself in.

'What are you watching?' Jamie followed her into the sitting room, glancing at the TV playing in the corner.

'*Peppa Pig*.' Phoebe grinned, not entirely sure she should admit to why. 'I haven't seen the ending of this one before.'

'I don't want to give you any spoilers, but all the episodes seem to end up with the whole family falling on the ground in a fit of uncontrollable laughter.'

'It's strangely hypnotic to watch. I hadn't even realised I still had it on until you asked, but Darcy was watching it before she went up to bed.' Phoebe shook her head. 'The other day I drove all the way back from dropping her off at nursery with the audiobook of *Winnie the Pooh* still playing.'

'It's all part of parenthood.' Jamie picked up the top book from the pile that was stacked on a side table. 'So what was the deal, buy one parenting book, get six free?'

'Not quite, it's just that I realised yesterday that I have absolutely no idea what being a parent is supposed to involve and I don't want to do it all wrong while I'm looking after Darcy. And what you see in the stack before you is the result of a dangerous mix of inadequacy and Amazon Prime.'

'You really think there's a handbook for this stuff?' Jamie smiled ruefully. 'I bet every one of these books has a different theory on parenting.'

'Yes, but most people *grow* into being a parent, find their way as they go along. I've landed in the role – albeit temporarily – with two feet.'

'In my experience, most people make it up as they go along.' Jamie gave her a quizzical look. 'You seemed to be settling into things really well until now. Has your mum been in touch?'

'God no. If she were to give me any advice as a parent, I'd make sure to do the exact opposite!' Phoebe shuddered at the thought. 'I met a woman at the nursery who seemed to be suggesting that I'm failing Darcy because she hasn't competed in her first horse show yet. Okay, maybe that's an exaggeration, but she definitely implied I should be doing more to encourage Darcy to develop her talents.'

Jamie shook his head and put a hand on her arm. She surprised herself by not immediately trying to shake it off. His hand was warm and, when he lifted it off again, she shocked herself even more by wishing he hadn't. 'Sorry, Phoebe, but it sounds like you've been Camilla'ed.'

'Sorry?'

'The woman you spoke to, did she have a son called Henry?'

'That's the one.'

'He's only just started at the nursery, but most of the other parents know her already. I'll let you in to a secret: when she comes to collect the poor little kid from forest school, he clings to me like his life depends on it and I can hear him shouting that he doesn't want to go with her halfway back down to the village.' Jamie sighed. 'She might think she's turning him into a leader of the future, but he just wants to be a kid and I'm not sure how putting constant pressure on a three-year-old, and signing him up for every activity going, helps anyone.'

'But I gave Darcy cheesy beans on toast for dinner tonight.' Phoebe tried to read his expression as she spoke, wondering if it would give away what he really thought – that she was doing a crappy job of holding the fort until Lucy got back. 'I made some chicken and broccoli stir-fry, but she wouldn't touch it. In the end I just gave in.'

'There's nothing wrong with beans on toast. What did you give her to drink, vodka or drain cleaner? As long as it wasn't either of those, I think you should stop beating yourself up.'

'I made a smoothie with bananas, summer fruits and orange juice and she seemed to really like it. It made me feel a bit better about the outright rejection of the broccoli.'

'You don't need these books, Phoebe. Trust me, you're doing more than okay.'

Phoebe nodded, unable to speak for a moment as relief flooded her body. Finally, she looked up at him. 'Part of me always envied Lucy, you know.' He was doing it again, getting her to tell him things she'd never confessed to anyone. Not even Scarlett. 'She seemed to be doing so well, raising Darcy, and still sticking around in Appleberry for Mum and Dad, despite everything. I know Darcy misses her mum, and I'm running out of things to say about when she's coming back. What if I mess her up while Lucy's away? What if I'm like my mum?'

'Neither you nor Lucy are anything like your mum. The fact that you've convinced yourself you're doing a rubbish job tells me how much you care.' Jamie held her gaze and there was nothing in his expression to suggest he didn't mean what he was saying. 'Lucy was envious of you too, you know. She always talked about how well you were doing with your career and the fact that you'd had the courage to get away.'

'I'm not sure running away is nearly as courageous as staying.' Tempting as it was to keep staring at Jamie as if he held all the answers, she dropped her gaze. If only Lucy would come back, even for half an hour, Phoebe could it explain it all to her too – tell her how wrong she'd been, thinking that her big sister somehow had it all worked out, and how much she wished she could do differently. 'It was so stupid, all that time we spent competing, when we should have told each other what a good job we were doing, without any real support from either of our parents. You must get sick of listening to me rattle on about them; I bet your parents are great. Did you grow up on the farm?'

'Until I was ten. Then I went to live with my grandmother.' There was such a sadness in Jamie's eyes when he looked at her, and she desperately wished she could stuff the words back down her throat.

'Oh God, I'm sorry. I shouldn't have assumed that you had the perfect life.'

'It's okay, it was twenty-five years ago now and, for a long time, I did have the perfect life.' Jamie breathed out slowly, as though he needed a moment to regain his composure. 'My parents hadn't had a holiday together in years. They decided to treat themselves to a break. Just a weekend, in a B&B, on the coast. I went to stay with my grandmother, and when they didn't come back on the Sunday night to collect me, she knew straight away something was wrong. Eventually the police went to the B&B, and they found the owner, and my parents... It was carbon monoxide poisoning from a faulty boiler. They wouldn't have suffered. They just never woke up.'

'Oh God, Jamie, I'm so sorry.' Phoebe had never known what to do in an emotional crisis. When colleagues at work burst into tears about relationship break-ups, or bereavements, she struggled to comfort them in a physical way. She'd happily cover their work for as long as it took until they could cope again. And she'd always take the lead on organising collections when anyone had suffered a loss, or was unwell themselves. But displaying her empathy in a demonstrative way had always seemed beyond her, until now. Maybe it was the parallel between Jamie's parents never returning, and what Darcy was going through. Whatever it was, she found herself putting her arms around him, as if it was the most natural thing in the world. 'Here I am whinging on, when the situation with Lucy and Darcy must be bringing up so many difficult memories for you.'

'You're not whinging.' He pulled back slightly, but somehow managed not to make it feel like he was pushing her away. They were still standing close enough for her to notice the flecks of green among the blue of his eyes for the first time. 'I've had years of counselling and I've worked through every possible feeling about my parents' death. I promise you I came to terms with it, long before I finally moved back to the farm after university. My grandmother had rented it out until I was ready, understanding how important it would be to be able to call it home again one day. She stepped in and stepped up and that's what you're having to do for Darcy. And if I can be here for you, and help even a little bit, it'll be like I'm paying my grandmother back.'

'I should be able to cope with it on my own, though. How can I stand here and offload on you, knowing what happened to your family?'

'Because I want you to, but only if you do too. You don't have to tell me anything, but if you think it might help to talk about it, I'm always going to be ready to listen.' Her eyes met his again as he spoke. This was what he was trained to do, she had to remind herself of that, and she couldn't let herself get too dependent on him either. If the worst happened, and Lucy really didn't come home, then sooner or later she was going to have to learn to stand on her own two feet. But for now, the words were already falling over themselves to spill out. She had to tell someone what she'd done.

'I wish I hadn't said the things I said to Lucy last time we spoke.' Guilt weighed her down, making her shoulders slump, just as it did every single time she recalled their last conversation. 'Lucy said something about how Darcy didn't want to listen to her when she tried to help her with her paintings, or how to hold the brush properly. I was a bit sharp with her and said she was only three. I think it hit a nerve, reminding me of every time my mother would focus on what I was doing wrong and never on what I was doing right. It probably hit the same nerve for Lucy, and she got defensive. After that, things just seemed to escalate, me giving out parenting advice I had no place to offer, and her getting more and more adamant that she knew exactly how to handle things. In the end, I told her she ought to be careful that she didn't end up like Mum, criticising everything we did, because she was halfway there already. Then I asked her if that was why she seemed so determined to bring Darcy up around our parents, so Mum could criticise her too. Lucy should have been able to turn to me, but I gave her nowhere to go and I don't think I'll ever forgive myself. She's a brilliant mother and, because of what I said, here I am now, trying to fill in for her, with absolutely no bloody clue what I'm doing, and knowing that it's all my own fault. I didn't mean it; she's nothing like Janet. But maybe I'm the one who is, if I'm capable of saying something like that.'

Phoebe's head was aching with the determination not to cry; the things she'd said to her sister were eating her up inside and her whole body had sagged ever lower by the time she'd finished recounting the story. If Jamie thought she was a horrible person, she wouldn't blame him, because she did too, but it was still a relief to finally admit what she'd done.

'I'm sure Lucy understood you didn't mean it.' Jamie frowned. 'One comment from you isn't what made her disappear.'

'It wasn't just one comment, though. Comparing each other to Mum, and letting her come between us, was always the worst way to lash out. I should never have made her doubt what a good mother she was. Just looking around the cottage, it's obvious she was devoted to Darcy in a way our mother couldn't even begin to comprehend.'

'Listen to me, this isn't your fault.' Jamie said the words slowly and put his hands on her arms, making her look him in the eye again. 'She'd been finding things more difficult than she'd admitted to anyone for a long time.'

'Did she tell you that?' Phoebe's eyes widened, and she wondered for the first time if Jamie knew more than he was letting on.

'Not directly.' He paused for a moment, his expression somehow less open than it usually was. 'But looking back now, with the benefit of hindsight, the signs were there.'

'What signs?'

'She felt she was being judged by people, even when she wasn't. Being a single mum might not be uncommon, but there aren't many people who share that experience in Appleberry and you can't get past the school at drop-off time for the Range Rovers double-parked on the pavement. She was worried she wasn't going to be able to give Darcy everything the other kids had. I think Lucy wanted to escape from that, as well as from your mother, but she didn't know how. And she was scared that disrupting Darcy's life, if leaving didn't end up working out, might make things worse for her little girl.'

Phoebe bit her lip, all too easily able to imagine her sister feeling that way. She still had a horrible feeling she'd contributed to it, and she knew for a fact that her mother had. Guilt was rising in her chest again, and the only way she could cope with it was to direct it somewhere else. 'People like Camilla don't help.'

'I know, but not everyone round here is like that; you should know that, given how long you've known Scarlett.' Jamie smiled. 'She said you went to school together. Cam and I have been friends for years.'

'She told me that when I wasn't sure at first whether to trust you.' Phoebe never blushed, but her cheeks suddenly seemed to be burning as she blurted out another secret she'd had no intention of revealing. 'Scarlett is one of the few people I don't have to explain the situation with Mum to. But she's been through a hell of a lot over the last few years, and she and Cam could do without me dropping my drama into their laps, just when things are finally settling down.'

'I know for a fact they're both desperate to support you in every way they can. Try not to shut people out, especially the ones who really care about you, even if you think you're doing it for their benefit.'

'Do you remember when we first met?' Phoebe folded her arms across her chest. It was almost impossible to believe, as she looked at him, that it had been less than a fortnight before. She'd worked with some of her colleagues for more than seven years, and they knew far less about her than Jamie did. 'You promised not to try and fix any of my problems.'

'You're right, I did.' Jamie held up his hands and smiled. 'It's a habit I can't seem to break sometimes.' It was obvious he just wanted to help, and she was tempted to admit he was right about letting Scarlett in, but then her mobile started to ring. It was the number that Bradley had given her, if she wanted to get in touch

with him, and her legs suddenly felt as though they were made of
jelly.

'Hello.'

'Phoebe? It's Bradley, PC Harrison.'

'Yes?' She couldn't force small talk. The poor man had barely
even had a chance to speak, and she still wanted to shout at him to
spit it out. But calling after hours on a Friday evening was hardly
likely to warrant good news. Just the idea of what he might be
about to say made nausea swirl in her stomach, and her hands
were shaking so much she was struggling to hold the phone.

'We've found something.' She sank down into a chair as he
spoke. This couldn't be happening, not to Lucy, and her reply was
barely a whisper.

'A body?' For the split second it took him to respond, it was like
someone was standing on her chest.

'No! Oh God, no, I'm sorry.' Bradley sounded horrified, and the
sense of relief was so overwhelming she struggled to catch her
breath. 'It's most likely to be something and nothing, just some
kids who read something online and think it's funny to try and
make some sort of practical joke out of all of this.'

'I'm sorry, you've lost me. What do you mean a *joke*?' There
were some sick people in the world if they thought a young mother's disappearance was funny.

'We've had a shoe handed in. It was taken into the station at
Craggy Head and brought down to us. Like I said, I'm sure it's just
some idiot's idea of a joke, Lucy's a grown woman after all, but it's
just that the shoe had her name written inside.'

Phoebe swallowed. It couldn't be a joke; no one else could
possibly know that Lucy still wrote her name inside her shoes
after all this time. Even Phoebe hadn't realised it was a habit her
sister had been unable to break, until she'd stayed at the cottage
and seen Lucy's shoes, still labelled up like they were when she

was a child. But there was one way to find out for sure. 'Which shoe is it?'

'The right one. Why?' Bradley's confusion was obvious. But only a handful of people would know why that question made a difference.

'And have you got it with you now?'

'I have, but it looks as if it's been in the sea for a while and the name was blurred too, but not so much that we couldn't read it. Like I said, I'm sure it's just a prank.'

'Can you see if there's an insert inside the shoe? Lucy's right leg is a bit shorter than the left and, ever since she's been old enough to buy her own shoes, she's always had an insert fitted just underneath the innersole.'

There was silence at the other end of the line for what seemed like forever and then the young police officer cleared his throat. 'Yes, there's one here. But I don't understand, why would she have written her name in her shoes?'

'It's something she did; it goes right back to when we were kids.' Phoebe didn't want to explain, at least not to Bradley. But glancing across at Jamie, she knew she was going to have to talk to him about it. He knew her sister perhaps better than she did these days, and he was the one person who might be able to convince her that finding one of Lucy's shoes in the sea didn't make her suicide any more likely than it had been before. 'Thank you for letting me know.'

'It might still be insignificant.' Bradley was trying his best not to put his foot in it again, but his tone wasn't exactly convincing.

'You'll let me know if anything else turns up?' Phoebe squeezed her eyes tightly shut as she spoke, silently praying that she'd be the one phoning next, to let him know that Lucy had just strolled back into her cottage, as if nothing had been going on. That sort of thing happened all the time. Well, maybe not *all the time*, but she'd spent enough evenings googling 'sudden disappearance' to know that it *could* happen. And she had to believe that it would with Lucy.

'Of course, I'll be in touch if there's news of any kind.'

Even as the call ended, Phoebe held the phone to her ear for a moment, listening to the silence, as she tried to make her brain process the discovery in a way that didn't lead to the one conclusion she couldn't accept: that Lucy was already dead.

'You okay?' Crouching down next to the chair, Jamie handed her a crumpled bit of paper. 'This fell out of your pocket when you grabbed your phone off the side.'

'It's Lucy's letter.' She looked at him, wondering if his expression would give anything away. 'Did you read it?'

'No.'

She stared at him for an uncomfortably long time, trying to decide if she believed him. Not that it really mattered, but this was *her* letter from Lucy – the last thing between the two of them. For now, at least. And she wasn't going to show it to anyone else unless Lucy said she could. She'd already refused to show it to her father, giving him a watered-down version that would appease her mother instead. It was pointless telling either of her parents the full story anyway; they only heard what they wanted to hear.

'Thank you.' Phoebe pushed the letter back into the pocket of her jeans. She'd take it out again as soon as Jamie had gone, trying to find the answers hidden among the words she'd already read a hundred times before. 'Could you hear both sides of the phone call?'

'I got some of it, something about one of Lucy's shoes?'

'It was handed in at Craggy Head, but it had been in the sea.'

'How can they be so sure it's Lucy's?'

'She'd written her name in it.' She didn't miss the look that crossed his face. 'I know it sounds crazy and that's why PC

Harrison thought it must be a joke. What twenty-seven-year-old woman writes her name in their shoe, right?'

'I have to admit the last time I did that I was about twelve and my grandmother had told me if I lost another pair of trainers at football club, she was going to confiscate my Game Boy.'

'Your grandmother's reaction sounds fairly standard; an infuriated parent acting like 99 per cent of people would in the same situation. But when Lucy lost one of her patent shoes, when she was about eight or nine, Mum raged about it for days on end. She kept telling Lucy she was disgusting for not appreciating how hard Mum had had to work to pay for those shoes, and didn't she realise what people would think of her, now she was having to send Lucy to school in old shoes. It was always about how things reflected on Mum. I remember how upset Lucy was, even before Mum started on her. She'd loved those shoes and having to go to school in an old pair was punishment enough. But not as far as Mum was concerned. She kept on about them for weeks, and I'm honestly not exaggerating when I say that – how ungrateful we were, calling us both spoilt little bitches who only thought about ourselves. I can still picture the spit flying out of her mouth as she shouted at us, she was so filled with rage.' Anger was coursing through Phoebe's veins as she recounted the story. She'd never understand how any mother could take so much pleasure from hurting her children. She wanted to weep for Lucy too, the little sister who'd never outgrown their mother's control, or been able to shake off the legacy of her bitter words.

'Over a lost shoe?' Jamie's head jerked back, his dark hair falling away from his forehead.

'I know it seems unbelievable but our whole childhood was like that. Walking on eggshells in case we upset the delicate balance that always seemed to be teetering on the edge. But it was useless anyway; we could never do anything right.' Phoebe screwed up her eyes again, her determination never to cry in front of someone else being sorely tested as she pictured the shoes her sister must have kicked off before she disappeared: marked and scarred – like Lucy herself – because of their mother. 'Both of us wrote our names in our shoes after that, and it took me years after I left home to finally stop. It's stupid, but if I bought a new pair of shoes and I didn't put my name in them, I couldn't sleep. Mum's words about how useless and ungrateful we were just kept playing in my head. Even now, I have to fight the urge to do it, but it was another habit Lucy clearly wasn't able to break. She's my little sister and I should have done more to protect her.'

'Oh God, I'm sorry. Lucy told me things were tough for you growing up, but I had no idea how bad it was.' Jamie was still crouching beside her, and she wanted to lean against him, to feel anchored and safe, even just for a minute, but she'd never been able to rely on anyone but herself and it was far too dangerous to start now. For a little while she'd thought that Eddie could give her that kind of support, but all that had done was make her vulnerable to being hurt, and she'd sworn she'd never lower her guard like that again.

'PC Harrison thought the shoe might be someone's idea of a sick joke. But even if there was a tiny chance that someone else knew what she did, it's definitely her shoe because of the innersole. She broke her femur bone when she was a teenager, jumping off a wall, but Mum refused to believe her and said she was just trying to get attention because it was Mum's birthday. She was in absolute agony, and it was two days before Dad eventually took her to hospital, when Mum went back to work. Poor Lucy had to have an operation to have it pinned. She always wore an insert in her shoe to level things out. So it's got to be Lucy's.'

Phoebe's voice had cracked on the words, but Jamie seemed

determined to try and reassure her. 'Maybe she left them on the beach with her coat and they just got washed out.'

'Maybe.' Try as she might, Phoebe's ability to hang on to any explanation that could lead to a positive outcome had all but disappeared, and her stomach was churning almost as fast as her brain. It could make sense for Lucy to leave her coat behind on a summer's evening, especially if she wanted to make sure the letter was found, but her sister walking off to start a new life without any shoes? That was much harder to believe. Yet the alternative meant that Lucy had done what the police had seemed to suspect since day one. And even the thought made Phoebe's heart hammer so hard she could feel it in her head, as panic surged through her. They could find a way to fix everything, whatever it took, as long as Lucy eventually came home. But if it was already too late, nothing anyone said or did could ever put this right. And the emptiness that always lurked inside of Phoebe would swallow her whole.

* * *

Jamie poured himself a large whisky. He wasn't in the habit of drinking alone, but it had been a difficult evening. Phoebe was clearly rattled by the call from PC Harrison and with what he knew about Lucy, he was too. He just had to hold on to the hope that there was some other explanation for all of this. They all did – Phoebe more than anyone.

If his role as a therapist wasn't legally and ethically binding, he'd already have told Phoebe everything he knew. He'd told the police, but that didn't mean he could tell anyone else. He had a duty of care to protect people who were at risk of harming themselves or others, but he couldn't just blurt out things that had been said in confidence, during counselling sessions, to everyone he thought deserved to know. As much as he wanted to help Phoebe, and give Darcy the answers the little girl needed, he was having to face an impossible choice. If he didn't say anything, Lucy's sister was going to continue to torture herself. But, if he did, it could rip apart the lives of another family forever. He just couldn't risk it, not even for Phoebe and Darcy.

'You don't know how lucky you are, Fisher.' Jamie swirled the whisky in his glass as he looked at the dog. 'All you've got to worry about is the fact that you'll never catch that duck who likes tormenting you so much.' The dog thumped his tail against the arm of the chair, not even bothering to move.

The alcohol burnt Jamie's throat as he took a huge slug. He'd promised Lucy that he wouldn't reveal her secret and client confidentiality bound him to keep other things to himself, but there was one way he might still be able to help Phoebe – if his client was willing to release him from that obligation – and it had to be worth a try. Sitting at his desk, he put down his drink, opened his laptop and started to type.

10

Daylight was already chasing night-time into submission by the time Phoebe finally dropped off to sleep. She'd considered giving up and accepting that the news about the discovery of Lucy's shoe was going to result in a completely sleepless night. Her brain wouldn't shut up, no matter how many sleep-inducing techniques she tried. It kept running through every possible scenario about why Lucy might have left her shoes on the beach, and still not coming up with an answer that would bring her sister home. She must have dropped off eventually, warm breath on her face jolting her awake. For a moment she forgot where she was, thinking Norma must have climbed up on the bed, and then she felt a tug on the sleeve of her pyjama top.

'Auntie Phoebe!'

'Sorry, darling, I didn't know you were awake.' Phoebe opened her eyes, the bright light making her squint.

'I'm hungry.' Darcy rubbed her tummy to emphasise her point and Phoebe had to laugh, despite exhaustion making her eyelids feel as though they weighed seven pounds each. Her niece was already dressed – in a tutu, gilet, tiara and wellies. For someone so young, she clearly had a pretty good handle on what British summertime could throw at you and she was ready for all eventualities.

'Well, we need to do something about that, then, don't we?' Phoebe decided not to remind Darcy that if she'd eaten her dinner the night before, she wouldn't be so hungry. She was determined not to be the tiniest bit like her mother, but that made it really difficult to tell Darcy off at all. That could have proved disastrous if she was really Darcy's mum, but surely it couldn't hurt in the short term. Phoebe got up from the bed and was about to take her niece's hand when Darcy threw herself against her aunt, almost knocking them both back onto the bed, squeezing her so tightly she could hardly breathe.

'This hug is very nice, but what have I done to deserve it? I haven't even made you any toast yet.' It was funny that, with this little girl, all of Phoebe's difficulties with showing physical affection didn't seem to apply. The first time Darcy had put her hand in hers had felt natural, instead of awkward. The hugs had taken a bit longer to come and, before now, they'd always been quite brief. But they'd felt precious instead of uncomfortable. Phoebe couldn't explain why all of that was so different with her niece; it just was. She could just have put it down to Darcy being so young, but Phoebe had never been given affection as a child and perhaps that should have made it harder. Whatever the reason, it had been great to know that it was one more way in which Phoebe was nothing like her mother.

Darcy didn't reply to her aunt's enquiry, she just nuzzled into her neck, the two of them standing in the shaft of light filtering through the gap in the curtains like contented cats, enjoying the moment for what it was. Lucy couldn't possibly have chosen to walk away from this.

'Make sure you eat everything up this morning.' Ten minutes later, Phoebe handed the little girl her requested breakfast, which was exactly the sort of compromise that Jamie had pointed out almost all parents had to make. There was a slice of wholemeal toast with Nutella on top to hide the seeds and grains that Darcy had objected to the day before. There was also a bowl of yoghurt with sliced banana and a glass of milk. They were doing okay and, for the first time, Darcy hadn't started the day by asking when her mummy was coming home. It was heartbreaking and a relief, all at the same time.

'Can we see the chickens today?' Darcy looked up from munching on her toast, a huge chocolate-spread smile stretching from cheek to cheek.

'Maybe later, darling, I'll have to ask Jamie. But we're going to see someone really special today.'

'Mummy!' Darcy dropped her toast, her eyes flying wide open, and Phoebe spun around, thinking for just a split second that Lucy would be standing in the doorway. But then she realised what she'd done; she'd raised Darcy's hopes for nothing and reminded the little girl all over again that her mother was missing, guilt tearing at her insides. Phoebe was barely coping as an adult, but it must have been so much worse for Darcy. Lucy's disappearance made it feel like they were all falling into a hole that had no bottom. At least if they hit the ground, they'd know the worst and she could work out what to do, how to explain things to Darcy. But instead, they were still free-falling, not knowing when they were going to hit the bottom, and the longer they fell the more damage it was going to do.

'Mummy's not back yet, darling.' Phoebe moved to sit next to Darcy, wishing she could take back the words that had raised the little girl's hopes, which were now going to be dashed again. 'But you're going to love Norma – she's my dog and she loves cuddles. She might even sleep on your bed if you want her to.'

'I want my mummy.' A big tear slid down Darcy's face, a million times more poignant than any storm of hysterical crying, and suddenly a new emotion swept over Phoebe. How the hell could Lucy be so selfish?

* * *

Deciding that Darcy needed as much cheering up as possible, Phoebe texted Jamie to ask if he'd be able to take her over to his place for a bit. He ran a Saturday club, once a month, with some of the children who attended the forest school, and it would give Darcy the chance to see her beloved chickens, while Adam was delivering Norma and some of Phoebe's other stuff. She didn't want Darcy to see quite how many things she'd asked Adam to bring, in case the little girl somehow worked out what that might mean: that Lucy wouldn't be back any time soon, if at all.

By the time Adam arrived, Jamie had already collected Darcy and taken her over to the farm. It was strange looking at Adam, who was exactly as Phoebe remembered him. But there was no reason he shouldn't be. It wasn't like his world had been turned upside down in less than a fortnight. Maybe it was because of what Adam represented – the link back to her old life – or maybe it was because he was bringing Norma with him, but either way, she ran down the path when he stepped out of the car, throwing herself into his arms with the same sort of enthusiasm Darcy had hugged her with that morning. He must have wondered what the hell was going on; they'd never had that sort of relationship.

Perhaps that was why his stay was so brief. Her behaviour had probably freaked him out, and they'd both been so resolute in the past never to blur the lines in their relationship. Even when

Adam's brother had been diagnosed with leukaemia, he hadn't really leant on her, at least not any more than he might have done another friend. And he clearly didn't want to take on her baggage now. Adam had said he had an interview early the next morning – the chance of a dream job and the kind of travel he'd been honest about always wanting. He was there to drop Norma off, that was it, and less than an hour after his arrival, he was gone again.

Phoebe tried to work out how she felt when Adam left, and whether or not she was hurt by his haste to get back on the road. But the truth was she was relieved. Her emotional reaction to his arrival had revealed something unexpected. As much as they had fitted together in London, and been what each other needed, they were entirely wrong for each other now. She didn't have the energy to pretend to be the easy, breezy, unemotional friends-with-benefits career woman he knew and resolutely did not love. Whether the person Phoebe had once been would ever come back, she had no idea. But she didn't live here, in Lucy's cottage, in Appleberry, that was for certain.

Ten minutes after Adam had driven away, Phoebe headed to the farm to pick up Darcy. The first person she spotted when she arrived was Scarlett. Her friend was making her way across the paddock, bumping an empty buggy across the rutty ground.

'I was hoping to catch up with you.' Scarlett gave Phoebe the kind of easy hug that didn't happen with anyone else, but Scarlett had never really given her a choice and, deep down, it was one of the reasons her best friend meant so much to her. 'I'm going to the lake tomorrow for a picnic, with Kate, Dolly and the kids, and we were hoping you and Darcy might fancy joining us?'

'I thought you'd want to put your feet up with a very big bottle of wine after a week at an adventure centre with Year Six. I know I would!' Phoebe laughed, briefly wondering if it would be really bad form to suggest that she and Scarlett got together over a bottle of wine instead. She'd happily have sat by the lake with Scarlett, but hanging out with her other local mum friends – who might be every bit as awful as that Camilla woman – held far less appeal.

'Tempting as that is, I'm desperate to spend some time with Ava and she'll love playing with Darcy. Kate's kids are a bit older, but I think Darcy already knows Dolly's second youngest, Chantelle, from nursery, and Matty, who's here today, is her youngest. I'm picking him up for her, while she's at the dentist with three of the others.'

'*Three* of the others? How many kids has she got?' Phoebe couldn't imagine coping with more than one. All of her energy seemed to be focused on Darcy right now, and she was still second-guessing her every move.

'She's got nine. Five birth children and four she adopted last year. She originally planned on adopting one child, but a sibling group needed a family and Dolly's one of those people who can't say no to helping out. She's amazing.' Scarlett smiled, and Phoebe found herself nodding. It certainly sounded as if Dolly was every-thing that Janet wasn't.

'She must be some kind of superhero. It makes me tired, just thinking about it.' Phoebe looked up as Jamie and the children came down the path towards them. 'Talking of which, it looks like Jamie might have worked his magic and managed to wear the kids out.'

'Hi!' he called out, his face seeming to light up when he saw them, and for a moment she found herself wondering if that had anything to do with her. It probably didn't; he was just that kind of person, friendly and kind, and it would have been big-headed of her to think she was held any higher in his affections than Scarlett. He'd known her best friend for far longer for a start. And it didn't matter either way; any bond between them had only grown because he cared about Lucy and wanted her home almost as much as Phoebe did. She wasn't special to him, and he wasn't to her – at least not beyond their shared concern for her sister. That was what she was telling herself as he walked towards them, because any other scenario was far too dangerous.

'Hey. How have the kids been? Have you had a good time?' Phoebe could tell by looking at her niece's face that Darcy had, without even waiting for an answer.

'They've all been brilliant.' Jamie's smile didn't waver, even as a little boy suddenly ran at him like a battering ram, hurling himself into Jamie's arms. 'And Matty here gives the most powerful hugs in the known universe.'

'I beg to differ.' Phoebe laughed as Darcy demonstrated her point, looping her arms around her aunt's waist and squeezing as tightly as someone trying to perform the Heimlich manoeuvre.

'It's so lovely to see them both looking so happy.' Scarlett didn't even bother trying to hide the fact that she had tears in her eyes. She was so different to Phoebe, and it was clearly making her emotional to see two children who'd been through such a lot being able to show so much affection. 'I was just trying to persuade Phebes to come down to the lake tomorrow to meet up with me, Dolly and Kate. I think Darcy would love it, don't you?'

'Absolutely.' Jamie's eyes met Phoebe's for a moment, but she gave a non-committal shrug.

'Adam's just dropped Norma off, so I'll have to see how well she settles in, and how tired Darcy is after today, but I do appreciate the invite.'

'We'd love to see you there and you'll enjoy it far more than you think.' Scarlett raised her eyebrows. 'Which I'm guessing you're expecting to be as much fun as root canal treatment.'

'Something like that!' Phoebe laughed for the first time.

'It won't be that bad, will it, Jamie?' Scarlett turned towards him for back-up.

'No worse than a gum injection for a buccal cavity, I promise.'
Jamie laughed too, as Scarlett pretended to push him, and Phoebe
suddenly found herself wishing that he'd been invited along to
join them at the lake, too. It shouldn't have made the decision
about whether to go or not easier, but as much as she tried to
convince herself that it wouldn't have done, deep down she knew
it would.

* * *

'Are you going to meet Scarlett and the others tomorrow?' Jamie
kept his words casual but there was something different about
Phoebe and he couldn't decide if it was just because Adam had
visited, or if maybe she'd had more news about Lucy than she was
ready to share. Everyone else had left, but Darcy had insisted that
the chickens' water needed changing again, because there were
bits of straw in it. So they were standing chatting while the little
girl busied herself with the job.

'I'm not sure.' She shrugged. 'If Darcy wants to then I guess I
will, but I just don't feel like doing much of anything at the
moment. I've got no problem with Scarlett seeing me being miserable and distracted, but I'm not sure I can put on an "everything's
okay" act for her friends.'

'How are you really?' Jamie caught hold of her elbow. 'I mean, I
know you can't really be okay with Lucy missing, but you just
seem different today, like you're losing hope, and we can't afford to
do that.'

'I'm sorry, I feel... God, this sounds stupid, but I seem to have
stopped feeling anything since that phone call about Lucy's shoes.
I still don't believe she's actually killed herself; I *can't* let myself
believe that. But it's like I'm watching myself going through all of

this, only I'm not really *feeling* it. Maybe I just don't function like other people, with a mother like mine...'

'Don't make this about your mum.' He cut her off before she could start comparing herself to Janet again. 'You'd be surprised how many people describe that emotion when they get a shock, and the initial reaction to the news gives way to numbness. It's a coping mechanism because your brain can't deal with all the emotions that are flooding in.'

'I suppose that makes sense. So you're sure I'm not a freak?' He might have thought she was joking if she hadn't been looking at him as though his answer really mattered.

'Far from it. Although I have been wondering about something.'

'You always look at me as if you're wondering about something. It's very unnerving.'

'I'm worried about you, that's all, but I promise to try and keep it to a minimum.' He laughed as they watched Darcy bossily shoo one of the hens out of the way, so that she could get to their water dispenser. The little girl was born for a life in the country. An unwelcome thought crossed his mind about how much that might change if Lucy never came home, and Phoebe eventually took her back to live in London. He'd miss them both.

'Go on, then, don't keep me in suspense – tell me what else it is that you were wondering about.' Phoebe's voice wavered, and he had a feeling she spent her whole life worrying that someone would say something to convince her she'd been right all along, and that she had turned out to be just like her mother.

'I was wondering why you've chosen to have a relationship with a man like Adam.'

'What do you mean *a man like Adam*?' There was no accusation in her tone. It was strange, given that he'd more or less implied he didn't think Adam was right for her, without ever having met him.

Maybe it was just part of her not feeling much about anything at all, but he'd expected a different reaction.

'I don't know, I mean, I've never met him, but the fact he didn't stay for a bit longer, with all that you're going through, and some of the things Scarlett said about him...' He trailed off for a moment, wondering if it was wiser to stop there, but for some reason he couldn't. 'I just think you deserve better.'

Phoebe shook her head. 'You don't know me, or what I deserve. But we've never pretended to be something we're not. We're not one another's emotional support animals, and at least it's honest.'

'And is that what you value the most, honesty?' If she ever found out what Jamie knew about Lucy's disappearance, it wasn't an opinion she'd have of him.

'You're judging Adam on what *you* expect from a relationship, but we aren't like that. Sometimes we're flatmates, sometimes we're friends and sometimes it's just a physical thing. We aren't a couple in a traditional sense of the word.' She laughed at the look that must have crossed his face. 'I know it doesn't make sense to 99 per cent of people, but if you'd witnessed a relationship like my parents', maybe you'd understand.' For the first time there was passion in her voice. She might feel absolutely nothing about most things right now, but when it came to her parents, her emotions clearly couldn't be dulled.

'Actually, it makes perfect sense, but I can't help feeling there's more out there for you than that. I know you hate the idea of anyone trying to fix your problems for you, but have you ever thought about therapy?'

'Wow, you really don't beat around the bush, do you?' She raised her hand to wave at Darcy, who was holding up a large brown egg she'd found in the chicken hutch. 'I've tried a couple of different types of therapy, but I can't see how any of them can overcome bad genes. Lucy and I are just broken from having the parents we've got, and some things can't be fixed. So what if I'm happier having a no strings kind of relationship, and Lucy likes burning lumps of driftwood and producing those huge, dark, swirly paintings that give me the creeps. We all have our ways of coping with what life throws at us, don't we? What about you? Single and hidden out here, spending most of your time playing make-believe in the woods. If we're asking probing questions, then I could turn that on you. Scarlett told me you were offered a job in really prestigious practice in Harley Street, but then you turned your back on most of your therapy work. So why exactly did you give up on your career?'

He turned to look at her, a burning sensation in his chest. 'My grandmother died five years ago and, with what happened to my parents, I realised life was too short to spend it doing something you don't love. Most people don't have the choice, but I did. When I moved back to the farm, I had to keep working as a therapist full-time to pay the bills. Then, when Nan left me some money, I suddenly realised it was the chance to try something else, start a business that would mean the farm wasn't just my home, but my career too. I could still pick and choose a handful of clients to work with, ones I felt I could really help with the kind of therapy I wanted to offer. But this – hiding out in the country, playing make-believe, as you put it – is what makes me happiest of all.'

'I'm sorry, I shouldn't be lashing out at you, but it's incredible that you had someone who cared about you the way your grand-mother did, someone you miss and who wanted the best for you even after they were gone.' Phoebe's voice was level as she looked at him, but her eyes seemed greyer than they ever had before. 'It must have been heartbreaking to lose your mum and dad, but that's something to be really thankful for.'

'I know.' He wished he could wave a magic wand and make things right for Phoebe, but it was never going to be easy to reach out to her. He wanted her to know that she could do for Darcy what his grandmother had done for him if the worst happened and Lucy never came home. But neither of them were ready to face that prospect. All he could do was hope that the message he'd written the night before might help, even just a little bit.

11

'Hey, sleepyhead.' Phoebe sat on the edge of Darcy's bed and looked at the little girl snuggled up with Norma on her pillow. The pug was fast asleep too, with her oversized tongue lolling out of her mouth, and snoring like a wildebeest. As Phoebe had expected, they'd hit it off instantly, and Norma was already following Darcy around wherever she went. That dog was no fool; she'd quickly worked out that soon-to-be-four-year-olds dropped a lot of biscuits and Phoebe couldn't work out if Norma was punishing her too for not being around lately. After her initial excitement at seeing Phoebe, the little dog had all but ignored her.

Maybe she was reading too much into it, but she couldn't seem to switch her brain off. Jamie was probably right that the numbness she felt was because she was too busy worrying about Lucy to process anything else. She'd barely slept, and her body felt as though someone had fed it through a mangle overnight. It was hard to believe she could ache that much, just from tossing and turning all night. One thing she'd decided was that Darcy needed to have as much fun as possible, and she couldn't rely on Jamie to entertain her all the time, so she texted Scarlett to say that she'd like to join them all for the picnic and had received an enthusiastic response. She only wished she could feel one hundredth of that same enthusiasm.

'Darcy, wake up, sweetheart.' She smoothed the little girl's hair away from her face as she spoke and caught her breath. Her niece had a tiny almost heart-shaped mole just before the start of her hairline, exactly like Lucy. If it was strange for Phoebe to notice that similarity, it must have been stranger still for Lucy, to see her own image so strongly reflected in that tiny likeness. It gave Phoebe an odd sort of comfort, to recognise she could still feel emotion at something so small. And more than that, to realise that a part of her sister had been here with her all along.

'Norma.' Darcy reached out, still half asleep, and put an arm around the pug, pulling the dog closer towards her.

'It's all right, darling. Norma's still here and I don't think she'll want to sleep anywhere else from now on.'

'I thought she might be gone.' Darcy rubbed her eyes with the hand that wasn't hanging on to Norma for dear life.

'I promise you that every morning when you wake up, Norma and I will both be here.' Phoebe didn't add *until your mummy comes home*. Somehow it was easier not to mention Lucy at all unless Darcy did. Making promises she had no power to keep had been something she'd wanted to avoid from the start.

'Can we take Norma to see the chickens today?' Darcy had pushed herself up into a sitting position against the bedhead with a still-sleeping Norma now draped across her lap like a rag doll.

'I'm not sure if that's a good idea; in fact, I don't even know if Norma's ever seen a chicken before. Sometimes when I take her for a walk in the park near where I live, she can actually break into a run trying to chase the pigeons.' Phoebe smiled as her niece looked down at the plump dog snuggled into her duvet, and then back up at her aunt, a look of disbelief on her face. 'I know it is quite hard to imagine, but I think that's part of her trickery, finding a way to sneak up on the pigeons by looking plump and innocent, and then suddenly moving quite fast and taking them by surprise.'

'Has she ever caught one?' Darcy furrowed her brow, obviously unimpressed at the thought of a pigeon getting hurt in Norma's pursuit of fun.

'Not even close.' Phoebe squeezed her hand. 'But do you know what we can do today? Take Norma down to the lake.'

'Really?' Darcy's face went from joy to worry in the space of about one second. 'She won't try to eat the ducks, will she?'

'I think they're more likely to peck her on the bottom.' Phoebe couldn't help joining in as Darcy laughed. But then the frown on the little girl's forehead deepened.

'That won't make her run away, will it?' Darcy was obviously terrified of someone else disappearing from her life, and Phoebe wanted to hold her niece in her arms and somehow make all of her fear go away. But it wasn't that easy.

'I'm just being silly; the ducks won't hurt Norma. All I meant is that she won't hurt them either. We might just have to watch our toes if we go for a paddle!' She tickled her niece's foot, and she squirmed in delight, the look of joy firmly back on her face. 'We're going to have a picnic at the lake too.'

'Me and Mummy do that sometimes.' The way Darcy's face could switch between happiness and melancholy was heartrending. But Phoebe hoped what she said next would cheer her up.

'We're going to meet Ava and Matty and their mummies down at the lake today too.'

'I love Ava!' Darcy was smiling so much now, it was impossible for Phoebe not to join in. 'Matty always wants to go worm hunting when we're at Jamie's, but I don't like it when they wiggle on my hand.'

'I'm not that keen either, but there'll be other children there, so

I'm sure Matty can find someone else to go worm hunting with.'
Phoebe wrinkled her nose and let the feeling of warmth wash over
her. They were doing okay. Darcy hadn't forgotten how to smile
and, when she did, Phoebe suddenly remembered how to
smile too.

'I wish Mummy was here; she was never scared of picking up
worms.' And just like that the feeling was gone.

* * *

'Oh, I'm so glad you could make it!' Scarlett, who was struggling
with carrying fold-up chairs and what looked like a food cooler
big enough to house a small family, set the chairs down on the
footpath, as Phoebe and Darcy caught up with her.

'Let me give you a hand.' All Phoebe had was a picnic basket
Jamie had lent her, a kid's fishing net, also courtesy of Jamie, and a
rolled-up blanket, which Darcy was carrying. Phoebe picked up
the chairs and Scarlett smiled in response.

'Thank you! I forgot that the last time I came down with all
this lot, Cam was with me.' Scarlett puffed out her cheeks. 'Thank
God Kate came and picked Ava up earlier so I could get the picnic
made, otherwise I'd never had managed to make it this far.'

'So is this a mums-only do?'

'Absolutely! Kate's husband, Alan, is on his way to a school
reunion in Yorkshire. And Cam is with Dolly's husband, Greg.
They run a football club that some of Dolly's older children, and
Kate's son, Barnaby, all go to. Dolly's just bringing the youngest
two, and Darcy is already friends with them both.' Scarlett's ready
smile was as easy as it always had been, when Phoebe had spent
every spare moment she could at her best friend's house. Scarlett's
mum and dad had been the parents Phoebe would have designed
for herself, if she'd had the choice. She'd never been able to invite

Scarlett or any of her other friends back to her place, and lots of them had grown to resent it. Some of them had thought she was a snob, before Janet had revealed her true colours often enough for word to get out, but Scarlett had always understood.

'How is Cam?' Phoebe had barely had the opportunity to catch up with Scarlett, let alone her partner. But she was hoping to put that right. It was really good to see her best friend so happy again, after what her ex-husband had put her through, and it gave Phoebe hope that even the most difficult situations could come right. She and Darcy both needed to spend as much time as possible around positive people, now more than ever. It was why she was doing her utmost to avoid her parents at all costs.

'He's really good. Enjoying the headship, but he's been approached about becoming an inspector.' Scarlett lowered her voice so much that Phoebe had to strain to hear.

'Why are you whispering?'

'Ofsted inspectors are about as popular as traffic wardens with teaching staff.'

'I've got nothing against Ofsted inspectors, but, living in London, I know exactly what you mean about traffic wardens.' Phoebe watched Darcy skipping in front of them, holding the blanket in one hand and Norma's lead in the other.

'You're doing really well, you know.' Scarlett paused for a moment, fixing Phoebe with a look that made her want to look away, but somehow left her powerless to do so.

'Do you really think so?' Apart from Lucy's whereabouts, wondering whether she was doing a good enough job of caring for Darcy was Phoebe's biggest worry.

'It's obvious. I'd have expected her to be subdued, but she's the same happy little girl she's been almost every time I've seen her.'

Phoebe breathed out slowly. 'It's such a relief every time she smiles. I think she's expecting Lucy to come home any time, so she's not as worried or sad as she would be if we knew for certain that wasn't going to happen. But if her birthday comes and Lucy still isn't here...'

'She'll be back.' Scarlett sounded so certain.

'What if she isn't? What if she's really gone for good? She tried to do it once before.'

'I remember.' Scarlett was the only person Phoebe could be more honest with than she was with herself, because her best friend knew the family's history better than anyone else outside of it. She'd understand how terrified Phoebe was as a result. If Lucy had been distraught enough to consider taking her life in the past, it made it all too easy to believe she could have reached that point again.

'What if she's done it this time?'

'She didn't have Darcy then.' Scarlett bit her lip. 'I know people in terrible pain still take their own lives, but I don't think Lucy would. But if she has, you'll find a way to protect Darcy, the way you always used to protect Lucy.'

'Not enough. I left her behind.' The end of her relationship with Eddie had been the catalyst for Phoebe. She'd got engaged when she was barely out of school, and it must have looked really odd to outsiders. Young people didn't decide to get married at that age any more, and Eddie had been almost fifteen years older than she was. Looking back, it was every bit as odd as it must have seemed. But she'd been desperate for love, and stability, and Eddie had seemed able to provide all of that. Except, in the end, he'd let her down too, and she'd had to get out of Appleberry to survive.

'You did everything you could to persuade her to come with you. I remember how hard you tried, but you had no choice other than to leave after all that stuff with Eddie. You set it up so she'd have a place at art school and worked every hour God sent so you could rent a flat with a spare room for her. It was Lucy's choice to stay.'

'I think she thought that it might somehow make a difference to how our mother felt about her, but we all know how that worked out.'

'You and Lucy don't see yourselves as other people do. You both amaze me, with what you've achieved after such a tough start. Mum and Dad have often said they thought you were brilliant too.'

'I always loved your mum and dad; how are they?' Phoebe resisted the urge to remind Scarlett how lucky she was, just as she had with Jamie about his grandmother. She had to stop having family-envy.

'Mum's great. She was really excited when I told her you were back in Appleberry, and she insisted I bring you over for Sunday lunch when you're free.' For the first time, Scarlett's face clouded a bit. 'Dad's a bit down. His best friend, John, has early onset dementia. It's quite advanced now and he's in The Pines care home. I don't know if you remember John, but he was at all the big family occasions. He doesn't have anyone else and so Dad is at The Pines a lot. I think he's finding it tough.'

'I'm sorry; I do remember him.' Phoebe felt sad for the lovely man she'd met many times. He might not have been biologically related, but he'd been very much a part of Scarlett's family, and Phoebe had seen a parallel with her place in their lives. But there was no justice in the world; how could that awful illness strike down someone like John and leave her mother still spreading poison everywhere she went?

'Thank God for Jamie.'

'Jamie?'

'He takes Fisher to The Pines and he's started a scheme up there for other animals to be assessed for pet therapy.' Scarlett smiled. 'Dad said it's been amazing. John's Jack Russell, Titch, was rehomed when he went into The Pines, and Jamie has even been going over to pick him up once a fortnight to bring him in to visit. He's a great guy.'

'He certainly seems to be.' Phoebe wasn't sure she wanted to hear any more about how great Jamie was. The comparison between him and Adam had been stark enough the day before, as it was.

It wasn't that Adam was a bad person. He'd always been honest that he wasn't looking for a commitment, because he needed the freedom to do whatever he wanted, whenever he wanted. When he and Phoebe had met, and decided to buy a place together, she'd been in a position where she wanted to be able to do those things too. But now it was different and, as much as she hated to admit it, part of her desperately wanted someone to lean on. Adam could never be that someone and he wouldn't want to be.

Jamie would have been perfect for the role. He was kind and caring, and he clearly adored Darcy as much as the little girl adored him. That's what made the prospect of allowing herself to lean on him such a risk. With someone like Adam, Phoebe knew where she was. There were clear parameters to the relationship, and no expectations of where it might lead. But if she allowed herself to start relying on Jamie for support, it would make her vulnerable if he ever decided to take that away. And Phoebe had promised herself, a long time ago, that she'd never let her guard down like that again. It was better to believe that the only person you could rely upon was yourself.

'I know Lucy has always been really grateful to have someone like Jamie living next door. Ava, Matty and Chantelle love the forest school almost as much as Darcy does, and you get far less competitive mum stuff there than you do at the nursery.' Scarlett pulled a face. 'Although you do get some of the mums trying to get Jamie's attention, not that he ever seems interested.'

'I'm sorry if this is going to put you into an awkward position, but I need to know, do you think there was anything going on between Lucy and Jamie?' Phoebe couldn't help holding her breath as she waited for her friend to respond. She could see now how easy it would have been for her sister to fall for her neighbour. His kindness would have slotted straight into the space in Lucy's heart that had been crying out for that since they were small. When she was still very young, Phoebe had come to the conclusion that she needed to rescue herself from the situation that fate had put her in – as Janet and Roger Spencer's daughter. She'd made the mistake once of thinking someone else could do it, but her relationship with Eddie had taught yet another harsh life lesson. Phoebe was almost certain that Lucy had hankered after something else: the hope that, one day, someone would turn up and rescue her from it all. Despite the fact that she'd sworn off men, too, after Callum, Phoebe had never quite believed it. And someone like Jamie could easily have tapped into that. If anyone could be mistaken for a knight in shining armour, it was him.

'Not that I know of, and I really don't think so.' Scarlett adjusted the weight of the food cooler, moving it to her other hand as she spoke. And some of the tension left Phoebe's spine. She desperately wanted to trust Jamie, which was why she was so glad he hadn't lied about that and shattered the hope that she could.

'Did she ever give you a hint that she was thinking of doing something stupid, like...' Phoebe still couldn't say the words out loud. 'You know, disappearing.'

'The last time I saw her, she looked happier than I can ever remember her looking.' Scarlett bit her lip again as she paused for a moment. 'But I know you well enough to realise that an upbeat persona can sometimes be your mask. Even if it was the same for her, it doesn't mean she won't come back.'

'What am I going to do about Darcy if she doesn't?' This thought was what shattered Phoebe every time it entered her head. As much as losing Lucy would break her heart, the impact of that on Darcy would be so much worse. If Lucy had decided to disappear, or even to take her own life, that was her choice. Darcy hadn't asked for any of this, though, and she didn't deserve it either. Deep down, Phoebe knew she wasn't really facing her own emotions, but there was no space to do that when she needed to be there for Darcy. She'd been a big sister for as long as she could remember, and she didn't know how she'd carry on without that. As much as she and Lucy had drifted apart in the fruitless pursuit of their mother's affection, she'd always assumed they'd find a way back to each other, and she'd always loved Lucy, even if she'd had no idea how to express it at times. Losing her altogether was too much to contemplate, not if she wanted to continue to function, or even to keep breathing in and out.

'Just keep doing whatever it is you're doing.' Scarlett gestured towards Darcy, who was now singing at the top of her voice about three speckled frogs sitting on a log. 'It looks like it's going pretty well.'

'I've got no idea what I'm doing.'

'I've got news for you, Phebes.' Scarlett turned towards her with a smile. 'None of us do!'

* * *

Kate and Dolly were as easy to talk to as Scarlett had promised, although it was impressive that Dolly could make conversation at all – given everything she had going on in her life. Matty, the youngest of her adopted children, was a complete ball of energy and Dolly had joked that she and her husband, Greg, had taken to man-on-man marking Matty, to stop him getting himself into dangerous situations. Luckily, Norma was proving a hit, and Matty's desire to hold on to her lead had anchored him to their spot by the lake. The little dog was surprisingly weighty and more than happy to revel in all the attention she was getting.

They spent the afternoon chatting about everything from Scarlett and Phoebe's escapades at school, through to Kate's unfortunate incident on a water chute at Center Parcs, which she was worried had scared her teenage nephew and his best friend for life, when her right boob had suddenly put in an impromptu appearance. Phoebe hadn't laughed like that in a long time and, despite a twinge of guilt at having fun while Lucy was still missing, a couple of hours after meeting them, it felt like Phoebe had known Kate and Dolly for years too.

'We've got eight snails now, Mummy!' Ava came rushing towards Scarlett, with Matty, Chantelle and Darcy in her wake, clutching an open Tupperware pot in her hands. Half an hour earlier it had contained sandwiches, but now it was lined with leaves and moss.

'Oh well done, darling.' Scarlett peered into the pot. 'Have you given them all names?'

'We're just thinking what to call them, but we're going to have two each, aren't we?' Ava looked around at the other children, who nodded enthusiastically, and Phoebe had to supress a smile. Given how horrified Darcy had been about the idea of hunting for worms with Matty, this was quite the turnaround. 'We're the super snail hunters!'

'You are, sweetheart, and a haul like that calls for a celebration.' Scarlett opened the cooler. 'Doughnuts and pink lemonade?'

The children took the proffered treats in a flurry of excitement, before heading off to continue their search, staying within an agreed distance of where Phoebe and the others were sitting – about twenty feet in each direction, and always away from the water's edge. Even though Phoebe barely took her eyes off her niece for a moment, there was still low-level anxiety bubbling under the surface whenever the little girl wasn't right by her side. But she had a feeling if she shared those worries with her friends that she'd be given another 'welcome to parenthood' speech.

'There's no denying I over-ordered on the doughnuts. I don't suppose anyone wants one?' Scarlett held out the box.

'God, yes!' Kate leapt forward and took hold of them. 'Come on, everyone's got to have one, to make me feel better about falling off the diet wagon for what might be the millionth time.'

'Diets are bad for you anyway.' Dolly grinned, taking a doughnut, before passing the box to Phoebe. 'And if you open the blue Thermos, you might just discover it's filled with Pimm's and not coffee.'

'I knew there was a reason I love you so much!' Kate blew her a kiss and quickly set about pouring them all a drink. Less than a minute later, Phoebe had a doughnut in one hand, and a plastic goblet of Pimm's in the other.

'I could get used to this.' As soon as the words were out of her mouth, she wished she could take them back. Horror at finding such joy in the moment, when her sister was missing, made her eyes sting. 'I meant if Lucy was home. I didn't mean—'

'It's all right, Phebes.' Scarlett cut her off, briefly reaching out and touching her arm. 'We know what you meant and it's okay not to be sad or consumed with worry all the time. That's the last thing Darcy needs to see.'

'It's just that I'd forgotten what summers in Appleberry could be like. I can see now why Lucy wanted to bring Darcy up in the village, even if it meant having Mum and Dad on the doorstep.'

'Why don't you come back? I'd love to have you home again,

and I know Lucy would too; it might even make it easier for her to come back if she knew you were staying.' Scarlett shook her head. 'Sorry, I shouldn't have said that. I don't want to put pressure on you, especially when I know how hard it is with your parents.'

'It's not even that so much.' Phoebe sighed. 'I've kept out of their way, and it's been like Darcy and I don't exist. They haven't even attempted to come up and see us. Dad did text for a while and tried to guilt-trip me into seeing them, but he's clearly not bothered enough to cross the village from one side to the other. And I don't see that changing if I moved back. It's just not the place for me any more. I couldn't see me, *the real me*, making a life here. It's great for families like all of you, but that's not my life. I feel like I'm just treading water, and trying not to let anything horrible happen to Darcy, before Luce gets back. I don't think I've got what it takes to do it full time.' She wasn't going to tell them, as she'd told Jamie, that she could never really be up to the job. Not when half of her genes came from Janet Spencer.

'Like I said before, apart from the bit about waiting for Lucy to come home, that's all any of us are doing.' Scarlett looked towards the others, who nodded in agreement. 'If anyone really analysed it, no one would ever have kids.'

Lowering her voice until it was barely a whisper, Phoebe leant forward. 'Do you think Lucy regretted becoming a mother?'

'Not from anything I ever witnessed, but sometimes it can get too much for anyone, and if people don't ask for the support they need, they can reach breaking point.' Dolly still had sugar from the doughnut on her lips, as she spoke. 'We were warned about it when we adopted the children. Maybe Lucy was struggling and just didn't know how to ask for help.'

'Maybe.' Phoebe wanted to believe that was true, but she couldn't shake the feeling that she'd ignored the signs of her sister's silent pleas for help. Or the very real prospect that it might now be too late.

* * *

Phoebe was walking along the edge of the lake towards Jamie. He'd arrived just in time to see Norma plunge into the lake in pursuit of two ducks, Phoebe quickly following her into the water and pulling her out again, getting soaked to the skin in the process. Her dress was clinging to every curve and Jamie was forced to remind himself that the last thing she needed was him blurting out how beautiful she was. Fisher trotted ahead of him, just as anxious to get to Norma as he was to Phoebe.

When they finally drew level, the little pug started wriggling to get free and he handed Phoebe Fisher's lead. 'Do you want to put this on her, so she doesn't go straight in for another swim?'

'Thank you.' As she took the proffered lead, he couldn't help noticing that her arms were covered with goose pimples, despite the warmth of the afternoon.

'Are you okay?'

'Apart from doing my best monster from the deep impression?'

'More like the Lady of the Lake.' He had no idea why he'd said that. The Lady of the Lake was an enchantress, and he didn't want her to think he was attracted to her, even if it was true. Their tentative friendship didn't need that kind of complication.

'Hmm, I think you're being far too generous, but that's why you've got a reputation for being so kind.' She obviously hadn't read anything into his comment. She had far more important things to worry about, and she probably didn't give him a moment's thought when he wasn't standing right in front of her.

'It's got nothing to do with being kind. There's only one monster of the deep around here and I think we both know who it is.' He ruffled the fur on top of Norma's head. 'Is she prone to running off?'

'Not usually, but if she wants something she won't come back to me no matter how much I call her. Despite being told not to, Matty threw half a doughnut that Norma had decided was hers into the lake. We didn't realise he'd unclipped her lead and, when the ducks looked like they were going to claim the doughnut, Norma had other ideas.' Phoebe wrinkled her nose. 'It's happened before. She ended up in the middle of the boating lake in the park near our flat in London once, when she decided she had more right to the sandwich that someone had thrown in than the birds did.'

'But she's good with the kids and other people?' An idea had taken root and Jamie was doing his best to convince himself it had nothing to do with wanting to spend more time with Phoebe.

'She's brilliant. In fact, looking after Norma was the only thing that could keep Matty in one place.'

'He's got so much energy and I think that's why he thrives at the forest school. He's a great kid, though. They all are.'

'You're amazing with them from what I've seen, and I wanted to thank you for everything you've done to help me with Darcy since I arrived, too.' She turned towards him, close enough that he could see how her dark brown eyelashes changed to a shade that was almost gold, right at their tips. 'I wish I could find a way to repay you. If you ever need my help with something, just shout.'

'I haven't done anything that anyone else wouldn't. But there is something I'd love to ask you.'

'As long as it doesn't involve clipping the chickens' claws or anything gruesome like that, I'm game.'

'I'm taking Fisher up to The Pines for pet therapy next week, but the residents can never get as much time with the animals as they'd like. So I've been thinking about adding some more dogs into the sessions. I think Norma could be perfect, as long as we keep her away from the chocolate biscuits, but I'd need you to come too to keep an eye on her the first time, just in case.'

'Well, if there are chocolate biscuits on offer...' Phoebe smiled. 'I owe you for something else too.'

'What?'

'For helping persuade me to meet Dolly and Kate. Talking to the two of them and Scarlett has reassured me that I might not be letting Darcy or Lucy down as badly as I thought I was. I've spent so much time worrying and not sleeping properly that I was starting to feel like a zombie, but after today I feel almost human again.'

'You look it too. Almost!' He laughed as she pretended to punch him on the arm. All he could do was be the best friend he could to Phoebe, until they found out what had really happened to her sister. After that, there was no way of knowing if she'd ever speak to him again.

12

After the picnic, Phoebe had managed a decent night's sleep for the first time since her arrival back in Appleberry. What Dolly had said to her about the possibility of Lucy finding things too much and needing to escape made sense. She'd been a working single parent with no support and a mother whose only goal in life was to criticise. It was a miracle she hadn't reached breaking point sooner.

Phoebe had been second-guessing her own parenting abilities since the moment she'd taken responsibility for Darcy, which had given her a tiny bit of insight into what her sister had gone through. It was nothing in comparison to facing that fear day in, day out, but it was exhausting, constantly questioning whether there were any traces of Janet Spencer's influence in the way she was handling things. It was no wonder it had driven Lucy to the edge, but things would be different when she came home. Phoebe would be there for her, to help reassure Lucy she was doing a great job, and to support her in finally breaking free of the self-destructive cycle of trying to win their mother's love. Phoebe could help her rent somewhere else away from Appleberry, if Lucy didn't want to stay with her in London. She just needed to find the strength to make that break, and she could start to heal. It might never be perfect, being raised by Janet had tainted them both, but Phoebe was proof that it was possible to find another life. She should have done more to help Lucy see that a long time ago but, when her sister came home, she was never going to let her down again.

The picnic had also allowed Phoebe to observe Darcy more objectively. There was no doubt her niece missed her mother and she cried far more often than she would have done if Lucy hadn't disappeared, but she was doing remarkably well considering what was going on in her life. The little girl amazed Phoebe with her resilience and she hoped that meant Darcy wouldn't be so badly affected by the whole experience, once her mother eventually came home. Her niece's laughter drifting on the breeze as she played with her friends had been a joy to hear. When she'd begun to get tired and had come over for a cuddle, it had felt like the greatest gift Phoebe had ever received. Things would be okay. They just had to wait for Lucy to clear her head and she'd be back. It was the thought Phoebe had clung on to when she closed her eyes, and it was the thing that had finally given her unbroken sleep, after so many nights without it.

When she'd told the others she could see the appeal of living in Appleberry again, it had been because she had people around her who weren't just there for the fun times. Scarlett had always been there for her, but the support she'd had from Jamie since Lucy had disappeared had been incredibly important too. He was starting to feel like Phoebe's friend, and she hadn't made a connection with a new person like that in a very long time. So long, in fact, she couldn't remember when it had last happened. She could already imagine a friendship with Kate and Dolly, too. So maybe the idea of settling back in Appleberry wasn't so crazy after all.

Phoebe was still feeling upbeat after she'd dropped Darcy off at nursery the morning after the picnic, but she should have realised it wouldn't last.

'Where have you been?' Her mother's eyes were wild as she turned to look at Phoebe. Even her father, the vision in beige at her mother's side, had an unusually animated expression on his face. Over the years he'd suppressed so many emotions that he'd ended up resembling Mr Potato Head before any features were added, but not today.

'I was dropping Darcy at nursery.' Phoebe fought to keep her tone level; reacting to her mother was like poking a wasps' nest. But it was hard to act casual when her parents' arrival was so unwelcome. There was almost nothing she wouldn't rather have found on her doorstep, including anything the local wildlife might leave to mark their territory, and her good mood was deflating like a punctured balloon.

'We've been calling.' Roger's face took on a pinched expression and, for a moment, she thought he might say they'd been worried. It would have been a normal response for any parent, especially when they already had a daughter who was missing, but she should have known better. Even if her father was terrified for her safety, he'd never dare admit that in front of his wife. Janet was the only person allowed to be the focus of his attention.

'We were in a rush. I forgot my phone.'

'And I suppose you forgot to look at all the messages I sent you, begging you to let us see our granddaughter?' Her mother's voice was shrill, the wild-eyed look even wilder.

'What are you talking about? What messages?' Phoebe clenched her fist, the pain of her nails digging into her palm a welcome distraction.

'These.' Janet thrust her mobile phone towards her, revealing a series of messages sent to a contact listed as Phoebe. None of the messages had ever arrived but, when she tried to grab her mother's phone for a closer look, Janet ripped it away again.

'I never got any messages from you. I had a couple of texts from Dad and that was it.'

'Oh, so I suppose this is all just my imagination?' Her mother's laugh was maniacal as she threw her head back, before fixing her gaze on her daughter again. 'How could you do this to me? You're evil. Everyone is saying so.'

'What do you mean *everyone is saying so*?' A familiar sensation tightened its grip on Phoebe's throat, and she could have guessed what was coming next, even before her mother answered.

'I put a screenshot of all my unanswered messages on Facebook, so everyone knows you're stopping me seeing my only granddaughter. I've been through enough, what with my other daughter disappearing without a word, and now you do this. I've had hundreds of messages saying how wicked you're being, lots of them from people I don't even know.'

'You posted it publicly?' It was no good Phoebe denying for a second time that she'd never got the messages. Janet was a master manipulator who had recorded countless arguments with her daughters in the past, editing them to make them sound one-sided, and then sharing the cruelty of her offspring with anyone who would listen. She liked nothing better than painting herself as the victim, to garner sympathy and attention. Faking the messages to Phoebe would have been child's play for her.

It was far easier for her father to buy into that and play along in front of Janet, the way he always had done, than to face up to the fact that his wife was a narcissist who'd driven both of their daughters to breaking point far too many times to recall. Or that he'd been too weak to do anything meaningful about it. Janet had hit the jackpot when she'd found an enabler in Roger, and it had sealed their children's fate. His occasional secret shows of affection hadn't saved them, and it didn't even begin to make up for all the times he'd gone along with what his wife wanted. It was too late now, anyway, and Phoebe couldn't think of anything her father could do that would change that.

'What else am I supposed to do when you won't even respond to my messages?' Her mother had adopted a tone of such faux sadness it made Phoebe's skin crawl, especially as it meant there was every chance this was another conversation Janet was recording. 'They said I should come here and take Darcy home with us.'

'Over my dead body!' It was as if a wild animal inside of Phoebe had suddenly been unleashed, and in that instant, she'd have fought to the death to protect her niece if she had to.

'It's okay, we're not going to take her.' Phoebe's father placed a restraining hand on her arm and for a split second a look of recognition passed between them. Deep down, he must know it was a fate no one in their right mind would willingly inflict on a little girl who was already missing her mother. But he couldn't say that out loud; it was more than his life was worth. 'We just want to see her, that's all.'

'What for?' Even as she asked, Phoebe already knew the answer. Her mother would want to take photos or videos, playing the doting grandmother and grieving parent. She'd already posted videos of herself crying about how much she was missing her daughter, linking them to the social media hashtags for Lucy's missing person campaign. Janet might have started off worrying how her daughter's disappearance would reflect on her, but she'd quickly realised there was an opportunity to exploit her own make-believe sadness and get the attention she so desperately craved. Being able to use Darcy as a pawn in that game would just raise the stakes.

'Because she's our granddaughter and we'll go to the authorities if we have to.' Janet thrust her mobile towards Phoebe again, this time with the Facebook app open. 'Look at all these messages from people advising us to do just that. Some of them have even offered to donate to a GoFundMe page to help pay our legal fees.'

'Jesus Christ, Mother! Every time I think you can't get any worse, you find a way to prove me wrong.' Phoebe was shaking with rage and a desire to cry that was so powerful, but so deeply repressed, it felt as if her head was in danger of exploding. 'Take me to court if that's what you want. Do whatever you like. But I'm going to do everything I can to keep Darcy as far away from you as possible, so there's no chance of her ending up doing what Lucy has done, just to escape you.'

'How dare you—' Her mother flew towards her, trying to grab hold of Phoebe's hair, but she was too quick, darting out of the way.

'I'm going to protect Darcy from you if it's the last thing I do.' Turning her back on her parents, she broke into a run, barely even hearing the torrent of abuse her mother was screaming. She'd been so hopeful after the picnic, and so sure that staying in Appleberry was the right thing for her and Darcy, but now she just wanted to run as far away as she could. Exactly like Lucy had. But Phoebe wouldn't be going alone if she left. She'd meant every word she said about protecting her niece and it was a promise she'd be keeping, even if that meant leaving Lucy behind for good.

By the time Phoebe got back to Lucy's cottage, her feet were covered in cuts. When she'd taken flight, leaving her parents on the doorstep, she'd been wearing flip-flop-style sandals that definitely weren't designed for running. But even when she'd been far enough away from her parents to be certain they weren't coming after her, she needed to keep going. Kicking off her shoes, she'd picked them up and continued to run, heading into the woodland, past the lake, and further into the dense thicket of trees that bordered Appleberry on one side, until she was in very real danger of getting lost. It had almost been tempting to keep going until she *was* completely lost, wondering if that was what Lucy had done. But then she thought about Darcy and Norma, Scarlett and even Jamie, and she knew she couldn't just disappear. Instead, she'd headed back, barely aware of how much damage she'd done to the soles of her feet until she was inside the cottage, with the door safely bolted behind her, and the certainty that her parents weren't waiting around the corner to stage another ambush.

As she'd run along the track through the woods, the sound of her feet making contact with twigs, stones and even fallen pinecones had been unmissable. She'd hardly noticed the resulting pain. It had merely served to provide the same kind of relief as when she'd dug her nails into the palms of her hands. But now, in the quiet of the cottage, she winced as the stinging sensations became a dull throb. Norma started to whimper in sympathy, her plaintive cries tightening the lump in Phoebe's throat all over again.

'It's okay, girl.' Scooping the little dog up, Phoebe headed into the kitchen, every step a reminder of how desperate she'd been to escape from her parents. Her mobile phone was still plugged in to the charger on the kitchen worktop, where she'd left it. Despite trying to fight the urge, she picked it up and scrolled through her messages, searching for the last exchange with her mother. She hated the power Janet still had over her, her ability to gaslight Phoebe to such an extent, that a tiny part of her wondered if her mother really had sent the messages. But there was nothing. Their last exchange a recrimination about Phoebe's decision not to visit for Mother's Day, every message before on a similar theme. It was all me, me, me with Janet Spencer and it always had been.

There were three back-to-back missed calls from her father,

from when her parents had been waiting on the doorstep, and an
email from Adam.

Hey Phebes,

I hope Norma is settling into country life okay. There was
something I wanted to talk to you about on Saturday, but it felt
like the wrong time.

I've been offered a job at the New York office and I'm going
to take it. The question is what we do about the flat? You could
buy me out, or, if you're staying down there with the carrot-
crunchers, we could sell it, or rent it out. Or if you're coming
home, you could rent out my room. I can cover my half of the
mortgage for a while, but the New York contract is for at least
three years, and I need to make a plan. The company is putting
me up in an apartment for six months as part of the relocation
package, but after that I've got to find my own place.

Sorry to land this on you. There's another job coming up in
the department I'm moving to and you'd have been perfect for
it, but I know you can't leave right now. However, if things
change at any point, just let me know. It's not that I'm asking
you to come with me, I just hate seeing all your potential going
to waste and I hope it's not forever.

Give me a call when it's a good time to talk, and don't let
the good folks of Appleberry persuade you to start making
compost out of your nail clippings, or anything else equally
gross.

Catch up soon,

Adamski

It was a nickname Adam claimed he'd been given at school,
and it was the way he'd always signed off his messages to
Phoebe. He'd sent her a link to an article, when she'd first

returned to Appleberry, about all the things people wanting to grow their own veg used to make compost. As a city boy all his life, he clearly thought anyone living in the country was bound to be odd. The email spelt out other things too. The fact that there was no mention of 'thinking of moving to NYC', but instead a fait accompli, said everything there was to say about their relationship. Phoebe wouldn't have expected anything else under normal circumstances, but she'd thought of Adam as one of her closest friends, regardless of any physical relationship they might have had. And with things the way they were right now, she needed her friends more than ever. It was clear now that it had been naïve of her to expect anything different. It was a shock to realise people could still disappoint her, despite having parents who reminded her of the possibility at every turn.

Phoebe was staring at her phone, contemplating a response, when it started to ring.

'Hello.' It was from a number she didn't recognise and her heart was hammering in her ears as she waited for an answer, desperately hoping that this might finally be the call she'd been waiting for. But it wasn't Lucy.

'Hi, Phoebe, it's Bradley. PC Harrison.' Whenever he called, the young police officer seemed to find it necessary to reiterate his job title, and Phoebe's mind was already racing, trying to work out whether he sounded like someone about to impart the best news possible, or the terrible kind.

'Have you found Lucy?' The hammering of her heart had reached a crescendo.

'I'm afraid not. But I wanted to let you know the initial results of the analysis of Lucy's laptop. Have you got someone there with you?'

'Uh huh.' Phoebe pulled the pug she was cradling in one arm

closer to her chest, sinking down onto the battered armchair in the corner of Lucy's kitchen.

'Good, because this might be difficult to hear.' Bradley coughed, as if he was unconsciously looking for a reason to delay speaking, but then he took a deep breath. 'It seems she was a member of a number of online forums. Some of them had discussions about how to drop off-grid and disappear to start a new life, but some of them were... more sinister.'

'Suicide forums?' It felt as if iced water was trickling down Phoebe's spine, even though she knew that was impossible.

'I'm afraid so. Some of the threads focused on the best ways to carry out the plan, and the other one that Lucy was a regular visitor to was aimed at finding a suicide partner. They all ought to be banned in my opinion. But the internet is like the hydra, and as soon as one site like that is shut down, more seem to pop up in their place.'

'Is there any evidence she met up with anyone she connected with on one of these sites?' Bile was rising in Phoebe's throat as she spoke. The fact there were people out there, sitting behind their laptops and encouraging other people to take their own lives, made her sick to her stomach. But the prospect that her little sister might have been influenced by someone like that was unbearable.

'We are investigating one lead in relation to that, but I can't say any more right now. I'm really sorry. As soon as there's anything to report, I promise I'll let you know straight away and, in the meantime, we're continuing to look into her online activity. Unfortunately, only the week leading up to Lucy's disappearance is accounted for within her search history and it looks like she went to a lot of trouble to clear any history before that point, as well as deleting any messages from social media and her emails. We've got ways of accessing deleted content, but it's going to take longer than we hoped to be able to do that. We're liaising with the service providers who host these sites, but they often hide behind data protection laws and it's a very protracted process.'

'This other lead you've got, how hopeful are you that it will come to something?' Every day that went past was a missed opportunity to bring Lucy home, and Phoebe was getting more and more worried that it meant she never would.

'We've conducted some interviews, but until we have some solid evidence to support what's been said, it would be wrong of me to speculate, and I don't think that will help you. But the missing person campaign is also generating a lot of engagement online and there are a couple of potential sightings we're looking into, but nothing definite yet.'

'Is there anything else I can do? Maybe if I went on TV and appealed to Lucy to come home, she'd see it and decide to come back. I think if I was holding a photo of Darcy, that might swing it.' Phoebe needed to do something, and she desperately wanted to believe that a grand gesture like that could work, when nothing else so far had.

'It's a possibility and we're liaising with the missing persons charity to explore other avenues. I'm sorry I can't offer you anything more than that, but I want you to know we're not giving up. Finding Lucy and bringing her home to her little girl is still a priority for us.' Bradley's voice caught on the mention of Darcy and his show of emotion gave Phoebe a tiny sliver of hope.

'Thank you.' Her words might barely be audible, but they were all she could manage. Lucy had reached out to someone for help after all, just in the worst possible way. If Phoebe had been a better sister that would never have happened, and whether Lucy eventually returned home or not, it was something she was going to have to live with for the rest of her life.

13

One of the things that had surprised Phoebe most about caring for a young child was how things got lost so easily. At breakfast, both of Darcy's shoes had been in the kitchen, but when it came time to leave for nursery, one of them had completely disappeared. A frantic search hadn't unearthed it, and in the end, she'd put Darcy into a pair of trainers instead.

'Come on then, confess. You ate the shoe, didn't you?' When she got back after dropping Darcy off, Phoebe looked at Norma, who grunted in response. But she was far too fussy an eater to have chomped down on the missing shoe. If it had been a sausage, or a packet of the pink wafer biscuits that Darcy loved so much, Phoebe wouldn't have looked any further for a suspect. This wasn't down to Norma, though.

The shoes had needed cleaning after Darcy had insisted on wearing them to Jamie's farm, and Phoebe had left them on the dresser in the kitchen afterwards, but the one they'd found had been by the front door. When she'd asked Darcy whether she'd moved the shoes, the little girl had been non-committal at first, but it seemed pretty likely she'd dropped it, or put it somewhere, and now couldn't remember where that was. The more they'd searched for the shoe, the more Darcy had got upset. And the last thing Phoebe wanted was to repeat history by making her niece so distressed that she wouldn't ever be able to own a pair of shoes without writing her name in them. That didn't mean Phoebe could just let it go either; the legacy of her own childhood couldn't be shaken off that easily, and she didn't seem able to stop searching for the shoe. She was supposed to be working, but instead she'd turned half of the house upside down.

'Do you think it could have fallen behind the dresser?' Phoebe spoke to Norma again, but the dog just rolled over and closed her eyes. If there wasn't the offer of a walk, a treat, or a cuddle on the cards, then sleep would always win. The trouble was, if Phoebe didn't find the shoe, there was a good chance that, unlike Norma, she'd struggle to get any sleep when she went to bed. She could almost hear her mum saying that if she couldn't even keep track of Darcy's footwear, how the hell did she think she had the ability to raise her.

Whenever she thought about the prospect of Lucy never coming back, it broke her heart, but it also terrified her that Janet might try and push for custody of her granddaughter, especially after the things her mother had said the last time she'd seen her. If Janet did that, it wouldn't be done out of love, or a desire to care for the little girl. It would be about presenting a certain image of herself to the world and, more than that, about having control. Janet would only want Darcy because she knew that Phoebe did, and she couldn't possibly allow her daughter to win. The stunt she'd pulled with the imaginary text messages was just a taste of what she would be capable of and, if it came to a fight, one thing was for certain, it wouldn't be fair.

'Okay, I'm going to pull the dresser out.' She was still speaking to the now snoring Norma, but this time she didn't even bother to glance in the little pug's direction. Talking to the dog was just a habit she'd got into, a way of thinking out loud. And even though she was never going to get an answer, she found it oddly reassuring.

Shifting the dresser a few inches forward, she heard a thud and put her hand down the gap that was now at the back. Thirty seconds later, she'd retrieved the shoe, an Alice band, two paint-brushes and another spiral-bound sketchpad. When Phoebe had searched through the house previously, she'd found eight sketch-pads in total. Some of the drawings were accompanied by a few words about what was depicted in them, and some just had titles, but none of the sketches had the same sort of detail written next to them as the drawing Lucy had done of the two of them as chil-dren, at Lake Pippin. So, when Phoebe started to flip through this sketchpad, she wasn't expecting to find anything significant. But then she got to a picture that was undeniably of Darcy, and Lucy had written a note beneath it.

I wish I could keep her like this forever, but she's growing up so fast, and before long she'll lose her innocent belief that everyone is good. I know, because I was like that once, until I realised I was someone not even a mother could love. I never want Darcy to feel that way because of her grandmother, or because of me. I could leave, I know that, but I can't ever escape the person my mother has made me into. Even if I move away from Appleberry, I'll never be able to undo that, and I'm terrified I'll pass all those insecurities on to my beautiful daugh-ter. I desperately want her to stay exactly as she is in this draw-ing, just like the girl I left behind all those years ago, who believed anything was possible. That's why Darcy needs to be raised by someone so much stronger than me, someone who still has that fire and belief, and who will never let my mother find a way of hurting my baby girl, whether she lives around the corner, or a thousand miles away.

Phoebe dropped the sketchbook on the kitchen table, and sank into one of the chairs, with her head in her hands, the pain in her sister's words making it feel as if someone had torn off the top layer of her skin. Phoebe wanted to escape from her own body, and the desire she'd had before – to run and just keep going – was back with a vengeance. But Lucy was right. It didn't matter how far they went, they couldn't ever outrun themselves and they'd never find their way back to the girls they used to be. Whatever happened with Lucy, and whatever stunts Janet tried to pull as a result, Phoebe was more determined than ever to protect Darcy from her grandmother. Or die trying. She just hoped to God that Lucy hadn't done that already.

14

The pile of post that arrived just before lunchtime looked innocuous enough. It was mostly junk mail advertising everything from a new pizza restaurant to the ultimate pre-pay-your-own-funeral package; there were also a couple of bits of mail that Adam had forwarded on from London. In among it all was a letter addressed to Phoebe sent directly to Lucy's address.

The letter was in a lavender-coloured envelope, which looked as if it might contain a birthday card or even a love letter, but with a pre-typed business-style label affixed to its front. It wouldn't be from Adam. He'd never written her a love letter in all the time they'd been together; texting to ask whether she was 'up for it' was a bit more his style. Lucy was the only person she knew who used coloured envelopes for everything. Phoebe had remarked on it once, during one of her infrequent visits back to Appleberry, not long after her sister had first moved into the cottage. There'd been a pile of pink envelopes on the dresser and, when Phoebe had asked what they were for, Lucy had explained they were for 'any-thing and everything'. Phoebe had pulled a face, but her sister had just laughed, insisting it could even make appealing against a parking ticket more fun, as long as you used the right stationery. Now, looking at the lavender envelope, there was only one person Phoebe could imagine the letter coming from. But, if she opened it, and it wasn't from Lucy, it was going to crush her.

'Well, it's not going to open itself, is it?' Phoebe addressed the empty room and Norma, who was sitting on the window seat, making the most of the late morning sun, didn't even look up this time. She clearly wasn't as engaged in their one-sided conversations as Phoebe was. Darcy was at nursery, despite objecting with a very well-thought-out argument for a pre-schooler that she'd much rather be at the forest school with Jamie. So it was just Phoebe and a lavender-coloured envelope that she was still finding it almost impossible to persuade herself to open.

'Right, one, two, three.' Ripping the envelope as she counted out loud, she felt like an idiot. She was terrified of what it might reveal, but almost as terrified that it might not be anything to do with Lucy after all. That would put her back where she'd started, with no idea where her sister was or what had happened to her. Then she began to read.

Dear Phebes,

I know you'll probably be veering between worrying yourself senseless about me right now and wanting to slap me for disappearing, and I'm really sorry for both of those things.

I hope whoever found it gave you the letter I left and that it helped you understand why I had to go. But I know by now you'll have started worrying that you aren't doing a good enough job of looking after Darcy.

So, I thought this would be a good time to let you know that I never expected you to be the perfect parent – God knows I haven't been – but I trust you more than I trust anyone else.

Remember when Mum and Dad started leaving us home

alone all the time because Mum wanted him to take her out dancing? You'd been in the school play, and everyone was saying you were born to be on the stage, and the teacher gave you a star-of-the-show trophy. Every time one of the other parents came up to say how well you'd done, all Mum kept on about was what a good dancer she'd been at your age, and how they should have seen her.

She and Dad joined that dance class and started entering competitions straight after. I can't count the number of times we were left on our own in the evenings, and sometimes for whole weekends. We can't have been more than seven and ten, but you were always the good big sister. We watched *Jaws* when it was being shown on TV that time, do you remember? And I was terrified a shark was going to come up the U-bend of the toilet and get me! Mum and Dad were out again, but you let me get into your bed and cuddled me until I fell asleep. Even though you were scared too, you always put me first, and that's why I want you to take care of Darcy.

I know we haven't seen each other as much as we should have done since you left Appleberry. I think we were both just so busy trying to prove something to Mum and Dad that we forgot about each other. I wish we hadn't, because I think if I'd had you, things could have been so different.

I left Appleberry once, did you know that? I lasted two whole weeks. I went to stay with an artist friend who ran a retreat in Devon. She offered me a job, and a place for me and Darcy to stay. But then Dad got in touch and said Mum was distraught, that she couldn't bear both her daughters moving away. He convinced me to come home, and I really believed that maybe things would finally be different. Of course, they weren't. She just didn't like the way us both leaving reflected on her. I was an idiot, and even now I can't trust myself to leave and not change my mind. Not unless I do something that leaves me no route back.

I'm not like you, I wish I was, but you never once looked back. So, please trust me when I say I know that you're the right person to take care of my baby girl. Give her a kiss from me.

Lucy-Lu xxxx

Just like the note she'd left on the beach, the letter was typed, except for the sign-off at the end and the kisses that followed it. Lucy-Lu was what Phoebe had called her sister when they were little, but it was a name she hadn't used, or even thought about, in years. Now, seeing it written down, was enough to bring a thousand childhood memories flooding back, and her head was throbbing with unshed tears. Part of her wanted the crying to finally start, but the other half was terrified that, if it did, she might never be able to stop. It wasn't just Lucy's disappearance she'd pushed down; there was decades of suppressed emotion buried beneath the latest pain.

Taking a deep breath to steady herself, Phoebe turned over the envelope. There had to be a clue to where Lucy had posted it, but the franking said London. That wasn't what she'd wanted to read; trying to find her sister there would be almost impossible if she didn't want to be found. But at least it was a start. And more than that, it meant Lucy was still alive. Relief flooded her body; it wasn't too late to help Lucy and it suddenly felt as though she was fizzing with energy. She just had to work out where to start, and she couldn't wait to tell Jamie and enlist his help.

Turning towards the kitchen counter to grab her phone, she caught sight of the last drawing Darcy had done for her and experienced a stab of something that felt very much like fear. If they found Lucy, eventually all of this would be over, and Phoebe would be free to go back to her old life if she wanted to. It was in that moment she realised she didn't want to, not if it meant bowing out of day-to-day involvement in Darcy's life. But she had no idea if Lucy would be willing to let her stay a part of it, if they ever managed to bring her home.

15

'Can you come over?' Phoebe's voice was breathy, as if she'd run for the phone before calling Jamie.

'What's wrong? It's not Darcy, is it?'

'No, it's Lucy.' It was impossible to tell without seeing her face whether it was worry or excitement making her catch her breath. 'If you've got time to come over, I'll explain everything, but it's proof she's still alive.'

'That's amazing! Give me five minutes and I'll be there.' Jamie put down the phone and unplugged the electric saw he'd been using to cut sections out of a large sheet of plywood. Putting together the templates for bird boxes was going to be the children's next project, and he'd been totally engrossed in the task until Phoebe had called. For the first time that day, he'd managed to do something without Lucy's disappearance constantly interrupting his thoughts. But if he went back to using the saw now, there was a very good chance of him cutting a finger off.

He'd wanted news of Lucy to give Phoebe hope, and it seemed to have worked. Only now he was second-guessing if it really was a good thing, because, if the worst turned out to be true, the fall would be even harder now. She was still holding on to the surety that her sister would make it home in time for Darcy's birthday and, deep down, he was hoping for that too. But knowing what he did made it much harder for him to be certain, and he hated the thought of what that might do to the little girl and her aunt.

Making the decision to leave Fisher at home, Jamie crossed the grass to the low hedge that separated his property from Lucy's cottage, barely even breaking his stride as he cleared it. The fact that Lucy's cottage belonged to him was another secret he hadn't shared with Phoebe. It had originally been a grain store, but he'd converted it to a holiday let not long after he'd taken over the farm. When Lucy had asked if she could rent it on a long-term basis, he'd taken a considerable hit on the income it had generated as a holiday cottage. But he recognised something in her, that sense of searching for a place where you felt you really belonged. Jamie had felt guilty about asking her to find another therapist, but the lines between their professional and personal relationship had become too blurred when she'd asked to become his tenant. He'd hoped that renting the cottage to Lucy, for a price she could actually afford, would give her that same sense of home the farm had given him. But sadly it hadn't.

Maybe he shouldn't have been surprised that even that wasn't enough for Lucy to ever truly feel at home in the same village where her parents lived. After all, she'd recounted enough stories for him to realise just how much poison Janet Spencer could spread. Lucy's mother had called her 'disgusting' and 'a failure' for falling pregnant and, worse still, for making her a grandmother. It had soon become clear that Janet had blighted the lives of both her daughters. From time to time, Phoebe would pay a flying visit to Lucy and Darcy and he'd always kept a low profile when he knew she was there. It had been clear from the start that Lucy loved her big sister, but she'd also admitted that their relationship could be tense as a result of the conflict their mother seemed to thrive on creating between them.

Jamie knew from the bank transfer that it was Phoebe who'd paid the first three months' rent on the cottage, and occasionally after that some of the payments had also come from her. The cottage was linked to a business account – *Appleberry Stays* – so there was no way Phoebe would know the cottage was his, unless he told her. Given that she'd questioned him more than once about his relationship with Lucy, he had no intention of adding any fuel to that fire, and it wouldn't do anything to help track Lucy down anyway. He couldn't even tell Phoebe that Lucy had originally been one of his clients, not without breaking confidentiality. As for what had happened with Lucy's friend Gerry, that was in the police's hands for now, and if he shared that with Phoebe, he'd be breaking a code of ethics, and risking his career too.

Until things had taken an unexpected turn, Jamie had been convinced Lucy was happy in the home she'd created for herself and Darcy. Every six months, when her contract was renewed, she'd ask him if he wanted her to move on, or if he was planning to increase the rent. She always had that same look of terror in her eyes as she'd had the first day she'd burst into tears in one of their sessions and asked if there was any way he'd consider renting the cottage to her. Her previous landlord was evicting her and Darcy for late payment, and she'd explained how there was no way she could go home to her parents, or even ask for their help. So, each time she'd checked whether the rent on the cottage was going up, he'd reassured Lucy that there wouldn't be any increase, because she was doing him a favour, being next door to take care of Fisher and feed the other animals on the very rare occasions he left the farm overnight.

They'd grown pretty close, once she was no longer his client, but he'd never thought of Lucy in any way other than as a friend.

She was far too vulnerable. And despite her own vulnerability, his feelings for Phoebe were a lot more complex and much harder to control, but that didn't mean he couldn't do it. Although, if he was going to keep the promise he'd made, he wasn't sure he could even truly be Phoebe's friend, because friends weren't supposed to lie to each other, not even by omission.

The first time he'd met Gerry had been two years before. She'd booked herself onto a mindfulness retreat he was running at the farm, and it was clear from the start that she was struggling with a range of issues, and that her mental health was very fragile. What he had no idea about at first was that Gerry only knew about Jamie's retreat because Lucy had told her. The two of them had met online, in a suicide forum, but none of that had come out for over a year.

Before Gerry left the retreat at the end of the weekend, Jamie had recommended some other therapeutic routes she might want to explore, and he'd been more worried about her than anyone else who'd attended the group. But even then, she'd never mentioned any intention to end her life. That was a plan he didn't discover for a long time.

Just over twelve months after that first visit, Gerry had got back in touch, begging for a counselling appointment, and telling him he was the only person she could talk to about what she was going through. It was during those sessions that she'd opened up and told him about the abuse and coercive control her husband was subjecting her to. She'd shown Jamie evidence of reporting it to the police, and their decision that there was insufficient proof to arrest her husband. He was clearly a clever man, and he was driving Gerry to the edge.

Gerry was terrified that if she left him, her husband would find a way of making sure he got custody of their children, but she couldn't bear the thought of staying simply for them either. That was when she'd first talked about suicide being her only option. She'd been so badly manipulated and horribly let down when she'd sought help, that the only way she could think of to provide evidence of what her husband had done was to blame him for the decision to end her life. Gerry was certain that would be the proof she needed to finally persuade everyone that her husband wasn't fit to have custody of their children. It didn't seem logical to anyone from the outside, including Jamie. After all, how could leaving her children help to protect them? But he'd seen it before, people who'd been so manipulated and backed into a corner that they genuinely felt death was their only way out. Gerry had told him that, even if she took the children, her husband would have continued to hound her and make all their lives a misery. By dying, she could leave the evidence behind so that the children were taken from him, but she'd no longer be around for him to try and get revenge. The battle would finally be over. Jamie had assured her that there were other ways for Gerry and the children to break away from her husband, and that losing her would devastate everyone who loved her. But by the time she came to him, she was already exhausted from the fight and he was scared she might not even have the energy to try and see an alternative.

Jamie often had clients who admitted to suicidal thoughts, but usually, when he asked how likely they were to act on them, the response was reassuring. It wasn't like that with Gerry, and he had a duty of care to protect her. He asked all his clients to sign up to an agreement safeguarding their wellbeing, which included details of their GP and next of kin, in case of that kind of situation. It meant he could liaise with a client's GP, then contact the next of kin to work closely with them on a plan to safeguard the client if the need arose. But as private clients, seeing him of their own free will, Jamie couldn't force anyone to provide information, and any details they did give him were taken on trust. It meant there was scope for a client to hide their identity, if they chose to do so. But so much about the relationship between a client and their therapist was built on trust, and if Jamie had started asking for verification of the details provided, that trust would have been broken before they even began.

The strange thing was that Gerry had seemed happy to provide almost all of those details, but had refused to give any information about next of kin because of her abusive husband. When Jamie had said he'd wanted to talk to someone about her intention to harm herself, she'd begged him not to contact her GP. She'd told him her husband worked at the same practice, and if Jamie contacted them, he might as well sign her death warrant. He'd agreed not to, because of how distraught she'd become, but they'd compromised on her giving him the name and number of the police officer she'd spoken to about her husband. When Jamie explained the situation to the police, they promised more help and that they'd look into her claims again. They also referred Gerry to further sources of support. After that, Jamie had continued to see her once a fortnight for another three months. She seemed to be making real progress, saying all the right things, but eventually Gerry had taken the decision to find another therapist, someone closer to home.

All that time, Jamie hadn't had any idea that she and Lucy were friends, and it took another crisis for him to find out. Lucy had been going through a really rough patch at the time and he'd been worried about her, popping in to see her more often as a result. It was only during a chance visit that he'd discovered Gerry was there too and, when he asked how they knew each other, Lucy tried to fob him off, but he refused to leave. Eventually it was Gerry who admitted they'd met on a suicide forum, and that it was Lucy who'd recommended him as a therapist. They'd discussed a suicide pact when they first met and had both decided against it, but Lucy had been raising the idea again. Jamie was horrified, but the fact that Gerry had admitted the truth gave him hope that she didn't plan to go through with it. Lucy was the one who'd scared him most, because she genuinely seemed to see it as a solution.

He'd followed all the protocols with Gerry when she'd been his client, and then with the two of them when he'd discovered their pact, doing the same again with Lucy, as soon as he'd found out about her disappearance, by contacting the police and sharing what he knew. They were already well aware of her vulnerability, but he'd been keen to stress that thoughts of suicide didn't always lead to action. He didn't want them to write Lucy off and stop looking into other possibilities, because he knew for a fact that she'd been close to wanting to die before and had changed her mind at the last minute. None of that stopped him wishing he could tell Phoebe everything he knew too, and the more he got to know her, the stronger that desire became.

Jamie was trying his best to trust the police, and they'd assured him that the matter was best left with them. But surely Phoebe had a right to know that her sister had become very close to someone she'd met on a suicide forum? But if he told Phoebe any of that, she'd want to track Gerry down, and he knew what that might mean for Lucy's friend. Any chance she might have of stopping her children being taken away by her husband could be severely compromised. And as much as he wanted to do whatever he could to help Phoebe, that was a line he didn't want to cross.

'Oh thank God you're here, I've been desperate to show you this letter to see what you think.' Phoebe looked totally transformed, her smile reaching her eyes for the first time since they'd met. 'It was all I could do not to run straight over to your place.'

'Who's it from?' Taking the letter that she was waving aloft, he desperately hoped she wouldn't notice his hand shaking. 'Can I open it?'

'It might be a good start.'

Pulling the letter out of the envelope, he read it, his mind racing so fast he had to go back over some of the sentences more than once. This hadn't been what he'd expected, and he had no idea if this letter had anything to do with the message he'd sent to Gerry. Looking up from the note, his eyes met Phoebe's and he struggled for the right thing to say, but the words wouldn't come. All he could do was wait for her to speak instead.

'Isn't it wonderful?' Phoebe moved another step towards him, so close he could smell the lemony scent of her shampoo still clinging to her hair. 'It came this morning and it's definite proof that Lucy's still alive!'

'It seems so.' He wanted to agree so badly, for them both to be able to believe there was no chance Lucy was dead, but he knew too much for that kind of certainty. And, even in the face of Phoebe's excitement, he couldn't bring himself to just nod and smile.

'What do you mean, it *seems* so?'

'Well, if it was handwritten, I might be more convinced.' He attempted a shrug, careful not to say too much. When he'd sent Gerry a message, he'd begged her to ask Lucy to get in touch with her sister, if she knew where she was, but there was no way of knowing if that was why the letter had arrived. And if Lucy was still alive, but didn't want to be found before she had the chance to end her life, Gerry might even have sent the letter herself, to cover for her friend. Their relationship had been intense and dangerous, and he wasn't sure he'd put it past Gerry to manipulate the situation so that Lucy had the breathing space she needed. The police didn't seem to have anything significant from talking to Gerry, at least nothing they'd shared with him, and he was starting to wonder if he should have confronted her face to face straight away instead. There was a possibility it could have put her at risk, but it might have given them the best chance of finding Lucy. And maybe it wasn't too late.

'But she's signed it Lucy-Lu, which was the nickname only I had for her. How could anyone have faked that, and why on earth would they want to?' Phoebe's eyes were searching his for reassurance, like a child who'd been told that Father Christmas wasn't real, begging their parents to promise he was.

'I don't know why anyone would want to do it, but I do know how they'd know about the nickname.' That was the trouble with lying, even by omission: it was so easy to get deeper and deeper into the mire. But whatever Jamie decided about going to see Gerry, he had no intention of getting Phoebe involved. He might have to put his career on the line by using information a client had given him, for purposes that had nothing to do with his work as a therapist. And if he did decide to confront Gerry, there was a possibility she could even claim harassment, given that she was already talking to the police. If any of that happened, he didn't want to add to the burden of guilt that already seemed to be weighing Phoebe down. Instead, moving over to Lucy's desk in the corner of the kitchen, he opened a couple of drawers and found one of the business cards he'd helped her to work on. 'She rebranded her business about three months ago and called it Lucy-Lu Designs. Loads of people in Appleberry knew the reasons behind the name, including all the mums at the forest school.'

'And you.' She shot him a look and he had to force himself to keep eye contact. If he wanted Phoebe to keep an open mind about who might be behind the letter, he had to accept that meant opening himself up to scrutiny and taking the chance about where that might lead.

'Yes, and me.' Jamie pulled the order book out of the open drawer. 'All of Lucy's customers knew the origin of the company name too; it was in the *About* page on her website.'

'But what about Mum and Dad taking up dancing, the thing with the *Jaws* movie, and the stuff about her leaving home? Even I didn't know that. There's so much detail in the letter; no one else could possibly know all of that, could they?' He knew whatever he said next had the potential to crush Phoebe, and he couldn't bear to see all the hope that had been in her eyes fade away. But he didn't want to tell her any more lies than he already had either. She had to know there was a chance this letter hadn't come from her sister. But she had no idea that Lucy had a friend she'd confided every detail of her life to, and he couldn't tell her that, not without breaking Gerry's confidence and putting her at risk. Phoebe was already struggling with how slow the police were moving and, if she discovered Gerry's existence, there was no way she'd be willing to sit around and wait. Telling Phoebe about everything that had gone on between Gerry and Lucy would have been like pulling the pin out of hand grenade and expecting it not to blow up in their faces.

'She told me those stories and there's a possibility other people knew them too.'

'She was always talking about how kind you were. There was no one else she spoke about in the same way. I can't think of a single other person she seemed close enough with to share those kinds of things.' Phoebe narrowed her eyes again, scanning his face. 'But you can, can't you? There was someone in her life. Why didn't you tell the police who she was seeing?'

Phoebe's voice had risen, but it was impossible to work out whether it was anger or fear bubbling to the surface, and Jamie shook his head. He had to tell her something, otherwise she was going to push him away, and then he wouldn't be able to help her at all. The problem was, if he revealed anything, the whole thing might unravel. But as he looked at her again, he couldn't bring himself to lie. 'She wasn't seeing anyone in that way, but there was a female friend she'd been close to in the past, who she started spending a lot of time with, before she disappeared.'

'Why the hell didn't you tell me?' Phoebe looked ready to launch herself at him and, if he'd had any question about how she might react when she knew that he'd kept something like this from her, there was no doubt now.

'Because the woman who Lucy was friends with came to me for counselling, and I was bound by client confidentiality.'

'How can that matter when Lucy's life is at risk? Surely you can tell the police in those circumstances?' There was a look of such intensity in Phoebe's eyes, it was almost frightening, but all Jamie wanted to do was comfort her, even when she screamed the next words at him. 'She could be dead now, because of you!'

'I *did* tell the police. As soon as I reported Lucy missing, when she didn't come back for Darcy.' He kept his voice level and tried to reach out to her, but she snatched her hand away.

'So where is this woman? She might know where Lucy is, and no one is doing anything about it. Not you, not the police. No one!' Her eyes were still blazing and he desperately wanted to reassure her that everything that could be done was being done, but he didn't know much more than she did. The last time he'd spoken to the police, they'd said they couldn't share anything with him. He'd already reached out to Gerry, despite his better judgement, but for all he knew she might not even have got his message and the arrival of 'Lucy's letter' could be pure coincidence.

'All I know is that the police have spoken to her, but they wouldn't tell me what she said. We've just got to trust that if she knows anything about Lucy, the police will find that out.'

'You might have to trust them, but I don't.' A muscle was pulsing in Phoebe's cheek. 'I need to speak to this woman, myself. The police already seem to have decided that it's too late, but I'm never going to give up on Lucy, not until I've got absolute proof that she's dead. What's this woman's name? Do you know how to get in contact with her?'

'Her name's Gerry, but it was only when I spoke to the police about her that I discovered she'd given me a fake address. She stopped coming to see me and the mobile number I had for her is no longer connected. I've got no idea if she even picks up messages from the email address I have, or if she's stopped using that too. There were things going on in her life that I can't talk about, but she'd had support from the police before, and they might have had details for her that she never gave me. They also had access to my bank records to trace her that way, if they needed to. But I don't have the same resources or access to confidential information as the police, so I've got no idea where she is, and they're certainly not going to tell me. Or you.' He looked at her levelly, desperate to make her understand that trying to trace Lucy's friend might only make things worse. Especially for Gerry. 'Even if I did know, I still couldn't tell you. I've already disclosed far more than I should, but I've felt terrible about keeping all of this from you. And if I really thought that giving you the little bit of information I do have would make a difference to bringing Lucy home, I'd take the risk of what that might mean for me and my career, as well as for Gerry, who's very vulnerable too. But the police do this kind of thing all the time and they're far more likely to get to the truth.'

'The police told me they'd found evidence of Lucy joining a suicide forum.' Phoebe's eyes had gone glassy. There was no doubting how devastated she was about her sister's disappearance, but Jamie had never seen her cry and it was clear how badly she needed to. 'Some of the discussion threads she was on were offering her advice on how to kill herself, and the others were about finding a suicide partner. Gerry was on those sites too, wasn't she?'

Jamie couldn't look at Phoebe, because if he did, she was going to see the answer written all over his face. When Gerry had first opened up about having suicidal thoughts, she'd talked about accessing those sites, but he'd had no idea at the time that Lucy was doing the same thing. It wasn't until much later that it had all come out. That was when he'd stepped in again and had spoken to Lucy's GP. The medical forms Gerry had completed when she'd first registered as a client had turned out to be as fake as her address. All he had was the number and name of the police officer he'd spoken to about Gerry before. She'd gone to extraordinary lengths to cover her tracks, and had told him she was terrified of her husband finding out she was seeking therapy, and using it against her for custody of their children. Despite all of that, he'd genuinely thought that his intervention after Lucy had pushed for a second suicide pact had helped. Lucy had seemed to get back on track and Gerry was doing much better too, talking to a women's aid charity who'd promised to help her keep her and the children safe if she chose to make the break from her husband. He'd done all he could think of, but it clearly hadn't been enough.

'Phoebe, I want to help, I really do, but telling you what I know about Gerry isn't going to do that. Since Lucy's disappearance and talking to the police, I've been going over and over every conversation I ever had with Gerry, and with Lucy. Gerry seemed completely genuine in everything she said about what she was going through, but there are people who lie so much, they end up believing their stories themselves. And that makes them even harder to spot. The police are investigating everything I've shared with them and, if Gerry knows something, they'll find out.' He was repeating himself now, vaguely aware that he was trying almost as hard to convince himself as he was Phoebe. Her agony at the thought of Lucy being on those forums was palpable, and he had no idea any more if his faith in the police was justified. He didn't even know if the things Gerry had claimed about her husband were true. She could be a complete fantasist who'd fabricated all the evidence of his abuse, or someone who got off on encouraging other people to take their own lives. After all, the police had seemed to doubt her when she'd first gone to them.

'If I could just talk to her. *Please.*' Phoebe's anger seemed to have given way to desperation, and that was a hundred times harder for Jamie to face. 'All I need is her second name and whatever other details you might have. There must be something in this house that links to Gerry if Lucy spent all that time with her. She might even have another number written down for her somewhere; I've got to try and find it. I know you think we should wait for the police, but whenever I talk to Bradley he says it's going to take time, and I'm terrified that's something we might be running out of.'

Taking a deep breath, Jamie looked at Phoebe again. His head told him he needed to shut this down now, but his heart didn't want to listen. He was going to offer her something. It probably wasn't going to be what she wanted to hear, but it was far more than he should be offering. 'Let me try to find Gerry first. The last thing Darcy needs is for you to put yourself at risk in any way. You've got to be careful.'

'I don't want to be careful! I want Lucy back and the letter is the closest I've had to believing it's really going to happen since I got the call saying she was missing. I need to know if it came from her, or if this Gerry is somehow involved.'

'I know, and so do I. I can't even imagine how hard this is for you.' When he turned towards her, the last thing he'd expected was for her to step forward and rest her head against his chest. There was always a part of Phoebe so restrained that it felt almost impossible to get as close to her as he wanted to. But now she was trusting him enough to lean on him, and he instinctively knew how big a step that was for her, which made him even more determined to do whatever he could to help. Even if it did end up costing him his career.

'She's got to come home. Darcy needs her and so do I. There's so much I want to tell her, and I can't bear the thought that I might never get the chance to say it.'

'I'll speak to Gerry and we'll find Lucy, I promise.' He whispered the words close to Phoebe's ear, making a vow he had no idea whether he'd be able to keep. But he'd do everything he could not to let her down; he'd done far too much of that already.

16

'Are you okay?' Jamie turned to look at Phoebe as they reached the car park at the front of the care home. They'd decided it was a good idea to walk there with Fisher and Norma to ensure that the dogs had burnt up a bit of excess energy before they arrived, but now they were about to go in. She'd promised not to keep asking him every thirty seconds whether there was any news on tracing Gerry, but it was really hard. So anything that offered a distraction should have been welcome, but Phoebe had never done anything like this before and her emotions were already uncomfortably close to the surface. She just didn't want to do anything to upset anyone.

'I'm a bit nervous. I know it sounds stupid, but what if I don't know how to act around the residents?' It was strange how she could be so honest with Jamie and not put up any pretence about keeping it all together, the way she would have done with Adam or some of her friends back in London. She only really had room in her head for thinking about Lucy and trying to be the best aunt she could to Darcy. Maybe it was selfish, but Lucy being missing made everyone else's problems seem meaningless.

Scarlett was always there for her, but she had enough going on in her own life without having to take on all of Phoebe's problems. The only person she could really talk to about any of this was Jamie. He'd been there to bring her back down to earth when the letter had arrived. He understood how much she wanted it to be from Lucy, but he was also the voice of reason, reminding her that things weren't always what they seemed.

She'd been angry with him at first for not telling her straight away about Gerry, but when she'd seen what he was willing to risk to help her, she'd started to understand how hard it must have been for him. Therapy might not have worked out for Phoebe, but she'd told the counsellors things she'd be horrified if they shared with anyone else. Now she was asking Jamie to breach that trust, and he was willing to do it, at least as far as trying to talk to Gerry on her behalf. She needed him more than she could remember needing anyone in a long time, and she was trying not to let that scare her as much as it did.

'There's no need to be nervous.' Jamie had a gravelly depth to his voice, but his tone was gentle. 'A lot of the residents have Alzheimer's, but there's also a wing for people with fewer high-end needs. We can start there, to let you get a feel for the place. But in all honesty, you probably won't need to do anything much at all. Even the residents with the most advanced Alzheimer's seem to come alive when they see Fisher, and I'm sure it will be the same with Norma. They talk to the dogs, and it might not make any sense to us, but you can tell by their faces that they are enjoying it. I promise, it'll be fine.' Phoebe really wanted to believe him.

'Hi, Barbara.' Jamie greeted a woman in a sky-blue uniform, with a badge identifying her as the deputy manager. 'I've brought Fisher for the pet therapy session, and I've cleared it with Daniel to bring a second dog in today. This is Phoebe, by the way. I would say she's Norma's owner, but I'm not entirely sure it isn't the other way around.'

'Oh, pugs are my absolute favourite – she's so cute!' Barbara bent down and patted Norma, who snuffled at her hand in response, always on the lookout for an unexpected treat. 'It's nice to meet you too, Phoebe, and the residents will be thrilled to have two dogs to fuss over.'

'I'm just hoping Norma behaves herself.' Phoebe couldn't keep the wobble out of her voice, despite Jamie's words of reassurance. What if she said the wrong thing? Tried to help a resident who didn't need her help, or worse still made someone's confusion even worse? She'd wanted to do this, mostly to forget her own problems for a little while, but the last thing she wanted was to add to anyone else's. It was strange to think that she'd never really been around older people at any point in her life. Her father had lost his parents long before either she or Lucy were even born and, as an only child, it could explain the unconditional attachment he had to his wife. There had to be some reason for it. They never saw anything of her mum's family either, which according to Janet was because they were all so jealous of her – although it didn't take a genius to work out the real reason. Either way, having grandparents had never been part of her life.

'She'll be fine; she certainly likes to be made a fuss of and that's all they want to do, really. You can go on straight through.' Barbara smiled and Phoebe found herself doing something she did all too often – imagining what it would be like to have someone like Barbara as a mother. Barbara looked like she'd be ready with a hug or a safe shoulder to cry on if things went wrong. Phoebe had never had that, and she never would, despite the countless wishes she'd made as a kid.

'Do they have a lot of other activities for the residents?' Phoebe could see a sand table out in the garden at the back of The Pines, and a badminton net strung much lower than it usually would be.

Jamie nodded. 'They do a lot of stuff outside; they were playing balloon tennis last time I was here, and I know they have music nights. Lucy was doing some art therapy here too, before…'

'Neither of us ever seem able to finish that sentence, do we?' Phoebe turned to Jamie and something seemed to flicker in his eyes. 'I understand why you didn't tell me straight away about Gerry, but you would tell me if you knew anything else, wouldn't you?'

'Of course.' Jamie bent down to adjust Fisher's collar as he spoke, and she looked at him again, shaking off the frisson of doubt that had prickled her scalp. She had to trust him, because, without Jamie, the agony of waiting for news of Lucy would be truly unbearable.

* * *

'Oh what a little darling – what's her name?' An elderly lady who'd been introduced to Phoebe as Olive was the third resident to have Norma sit on her lap. None of them seemed to mind that the little dog was living up to the breed's reputation for shedding hair faster than the needles on a Christmas tree when the heating was turned up too high.

'She's called Norma and she looks completely at home sitting on your lap.' Jamie had been right, there'd been nothing to worry about. After years of being told that everything Phoebe had ever done was wrong, it was hard for her to believe she might actually do something right. Especially something new. It was part of the reason she'd been attracted to working with data, which wasn't something many people could claim. She liked the certainty of it and the rules that meant it wasn't based on someone's opinion; it made her feel safe.

'I'm not surprised she feels at home. When my husband, George, was alive, we always had a dog, and the last two we owned were pugs.' Olive turned her watery blue eyes towards Phoebe, and gave her a smile she suspected she'd remember forever. 'Thank you so much for bringing her in, you're an angel.'

'Hardly.' Phoebe concentrated on watching Olive's hands move slowly up and down Norma's wrinkled back – the paper-thin skin on the old lady's hands another reminder of just how much life she'd lived – and swallowed against the lump in her throat that now felt more present than ever. No one could see it from the outside, but it was there, always ready to remind her of its presence when her emotions were threatening to overwhelm her.

Like Barbara, Olive was a reminder of all the things she and Lucy hadn't had. They'd talked about trying to find their maternal grandparents, but the fear of rejection had won again. Now it might be too late for them to ever try, and not just because their grandparents would be a similar age to the woman sitting opposite.

'My George and I could never have children, you know?' Olive raised a quizzical eyebrow, as if Phoebe might somehow have been party to that information.

'No, I didn't know that.'

'The dogs were always like our babies; we had different breeds over the years, always small ones, though, like Jack Russells and Westies, so they could be proper lapdogs and get cuddles like Norma.'

'There's nothing like it, is there? I didn't have her with me when I first came down here and I missed her more than I would ever have thought possible.'

'Oh I know! Each time we lost one of our little dogs to old age or illness, we swore never again, it was just too painful to let them go. But then, after a month, sometimes less, either George or I would bring up the subject again, and we'd both admit how much we missed having a dog around, which meant we always ended up with another one before too long. Our pugs were called Betty and Doris after my two sisters.' Olive laughed, making Norma open her eyes for just the briefest of moments before she shut them again, sighing contentedly as she nestled into Olive's lap. 'It was George's idea; my sisters were always a bit bossy and made me feel like a failure for never having a family of my own, so it was his little bit of revenge to name the pugs after them. He said they had exactly the same sort of faces! He could always make me laugh, George, even at the worst of times. I miss that too.'

'I'm so sorry.' Phoebe laid her hand on top of Olive's, which was still resting on Norma's back. For a moment, she considered confiding in her that Lucy was missing, but it didn't seem right to encroach upon the older woman's loss. Although it was comforting to know she wasn't the only one grieving for the empty space left in her life, even if she wouldn't have wished that on her new friend for a moment.

'It's funny what you miss, isn't it?' Olive's voice was wistful. 'I used to love Friday evenings when George would get us cod and chips, then we'd share a whole packet of garibaldi biscuits with a pot of tea. We'd both be so stuffed that we could barely move, with the dogs curled up between us on the sofa. It might not sound very exciting to most people, but I'd give all the money in the world to have one more of those Friday nights.'

'It sounds pretty amazing to me.' The lump in Phoebe's throat seemed to be growing by the moment. And if wishing for something made it so, Olive would be back with her George, and Lucy would come home.

'Will you bring Norma to see me again, please?' Olive had the same pleading look on her face that Darcy always wore when she asked to go over and see Jamie's chickens. Even if Phoebe hadn't wanted to come back to The Pines – which to her surprise she found she did – she'd have been powerless to resist Olive's request.

'Of course I will.'

'You promise?'

'Absolutely. I'll make sure Jamie puts Norma on the rota to visit as often as possible. And I'd like to come back and see you too, if that's okay?'

'That will be an added bonus.' Olive gave her a cheeky wink. 'And if you could see your way clear to sneaking me in the occasional packet of garibaldis, I might even love you as much as I love Norma.'

'It's a deal.' Phoebe smiled and settled back into her seat next to Olive's, neither she nor Norma in any hurry to move on.

* * *

By the time Phoebe met up with Jamie again to go through to the main part of the care home, where the lounge for the specialist Alzheimer's care was located, she was feeling far more confident. There wasn't the same sort of meaningful conversation she'd had with Olive, of course, but the residents were just as delighted to see Norma and they made even more of a fuss of her if that were possible, with one old gentleman singing the same song to the little dog over and over again, so that even Phoebe knew all the words of the previously unfamiliar tune in the end. Norma was obviously in her element and Jamie had been right about that as well.

'Phoebe! Scarlett told me you were back.' Before she even had the chance to respond, Scarlett's mum, Christine, had folded her into a hug and held her for a good ten seconds before she let go and took a step back. 'It's been too long; I was always hoping we'd see a bit more of you in the village, but I hear you've been busy building a brilliant career in London.'

'Who told you that?'

'Scarlett and Lucy.' It wasn't a surprise to hear that Scarlett had been singing her praises, but the fact that Lucy had too made her heart feel heavy. There were so many missed opportunities to say how proud they were of one another when they still had a chance.

'I'm not sure you can call designing data analytics systems brilliant, but it pays the bills.'

'Don't sell yourself short – you were always doing that!' Christine wagged a finger at her affectionately, before donning a more serious expression. 'And how are you? With everything that's been going on?'

'Worried sick about Lucy half the time and walking around like a zombie the other half.' Christine wasn't the sort of person who could be bought off with a half-truth, so she might as well tell it as it was.

'Oh darling, I wish there was something we could do.' Christine pulled her into her arms again and this time Phoebe didn't even stiffen.

'I wish there was too, but Scarlett's been great and being back here has reminded me that there was always more to life in Appleberry than Mum and Dad.'

'I know you had a difficult time, sweetheart, but don't cut them off completely, will you? Deep down they'll be worried about Lucy too, and I know your dad doesn't always know how to show it, but I do think he loves you both.'

'You always did see the best in people, didn't you?' Phoebe couldn't help wishing that her experiences hadn't made her so different to Christine. After what Janet had put her through, she tended to assume the worst of people until she was proven wrong,

rather than the other way around. 'Sadly I don't think my relationship with my parents is ever going to change. I might as well go
into the woods beyond Lake Pippin and talk to one of the trees, for
all either of them are prepared to listen. I can't even share my
worries about Lucy with them. We should be pulling together at
the moment, but I genuinely don't think they care.'

'Oh darling, you have got things tough, haven't you?' Christine
took a piece of paper out of her bag and wrote something down on
it. 'This is my new number and I want you to call if you ever need
to chat, and Scarlett isn't around. It must be so hard not to have
anyone else you can talk to about how you're feeling.'

Phoebe took the proffered number, feeling disloyal for not
telling Christine how much of a difference having Jamie around
had made. But there was a good chance that Christine would put
two and two together, and come up with the ridiculous notion that
Phoebe and Jamie were more than friends. He might be willing to
risk his career to help her, but that was because of Lucy, not
Phoebe.

'I know Scarlett would do anything for you, but if things get
difficult, I want you to know that I'm here for you too. You were
like my second daughter when you were younger and Steve used
to swear you were in our house more than your own!'

'He was probably right.' Some of Phoebe's happiest memories
were of spending time at their house, but it made her feel guilty
too. Lucy had never had a friendship like she'd had with Scarlett
and, looking back, it must have given her yet another reason to
feel left out. Phoebe should have done more to include her little
sister. She didn't deserve Christine's affection, but that didn't stop
her wanting it.

'I mean it, sweetheart. You're welcome any time.' Christine gave
her one final hug before finally letting her go and it was all Phoebe
could do not to run after her.

* * *

'Thank you for suggesting I brought Norma up to The Pines this afternoon.' Phoebe spoke, falling into pace next to Jamie as they walked back through the village. 'I can't quite decide who enjoyed it more, me or Norma.'

'I'm really glad it gave you something else to focus on, even if it was only for a little while.' Fisher stopped to sniff another lamp post and Norma immediately sat down, obviously worn out by her afternoon of cuddles. 'It always makes me feel better, helping others, and I think that's what's kept me going since my grandmother died. It was really hard not to have anyone left who gave me the kind of unconditional love she did, and it made me feel so much better to be able to reach out to other people who might be feeling the same way. I know you can't forget about Lucy being missing, even for a minute, but just having something else to think about from time to time might make it a tiny bit more bearable.'

'I hope so.' They moved off again and a white cat shot out from a bush on the edge of someone's garden, causing Norma and Fisher to lurch forward together, making Phoebe stumble so that Jamie had to catch her with his free arm to stop her knocking him flying too. For a moment they just looked at each other and she really thought he was going to kiss her. She couldn't admit how much she wanted him to, even to herself. But he steadied her again and then stood back, the spell broken. Clearly Jamie was a much nicer person than she was.

Her sister was still out there, God knows where, but all she could think about was what it would be like to kiss him. And the awful thought that she might be far more like her mother than she ever wanted to believe struck her all over again.

17

Jamie had never spent so much time online in his life, and staying up for most of the night carrying out internet search after internet search wasn't something he'd ever done before either. But it had become a regular occurrence in his determination to track Gerry down.

All he'd had to go on was her name, the email address she'd provided and the details she'd shared during their sessions. Her name had matched the details on her bank card – G. Clark – otherwise he'd have been convinced that such a popular surname had been another one of her ruses, and that she really was the Walter Mitty-type character he was starting to fear she might be. Whatever the reality, tracking down someone with the surname of Clark, with only the county she lived in to go on, was not proving easy. There'd been no reply to the email he'd sent and, when he followed it up with a read receipt to check if the message was opened, there was no indication Gerry was still accessing her email address.

When Phoebe had stumbled against him the day before, he'd wanted to hold her. It was only the fact that he still couldn't be completely honest with her that stopped him. Phoebe already suspected that Gerry and Lucy had met on a suicide forum, but he knew for a fact that they'd planned to carry out a pact at least once. He'd been so close to telling her, but it would have gone against everything he believed in. The police already knew all of this, and Phoebe knowing wouldn't change anything, yet he still wanted to tell her. As it was, she'd feel horribly betrayed that he was still holding something like that back, and he couldn't expect her to understand his dilemma when the person at the centre of it was her little sister. If they'd kissed, or gone beyond that in some way, it might leave Phoebe feeling even worse about herself than she already did. That was something he wasn't willing to add to the list of things he already had on his conscience.

During their sessions, Gerry had told him she was a head-teacher at a primary school. And, from what she'd described, she'd spent almost fifteen years under the coercive control of her violent and abusive husband. According to her, no one outside the marriage could see it, and she was terrified she wouldn't be believed. After all, it would be hard to persuade the world that her husband – a GP and lay minister in their local church – was capable of the kind of evil she described.

Her husband had convinced her that if she left he'd get custody of the children and that he'd paint her as the 'psycho' he regularly told her she was. Her plan had been to end her life, but leave behind all the evidence she'd compiled of his abuse that no one would take seriously while she was alive. Gerry had said that the police wouldn't act on her claims of abuse, because she hadn't been physically hurt. She'd asked them whether she needed to die before they took any notice, and when one of the officers she'd spoken to had laughed, she'd convinced herself it was her only option. It was twisted and wrong but given that Gerry had been cut off at every attempt she'd made to solve the problem in some other way, Jamie could understand how she'd got there.

As horrifying as it was, the suicide pact with Lucy had seemed the solution to a situation Gerry could see no other way out of at the time… But, in the end, she'd decided she couldn't bear to leave her children. Ending her life wouldn't have solved anything, it would just have caused them unimaginable pain. It was only after Gerry had come scarily close to fulfilling the pact with Lucy, that she'd discovered even greater resources of strength than she'd exerted already, to continue fighting to unmask her husband. If she could do that, the children would be able to stay with her and the three of them could eventually try and build a new life together. But Gerry was terrified that if her husband ever found out she'd been active on suicide forums, he'd use it against her, and that it would guarantee him custody of their children. She was paranoid it might result in the loss of her job too. There was so much at stake. It had been an incredibly hard story to hear, and Gerry had been utterly convincing. But now he had to speak to her again, to know for sure if she'd been telling the truth, and to discover just how much she knew about Lucy's disappearance.

Searching for headteachers with the first name of Gerry or Geraldine hadn't thrown anything up that matched with the person he'd met. Then he'd remembered something else she'd said, a throwaway comment: 'If only the parishioners at St Mark's knew what their beloved minister was really like.' It had kick-started the next phase of his search. There were far more churches bearing the name St Mark's than he would ever have imagined, and the attempt to make the link between one of those churches and Gerry had been long and painful. He'd looked through the details of all the lay ministers he could find listed on church websites, and eventually found one called Robert Clark, whose occupation was listed as being a GP. His bio also detailed that he lived in the parish with his wife and two children, and it even mentioned that they'd married at the church, sixteen years before, with a link to a newspaper announcement celebrating the nuptials of Robert Clark and Grace Gerald. Suddenly it all clicked into place. Gerry wasn't her first name; it was a shortened version of her maiden name. What he couldn't understand was how none of this had come out on any of the occasions when he'd spoken to the police about her, but that was just one of the questions he was planning to ask, and it was far from the most important.

A quick Google search revealed that the headteacher of the nearest primary school, opposite the church where Robert was lay preacher, was a woman called Grace Clark. The photo on the school's website confirmed it: Grace Clark and Gerry were one and the same. Jamie hadn't been sure whether to be relieved that everything seemed to be lining up, or to feel even more guilty about potentially putting a former client at risk. But at last he had a way of contacting Gerry, and he didn't intend to waste any more time.

The number for the school was readily available, but it was the summer holiday and there was a good chance none of the teaching staff would be around. If he had to, he'd call the school and ask one of the admin team to pass on a message, but involving a third party could cause problems. In a small community, where the school and the church were linked, there was no way of knowing how many people Robert Clark had dancing to his tune. Jamie would have to explain how urgent the message was, but if he said anything that could cause Gerry problems, there'd be no putting the pin back in the grenade for her either. The website listed email addresses for key staff, and there was one next to Gerry's name.

He had no idea if she was the sort of person who picked up emails when she was on leave, but he made a bargain with himself. He'd give her forty-eight hours to reply before he called the school. Typing out his message, he kept the wording brief and vague, just in case her emails were filtered out by admin staff too. He just hoped that giving his message the heading of Lucy's name would make Gerry take notice.

Subject: Lucy Spencer

Hi Grace,

    I tried to reach you on your private email address, without any luck, and I need to speak to you about Lucy. I know you're on leave, so if I don't hear back from you by Wednesday morning, I'll try calling. But I'm in your area later this week, so I can always pop in if that's easier.

    Best regards,

    Jamie Shepherd

All he could do was pray that the veiled threat of him turning up would be enough to persuade Gerry to email him back. She had until first thing Wednesday, otherwise he was calling and, if that didn't work, he would be taking a trip up to Sandlethwaite.

* * *

Phoebe had left a message for Bradley as soon as Jamie had mentioned Lucy's friend Gerry. She wanted to know what the police were doing about it, and she needed them to understand that Lucy hanging around with someone new was much more significant than they might expect. After all, making new friends wasn't that unusual, unless you were one of the Spencer girls.

Being guarded had become a way of life for both of them and, if Phoebe was honest, the 'friends' she had in London were little more than acquaintances. They knew a sanitised version of her life, a form she could present from the safety of a city more than sixty miles away from the village where she'd been brought up. But Lucy had actually been spending time with this new friend in Appleberry. There'd have been little chance of doing that without revealing the warts-and-all reality of life in the shadow of their mother. For Lucy to trust someone enough to risk that, the relationship had to mean a lot to her, and there was every chance this woman held clues to where Lucy was now, even if Gerry had nothing to do with the letter that had arrived.

When Bradley's number flashed up on her phone, she was ready – whatever the news was – as long as there was some kind of progress in finding out what on earth had happened to her sister.

'Can you tell me what Gerry said when you spoke to her?' Phoebe cut to the chase, before Bradley even had the chance to speak.

'Unfortunately, the information we discussed is confidential and I'll only be able to share it with you if we think it has any relevance to the enquiries about Lucy's disappearance.'

'What do you mean if it has any relevance to Lucy's disappearance? Of course it does! You said it yourself: she was on suicide forums, places where people find partners to kill themselves with. Then she starts hanging around with this Gerry out of nowhere. How the hell can that not be relevant to Lucy's disappearance?'

'I understand your frustration, Phoebe, I really do, but I promise you if there was anything I was at liberty to share, I would. And, if that changes, I'll be in touch straight away, but I have got some further results from the computer analysis.' Bradley cleared his throat. It was a habit she'd noticed he had, whenever he was about to say something she might not want to hear, and it didn't bode well for there being good news. 'There's evidence of Lucy being active on several suicide ideation forums in the weeks leading up to her death. The computer history revealed she'd been active on these in the past, but then there was a hiatus of around six months, before it suddenly started again, two weeks before she disappeared.'

'Oh God, that's what I was afraid of.' She'd seen films where people's legs had buckled from beneath them, but she'd never believed it really happened until that moment. Sinking down on to the chair in the corner of Lucy's kitchen, she gripped the phone. 'Can you trace the people she spoke to, to find out if they know anything that isn't on the forums?'

'We're working on it, but some of the forum messages were sent on pay-as-you-go mobiles, which makes the job of tracking them down more difficult, and as I keep saying, these things take time. But that doesn't mean we aren't trying. What we do know from some of Lucy's previous interactions online, which might offer you reassurance, is that she didn't proceed with any plans she made in the past. She'd agreed a date to carry out a pact with someone else, before she stopped using the forums for all those months, and she clearly didn't go through with it. Which means there's a chance this was only ever a fantasy about leaving her problems behind, and that she never really intended to go through with it. If that's the case, she may well have found another way to escape, by choosing to disappear and start a new life. We're still working with the missing persons charity, and I know they've been in touch with you too. I promise you that we are continuing to explore all avenues.'

'But there's also a chance that this time she didn't change her mind.' Phoebe felt as though someone had laid a concrete slab on her chest that she couldn't get out from under. Every day that passed without Lucy, and every bit of negative news that came in, seemed to increase the weight. It wasn't until that moment that she'd realised how much hope she was pinning on Jamie finding

Gerry, and finally getting an answer to where Lucy was. But if Gerry wasn't one of the people her sister had been talking to recently, she might not be able to provide any answers at all.

'I'm sorry, this must be incredibly difficult to hear, and I know you just want solid evidence that Lucy is okay. It's what we're all still hoping for, and we're working hard to find definite news, but there's a possibility we might never know for sure what happened.' Bradley sighed. 'That might be something you and your parents find it useful to discuss with specialist counsellors from the missing persons charity. I know you said before that you weren't interested, but they're experienced in helping children too, and it might be something Darcy needs in the future.'

'I'll think about it.' Phoebe shivered. Accepting that they might never know for sure what had happened to Lucy was the last thing she wanted to do, because that would mean giving up. Her mother, on the other hand, would probably relish the attention, and the opportunity to play the role of heartbroken mother, at least until the mask slipped. But Phoebe would keep pushing for answers until her last breath if that was what it took, and she had to face up to every possible explanation for Lucy's disappearance, no matter how hard. 'Do you think there's any chance that one of these people Lucy was talking to could have hurt her?'

'Anything's possible, and we considered the potential for someone else to be behind Lucy's disappearance when she first went missing. But from what we know about her previous suicidal thoughts and the letter she left you on the beach, and the fact that the messages online all seem genuine, there's no reason to suspect foul play. But, like I say, if any evidence suggesting otherwise came to light, of course we'd look at it with an open mind.'

'There's something else I haven't told you. I got another letter, supposedly from Lucy.' Phoebe fiddled with a loose thread on one of the buttons of her shirt. When she'd left the message about

Gerry, she'd considered mentioning the letter to Bradley, but she hadn't wanted to be made to hand it over. If it really was from Lucy, it would feel like giving another part of her away. And if analysis proved that it wasn't, another shred of hope that Lucy was still out there would be taken away from her too.

'When did you get it?' The shock in Bradley's voice that she was only just mentioning this was evident.

'A few days ago, but I wanted to speak to you about Gerry first.'

'It's important that we examine the letter as soon as possible.' There was a harder edge to Bradley's voice this time. He clearly didn't like being kept in the dark about anything. 'Please tell me you've kept the envelope, because that might be able to tell us more than you'd think.'

'I have and I can drop it off at the station tomorrow.'

'We'll send someone round for it today. If it does contain evidence, we don't want to delay any further than we already have.' Despite the fact he'd said 'we', it was obvious he was placing the blame for the delay with Phoebe.

'I really don't think it'll tell you anything new; the letter just explains why she left Darcy with me.' Phoebe swallowed hard against the ever-present lump in her throat. 'And I know she wouldn't have wanted my parents to see it, or for the contents to get out to the media.'

'I can't make any promises, but we'll do what we can to protect Lucy's privacy as much as possible. We only release information about the personal lives of missing people if we believe it increases the chances of finding them.'

'Okay.' Phoebe put her hand in her pocket, tracing the outline of the letter she'd put there. Lucy would hate the idea of anyone analysing her words, but if it increased the chances of bringing her home – even a little bit – Phoebe was willing to do anything.

18

Finishing the second plait in Darcy's hair, Phoebe leant back to look at her handiwork. She was getting better at this. Okay, so she was still no Vidal Sassoon, but at least Darcy came back from nursery now with her plaits largely intact and the little girl didn't cry out to complain that Phoebe was pulling her hair so much.

'Are we still going to the park?' Darcy gave her the sweetest smile, but she might not be in such a good mood when she found out where they were actually going. It had been a week since Phoebe had got the letter from Lucy and she couldn't put it off any longer, especially as Bradley said he might need to talk to her parents about it. If her mother found out she'd been withholding the arrival of Lucy's letter, it would give her the perfect opportunity to paint herself as a victim again, and Phoebe as the villain.

'Yes, later, but we're going to see Nanny and Granddad first.'

'Do we have to?' Darcy wrinkled her nose, which was liberally sprinkled with freckles, just like her mother's had been when she was a little girl. Lucy had tried to scrub them off once, when Phoebe had teased her about them and told her it made her look like she had spots. Of course it hadn't, they'd always been as cute as Darcy's, but their next-door neighbour had commented on how pretty they were in front of Janet. When their mother hadn't reacted by belittling Lucy in some way, Phoebe had been jealous. She'd got it into her head that freckles might be the one thing that would make their mother love Lucy more. It seemed ridiculous now, but at eight years old it had made perfect sense.

'I know it's not much fun there, but I need to speak to them about something and I want you to come with me, because I miss you when you're at nursery.' It wasn't a lie; she did miss Darcy when she wasn't around, more than she'd ever thought possible. But the real reason was because she couldn't help holding on to the tiniest hope that her parents might finally react to their granddaughter visiting in the way that any normal grandparent would. Experience told her that it was never going to happen, but that was the thing about hope: it was hard to kill.

'Nanny always says I'm naughty.' Darcy looked at her, tears welling up in her eyes, and guilt gripped Phoebe all over again. She shouldn't be putting the little girl through this too. The note in Lucy's sketchbook had said she wanted to preserve Darcy's innocence about the good in people, by making sure her grandmother never made her feel inadequate. But it felt like it might already be too late.

'Nanny says a lot of things she doesn't mean.' Phoebe lifted Darcy into her arms and held her close for a moment. 'You're such a good little girl and your mummy and I couldn't love you any more than we do. So does Jamie, and Norma and Fisher. Everyone does.'

'Not Nanny,' Darcy whispered, her breath warm on Phoebe's neck.

'Nanny's got a poorly head and it means sometimes she isn't kind, but it's not your fault.'

'Promise?'

'Oh darling, I promise.' Phoebe held her close again, wanting to protect her from everything, no matter what. Just like her sister had. There was no way she was letting Darcy go through what she and Lucy had suffered for so long – wondering if anyone in the world loved them. 'I tell you what, I'll phone Scarlett and see if you can go and play with Ava while I go in and see Nanny and Granddad on my own. Would you like that?'

'Yay!' The little girl wrapped her tiny arms around Phoebe's neck and squeezed with all her might. 'I love you.'

'And I love you. To the moon and back.' It was true and even if that meant seeing her parents on her own, with nothing to distract her from the horror of it, she'd do anything for Darcy. Absolutely anything.

* * *

Scarlett had been more than willing to look after Darcy, but it had taken all of Phoebe's strength to walk back out of her best friend's house and in the direction of her parents' place.

Their house looked so normal from the outside, and it was almost impossible to believe it could harbour so many bad memories. It was just an ordinary semi, kept neat and tidy by Phoebe's father's hard work and her mum's nagging. After all, the house reflected on Janet, so it had to be perfect. Her need for admiration meant they'd spent more money on the house than they could really afford, and that the car sitting squarely on the driveway absolutely could not be more than two years old. As a result, there'd never been enough money for family holidays or days out, to make the kind of memories that other people valued way above material things. And it was another reason why the vitriol their mother spouted when they scuffed their school shoes, or lost a button from a coat, was all too frequent. Over the years, Phoebe and Lucy had learnt to be extra careful, and they both bore the physical scars of their mother's violent overreactions, as well as the emotional ones. But sometimes it had been almost a relief to Phoebe to be hit; it was some form of contact – an acknowledgement that she existed in her mother's consciousness. If they somehow managed to tread carefully enough to comply with Janet's demands and expectations, they were ignored. It was only when Phoebe upset her mother that she even felt noticed.

Roger had gone along with his wife's behaviour their whole married life and he'd lost all of his other relationships over the years as a result. Janet would convince herself, and Roger, that his friends wanted her, goading him until he accused them of being in love with his wife. Phoebe's mother had relished the drama of it all, and being at the centre of a fantasy where everyone was fighting over her. So much so that she'd recount the stories to her daughters, who were far too young to hear the things she told them. But as long as it made Janet feel like the whole world revolved around her, nothing else mattered.

'Hello, love.' Roger Spencer looked furtively around the front garden as he addressed his daughter, as if he was terrified his wife might overhear the term of endearment. For a moment, Phoebe felt sorry for her father, despite the pain his unwillingness to stand up to Janet had caused both his daughters. He'd been digging the garden when she arrived, even though it was a boiling-hot day and he'd been advised to take early retirement because of a problem with his heart. She'd have bet her last pound he was out there on orders from her mother.

'Dad.' She gave him a perfunctory kiss on the cheek, his breathing rapid in her ear. If he dropped down dead in the garden, her mother would still find a way to make it all about her. Roger would be accused of abandoning her, no doubt. But it might take that for her mother to finally realise that he was probably the only person in the world who loved her. God alone knew why, but he clearly did.

'Any word from Lucy?' Phoebe's father might have looked hopeful, but she couldn't help questioning whether he *really* cared. Was he lying awake half the night, like she did, imagining Lucy sleeping rough or, worse still, lying in a ditch somewhere, undiscovered? Had he driven up to Craggy Head, just to look at the stretch of beach where she'd disappeared? She was certain he hadn't put posters in the windows of every shop that would take them, like she had, asking people to contact the police if they'd seen her, or scouring every comment on social media posts about Lucy, just in case Bradley and his colleagues had missed something.

'Where's Mum?' Ignoring his question, she looked past him. She wasn't going to go through the process of explaining the letter twice. So, until she knew where her mother was, she wasn't going to tell him anything.

'Lying down. She's been very tired since Lucy disappeared.'

'It must be awful for her.'

'Don't be like that, Phoebe. I know she doesn't show it in the way people usually do...'

'You mean the way anyone normal does?' She cut him off before he could make probably his millionth excuse for his wife's unacceptable behaviour.

'She can't help it.'

'She won't even try.' It was a conversation they'd had almost as many times as he'd made excuses for his wife. She'd been offered psychotherapy, but as far as she was concerned it was everyone else who was at fault. So she'd always refused any attempt to get help. Not that Phoebe could remember her dad ever trying that hard to persuade her.

'Mum's just different, but we've all got used to it over the years, haven't we?'

'We might have put up with it, but we never got used to it.' It was really difficult not to scream when there was already a voice inside her head doing it. 'Haven't you even considered that might be the reason Lucy disappeared, because she couldn't live with it any more?'

'But she's been moved out since before Darcy was born.' Her father had an answer, and an excuse, for everything.

'What, so you think all those years of Mum putting us both down was just forgotten when we moved out, that it hasn't done any lasting damage?'

'You girls always make too much of stuff.' Her father sighed and started to dig a hole in the border for the next of his delphiniums, his breathing still laboured as he bent down again. 'There are children who have far worse upbringings than you.'

'If that's what you honestly think, then there isn't much I can say, is there?' If her father really believed Lucy hadn't been affected by Janet's behaviour over the years, then he didn't know his daughter at all. Either of them. And he'd be no use in helping her work out whether the letter she'd been planning to show her parents really was from Lucy. The worst part was she wasn't sure they'd even care.

'It's not that I think it was easy for you and I know there were times when I could have been—'

'Well, look what the cat dragged in.' Phoebe's mother suddenly appeared in the front garden, cutting off whatever it had been that her father was about to say, and it was like the sun going behind a cloud, with any last shred of hope she might have had disappearing with it. 'Finally found the time to come and visit, have you?'

'It's not a social visit.'

'Well, why would it be? You're far too wrapped up in yourself to think about me; you always have been. Just like your sister!'

'This was a mistake.' White-hot rage was bubbling up inside her, but she knew better than to react. People like Janet fed off the misery of others, and Phoebe didn't want to be part of giving her mother anything she craved. She didn't want to share the letter with her parents. If they really were Lucy's words, they didn't deserve to read them. Even if they weren't, there were still things in that letter that she and Lucy had shared, and her parents hadn't earnt the right to hear them.

'Running off again? Like you always do, just like Lucy!' Janet's wounded look would probably have convinced a passer-by that she had every reason to be upset by her daughters' behaviour. The strangest part was that she clearly believed it too – no one was that good an actress. Once upon a time, Phoebe might have followed her father's example and tried to excuse her mother's behaviour. After all, she was clearly ill. But Janet didn't want to get better, and Phoebe was way past letting her off the hook, especially as her vitriol was now aimed at Lucy. 'She's a selfish bitch, going off like that and leaving us to face the shame. She failed at everything she's ever done, and yet she's gone around telling people it's my fault. One of her old school friends put a long post about it online. How am I to blame for the fact that she can't keep a man around? Or because you'll find cowpats in any field around here with more merit than her so-called artwork?'

'Well, it was fantastic to see you both, as always.' Phoebe's voice was calm, despite her tone dripping with sarcasm. It was amazing the emotion that could be raging inside her that she still managed to hold in. 'Hatred' was a strong word, but it was the only one that fitted how she felt about her mother. And, in that moment, she made a decision. She couldn't take her mother's relentless poison any more, and she was never going to let Darcy be subjected to it. In the past, there'd been periods when her mother could be charming; it was part of what had kept Lucy dancing to her tune for so long and holding on to the hope that those snapshots in time might become the norm. Instead, even those brief moments were gone. These days Janet was relentless, and there didn't seem to be a moment's respite from her put-downs. Even if Phoebe was forced to see her parents again, there was no way she'd ever take Darcy. It was just the two of them now, until Lucy came home, and then they'd all find a way to break free. Forever.

19

Along with visits to The Pines with Jamie and the dogs, where the highlight was always chatting with Olive, Phoebe's meet-ups with Scarlett, Dolly and Kate were increasingly becoming her salvation. She could talk about Lucy and her parents as much as she wanted to without experiencing a roll of the eyes. But more than that, they laughed together and it made her feel normal – if only for a moment.

Going to The Pines with Jamie helped in a different way. It made her realise she wasn't the only person in the world going through something she couldn't control, and the residents had taught her more than she'd ever have imagined about finding joy in the little things. Watching Jamie interacting with people who might never remember his visit had made her like him even more. When she'd noticed how tired he was looking, he'd admitted to having spent hours online trying to track Gerry down, and he'd promised to keep her updated. Part of her had questioned whether he was just fobbing her off, since he clearly felt torn about the ethics of contacting a former client, but in the end she'd decided that all she could do was trust him to be honest with her. Unless he did anything to prove her wrong.

With her friendships in Appleberry developing, she was starting to see the village in a whole new light, but it wasn't all plain sailing. Phoebe's mother had turned up at the cottage a couple of times, but Phoebe had refused to let her in. After that, Janet had sent her latest 'disciple' to come and tell Phoebe what an awful daughter she'd been. This woman, who Phoebe had never seen before, came to the door and announced that as Janet's best friend she felt it was her duty to give Phoebe some home truths.

The woman, who'd said her name was May, asked how Phoebe could live with herself after the way she'd treated her mother – refusing to let Janet see her granddaughter, and taking out her guilt at how badly she'd let her sister down on their mother. It was like Janet had twisted all the things she'd done to Lucy, and blamed Phoebe for them instead. May had been completely taken in, and God knows what 'evidence' Janet had cooked up to prove what she was saying. But it wasn't even worth Phoebe's breath protesting against her mother's version of events. It was pointless, a waste of energy that she needed for finding Lucy, and caring for Darcy. As much as she might want to tell her mother exactly what she thought of her, if Phoebe was going to be able to stay in Appleberry with the friends who'd already come to mean more to her than she could ever have imagined, the only solution was to pretend her mother didn't exist, even in the wake of her painfully obvious presence. So Phoebe shut the door in May's face and left her on the step, exactly as she had her mother. Being ignored must have been torture for Janet.

'Let's get you ready.' Phoebe plaited her niece's hair, her fingers now threading the silky-soft hair into braids like an expert. At least she'd got this part of being a stand-in parent down pat.

'Auntie Phoebe?' Darcy's voice lifted at the end, so it was obvious a question was coming and Phoebe braced herself. That had been another part of parenting that had taken her by surprise. The constant questions. Watching a documentary the night before about a farm in Yorkshire had seemed safe enough, until the farmer had taken a large syringe to artificially inseminate some of his cows. Not quite quick enough with the remote, it had led to some questions that had been really difficult to answer and in the end she'd settled for something vague about seeds growing, and eventually becoming baby cows. The poor kid was going to be so confused by the time her mum came home.

'Yes, darling?'

'Is Mummy coming to watch?'

'Oh sweetheart.' Phoebe held the little girl and suddenly wished what she had to say next was as easy as explaining how calves sometimes came about. 'I don't think she's going to make it back for sports day today.'

'When will she come home, then? It's been ages.'

'I know, darling, but Mummy's not well at the moment and she doesn't want to come home until she's better, so she doesn't make you poorly too.' It wasn't an outright lie. However misguided, it was clear from her letters that Lucy had disappeared in an attempt to protect Darcy.

'You could look after her, like you look after me.' Darcy rubbed Phoebe's earlobe between her fingers when she was tired or upset; it seemed to bring her comfort.

'I could and I will, but we just have to be patient. I know it's hard, darling.' She kissed the top of the little girl's head, burying her face in the strawberry scent. If Gerry couldn't share anything useful, and the police couldn't track down the people Lucy had been speaking to online, they'd be no further forward in knowing what had happened to Lucy than they'd been the day she disappeared. It already felt like forever to Phoebe, so she couldn't even imagine how endless the wait must seem to Darcy. The days left until her birthday were ticking down too, and just the thought of how she'd react if her mother missed it made Phoebe feel sick. If Jamie couldn't track Gerry down, maybe she should try. Except she had no idea where to even start.

'Can we go now?' Darcy wriggled out of her arms with a smile that looked painted it on. She wasn't even four and she'd already learnt to put a brave face on things.

'Yes, darling. Remind me again, how many races are you doing?'

'Four.' Darcy held up the appropriate number of fingers as she spoke and, for once, it was Phoebe's turn to ask a never-ending stream of questions about the day ahead. Anything that might take their minds off Lucy's absence had to be worth a try.

* * *

There was a lot of crossover between the work Jamie did at the forest school and the nursery, and he often helped out when they had big events, like sports day. The nursery was open all year round, rather than just in term-time, and they only closed for a summer break in the final two weeks of the school holidays. So, sports day was their version of a big finale to their academic year.

Setting the last of the coloured cones out to separate the running lanes, Jamie stepped back to check the lines were straight. Not that there'd be much running. If previous sports days were anything to go by, there'd be lots of dropped eggs, at least one broken skipping rope, a couple of falls and a few tears. He loved that the nursery were willing to have a competitive old-fashioned sports day, but all of the children would be awarded a medal at the end for taking part. Although it was the parents' races that got the most competitive. If he hadn't seen it with his own eyes, he'd never have believed grown-up people would resort to such dirty tactics to try and win a cheap bit of metal threaded onto a ribbon. People like that were just lucky they didn't have real problems. Not like Phoebe.

He spotted her before she saw him, and she looked exhausted. When he'd told her there was a chance the letter from Lucy might not be genuine, he'd wanted to take the words back. Everyone needed hope and she must have felt like he'd robbed her of that. He'd worried she might want to keep her distance from him once she'd found out that he'd kept Lucy's friendship with Gerry from her, but instead she'd asked when they could go back to The Pines, and he'd understood why. From the outside it might look like it was them providing therapy to the residents by taking Norma and Fisher along to visit, but they were getting a different kind of therapy of their own. Helping other people had always done more to solve Jamie's problems than anything else, and second-hand joy could be almost as good as the first-hand kind, especially when that was so far out of reach.

It had helped him cope with the fact that he was keeping something from Phoebe again. Gerry had replied to Jamie's email and had agreed to meet him when her husband would be away at a conference. But only on the proviso that he didn't make contact again before then. If he did, all bets were off. Jamie had gone back and forth about whether to tell Phoebe, but he knew she'd want to come with him. And, even if he persuaded her that he was better going alone, she'd build up her hopes to ridiculous heights, pinning everything on Gerry having all the answers about Lucy. He'd rather take the hit for disappointing her than have to watch her be crushed by reality yet again.

Right now, she looked like she could use some joy of any kind, and if anyone could supply that it would be Darcy. Phoebe and her niece were heading towards where Scarlett and Dolly had already set up camp, close to the finishing line, but she stopped as they reached the point where Jamie was standing.

'How have you been?' He'd heard about Janet turning up at the house; he just hoped she hadn't created any more dramas. That was the last thing Phoebe needed.

'We're doing okay.' The dark circles under her eyes told a different story and he silently cursed himself again, because if the latest sleepless nights weren't down to Janet, they could well be down to him. Telling Phoebe half the story about Gerry was probably worse than having told her nothing at all. Waiting for more news must have been unbearable.

'That's good.' He wanted to tell her he was always there, but it would have sounded ridiculous, especially when he hadn't been nearly as good a friend to her as he should have been. Instead, he smiled down at the little girl, who sometimes looked so much like her mother it was heartbreaking. 'Good luck, Darcy. I reckon the sack race is yours for the taking this year with all that practice Sally tells me you've been doing.'

'I want to win lots of medal so I can show Mummy... later.' He exchanged a look with Phoebe as Darcy spoke, a physical pain in his chest that he might be even a tiny part of the reason why Darcy didn't know where her mother was.

'I'll be cheering you on, sweetheart.' He turned to looked at Phoebe again. 'And lots of aunties, grandmas and big sisters take part in the parents' race too, so don't think you can get out of that!'

'Oh yes please, Auntie Phoebe!' For the first time Darcy looked more like her old self, excitement replacing the look of sadness she'd been wearing.

'Well thanks, Jamie, I can hardly say no now, can I?' Phoebe shook her head but there was a smile on her face for the first time too, and he sent up a silent thank you that he'd somehow managed to say the right thing, for once.

* * *

'Oh my God, I think I might actually be incapable of moving.' Scarlett's attempts to shift position in her deckchair were nothing short of comical.

'That's what you get for actually training for the parents' race!' Kate, whose children had long since left nursery, had arrived halfway through the sports day as an excuse to catch up with her friends. 'Fancy pulling a ligament practising for that.'

'At least Scarlett can get out of it now.' Dolly lifted up her legs so that they stuck out in a straight line from the front of her deckchair. 'With legs this short, I've got absolutely no chance of coming anywhere but last! But try telling Chantelle that. When they send the kids over to get the parents to join in, she'll be the first one to drag me up there. And when she makes her mind up about something, it's almost impossible to say no.'

'I can imagine.' Phoebe looked over to where Chantelle was entertaining the other kids, doing a dance that had them in fits of giggles that had pealed across the playing field. Scarlett had told her how shy the little girl and her siblings had been when Dolly and Greg had first started the process to adopt them, and being with such a loving family had clearly transformed her. Phoebe tried not to think about how different things might have turned out to be if she and Lucy had been given that chance. For a start, her sister would probably never have felt the need to run away from her own life. Shaking herself, she painted on a smile, mirroring the one her niece had worn just before they left the house. 'Thanks to Jamie, I've been roped into the parents' race too.'

'Does Darcy know you're doing it?' Scarlett made another futile attempt to move into a comfortable position.

'She's the only reason I am. Her face, when Jamie suggested it, was the happiest I've seen her in days.'

'He knows how to bring the best out in kids, even at the hardest of times.' Dolly raked a hand through her hair.

'I know, but sometimes I can't help wishing he wasn't so bloody insightful.' Phoebe twisted her watch around her wrist, so that the face was lined up with the centre of her hand; she didn't want to have to look any of the others in the eye as she spoke. 'When I got the second letter from Lucy, I just wanted someone to tell me it was from her, and that it meant we were a step closer to her coming home.'

'So what did Jamie say?' Scarlett pushed her sunglasses up into her hair as she spoke, lifting her fringe away from her forehead.

'He said we couldn't just assume it's from her. It could be from the woman she got friendly with just before she disappeared.' As much as she valued her friends, Phoebe had been cautious of how much she'd revealed about Gerry. Jamie was putting his career on the line to try and find her, and the least she could do was keep that close to her chest.

'Don't be too hard on him.' Dolly's tone was gentle. 'I just don't think he wants to see anything hurt you more than it already has.'

'I know.' Phoebe swallowed hard, the lump in her throat suddenly feeling as though it had grown bony nodules. She hated herself for having feelings for Jamie that she couldn't quantify when all she should be doing was focusing on Lucy's disappearance. She wouldn't blame her friends if they judged her for it, but she had to tell someone. 'It's not even just that. A couple of weeks ago, we sort of had this moment, and I don't know, maybe I just wanted a hug. I can guess what you're thinking, Scarlett – me of all people! But whatever the reason, it was like the idea of touching me repulsed him. I've never seen anyone step back so sharply. He probably thinks I'm the worst person in the world for even thinking about something like that, with Lucy missing, and now I just feel embarrassed.'

'He doesn't think that about you.' Scarlett was shaking her head.

'How do you know? Has he said something?'

'I know because it's obvious. The way he looks at you leaves me in absolutely no doubt, and then there's the fact he brings your name up at every opportunity.' Scarlett sighed. 'But he knows what you're going through with Lucy missing, and there's no way he'd cross a line with that going on.'

'In my experience that's not the way men are wired.' Phoebe bit her lip. Comparing Jamie to Adam wasn't fair, but she couldn't help comparing him with Eddie. Her ex-fiancé had promised her the world and he'd found a way to make her believe she was worthy, despite all the things her mother had told her. She'd trusted him completely and he'd taken down the wall she'd built up, brick by brick. But then he'd let her down in the worst possible way, and had proven that all the things her mother had said about her were true – she was unlovable, she was nothing, not even worth the dirt on her mother's shoe. Now here was Jamie, making her feel like she was worth something and prioritising her so clearly that he was willing to risk his livelihood to help her out. And yet part of her couldn't trust him, because of what Eddie had done. He'd professed his love for her but he'd been willing to lie to her, to betray and humiliate her. Risking letting Jamie in meant she was also risking allowing that to happen again. So just because Scarlett thought he genuinely cared for her, it didn't mean it was true. 'Unless it's because he knows more about Lucy's disappearance than he's admitting, and he feels guilty.'

'There's no way he'd keep that from you.' Scarlett shook her head again. 'He's a good guy, Phebes, maybe even too nice for his own good sometimes.'

'She's right.' Kate's tone was insistent. 'Over the years, we've all trusted Jamie with the most precious things in our life – our children – and Lucy does too. He wouldn't do anything to deliberately hurt anyone. Dolly's more likely to finish first in the mothers' race. And have you seen those women? Some of their running shoes cost more than my wedding dress, and most of them have got at least fifteen years on Dolly!'

'Well, with friends like you, who needs teenage children to remind me what a cringeworthy embarrassment I am?' Dolly nudged Kate and laughed. 'But in anticipation of me causing the biggest upset that Appleberry has ever seen, and clinching first prize in the parents' race, you're all invited to a barbecue at mine tomorrow afternoon from one o'clock. Kids are welcome, of course. In fact, it's mandatory they attend.'

'Nothing could keep me away.' Scarlett smiled.

'And I'd go to any event on offer it if meant I don't have to cook!' Kate dropped the perfect wink.

'We'll be there too.' Phoebe caught herself for a moment. It was strange how quickly she'd come to think of herself and Darcy as a unit, a 'we', in the way she hadn't done with anyone since Eddie.

'Fantastic! I've invited Jamie, too – I hope that's okay?' Dolly looked pensive for a moment.

'Of course it is. I was just overthinking things, but you've all really helped.' Phoebe nodded to add extra emphasis to what she was saying. They were right: Jamie was one of the good guys, and she had to stop being so suspicious of everyone or Darcy would be the one to suffer.

'Oh look, they're about to start!' Scarlett gesticulated towards where the children were beginning to line up at the other end of the playing field. 'Get the camera ready, Phebes; it looks like Darcy is in the first race.'

'Come on, Darcy!' Scarlett was the first to call out her name. She was tiny in comparison to the others, at least half a head shorter than the next nearest child to her in height, and soon everyone in the crowd who didn't have a child of their own to support was rooting for the little girl. Phoebe was recording the race on her mobile, so that Lucy could watch it back when she came home, and she was trying not to shout too loud so she didn't ruin the recording. But, as her niece started to take the lead, it was too hard not to. It was a dressing-up race and Darcy was first to get the coat on; she was still in front when it was time to put on the hat and scarf, but when it came to the rubber gloves, it all got a bit tense.

'Just put them on the ends of your hands – don't try to get all the fingers in!' Phoebe couldn't stop herself from shouting out advice. She so wanted her niece to win and have something to smile about. But as 80 per cent of the crowd urged Darcy on, the little girl steadfastly ignored her aunt's advice, struggling to put the gloves on properly, as the other children started to catch up with her.

'Come on, darling, just run.' Phoebe had got her feet too and Jamie drew level with where they were standing, to help the kids who were having the most difficulty getting the next item of clothing on.

'You've done a great job with your gloves; you can just run now.' Jamie urged Darcy on. She looked up at him and, as he nodded, she finally decided it was time to move. With the rubber gloves only half on, she made a dash for the line, with a boy who looked almost twice her size hot on her heels. As Darcy crossed the finishing line first, by a matter of centimetres, the whole crowd erupted in a roar and, to her surprise, Phoebe realised she was crying – something she hadn't done in front of other people in years. She was completely and utterly in love with the little girl she'd barely known before being forced back to Appleberry, and more bewildered than ever by the idea that Lucy could have left her daughter behind.

20

Jamie had spent another sleepless night tossing and turning. He'd been so sure that not telling Phoebe about meeting Gerry had been the right thing to do until he'd watched her at the sports day. She was devoted to Darcy, and the love she had for the little girl was tangible. It was an extension of the love that Phoebe felt for her sister, and if anyone had a right to speak to the woman who might hold the secrets of Lucy's disappearance, it was her.

There was no way of knowing what would come out in that conversation with Gerry, and what Phoebe would think of the steps Jamie had taken when he'd tried to help both women, especially not when it looked as though he'd failed miserably with Lucy. But it was a risk he was willing to take, because he didn't want to keep anything else from her. As soon as it got light, he sent Phoebe a text.

I've managed to find Gerry and she's agreed to meet me at Lake Pippin today, at ten o'clock. You're welcome to meet us there, but if you don't want to, I'll call you as soon as she's gone. J x

He turned off his phone after that, in a deliberate effort to avoid any contact from Phoebe. She'd have too many questions, ones he couldn't answer without making her lose any trust she might have had in him. That was all on Jamie, but he didn't have the headspace to deal with any of that right now. He needed to focus on how to approach Gerry, to give them the best chance of getting the answers Phoebe so badly needed. The rest was a problem for later. But he already knew that Phoebe would never forgive him if he met Gerry alone.

Despite being man-made, Lake Pippin could rival any natural beauty, and it had always been one of Jamie's favourite places to spend time. But not today. The early morning mists that usually cleared quickly were still lingering – as if they'd decided to settle in for the day – and there was an eeriness about the place that made it look more like the set of a big-budget horror movie than a local beauty spot. None of that helped the sense of foreboding weighing heavily as he waited for Gerry to arrive. Jamie hardly knew her and, if she was behind Lucy's disappearance and planned to make him disappear too, there'd be no witnesses. At least not if Phoebe didn't show up. As far-fetched as that sounded, even in his own head, it was always a possibility. And Lucy had already proven that someone could disappear, seemingly without a trace.

Ever since she'd gone, Jamie had been desperate to cling on to the hope that she could still be found safe and well. He'd read more articles than he could count about the likelihood of a body lost at sea being recovered. If she really had stolen the boat on the day she'd disappeared, she could have plunged into water so deep, and so cold, that her body might never be recovered. But if she'd waded in from the shore at Craggy Head and had drowned in the relatively warm and shallow water there, the likelihood was that the sea would have given her body up within days.

Reading the articles had been painful, especially the ones about other suicides at Craggy Head. Every story was a tragedy in its own right, and he couldn't bear to think of someone one day writing about Lucy like that. He had to believe she'd had another plan, something she might have discussed with Gerry. It was the real reason he was feeling so apprehensive about agreeing to meet her. So much was riding on Gerry having some of the answers, and, if she turned out not to, it would be even harder to continue holding on to hope. If he was feeling like that, he couldn't even imagine how Phoebe was feeling. Maybe that was why she hadn't turned up yet.

'Thank you for keeping your promise not to contact me again before we met.' He heard Gerry's voice a good twenty seconds before he saw her. If she'd planned the whole thing out to make it as spooky as possible, she couldn't have done a better job. And, when she finally emerged from the mist, it was almost an anticlimax to see her looking so normal: exactly as he remembered her. Gerry was just an ordinary woman in her forties, with wavy salt-and-pepper hair cut into a bob, heavy framed glasses and a linen smock-style dress that left everything to the imagination. If Jamie hadn't known her, and had been asked to guess her occupation, he'd have said art teacher, and he wouldn't have been far wrong. But anyone judging Gerry by her appearance would have no idea about the realities of her life. She didn't look like the kind of woman who'd stay in a marriage even after her husband had held her against the wall by her throat until she'd blacked out. The truth was, stereotypes and judgements about people who found themselves in those sorts of situations didn't help anyone, certainly not the victims of abuse and coercive control.

'I don't even know what to call you. Gerry? Grace? Or is there another name you go by? When I spoke to the police about you, they wouldn't tell me what they knew, or whether you'd used your real name when you went to them about Robert.' He was scrutinising her every expression, trying to work out whether all of this was some kind of elaborate game she was playing, to manipulate the unwitting participants. He'd always thought of himself as a good judge of character, and someone who had the ability to encourage others to be open and honest, but just lately he was starting to doubt himself more and more.

'It took a while for me to be honest with them, but I had to in the end because they couldn't investigate my claims otherwise. They knew I used a different name with you and I made them promise not to tell you my real name, in case Robert somehow found out. Gerry's an old nickname from when I was at uni, that he never knew about. It helps me remember there was a time before my husband, and that if I fight hard enough, there'll be a time after him too.' Everything about the woman standing in front of Jamie told him she was genuine but whether he believed her or not didn't matter, not unless she was willing to tell him everything she knew about her friend's disappearance.

'Did you lie to Lucy, too?' Jamie couldn't keep the accusation out of his voice and he wasn't sure he'd ever felt more on edge. He was expecting Phoebe to turn up at any moment and there was no way of knowing how she'd react.

Gerry shot Jamie a look. 'I'm not sure you're in any position to take the moral high ground. You know I could report you for using the things I told you in confidence to find me.'

'If that's what you feel you need to do, then do it.' Jamie shrugged. He was past caring about any of that now; all he wanted was to find a way of helping Phoebe. Whether that was by finding Lucy, or coming to terms with losing her. Somewhere along the line, doing that had become more important to him than his career. 'Phoebe and Darcy deserve to know where Lucy is.'

'You're right.' Gerry's response surprised him. All the bravado she'd displayed had clearly been false, and she suddenly looked desolate, making Jamie's breath catch in his throat. At that moment he wasn't sure he was ready to hear what she had to say and Gerry steadied herself against a large tree stump. 'I'm so sorry, but I really think she's gone this time.'

'How do you know that?' Tears were stinging his eyes, but anger was bubbling up inside him too. He'd fought so hard to help the two women find another path, but if Gerry had continued encouraging Lucy to believe that death was the only way out, he would never be able to forgive her.

'Because she wrote and told me.' Gerry's chin wobbled, and she was clearly struggling to control her emotions. 'She told me that by the time I got her note, she'd be gone, and she was right; her disappearance was all over the news and social media on the day it arrived. Lucy said she'd tried her hardest, and that you'd done everything you could to help, but, even after all of that, it was still the only way out she could see. She told me she'd left a letter on the beach for Phoebe, and she also asked me to pass on two more letters to her sister. Lucy was terrified Phoebe might think she wasn't up to the job of caring for Darcy, and she wanted to make sure she never doubted it enough to walk away. I know I should have gone to the police as soon as I got Lucy's note, and told them about it when they got in touch. But, if I had, it might have got in the middle of everything I've been trying to do to build a case against Robert. I've finally got the police on side, but if they thought I encouraged Lucy in some way, because of the pact we made before, all of that might change. So I told them I didn't know anything and that we hadn't been in touch for months. I'm so close to getting a decision about whether there's enough evidence to prosecute him, and I can't jeopardise that. If I get into trouble with the police after that, I can live with it. As long as I know that whatever happens, Robert won't get the children. But I'm not going to tell them everything I know until I'm sure of that. I'm sorry, Jamie, I just can't.'

'We have to tell Phoebe you're the one who sent the letter. She's convinced herself that Lucy is alive because of it.' Jamie felt sick. If he'd been torn before, he was ripped to shreds now. He had no doubt any more that Gerry was telling the truth about her husband; what she'd been through was obvious in her eyes. But he couldn't help picturing Phoebe too, and the hope that had changed her whole face when she'd first shown him the letter. He couldn't let that keep building, if another letter came. When she discovered that Lucy was gone, she was going to need her friends, including him, he hoped, more than ever. But there was no way on earth she'd ever be able trust him after she discovered he'd known that it wasn't Lucy posting the letters.

'I understand she needs to know, and I wish we could tell her now and that I could hand her the last letter myself and explain.' Gerry's teeth were chattering, but the early morning mists had finally begun to clear and it was getting warmer, so her reaction had nothing to do with the cold. She was clearly terrified. 'But there's no way Phoebe won't go straight to the police, or stop trying to find me to tell me what an arsehole I am for letting her think these letters have come straight from Lucy. And if she asks you where I am, are you really going to be able to refuse to tell her when she finds out about this? I wanted to put a note in with the first letter, explaining that I was posting it on Lucy's behalf, but she'd have gone to the police too. I know it probably sounds really selfish, but I couldn't risk any of those things, and Phoebe would be a loose cannon.'

'Why did you post the letter? You could have just kept it until the police confirm they're supporting your case against Robert. Can't you see that giving Phoebe hope like this was incredibly cruel?'

'I thought about that, I really did. But this was the last thing Lucy asked me to do, and I couldn't let her down.' Gerry was sobbing now, and Jamie felt like the worst person in the world. He took a step towards her, putting an arm around her shoulders.

'It's okay and I'm sorry; I know how hard this must have been for you and we're all trying to do right by Lucy, as well as Phoebe. But somehow it seems impossible to do both.'

'It does.' Gerry's voice caught on the words. 'I went back and forth trying to decide what was for the best. But Lucy saved my life. If she hadn't put me in touch with you, I'd never have got the help I needed to find another way of getting Robert out of my life and away from the children. I didn't have the strength left, but she let me lean on her, even when she was crumbling. And the help you gave me changed everything; I just wish it could have done the same for her.'

'Me too.' Jamie tried to clear his throat, but it was choked with tears. The worst part of all of this was that he'd let Lucy down by not being able to persuade her that there really was another way. He wanted to support Gerry and help her fulfil the last thing Lucy had asked for, but he had no idea how to do that without letting Phoebe down too.

'That's the other thing about telling Phoebe. If she reacts really badly to finding all of this out, it will be understandable. But if she comes to find me and loses it because she's in no fit state to listen, anything could happen. I can't lose the chance to escape when I'm so close. If it came down to it, I'd have to call the police and say she was harassing me, to get rid of Phoebe before Robert found out why she was really there. All of that could play right into her mother's hands, and that's the one thing Lucy was most scared of.' Gerry sniffed, wiping her eyes with the back of her hand. 'We can't let Janet have any chance of getting Darcy, any more than I can risk Robert getting custody of my children. So, as horrendous as I feel for keeping Phoebe in the dark, I just can't see another way. Lucy must have felt it was vital that Phoebe got these letters, even after she was gone, to give her the confidence she needed to fight to keep Darcy. And I can't jeopardise that either.'

'I texted Phoebe and told her to meet us here. Even if you go now, what am I supposed to tell her when she turns up, or asks me what you said?' Jamie grabbed his phone out of his pocket and switched it on.

'Why the hell did you do that? You promised it would just be us.' Gerry pulled away from him; her entire body was shaking now and there was every chance she'd turn away and break into a run before he even had a chance to answer.

'I'm sorry, I just couldn't keep lying to her. I really thought she'd be here; she was so desperate to find you, and she was pinning everything on you having answers about Lucy. But maybe she decided she wasn't ready to hear them first-hand.' Jamie looked down at his phone as it lit up, and clicked on the messages app. There was a red failed notice on the text he'd sent Phoebe. She wasn't coming, because she'd never got his message.

'She didn't get my text; it didn't send. She doesn't know I've found you.' Jamie was saying the words, but his brain was struggling to process them. It wasn't too late to go back to pretending he still hadn't found Gerry. He could wait, just long enough for her to get confirmation from the police that Robert would be arrested. But he still wasn't sure. Every time he looked at Phoebe, it killed him knowing that he was lying to her.

'I don't usually believe in these things, but maybe it's a sign.' Gerry took hold of his hand, her eyes pleading with him. '*Please.* Everything's lined up, I just need a few more days. Lucy asked me to make sure Phoebe got her last letter on Darcy's birthday and, by the time she does, I'll have made the break from Robert either way. He doesn't know it yet, and neither does anyone at the school, but

I'm not going back for the start of term. One of the charities you put me in touch with has got a place for me and the children, over two hundred miles away from Sandlethwaite. This time next week I'll be there; it's all sorted, and I can't change any of the plans without risking him discovering what I'm doing. A few more days, that's all I'm asking. It won't make any difference to Lucy coming home, but it could change everything for me. And it could also give Phoebe the best possible chance of keeping Darcy away from her grandmother. Lucy was so insistent in her note that the letter had to arrive on Darcy's birthday. We've got to do this one last thing for her; it's what Lucy would have wanted and that makes it the right thing to do.'

'God, I hope so.' Suddenly, Jamie could almost hear Lucy's laugh when she threw her head back. But even in the rare moments of pure joy he'd witnessed, her smile had never once reached her eyes. Not until that last time he'd seen her, when she must already have put all of her plans in place. All he could do was pray that Gerry was right, and that honouring Lucy's final wish was the right thing to do. It was too late to change the outcome for Lucy; he just hoped to God that the letter Phoebe received on Darcy's birthday would be enough to give her some peace of mind.

* * *

Phoebe had got up at four thirty in the morning to get some work done so she could finish early enough to take Darcy dress shopping before the barbecue at Dolly's house. The little girl was changing quickly, almost every day it seemed, and Lucy was missing so much. She'd only been gone for six weeks and yet her daughter already seemed to be outgrowing her clothes. She wasn't the only one who'd outgrown everything in her wardrobe, but the unsuitability of Phoebe's clothes wasn't because they didn't fit her any more. They just didn't fit her new life.

Phoebe was hesitant to borrow anything of Lucy's that might bring back memories for Darcy, either. She'd thought about asking Adam if he would bring some more of her stuff down, but there was probably nothing she owned that would have fitted with her life back in Appleberry. In any case, Adam was busy packing his half of the flat up for the move to New York, and that was something else she was eventually going to have to deal with. Despite an initial urge to run back to London, taking Darcy with her, she was certain now that she wouldn't be going back any time soon, even if Lucy came home. Phoebe and her sister had so much lost time to make up for, and all the things her job had seemed to once offer had lost their sheen. Against all the odds, Appleberry was starting to feel like home, despite her parents' presence. And she was getting pretty good at pretending they didn't exist.

By the time they'd finished shopping, Phoebe had bought Darcy three new outfits, and had found herself a pretty summer dress in forget-me-not blue, with a pattern of tiny white flowers. It was the sort of thing she'd never have worn back in London, but it was perfect for a get-together at Dolly and Greg's. Darcy had chosen one of her new dresses to change into too. But, when they went to leave, Norma was sitting by the front door of the cottage, giving them a beseeching look.

'Sorry, sweetheart, you can't come this time. The barbecue will be too much of a temptation.' Phoebe scooped Norma up. Putting her in her basket, she turned on the radio to give the little dog some company, and put a couple of chew treats on the blanket next to her. 'We won't be late.'

'Poor Norma.' Darcy put her arm around the dog, leaning against the blanket as she did so, not caring a jot if her pretty pink party dress got covered in the hairs the pug seemed to shed everywhere she went. 'You can come to my party, 'cos it's going to be here.'

'You want to have your party at home?' Phoebe crossed her fingers as she spoke, desperately hoping that her niece wouldn't repeat the question she'd asked so many times about whether her mother would be back for her birthday.

'Yes, but can we have a princess?' Her eyes were wide as she looked up, and Phoebe didn't know whether to sag with relief that she hadn't mentioned Lucy or give in to the tears that seemed so close to the surface just lately. Her tears at sports day had been the happy kind, and so brief that no one even noticed. But if she started crying because there was a chance that at some point Darcy would no longer ask about her mother at all, there was no knowing if she'd ever be able to stop. Focusing on her niece's request was much easier.

'A princess?'

'Ava had Belle, but I want Elsa.'

'From *Frozen*?' They'd streamed the movie enough times since Phoebe had arrived for her to be able to quote some of the lines word for word. She'd have to ask Scarlett how you went about booking a princess for a party.

'Yes, *Frozen*'s my favourite.'

'I know it is, darling.' She'd sort it tomorrow and, whatever Darcy wanted, she'd get it for her, as long as it was in her power to do so. 'Of course we'll get you a princess.'

'I love you, Auntie Phoebe.' The words that now seemed to trip so easily off her niece's tongue stirred something in her every time she heard them.

'I love you too, darling.' Gently brushing the dog hair off the little girl's dress, Phoebe breathed out. She could make sure Elsa attended Darcy's fourth birthday party. Sadly, the arrival of the person they most wanted there was completely out of her hands.

21

Jamie had considered not turning up to the barbecue. He had no idea how to look Phoebe in the eyes without telling her that he knew where Gerry was, or that she was behind the arrival of the letter from Lucy. It had been easier when there was still hope that she might come home, but now he was almost certain Lucy had taken her own life. He still wasn't sure whether he could trust Gerry to tell the police the full story, but he'd given her until the Monday after Darcy's birthday to contact them, by which time she'd be in the safe house set up by the charity, or he'd go to the police himself. It would also give Gerry enough time to get Lucy's final letter to Phoebe.

If Jamie ended up having to talk to the police, Phoebe would realise his betrayal, but if Gerry did speak to them, Phoebe might never discover how much he knew. Wanting to find a way of keeping that from her compounded the guilt he already felt, but the alternative was even worse. Developing feelings for Phoebe had been the last thing he'd wanted, but it had happened anyway. All his attempts to convince himself that he wanted to stay in Phoebe's life for the benefit of Darcy were futile. He wanted to stay in her life because it was already impossible to imagine his life without her around.

In the end he'd decided to go to the barbecue. It would have looked odd if he hadn't gone, after accepting Dolly's invitation, and he really wanted the opportunity to talk to his best friend. Cam was Scarlett's fiancé, and the headteacher of Appleberry's primary school. He'd been head-hunted to work with Ofsted and had spent most of the summer holidays consulting with senior leadership teams from schools that had recently received disappointing inspection reports. It meant he'd been incredibly busy for the past couple of months and away on training courses most weekends. Usually, Cam and Jamie would have hung out together at least once a week, but the barbecue would be the first time they'd seen each other in over six. Jamie was desperate to get Cam's advice, but there was only so much he could ask without revealing information he couldn't share.

'You look exhausted, and as if you could do with at least two of these. One for each hand.' Cam handed Jamie a beer almost as soon as he arrived.

'This is why you're my best mate.'

'Some best mate.' Cam frowned. 'You've been going through all this stuff with Lucy missing, and her leaving Darcy with you, not to mention supporting Phoebe. I should've been there for you.'

'You've got your own stuff going on.' Jamie took a swig of beer, mostly to avoid having to look at Cam. Not only had he lied to Phoebe, now he was going to have to lie to his best friend, too.

'That's not a good enough excuse, but I'm here now, and if you want to offload, I've got all night to listen.'

'I'm not sure how Scarlett will feel about that, and the last thing I want to do is cut into your family time when you've been away so much.' Jamie had wanted to ask Cam what he should do, from the day Lucy disappeared. But now that he finally had a chance, he had no idea what to say.

'Scarlett would be the first one to order me to get my arse over here and talk to you.' Cam's tone brooked no argument. 'Now tell me what I can do to help, or just tell me how crap the whole situation is. Scarlett's been finding it tough enough trying to find ways of helping Phoebe through this, but you've had to be there for Darcy too. How's she coping?'

'Remarkably well, mainly because Phoebe's doing such a great job with her. But I think her birthday might be the turning point, when Lucy doesn't turn up. I mean *if* Lucy doesn't turn up.' Jamie shook his head, but the words were already out there, hanging in the air between him and Cam, and more loaded with meaning than he'd ever intended.

'Do you really think she won't come back?' Cam held his gaze. 'That she really went into the sea and never made it out again?'

'I don't want to believe it, but it's looking more and more likely. Phoebe's terrified that the police have already decided that's what happened, and they're going to stop looking for Lucy altogether.' He could still see the look on her face when she'd confided those fears to him, and it made it all too easy to imagine how she'd react after Gerry had spoken to the police, and made the decision to stop the search so much easier. He didn't want Phoebe to go through that kind of pain, especially when the hope he'd allowed her to hold on to by not speaking up sooner would make it so much harder to bear. 'What the hell am I going to do to help Phoebe and Darcy to get through it, if that ends up happening?'

'All you can do is carry on what you've been doing so far: be there to listen to both of them, and step in to support Phoebe if she needs it.' Cam made it sound so easy.

'What if they don't want to talk to me any more?'

'Why wouldn't they, when you've been there since day one?'

'It might be different if the police decide Lucy isn't coming back.' And it would definitely change things between him and Phoebe, if she ever discovered how long he'd known about the plans Lucy had made with Gerry. He couldn't seem to stay still; it was like he was constantly being pulled in two directions, and he'd found himself looking over his shoulder for no reason. He was on high alert, waiting for some kind of ambush, and it would almost have been a relief if it had finally come. Honesty was one of the qualities he valued most highly, and he hated what this situation had turned him into. He didn't like himself, so how could he expect anyone else to, when the truth eventually came out? Losing Phoebe would be agony, but it might not be the only price he had to pay.

'You're right, and I suppose there's a good chance they might want to talk to counsellors who specialise in that kind of loss.' Cam clapped him on the shoulder. 'But no one's better qualified than you to point them in the right direction. You've supported children and families with parental loss before, and you've been through it yourself. Trust me, having you around is going to make the world of difference to Phoebe and Darcy, whatever the police decide about Lucy. But you've got to look after yourself too, and you know where I am if you need me.'

'Thanks, Cam.' Jamie managed a half-smile, feeling like the lowest of the low for allowing his friend to talk about him like he was some kind of hero, when the reality was, he was a fraud.

* * *

Darcy had decided to change outfits at the last minute. She wanted to save the first dress she'd put on for her birthday party, because she thought it was the one her mum would like best. When she'd looked at her aunt and explained her reasoning, Phoebe had experienced a physical pain in her chest, as if her heart might actually be permanently damaged. When her niece had skipped along the hallway ten minutes later, wearing her second choice of dress, a surge of anger towards Lucy had almost overwhelmed Phoebe. It wasn't the first time she'd felt that way since her sister's disappearance, but this was different than before. It came from a love of Darcy so powerful that she hadn't known it was possible to feel that way about anyone. She'd heard parents say they'd die for their children. And, while she hadn't doubted the sincerity of their words, she'd had no idea what such a strong desire to protect another person felt like. Now she knew, and it was breathtaking. She'd do anything to stop Darcy getting hurt.

When Phoebe had first started caring for her niece, her overriding emotion had been fear of doing something wrong and terror that Lucy wouldn't come home. That had gradually been replaced by far more complex emotions. The anger had crept in slowly and, when she'd first realised what she was feeling, she'd wondered if it came from resenting the fact that Lucy's disappearance had wrenched her out of her old life. Except that wasn't it.

All of the anger she'd felt at first had been directed at her parents, but the first time she'd realised she was angry with Lucy too, it had shocked her. Her sister was the victim; she couldn't be to blame. Yet she'd walked away from a little girl who was the only completely blameless person in all of this. The same little girl who'd been lost and confused and had asked for her mother at least ten times a day when Lucy had first disappeared. That was where the anger had come from when Darcy changed her dress for the party. It was like a heat rising up inside Phoebe's body, and if Lucy had been standing in front of her, she'd have wanted to shake her sister.

She was so angry with her for putting Darcy through this. But when she pictured Lucy, she wanted to cry, too, for all the things that had pushed her beyond her limits, and made her lose sight of the one thing that really mattered. It was an ugly mess of feelings, and just trying to keep a handle on them had left Phoebe exhausted. So, when a new emotion had begun nagging at the back of her mind, she'd dismissed it as a symptom of that exhaustion, because it was crazy. But in the quiet moments, when Darcy was asleep and Phoebe had far too much time for thinking, the thought kept creeping back. When Lucy came home, she'd take over again, exactly as a mother should, and exactly as Phoebe wanted her to. But that would change things between Phoebe and Darcy too. She wouldn't be the one her niece ran to, with arms outstretched, at pick-up time, or the person whose lap she wanted to curl up in at the end of a long day. Darcy would have her mother back for all of those things, and there'd suddenly be a gaping hole in Phoebe's life.

She'd been closed off for so long, not wanting to risk allowing anyone to really get past the barriers she'd put up, not even Lucy. Loving someone, unconditionally and with her whole heart, was far too great a risk. Except Darcy had crept under that barrier, and she'd brought an army with her.

Letting the little girl become her whole world had meant allowing other people in too. She'd become closer than ever to Scarlett and built new friendships with Kate and Dolly. But the bond she shared with Jamie went even deeper, because he was the one who'd taught her how to be Darcy's stand-in mother and had been there to witness the transformation of their relationship. All of these people were in her life now – truly in it – and they'd filled up pockets of loneliness she hadn't admitted existed, even to herself. The idea of losing what she had with Darcy was terrifying and she couldn't imagine anything else ever being able to take its place.

Throwing herself into her job again wouldn't work. Darcy

already meant more to her than her work ever could, and the thought of giving up her role as her niece's stand-in mother was more painful than she could ever have imagined. She hated herself for even thinking that way. She desperately wanted Lucy back, and so did Darcy. It would make the little girl she loved happier than anything else in the world. But Phoebe couldn't control the unwanted thoughts, any more than she could control if and when Lucy came home. She'd just have to work hard to discover what her new place in her sister and niece's lives was, that was all.

As soon as Lucy came back, she'd do everything she could to put her relationship with her sister back to how it should always have been. Nothing else would do, because she couldn't lose Lucy a second time, and the prospect of losing Darcy was like someone asking her to imagine life without her arms or legs. Her niece was a fundamental part of her, and her identity had shifted so much. She wasn't Phoebe Spencer, the corporate go-getter, who'd happily step over anyone to climb the career ladder in her industry. She was Darcy's auntie, and if that was taken away from her, she didn't want to be anything else. There was no life without Darcy, at least not one she even wanted to try to envisage.

'Sorry we're so late.' Phoebe joined Scarlett and Cam, who were standing with Jamie, while Darcy went over to where other kids were playing on the swing set and slide in Dolly's garden. 'First of all, Darcy wanted an outfit change, and then Norma decided to make a dash for it as we were leaving. She got all the way to your chicken coop before I managed to catch hold of her. I thought I'd shut the kitchen door, but somehow she made it out of her basket and got through the gap in the door in the time it took to find my house key. It's all right, though, she didn't actually get hold of any of the chickens, but Fisher was barking his head off standing by your patio doors.'

Phoebe was aware that she was babbling, but she seemed to be doing that around Jamie a lot lately. She tried to convince herself it was because she didn't want the subject of Lucy's disappearance, or the search for Gerry, to come up and bring the mood down straight away. She promised not to mention Lucy's friend in front of anyone else, because she knew how much Jamie was putting on the line just trying to find her, and how keen he was to protect Gerry, who'd clearly been very vulnerable when she'd been his client. But it wasn't just all of that. He'd been such a big part of helping her fall in love with Darcy, and her brain was playing tricks on her as a result. It was as though her subconscious had neatly packaged up the three of them, like they were pieces of a jigsaw that could only fit together. But the reality was Jamie helped everyone. He was a natural with children, too. It was probably just a transference of the gratitude she felt towards him, and the relief it had been to have someone to lean on, masquerading as something else. It would pass, once Lucy was home.

'As long as you're okay?' Jamie smiled and she cursed the way she felt when he looked at her like that.

'I'm fine. I think Norma just needs a bit more attention than I've been giving her, so maybe I should come to The Pines with you more than once a week?'

'Any time you like – I'm up there at least twice a week. The offer's always open, and they loved you. Both of you.' He was looking at her again, making her grateful they weren't alone, otherwise she'd really be in danger of making a fool of herself.

'So how are you guys?' She turned towards Scarlett and Cam and the spell was immediately broken. 'How are the plans for the wedding going?'

'Okay, but the list of guests is starting to get a bit out of hand. Manly because of Mum.' Scarlett wrinkled her nose. 'I'm not sure I'd have recognised some of the distant relatives she's invited, even if I passed them on the street. But she's so happy for me, and she keeps saying she wants to make the wedding a huge party to celebrate. Even my great-great-aunt Morag, who lives in Aberdeenshire, and is ninety-two, has an invite. We could end up having to look for a bigger venue at this rate.'

'Yep, between your mum and mine, we might need to see if Westminster Abbey can squeeze us in.' Cam grinned. 'My mum keeps talking about the choir she performs in singing at the service, and the choir master is already working on a new song, just for us. Not that we've got any say in the matter!'

'Mums, eh? They can't help interfering sometimes, but I suppose they only do it because they love us.' As Scarlett spoke, she caught Phoebe's eye, her cheeks suddenly blazing. 'I'm sorry, I...'

'Don't be daft.' Phoebe shook her head, suddenly in desperate need of a glass of wine to drown out all thoughts of her own mother. For a little while she'd gone quiet. But Bradley had shared the new information the police had found on Lucy's laptop with her parents, and it had stirred Janet up again. She was badgering Phoebe with texts and calls, posting all over social media and putting comments on the missing person posts. She'd tagged in online friends, some of whom Phoebe was also friends with. That was how she found out about one of Janet's latest posts. She'd talked about having one daughter who was missing, and another who was refusing to speak to her about whether she'd known that Lucy had been on suicide forums. Janet had written: *makes you wonder what she's got to hide*, at the end of the post, which had sparked a whole series of comments. It shouldn't have hurt any more, not after all the times her mother had lashed out, or blamed Phoebe simply for existing. But the sting was still there. Perhaps it was the injustice of other people believing her mother's words, or maybe there was a tiny part of her that was still clinging hopelessly to the idea that Lucy's disappearance could finally make Janet change. But all it seemed to be doing was making her even more of a monster.

None of her mother's online activity was helping the search for Lucy; it was just muddying the water, and giving Janet the kind of attention she craved. So, the idea of having a mother who interfered because she loved you was as alien to Phoebe as a three-headed space creature. And she knew which one she'd rather spend time with. 'I'm definitely ready for glass of wine. Can I get anyone else a drink?'

'I'll have a white wine too. It'll be something to fill up my big mouth with.' Scarlett still looked mortified, but Phoebe shook her head.

'It's fine, honestly. Don't let my mother make you feel bad; she's done enough of that with me and Lucy.' She turned towards Cam. 'Right, wine for Scarlett – what can I get you?'

'A beer would be great, thanks.'

'I'll come with you.' Jamie followed her as they moved away, not speaking again until they were out of earshot of the others. 'Are you sure you're okay?'

'I'll be fine, it's just been one of those days and it's got nothing to do with what Scarlett said. Darcy mentioned seeing her mum on her birthday and it breaks my heart thinking about how she might react if Lucy isn't back in time. What am I going to say? We're no closer to finding Gerry, are we? And I can't keep putting off the difficult conversations with Darcy. I need her to be able to trust me and, even though I'm trying to keep giving us both hope, I'm terrified of what will happen if it turns out I'm lying to her.' Her eyes were stinging and, ever since she'd cried watching her niece on sports day, it seemed much harder to hold back the tears. Darcy had changed her. Caring for her niece had forced her to open up and get in touch with emotions she'd previously buried beneath the protective layers she'd wrapped herself in for years. The problem was, there was no way of turning that off and now she couldn't stop herself from experiencing difficult emotions, no matter how much she'd rather not face up to them.

Jamie looked close to tears himself as he shook his head. 'I wish I could tell you something useful about Gerry, I really do. But I think you're right that you need to start having a conversation with Darcy, where the outcome might not be the thing we all want. I'm sorry, Phoebe, I'm really sorry for everything you're going through.'

'None of this is your fault and I wouldn't have got this far without you. But I've still got no idea how to even start a conversation like that with Darcy.' She felt sick just thinking about it.

'Maybe you should talk to Dolly about it; she's dealt with similar kinds of issues since the adoption.' Jamie stopped as they reached the stairs leading up from the garden to the deck outside the kitchen, where Dolly and Greg had set up a serve-yourself bar. 'I know it's really hard even having to think about it, and that you hate it when I say this, but if there's even a chance that Lucy is never coming home, Dolly will be able to give you some great advice on what worked for her and the kids. I've supported some families with parental loss, too, so I might be able to recommend professionals you can speak to. But that's probably not something you want to think about doing until you know for sure. Reaching out to a friend in the meantime can't hurt, though.'

For a long moment, Phoebe couldn't find the words. Part of her wanted to confess that she was starting to think that the faith she'd had about Lucy still being alive was almost certainly misplaced. But she wasn't ready to admit that yet. Just the thought of saying those words out loud made the tears, which she was so desperately trying not to give in to, choke in her throat. It was unbearable, and she refused to accept it, even if deep down she knew she was burying her head in the sand. Denial was the only route to survival right now, and not just about Lucy. 'I still don't believe she's dead. But I've got to do something if Lucy doesn't come home soon, for Darcy's sake.'

'Not just for Darcy's sake, for yours too.' Jamie moved forward, and for a moment she'd been certain he was going to pull her into his arms, and she was powerless to stop herself from leaning forward, but then suddenly he bent down to pick up a tennis ball, which had been lying on the middle of the bottom step. 'I'd better move this, or someone could have a nasty fall.'

'Good idea.' Mumbling the words, Phoebe was just grateful Jamie couldn't see the flaming of her face. Even if her brain was just doing its best to distract her from the horrors of Lucy's disappearance, she had to stop focusing on the stupid things she was obsessing over and do more to find her sister. And if Bradley didn't have an update the next time they spoke, Phoebe would take things into her own hands. She'd promised Jamie she wouldn't try to find Gerry and the truth was she wouldn't even know where to start. There was something she could do, though. She could find a way to start facing up to the prospect of Lucy never coming home, so she'd be ready to help Darcy through her grief if that turned out to be true. It would be incredibly difficult, and Phoebe was certain it would have broken her completely if she'd had to face it alone. Except she had Darcy now, and she had to be the strong one, so she had to find a way for them to get through this together.

22

'How adorable do they look?' Phoebe got out her phone again. The photos had been almost exclusively of Norma until she'd come back to Appleberry, but now the little pug had been relegated to about 5 per cent of the phone's photo album; everything else was filled with Darcy. At that moment, her niece was organising Ava, Chantelle and some of the other children into a conga-style line and jumping up and down in tandem. As usual, Chantelle's infectious laugh was ringing out, even over the music that one of Dolly's older children had taken charge of.

'Darcy's such a great kid, especially with everything that's going on at the moment. She's always looking after the others.' Scarlett smiled and Phoebe nodded in response. Her niece made her proud every single day. They were standing at the edge of the garden, and Phoebe was incredibly grateful that her best friend had instinctively understood her need to hide out. She'd lasted for all of an hour, before the questions from old acquaintances about what she really thought had happened to her sister got too much.

'She loves other kids. I think she's just a natural mother hen.' Phoebe shot another look at her niece, who had now taken hold of the hand of a little girl who'd been sitting on the ground, watching the others from under her blonde fringe. Darcy wasn't taking no for an answer and soon had the little girl joining in.

Suddenly the music changed to the song behind the latest TikTok dance craze, and the younger children were joined by some of the older ones. A few seconds later, Dolly's teenage daughter, Molly, had grabbed hold of her father's wrist, loudly urging him to join in. Clearly not wanting to be the only adult forced to perform, Greg was soon busy persuading Cam and Jamie to join him too. As soon as they started to dance, it was obvious none of them had the faintest idea how to perform the moves, but their attempts at freestyling were nothing short of hilarious.

'If this was the first time I'd ever seen Cam' – Scarlett was giggling now – 'I'm not sure we'd ever have got to a first date, let alone be planning a wedding. Those dance moves aren't exactly what you'd call sexy.'

'More of a contraceptive than seduction technique, I think!' Phoebe was laughing too, as Cam made a move like he was lassoing an imaginary head of cattle, and Jamie did the sort of spin made famous by cheesy boy bands. The kids were absolutely loving it, and so was she. But then it came, out of nowhere: the all-too-familiar stab of guilt at realising just how hard she was laughing, when her sister was still out there somewhere, missing. How the hell could she be so selfish? But then maybe it was hardwired into her DNA. It was just one more thing to hate herself for. And there was no denying another emotion was back too: fear that all of this could be taken away. She'd never expected to find her reason for living, or the things that made her happiest, in Appleberry, the place she had so decisively run away from. If Lucy came home and didn't need her around – or worse still, didn't want her – then all of this could disappear. As impossible as it might feel to walk away, she'd be prepared to do it, if it meant Lucy was still alive. But what Phoebe really wanted was *all* of it – this wonderful new life with her sister at its centre – and she wasn't sure how she'd go on if she had to let go of any part of that dream.

* * *

Nine o'clock had been and gone, and it was way past Darcy's bedtime, but Phoebe had decided to let her niece keep dancing until she dropped. When Chantelle had begged Dolly to let Darcy and Ava sleep over, Phoebe had been powerless to say no. The girls were having so much fun, and it was wonderful to see Darcy like that. She could spend the rest of the weekend catching up on missed sleep, if she needed to, and there was no way of knowing how many more moments of pure happiness she'd get. Not if Lucy didn't come home.

Most of the other parents seemed willing to let the kids stay up way past their bedtimes too, and the children were showing no signs of slowing down yet. Phoebe only wished she had half their stamina. She was just thinking about saying goodnight to Darcy and heading home, when a familiar figure crossed the garden towards her.

'What are you doing lurking over here in the dark? Is this your genius strategy to make sure the kids don't pull you up to join in with the next dance routine?' Jamie raised a questioning eyebrow as he reached Phoebe's side.

'No one needs to see my attempts at dancing.' Phoebe had got so used to putting herself down, before her mother got that chance, that she'd almost forgotten how much she'd loved performing when she was a little bit older than Darcy. Janet had a real talent for sucking the joy out of every situation and, even now, twenty years after she'd managed to kill Phoebe's love of performing, her criticism cast a long shadow.

'Oh, I think we'd all very much like to see that.' Jamie smiled. 'I know I would.'

'If I didn't know better, I'd think you were flirting with me.' The words had undoubtedly come out of Phoebe's mouth, but she still couldn't believe she'd said them. It was like she'd suddenly turned into a ventriloquist's dummy, and somebody else was working her mouth with their hand shoved up her back.

'What makes you think you know better?' He was looking at her again, in a way that made her feel like she was the only person in the world he was interested in talking to. But she wasn't that special; she'd been told so often enough.

'Because someone as nice as you wouldn't be flirting with the sister of a missing friend. You wouldn't even think about stuff like that, when we've got no idea where Lucy is.'

'I'm not sure how I feel about being described as nice.' Jamie was standing so close to her that she could make out the graze of stubble on his cheeks, even in the darkness. 'But I wouldn't say that being attracted to someone in the midst of a traumatic event necessarily means a person isn't nice.'

'What does it mean, then?' Phoebe had to know, because she couldn't deny her attraction to Jamie any more. If he had a way of explaining it, without it proving she was exactly like her mother, she desperately needed to hear it.

'It just means that person is human. They're going through an awful time, something that's almost more than they can bear. But being attracted to someone releases endorphins, which reminds them they're still alive and capable of feeling something other than misery. That might be the one thing that gets that person through, when everything else feels hopeless.' Jamie's eyes never left her face, and all the time she kept telling herself that in another place, another time, maybe she could have acted on her feelings. But not now, not here.

'So, it doesn't make that person a selfish narcissist, then?'

'Not unless they already were one, and you definitely aren't.'

'I thought we were talking about you.' She was still trying to act casual, but it was suddenly hard to catch her breath.

'I think you know I was talking about both of us.' He took a step forward and she was frozen to the spot, the sensible part of her half-hoping that he'd bend down to pick up another stray tennis ball, but the rest of her desperately wanting him to finally reach out and touch her. He took another step forward as she held her breath and seconds later they were kissing. In that instant, she understood exactly what he'd meant. When he was touching her, she couldn't think about anything else and, for a few blissful moments, the pain of Lucy's absence receded so far into the shadows that she could no longer feel it.

'I've been wanting to do that from the first day we met.' Jamie's voice was low as they finally pulled apart.

'Me too.' The ventriloquist's voice was back, and it was forcing Phoebe to admit things she'd tried denying even to herself.

'I really like you, but I'm not expecting anything from you; I need you to know that. I understand how hard everything is for you right now. And I know there are things you wish I could tell you about Gerry. I promise, like I said before, that I'd tell you everything she ever said to me if I thought it would make any difference to finding Lucy. But I can't do that if I know it won't do anything to change the situation, not even if something happens between us. I don't want you to regret anything later, because there are things I know about Gerry that I have to keep to myself to protect her.'

'I know that, and I understand. Just the fact that you're prepared to try and find her, and ask her to talk to me, when you could lose your job over it, means more than you'll ever know. And I'm not expecting anything of you either, but what you said about the attraction between us makes sense. I need to feel something again, anything other than terror about what might have happened to Lucy. And I'd like you to come back with me when I leave.' Whoever the ventriloquist who'd taken control of her was, they had a lot to answer for. Phoebe would never have dreamt she'd be able to say those things to Jamie, but, despite her shock, she was glad she'd finally found her voice.

'You want me to come back to Lucy's with you?'

'It might be better if we go back to yours.' The last thing she wanted was to end up having a meltdown when she spotted something of Lucy's lying around.

'Are you sure?' Usually she'd have questioned whether Jamie was trying to find a way of backing out, but not when he was looking at her the way he was, and his hand was still resting on the small of her back.

'Absolutely certain. I'm going to say goodbye to everyone, but I'll meet you out front in ten minutes.' Not waiting for him to answer, she moved out of the shadows and headed across the garden to say goodnight to her friends, and her niece. She refused to think about whether she might end up regretting what she was about to do. She needed Jamie and the chance to block out all the difficult feelings she'd been having; just for tonight, nothing else mattered.

23

Waking up next to Phoebe, Jamie felt even worse about himself than he had when he'd been talking to Cam. He'd wrestled with the decision about whether to spend the night with her, right up to the point when she'd taken his hand and led him upstairs. It wasn't because he didn't want to be with her – that was the easy part. He'd tried to be as honest with Phoebe as he could and reminded her that he was keeping things from her, but she still had no idea the extent of that deception and that he'd managed to track Gerry down. He could tell himself as often as he liked that he'd done it for the right reasons, and that the fact he'd tried to text to let her know, and it hadn't gone through, was some kind of sign. But it didn't change the reality that he'd lied to her.

He should have stopped it or told her the truth and given her the chance to tell him to go to hell. But he couldn't do that either. He knew in his heart Gerry was telling the truth about everything and he couldn't risk blowing her opportunity to escape for the sake of a few more days' silence. So, it had been down to him to stop anything happening with Phoebe, and he'd had plenty of chances.

They'd stopped off to pick Norma up, so she could sleep down in his kitchen with Fisher. He could have told Phoebe then that it wasn't a good idea, and that there were things she didn't know about him that would eventually make her realise that. But she'd want to know what those things were. If he refused to tell her, knowing Phoebe, she'd take it as a rejection: yet more proof that she was unlovable and unwanted. That was so far from the truth it would have been laughable, if it wasn't so sad.

He told himself he was making decisions for the right reasons, but that didn't stop him feeling like he'd betrayed her all over again. To add to his misery, a realisation had hit him as he'd watched her sleeping, when he lay awake too riddled with guilt to even close his eyes. Somewhere along the line, the feelings he had for her had turned into something that felt a lot like love.

Everything about her was extraordinary, and yet she had no clue. He'd known her for such a short time, but he'd watched her push her own feelings aside to ensure that Darcy was happy and secure, despite her mother's disappearance. He'd seen her with the residents at The Pines, her unending patience and fearlessness in situations others backed away from, just because they felt awkward. When she'd happened across an elderly man in a corridor, who'd been confused and frightened, not to mention totally naked, she hadn't panicked. Instead, Phoebe had comforted him, gently persuading him back to his room, and striving to protect his dignity, even though he had no idea he'd lost it.

According to Lucy, Phoebe had protected her for years too, and the guilt she felt about failing to do that now was horribly misplaced. Just the fact that Phoebe questioned it said so much about her. She couldn't have been more unlike her mother, but the saddest part was that she didn't believe that either. Phoebe was complicated and broken, yet somehow perfect all at the same time. And it turned out that loving her had been impossible to resist, which made the things he'd done even worse.

'Stop staring at me like that, I know I'm an idiot.' Jamie looked at the two dogs, who'd been curled up in the basket together when he'd crept downstairs to make coffee. They turned their attention to him as soon as they'd woken up. And they might not be able to speak, but their eyes said so much.

'Why are you an idiot?'

'Oh my God, you nearly gave me a heart attack!' Jamie dropped the spoon he'd been holding, scattering ground coffee all over the worktop as Phoebe suddenly appeared out of nowhere.

'Sorry.' A smile was tugging at the corners of her mouth, and he tried not to think how much he loved it when something made her happy, knowing that at any moment it could be taken away. 'So come on then, why are you an idiot?'

'I forgot to buy more milk when I was at the shop yesterday.' He shrugged, wondering if she'd see through him as easily as Norma and Fisher clearly could; there were still two pairs of canine eyes trained on him, expertly conveying their disdain.

'I don't think that warrants describing yourself as an idiot.' Phoebe looked at him, but the maelstrom of emotions he was battling made it hard to hold her gaze. He wanted to ask her to stay, to tell her he hadn't felt this way about anyone since... He couldn't even finish the sentence, because he'd never felt this way about anyone else. But even if she felt half as strongly about him, it could never work, because the whole basis of whatever this was had been built on a lie. He'd ruined something that had the chance to be amazing, before it had even really begun.

'You don't know the half of it.'

'What, so you've forgotten the sugar too?' She smiled again and it was so hard not to kiss her, but they'd spent the night together on her terms. Phoebe had taken the lead, and it was the only reason he could live with what he'd done. If he made a move now, he'd be even deeper in the wrong than he already was. 'I didn't come here for coffee. I came here to feel like someone other than the sister of a missing woman, and you made that happen. Last night was great. But the best part about it is that I know you don't judge me for it, and that it doesn't mean I love or miss Lucy any less. I'm not sure I'd ever have believed that if we hadn't talked.'

'You can miss someone desperately and still carry on with other aspects of your life, most of the time because you've got no choice. You still have to work, look after Darcy and Norma, feed them and yourself. Sometimes people looking in will wonder how you can even function, but the world doesn't stop just because you might want it to.'

'I do feel like it should have stopped the moment I got the call about Lucy, but even the police are moving on. And I've got a feeling I might be the real idiot.' Phoebe bit her lip and the hairs on the back of Jamie's neck felt as if they were pulsing with electricity. If she'd somehow discovered he'd found Gerry, she'd feel like an idiot for ever believing a word he'd said. Only when he looked at her, it wasn't anger written on her face, it was fear.

'Why would you ever think you've been an idiot?' He told himself not to reach out and touch her, even though every muscle in his body was urging him to do so.

'Because last night, just before you came over and found me hiding in the dark, I emailed a therapist to confirm that I wanted to arrange a consultation with her.' Phoebe ran a hand through her hair.

'How on earth does that make you an idiot?'

'Because it's never worked for me in the past.' Phoebe sighed. 'If they couldn't fix me, before all of this, how the hell can I expect them to fix me now?'

'You don't need fixing.' Jamie took hold of her hand, wishing he could find a way of saying all the things he wanted to say – that she was perfectly imperfect and that he'd never met anyone like her. But he'd promised not to put any pressure on her, and those kinds of things were far too intense for her to hear. Even if they were true. 'What is it that you'd like to achieve from seeing someone?'

'If Lucy has gone forever, I've got no idea how I'll handle that, and as for Darcy...' She shook her head, looking so vulnerable that he couldn't stop himself from pulling her into his arms. 'And I'm an idiot because of that too. I'm putting myself in a situation where I'll be asked to confront something I'm nowhere near ready to face. I still don't know whether or not to go.'

'No one would ever be ready to face something like that, but not knowing how to deal with it will be even worse.' He could tell her now that he was almost certain Lucy's death was something she needed to be ready to deal with, for herself and Darcy, to make sure Phoebe didn't back out of seeing the therapist. But he didn't.

'Lucy was so lucky to have you around, and so am I.' She leant forward, pressing her lips against his, her hands moving up his arms, until her body was touching his, and it was as if there was a storm raging inside of him. He couldn't let anything happen between them again, not until she knew everything. But as soon as the words came out of his mouth, she'd push him away and out of her life for good. Jamie had spent his whole life doing the right thing, but it had never been so blurred before.

'There are things you should know; I tried to help Lucy as much as I could, and—'

'Don't.' Phoebe cut him off, putting a finger against his lips. 'I've beaten myself up a thousand times for the things I should have done or said. No one could have done more for Lucy or Darcy than you. So don't say it, or I'll be spiralling straight back down the well of guilt with you. I'm not picking Darcy up until this afternoon; please let's just have until then to be like any other people getting to know one another better.'

'Is that what you really want?' She was driving the situation again, and he was desperately trying to convince himself that it would make whatever happened next okay.

'It is. We can have coffee, without sugar or milk.' She laughed, and seeing even a snippet of happiness was enough to help convince him, because he was looking for any reason to be with her. 'Either way, we could take the coffee back up to bed with us, and later we could walk Fisher and Norma, maybe even go to the village shop so we can get some lunch and stock up on all the essentials you've forgotten. You know, just the sort of stuff that normal people do on a lazy Sunday. I just need one day that's not about... *one day*, that's all, and I want it to spend it with you.'

'Everyone deserves one day of doing what they want.' Jamie said the words aloud, but he was justifying it to himself as much as Phoebe. He was going to have to pay for the choices he'd made eventually. But, when it came down to it, deciding whether or not to spend another day with Phoebe, while he still had the chance, had never really been in question.

* * *

Phoebe had expected the guilt about spending time focusing on something other than Lucy's disappearance to catch up with her. But it hadn't. By the time she'd gone to Dolly and Greg's to pick Darcy up, late on Sunday afternoon, she felt as though she'd had two weeks away from everything. There was that post-holiday sense of relaxation, something she hadn't often achieved even after a real break away. Her energy levels were back too, but something else had shocked her even more than that – just how much she'd missed Darcy.

'Auntie Phoebe!' The little girl had hurtled towards her, like a human cannonball, almost sending Phoebe spilling backwards into one of Dolly's flowerbeds. Given that Darcy had been playing with Chantelle and Ava when her aunt had arrived, Phoebe hadn't expected her niece to even notice her arrival at first. She'd braced herself for Darcy to plead to stay at Dolly and Greg's for longer, and being sulky or tearful when she was told that wasn't possible. What she'd hadn't expected was to have her face covered in kisses by her niece, or for her to squeeze Phoebe so tight it was hard to breathe. 'I've missed you millions!'

'I've missed you millions too, sweetheart.' Phoebe had leant the side of her face against the top of Darcy's head, so that no one would spot the tears that had filled her eyes. She hadn't cried in years and yet now she was doing it every five minutes. That was what love did, apparently, and it was terrifying and wonderful all at the same time.

It was Darcy's final week at nursery, and then she had less than a fortnight before she went to school. Just thinking about her starting at the village primary, and being the youngest in the class, twisted something in Phoebe's chest. Lucy had bought all her daughter's uniform before she disappeared, and it was something else that didn't make sense. It was almost impossible to believe that someone so tortured that they were considering ending their life would think that far ahead. Or maybe that was just wishful thinking.

Dotting from thought to thought was how Phoebe's mind seemed to work these days. So, it was no surprise she was in a world of her own when she got back to the cottage after dropping Darcy at nursery. It was why she didn't notice the woman standing by the front door, almost until the moment she took out Lucy's key.

'Bloody hell.' Phoebe clapped a hand to her chest, her handbag dropping to the floor and half of its contents spilling out onto the path, when she finally realised there was someone standing in front of her. For a split second she wondered if the stranger might be Gerry, but then she thrust a lanyard towards Phoebe, almost garrotting herself in the process.

'I'm so sorry I startled you. My name's Rosie Dawkins. I'm a social worker, from the local authority.' The woman smiled, but Phoebe's fight or flight response already seemed to have kicked in. If this person thought for one moment she was going to come and take Darcy away from her, Phoebe wouldn't be responsible for her actions. There it was again, a lightning-bolt reaction, convincing her she'd do anything for her niece, or die trying. They couldn't take Darcy from her; the little girl meant everything, and in all her terror that she might one day lose her niece, she'd never imagined it would be like this. Her heart was pounding, and it took all she had not to scream at this woman that she wasn't taking Darcy away. Not now, not ever.

'Social services cleared me to be my niece's temporary guardian, so I've got no idea what you're doing here. And I'm not speaking to anyone without a lawyer.'

'Oh God, no, it's nothing like that, and I'm not the police.' Rosie smiled again. 'So you don't need a lawyer. I just wanted to check in on you, that's all, to see how things are going, and how Darcy's doing.'

'She's at nursery, but she's doing fine.' Phoebe bent down to gather up the contents of her bag, praying that Rosie hadn't spotted her Gin Lover's notebook.

'That's good, and she must be so excited about starting school. She was already talking about it non-stop the last time I saw her.'

Phoebe's head jolted upwards. 'You've met Darcy before?'

'Oh yes, a couple of times. I was the social worker assigned after we had the concern-for-safety calls about Darcy suggesting there might be parental neglect.' Rosie made it sound so everyday, but if Phoebe hadn't already been crouching on the floor, she wasn't entirely sure her legs would have held her up. Something as huge as that had happened in her sister's life, and Phoebe hadn't known anything about it. Guilt was twisting the knife in her gut once more. Lucy must have been every bit as terrified as Phoebe had been when she'd discovered Rosie on the doorstep, maybe even more so. But she hadn't felt able to turn to her big sister, and the concrete weight was pressing down on Phoebe again. She'd let Lucy sink, all because she'd never made the effort to be around. But there was a flicker of something else as she looked at Rosie. How dare this stranger think she knew anything about what Lucy was like as mother?

'You had concerns about Darcy being neglected?' Anger at the way her sister had been treated was starting to overshadow everything else, and the roots of Phoebe's hair bristled as she got to her feet. 'Lucy's an excellent mother.'

'That soon became apparent, believe me.' Rosie glanced over her shoulder as she spoke. 'Perhaps it would be better if we went inside.'

'Okay, but I need to start work in half an hour, so you'll have to make an appointment if it's going to take longer than that.' Phoebe clamped her handbag to her chest like a shield. She could start work whenever she wanted, but there was no way she was admitting that to a social worker who'd turned up on her doorstep unannounced. If she needed to get the woman out of the house, this would give her the perfect excuse. Even with an exit plan, she couldn't help wishing Jamie was there, and the realisation jolted her all over again. She could handle anything on her own; she'd had to do it for as long as she could remember. So the idea that she might be starting to rely on him was almost as scary as facing a social worker across Lucy's kitchen.

'Can I get you a drink?' Even to her own ears, Phoebe's offer sounded reluctant, and she was relieved when Rosie shook her head.

'No, I don't want to keep you. I really just wanted to make sure that you aren't getting any... I'm not sure how to put this, I suppose *interference* is the best word, in taking care of Darcy.'

'Interference from whom?' Phoebe looked across at Rosie, but things were already starting to click into place. A malicious concern-for-safety call had the hallmarks of Janet Spencer written all over it, and the anger that she'd felt towards social services was immediately directed somewhere else.

'Lucy believed the call came from your mother, but I'm not at liberty to say.' Poor Rosie had flushed red, right to the roots of her hair, and Phoebe suddenly had the urge to hug her. First she'd started crying at the drop of a hat, and now she was tempted to hug a stranger to offer comfort; what on earth was happening to her?

'I only wish someone had put a neglect call in for us when we were kids.'

'That's exactly what Lucy said and, even after I visited and confirmed there were no concerns about Lucy's parenting, the anonymous reports and calls remained relentless.'

'Oh God, poor Luce, why didn't she tell me?' Phoebe was speaking more to herself than Rosie, but the other woman shook her head all the same.

'I think she was probably embarrassed. Lucy was mortified at the idea that it might get out that she'd had visits from a social worker. I assured her it wouldn't, but she was worried the person reporting her wouldn't stop until they got what they were after.' Rosie sighed. 'I told her there was a note on the system and gave her a copy of the report, which detailed how well she was caring for Darcy, but then I heard that she'd disappeared... I'm sorry, I shouldn't be here, and the truth is this isn't an official visit. You and

Darcy would have been assigned a social worker of your own after Lucy's disappearance. But we're so under-resourced, and you probably haven't even had a phone call to see how you're getting on. I was worried that you might have slipped through the net, and that if your mu... the malicious behaviour had started again, you might not know where to turn. I felt awful wondering whether Lucy's disappearance might have had something to do with our investigations, but I wanted to let you know that I'm here if you need to speak to someone from social services. I just wish I'd done more for her.'

'Thank you.' Phoebe took the card Rosie was holding out towards her, knowing that the social worker was almost certainly risking her job by being there. So many people had been left feeling they should have done more to help Lucy, yet there was only one person who should have been blaming herself for Lucy's disappearance. Anger didn't even come close to what Phoebe was feeling towards her mother: it was more like a murderous rage. Since returning to Appleberry, Phoebe had begun to understand what it meant to be willing to die for a child, but now she understood the concept of being willing to kill for one too. And that feeling wasn't just reserved for Darcy. In that moment, Phoebe would have been capable of doing it for Lucy too. But none of that anger was aimed at Rosie any more.

'You need to know this isn't your fault. It sounds like Lucy was comfortable enough with you to open up, and she isn't like that with everyone. You were just doing your job; you can't blame yourself for that.'

'It's hard not to, when something like this happens.' Rosie's eyes were glassy and all Phoebe could do was nod, because despite the advice she'd given the social worker, she was finding it impossible to shake her own guilt, and part of her was scared she never would. There was also a very good chance she might never be able to get past another emotion, the white-hot anger that was boiling up inside of her at everything Janet had put Lucy through and was continuing to put Phoebe and Darcy through too. There was only one solution she could think of to getting past that, but it could cost her everything.

24

———

On the morning of Darcy's birthday, sunlight was streaming through the window by 7 a.m., but Phoebe had only managed a couple of hours of broken sleep before she'd given up altogether, long before it started to get light. It was early September but, instead of beginning to cool off, the summer seemed to be getting a second lease of life. The bouncy castle Phoebe had booked, along with Princesses Elsa and Anna, were all due to arrive half an hour before the party started. It had taken Phoebe almost twenty phone calls to find princesses who were free at such short notice, and she hadn't had any idea they'd be in such high demand. But luckily a company forty miles from Appleberry had received a last-minute cancellation and she'd been more than happy to pay a premium for them to travel a bit further. The kids would be able to use the paddling pool and sandpit, and eat outside, picnic-style, just as Darcy had requested. So it wasn't the threat of rain stopping play that had caused Phoebe such a sleepless night. It was the fact there was no sign of Lucy.

Phoebe had called her sister's old mobile phone number the night before, hoping for some kind of miracle, only to hear an automated message telling her the number had been deactivated. She'd then spent the next few hours going through Lucy's things yet again, desperately hoping to find a clue she'd somehow missed before, or a way of getting hold of Lucy and bringing her back home in time for the party. If she didn't manage to do that, it didn't matter what else Darcy got for her birthday; it was still going to be a miserable one. But Phoebe was finding it almost impossible to face up to the reality, because it made it far more likely that her sister was never coming home.

She'd been so certain for so long that Lucy would come back for Darcy's birthday. Every sound she'd heard the day before, the distant hum of a car travelling through the village, or a door slamming, had put her on high alert. She'd lost count of the number of times she'd gone to the window, craning to catch sight of her sister coming down the path. She'd barely slept at all, but she must have drifted off at one point, and she'd woken with a start, fully expecting that when she got downstairs Lucy would be sitting at the kitchen table or curled up on the sofa in the tiny living room. But it had been quiet and empty, the kind of emptiness that seemed to echo through Phoebe's whole body. Lucy was nowhere and for the first time Phoebe got the feeling she'd been dreading. She'd always said she'd know if Lucy was dead – that she'd somehow sense it – and in that moment she did. But she'd shaken it off, giving herself a good talking-to. All that stuff was just make-believe, and it didn't mean that Lucy was really gone. Except she was finding it harder and harder to believe the stories that she insisted on telling herself.

'Morning, I just wondered if you needed a hand with anything?' Finding Jamie standing at the door of Lucy's cottage, Phoebe hadn't been able to stop herself from launching at him. If he was shocked at her reaction, he didn't show it. Instead, Jamie put his arms around her and held her close. He didn't say anything, neither of them did, and Phoebe found herself wishing she didn't have to let go. As surprising as it was to realise it, Jamie made her feel the way no one else, not even Eddie, ever had: safe.

'What am I going to tell Darcy when she wakes up?' Silent tears were streaming down Phoebe's cheeks as she stared up at Jamie, when she finally forced herself to pull away from him, and there was nothing she could do to stop them. She didn't need to explain to him what she meant, and that made it so much easier to allow her emotions to come out. 'She's still in bed because she was too excited to get to sleep until late last night. But the party starts in two hours, so I'm going to have to wake her up soon.'

'You've just got to keep telling her the truth, like you've been doing all along.' Jamie looked as though he'd barely slept himself. It had only been her determination not to confuse Darcy that had stopped her going over to his place every night, with her niece in tow. The last thing the little girl needed was to form any more attachments that might not last. If she started to see Jamie as anything more than her teacher or family friend, she could get hurt if whatever was going on between him and Phoebe ended as quickly as it had begun. She didn't need an 'uncle' who disappeared from her life as suddenly as her mother had.

'What's the truth, though? That's the problem; I don't even know where Lucy is, what she's thinking, or even if she's thinking at all any more. How long do I leave it before I tell Darcy that the likelihood is her mother is dead?' Phoebe's voice cracked on the last word, and it felt like another hairline fracture had appeared on her heart. She'd clung on to hope, with no real evidence that her sister was still alive. But whatever stories she tried to tell herself, or excuses she made, Lucy would never have missed Darcy's party; she wouldn't do that to her little girl. This was the day she'd been waiting for. The day when Lucy would come home, and they could work together to try and heal from everything their mother had done to them. But it hadn't happened, and the slow realisation that this meant it almost certainly never would wasn't just fracturing her heart, it was smashing it to pieces.

'I don't know, but whatever you need, I'm here for you as long as you want me to be. I just wish with all my heart that it hadn't come to this.' Jamie sounded almost as defeated as she felt.

'I asked Dolly how she helped the children cope, when the adoption was going through, and they had to say goodbye to the idea of living with their birth mother. She told me it was easier than what Darcy is facing, because they knew the outcome from the start. They explained to the children that their mother was too poorly to be able to care for them herself, and that the doctors couldn't fix the things that were wrong with her. Dolly said that worked okay until the contact visits stopped, after their mother's behaviour spiralled completely out of control, and she became much more violent and unpredictable. That's when the courts decided continuing contact wouldn't be in the children's best interests.'

'Those poor kids.' Jamie's grimaced. 'Did Dolly say how she handled that?'

'She told them that their mum had become even more poorly and that her illness meant she couldn't cope with the contact visits, but that it didn't mean she didn't love them. And that Dolly's family loved them very much, too. It amazes me how well the children have adjusted; I don't know how she did it.'

'Yes, you do, because you've done that with Darcy from the moment you arrived, whether you realise it or not.' Jamie held her gaze. 'Darcy knows how much you love her, and I've heard you talk to her about the things she and Lucy did together, and how much her mum loves her, even if she can't be here right now. So I know you'll find a way to do that today too.'

'I wish I didn't have to.' Hot tears were burning Phoebe's eyes again and no amount of trying to blink them away made any difference.

'I know you do; so do I.' Jamie brushed the tears away with this thumb, and she put her hand over his, holding it against her face, until she was finally ready to ask the question she already knew the answer to.

'I think I need to wake her up now, don't I? To give her a chance to process everything.' Phoebe looked up at him, more grateful than ever that he was there. He was the only person she'd been completely honest with about how difficult today was; she hadn't even admitted that to Scarlett or Dolly. He understood what it was like for her to have to face the prospect of talking to Darcy, with the very strong possibility that her mother would never be coming home. And she wouldn't have survived it without him. 'The party starts at eleven, it's already gone nine and the princesses will be here in about an hour and a half, to get Darcy ready before everyone else arrives. It doesn't feel like enough time for her to have to deal with all of this. I don't know, maybe I should cancel the party?'

'This day is going to be tough enough as it is, but a birthday with no party won't make any of it better. You can do this, and I promise that Darcy is going to be okay, as long as she's got you.'

'Thank you.' Swallowing hard, she leant into him again, wrestling with the idea of admitting just how much it meant to have him there too. In the end, as they so often did when Jamie was around, the words came out all by themselves. 'And I'll be okay too, as long as I've got you.'

'Like I promised you, I'll be around for as long as you want me to be.' The emotion in his voice was undeniable, and for the first time in days Phoebe's shoulders relaxed just a little bit. If Jamie believed she could get this right, then maybe she could, because she trusted him more than anyone else in her life right now.

* * *

'Is Mummy here?' They were the first words Darcy said, the moment she opened her eyes. Not a desire for presents, or excitement about the impending arrival of Elsa, but a simple request to see the one person who should have been there to greet her on the morning of her fourth birthday. And it broke Phoebe's heart.

'I'm so sorry, darling, she isn't.'

'But it's my birthday.' Darcy's bottom lip was trembling and the inevitable tears were already filling her eyes. All Phoebe could do was lift Norma up to sit on the end of Darcy's bed, and kneel down by the side of it to take hold of her niece's hands. The ache in Phoebe's chest was so powerful that she could barely speak. But she couldn't give in to her own feelings; she had to do this for Darcy.

'I know you were hoping Mummy would come back today and I was too.' Her head was throbbing with the effort of keeping her tone light, when she wanted to rail and scream alongside Darcy at the unfairness of it all. This was the hardest thing she'd ever had to do, but she had no choice. Lucy had trusted her to protect Darcy, the way the two of them had never been protected. And she was going to do that, no matter how badly she was hurting. She could survive anything, as long as Darcy was okay, and she didn't let Lucy down again. 'But the reason Mummy's not here isn't because she doesn't love you or doesn't want to spend your birthday with you. Mummy still loves you much more than anything else. Do you remember your party last year?'

Phoebe picked up the iPad she'd brought into the room, opening the album of photos that she'd downloaded from her sister's social media pages. 'Look, here's you with Mummy at your fairy party. She made all the wings for you and your friends from nursery school, out of pink tissue paper, and she baked the cake because she wanted the day to be perfect. Just like you.'

'But. Why. Can't. Mummy. Come. To. This. Party?' Darcy's words were interspersed by sobs, making her pause between words to take a shuddering breath, and Phoebe bit her lip so hard she could taste the blood. No child should have to go through this, and all the blame for it lay at the door of Darcy's own grandmother. Yet somehow, she couldn't let go of the last shreds of anger she felt towards Lucy, for allowing their mother to take her away from Darcy. She should have fought harder, just like Phoebe was fighting now. It wasn't fair to blame Lucy for any of it, but the tangle of anger and sadness wrapped up inside of her couldn't be separated nearly as neatly as she wished. It was just one more type of agony she never wanted Darcy to feel.

'I know she would have come if she could.' Phoebe put down the iPad, sat on the edge of the bed and pulled her niece onto her lap. 'But Mummy got very sad about some things and, even though she loves you more than the whole world, she needed to go away.'

Darcy didn't answer as her sobs began to intensify; all Phoebe could do was hold her. Sometimes words just weren't enough, and her niece needed to be able to express how she was feeling. Phoebe didn't want to shut off her emotions by talking, or trying to pretend it was all okay, when they both knew it wasn't, and her own tears fell silently into the little girl's hair. Gradually Darcy's sobbing started to subside and eventually she looked up at her aunt, an expression in her eyes that no four-year-old should ever have to wear.

'Is Mummy ever coming back?' As she spoke, Norma clambered into the tiny space between Darcy and Phoebe, nuzzling her face against the little girl's chest, and for a moment Phoebe couldn't even speak. It was the question she'd been dreading the most and she couldn't give a definite answer, not without risking a lie. She wouldn't do that to Darcy, so she had to say something that would be true no matter what happened with Lucy. Promising her niece a future where Phoebe would always be there for her suddenly felt like the only thing she could do. And nothing on earth would stop her doing that, whatever it took.

'I don't know, darling. I hope so. But even if Mummy can never come back, she'll always love you.' Phoebe stroked Darcy's tear-soaked hair away from her eyes. 'And I love you and so does Norma, and we'll always be here to take care of you. I promise.'

'Forever and ever?' Darcy wrapped her arms around Norma, clinging on to the little dog as if her life depended on it.

'Forever and ever. I know that won't stop you missing Mummy, and that's okay, because I miss her too. But we can still include her whenever we do something, by talking about her, and thinking about all the fun things we did with Mummy.' Phoebe was still stroking her niece's hair. 'She'd have loved to meet Elsa and Anna, wouldn't she? And she'd probably have wanted to dress up with you, too. She always loved dressing up when we were little.'

'What as?' For the first time there was a spark of something other than sadness in Darcy's eyes, and Phoebe managed a half-smile in response.

'We used to make our own costumes out of things we had in the house. There was a lovely white lacy tablecloth, and we used to take turns wearing that to make-believe we were princesses. But mostly your mummy liked pretending she was a pirate, and there was a black tie that belonged to our dad, which she used to make into an eye patch. She always had the best imagination, and she made games so much fun.'

'You're good at making games fun and you always look pretty, just like Elsa.' Darcy put her hand on top of Phoebe's, and a rush of overwhelming love washed over her. 'If I can't have Mummy, I'm happy I've got you.'

As the little girl spoke, Phoebe suddenly realised it was possible to feel intense joy and utter heartbreak all at the same time. She'd spent most of her life suppressing her emotions, but because of Darcy they were tumbling over one another to get out. 'And I'm the luckiest auntie in the world to have you, sweetheart. I love you so much.'

Phoebe barely got the words out before a sob caught in her throat. But it was okay to cry, Darcy had taught her that, and so much more than she'd ever have learnt if she hadn't come home to Appleberry. She just wished with all her heart that her sister's disappearance hadn't been the price she'd had to pay.

25

The arrival of Elsa and Anna had done wonders to cheer Darcy up, but every so often Phoebe would catch her staring into the distance. There was no doubt she was thinking about her mother, and Phoebe hated the fact that, at just four years old, her niece couldn't enjoy the party for what it was. She was surrounded by her friends, and she should just have been having fun. Phoebe and Lucy had never had birthday parties as children. It would have involved far too much mess and noise, and there'd have been absolutely nothing in it for their mother.

'You don't need friends; they always let you down in the end, anyway.' It was the snippy response Janet had always given whenever Phoebe or Lucy had asked if they could have someone over. As far as she was concerned, she'd been let down by everyone who'd ever tried to be her friend. When the reality was they'd seen her for who she was, and had ducked out of her life as quickly as possible. What she failed to see in all these broken friendships was that she was the common denominator.

Not being allowed to have friends over, the girls had developed a rich fantasy world, and had found the perfect place to stay out of their mother's way in the upstairs of their childhood home that had been converted from what had once been the loft. There were eaves running along both sides, meant as storage spaces. But since Janet wasn't remotely sentimental, there was nothing much kept there, and it provided the perfect place for the two girls to play dressing-up games with bits and pieces they'd managed to find, and to hang out with the group of imaginary friends they'd created together.

Darcy didn't need to hide somewhere, or to play in secret, and she didn't need to create a group of imaginary friends. And yet she was still shrouded in a blanket of sadness because of her grandmother.

'How are you doing?' Jamie came up beside Phoebe, who was watching when Darcy finally broke off from her trancelike state, and started laughing as Ava attempted an ambitious somersault on the bouncy castle.

'I'm okay. But I just still can't believe Lucy's not suddenly going to walk in.' Turning towards Jamie, she sighed. 'I know the likelihood is that can only mean one thing. But unless they find evidence of that, I don't think I'll ever really accept it.'

'I wish there was something that could give you the concrete proof you need, but—'

'The kids are having a great time!' Scarlett called out, cutting Jamie off, as she walked towards them, with Kate and Dolly just behind her. 'If you ever get bored of whatever it is you do with data, you could always think about becoming a kids' party planner.'

'I should probably be offended about the data comment, but the truth is, I have started to think about changing my job.' Phoebe had decided that saying it loud constituted a commitment. 'I've managed okay working from home. But I don't know... since I started taking care of Darcy, it suddenly feels like what I do is meaningless in comparison. So I've been thinking about maybe re-training to be a counsellor, for kids who've been through the same kind of stuff as me and Lucy have.'

'Wow, I had no idea.' Jamie was staring at her as if he was seeing her for the first time, which was exactly how she'd felt looking at herself in the mirror after her counselling session.

'Who'd have thought it from me? The woman who said coun-selling didn't work.' Phoebe gave him a wry smile. It was a huge turnaround, she knew that, but she was in a very different place to where she'd been when she'd had counselling before. Back then she'd wanted it to fix her problems with her mother, and now she knew nothing could do that. Even in a thirty-minute initial consul-tation, her new therapist had helped her see that she'd never be able to change her mother's behaviour. The only thing she had power over was changing how she allowed it to make her feel. She wanted to help children going through something similar to realise that long before they got into their thirties. 'I had a bit of an epiphany after my therapy session, and it feels like what I'm meant to do. It's almost as if it's the reason why I had to go through all of this. If I'm able to support children in the toughest times, it will mean some good comes out of everything Lucy and I had to endure. It'll be the start of a whole new life for me, but it feels right.'

'You'd certainly have the empathy and understanding for that.' Dolly's tone was encouraging. 'And God knows it's needed. I've seen that only too clearly with my four.'

'Will you have to go through more counselling yourself first?' Scarlett was clearly struggling to process Phoebe's change of heart, and she could hardly blame her.

'Quite extensively from what I understand, but I want to set a good example for Darcy, too. If she gets support now, it could have so much more of an impact.' Phoebe shook her head. 'It might be ridiculous, thinking I can do this, but maybe this time I'll be ready to open up enough for it to have more chance of helping.'

'For what it's worth, I'd much rather have a counsellor who understands what I'm going through, and who knows that not everyone finds it easy to embrace the process.' Kate pushed her sunglasses up into her hair as she spoke, looking Phoebe straight in the eye. 'And when I had counselling, it took three goes before I found a therapist I could click with. Maybe that's what you needed, just to keep going until you found the right person.'

'Being here has helped me see that.' Phoebe caught Jamie's eye, and she wanted to tell him how much he'd helped with everything, but she didn't want to say it in front of the others. In any case, she owed them *all* a debt of thanks, and now wasn't the right time to single anyone out. 'You've all been brilliant since I came back to Appleberry.'

'It's been so lovely having you home.' Scarlett slipped an arm around her waist and squeezed, but Phoebe didn't even flinch. Not so long ago, her instinctive reaction would have been to shy away from physical affection, but so much had altered in less than two months. Back then she'd been determined to secure the big contracts for her company, and the idea of becoming a parent would have horrified her. Even when she'd first got to Appleberry, she'd had some certainties, the first of which was that she'd be leaving again as soon as she could, but the biggest certainty was that Lucy would eventually come home. Now all of that had changed.

'I'd never have believed it, but Appleberry is really starting to feel like home again and—'

'Phoebe!' Her mother's all-too-familiar voice boomed across the garden, and the muscles in her jaw clenched in response to Janet shouting her name. Her mother hadn't been invited, and her arrival was almost certainly going to change the atmosphere for the worse, even if for once in her life she didn't make the kind of scene she was almost sure to make. Darcy deserved the perfect day. Phoebe hated that Janet was still a part of their lives and that she could lay any claim at all over Darcy. It was impossible to believe there was any link between the sweet little girl that Phoebe loved so ferociously it scared her, and the woman who made her flesh crawl just by being near her. Seconds later, Janet had reached her side.

'What are you doing here? I agreed with Dad that it would be better for you to see Darcy and give her your gift on her own. There's too much else going on for her today, and I knew you'd want her to be able to focus.' Even as Phoebe fought to keep an even tone, she knew she was wasting her time. Any attempts to placate Janet seemed to have the opposite effect, and there was no point trying to divert her from causing a scene, because that's exactly what she wanted.

'Your father's told me what you said, but I thought the child should have her gift on her birthday. After all, what's the point of giving a gift late, and this one is *really* special.' Janet was clutching a bag from a very expensive jeweller. Whatever she'd bought in a store like that, it wouldn't be appropriate for a four-year-old, and Janet was wrinkling her nose as she looked at Phoebe again. 'I suspect the real reason you didn't invite me to my only granddaughter's birthday was because you didn't want my gift to overshadow whatever bit of plastic tat you decided to get her.'

'I got Darcy a dolls' house, which was exactly what she asked for.' Phoebe hated the fact she was trying to justify herself to her mother, but years of programming were hard to undo.

'Why don't we go and get you a drink, Mrs Spencer? It is a party after all.' Scarlett was smiling, although the tension in her friend's face mirrored Phoebe's own. She couldn't have asked for a better friend, but Scarlett was still a complete amateur when it came to dealing with Janet.

'I'll have a vodka and tonic. A double, with two cubes of ice, no more, no less. But I'm not going anywhere until I've seen my granddaughter.' Janet flicked her hand towards Scarlett, dismissing her like a servant.

'Where's Dad?' Phoebe had expected to see her father trailing along behind his wife, the way he always did, but there was no sign of him.

'On your side, apparently.' Janet sniffed, and Phoebe was too shocked to even respond. It was something she'd wanted to believe her entire life, but her father had only ever shown support for either of his daughters when there was no chance of his wife witnessing it. So she had no idea how to feel and she wasn't even sure she could believe it. After all, her mother was capable of twisting everything. 'Now are you going to get *my* granddaughter, or do I have to go over there myself?'

'She's playing with her friends at the moment, and everyone has left their gifts in the kitchen. Darcy's going to open them after the party, so we can make a list of who to thank.' Phoebe held her mother's gaze, daring her to make some comment about how well brought-up she must be, to encourage Darcy to do that.

There'd never been piles of gifts for Phoebe and Lucy, and no risk of losing track of who'd sent them. She wasn't sure whether it was because her mother had driven all their relatives away, and that she went through friends quicker than other people got through teabags, or whether there had been gifts, and Janet had just decided to keep them from her girls. After all, there was no such thing as a special day unless it was all about her. One thing she had done was to start playing them off against one another from an early age, by providing an extravagant Christmas gift for the daughter who'd pleased her most, and buying nothing for the other. Janet was a purveyor of evil, and Phoebe wasn't going to let Darcy fall victim to it.

'I want her to have my present now!' Janet's eyes flashed and she grabbed a long, slim box, covered in midnight-blue velvet, from the gift bag she'd been holding.

'Phoebe has already explained why it's best to wait until later to give Darcy her present.' Jamie might have sounded amicable, but there was a muscle going in his cheek, even before Janet moved uncomfortably close to him.

'Jamie, the knight in shining armour of the Spencer girls. What's it like to have both of my daughters following you around like lovesick puppies?' Janet put one of her hands on his shoulder, the other still clutching the velvet box. 'I suppose you feel sorry for Phoebe. But I must confess I did wonder if there was something going on between you and Lucy. She was always the pretty one, after all, so much more like me than Phoebe ever was.'

'Why are you talking about Lucy in the past tense?' Whatever Jamie had been about to say, Phoebe didn't give him the chance. She didn't care about her mother's game-playing, or her blatant attempts to put Phoebe down. All she cared about was the fact her mother was so casually discussing Lucy as though there was no doubt that she was dead and gone.

'Oh, for Christ's sake, grow up! She's not coming back.' As Janet began to shout, Phoebe was vaguely aware of everyone else in the garden falling silent. And the last thing she wanted was to allow her mother to ruin Darcy's birthday.

'Let's just talk about this later. If I get Darcy now, you can give her the gift, and I'll come and see you and Dad to discuss everything another day.' Backing down had become a way of life when she'd still lived at home, and it was one of the reasons she'd had to get away from Appleberry altogether. She'd stopped wanting to keep the peace with her mother a long time ago, but this wasn't about her. Keeping it now was all for Darcy.

'There's nothing to discuss; you've both been a pair of attention-seekers since the moment you were born. Lucy threatened to kill herself every other week, and once you'd slept with everyone in Appleberry, you decided to do the same with half of London. You'd do anything to get noticed, and this time Lucy has gone the whole hog.' There were veins bulging in Janet's neck and everyone, including the children, were now looking in their direction. Any chance Phoebe had had of containing the situation for Darcy's sake was long gone, as Janet ripped a diamond-studded bracelet out of the velvet case and threw it towards Phoebe. 'You even had to ruin this for me, didn't you? I wanted to give my granddaughter something beautiful, so everyone can see how much I love her. But, no, you had to make it all about you. Are you satisfied?'

For a moment Phoebe couldn't answer, even as hands reached out to comfort her, and several voices were raised in her defence. But this was her battle to fight, and it was far too late to protect Darcy from having to witness it. She was done, exhausted from trying to keep some kind of relationship going with her parents. It was just about manageable from a distance, and even then it had been because deep down she loved her father, despite all his failings. What she felt towards her mother had mostly been fear. There'd been love for far longer than there should have been, and a determination to try and make her mother love her back, but all she got in return was more poison. She wasn't even sad any more. That white-hot anger was back. At times in the past she'd lacked the courage to act on her feelings, afraid of the reaction it would provoke. But looking at Darcy, she knew she could do anything. And when she finally found her voice, it was icily calm. 'Get out and don't ever come back. The last person Darcy needs around is you. You've already ruined mine and Lucy's lives, and Dad's too. But I'm not going to let you ruin another one.'

Picking up the bracelet as Janet spluttered a response, she thrust it against her mother's chest and repeated her instruction, much more loudly this time. '*Get out!*'

'I knew you'd do this.' Her mother spat the words at her. 'Try to turn my granddaughter against me, just like you did with your sister and like you're trying to do with your father. It's always all about you! But mark my words, I'll make sure everyone knows what you did. Everyone.'

With those final barbs, her mother turned on her heel, and Phoebe's whole body seemed to slump. Tears were streaming down her face, and she desperately tried to wipe them away so she could see her niece through the blur and tell her it was all okay, and that she couldn't allow her horrible excuse for a grandmother to ruin the party. Then Jamie put his arms around her.

'You're okay, it's going to be all right. Let's take Darcy inside for few minutes, while Scarlett gets the party back on track. Then we can all come back outside with the cake and forget this ever happened.'

Feeling like a limp rag doll, it was only too easy to let Jamie take over. It was a relief to be away from the rest of the guests, who were probably trying to work out what the hell they'd just witnessed.

'I'm so sorry, my darling.' Phoebe scooped Darcy into her arms the moment they were inside. 'You know I told you before that Nanny has poorly things in her head, and today was really bad. But she's gone now, and you don't need to worry about it any more. This is your party and it's all about having fun.'

'Is Mummy's head poorly like Nanny's?' Darcy had the most soulful eyes Phoebe had ever seen, and it would have been impossible to lie to her, even if she'd wanted to.

'No, darling, but because of some of the things Nanny does, it made your mummy really sad. That made her poorly in a different way, so she had to go away and she couldn't take you with her. Even though I know she really wanted to.'

'Will Nanny make you poorly too?' Darcy's eyes widened even further.

'No, darling. I'm never going to leave you.'

'What if I get poorly like Nanny, or Mummy?'

'You won't, sweetheart, but if you do ever get poorly, I'll be here to take care of you and make sure you get better.' Phoebe couldn't see Jamie, but she felt his hand on her arm and knew he'd read her mind. *If only she'd been there to help Lucy get better.* She understood what his gesture meant, and what he'd have said in response; there was nothing she could have done differently and going over the past wouldn't change anything. But none of that stopped the guilt that would probably always be there from thudding inside her, as ever-present in the background as her heartbeat. All she could do was focus on her niece and make sure there was no chance of history repeating itself.

'I love you, Auntie Phoebe.' Darcy squeezed her tightly for a moment. 'Can we have cake now that Nanny's gone? I really want to eat the pink icing!'

'Of course we can, darling.' Pulling away from her niece, Phoebe's smile felt genuine for the first time that day. And she turned to mouth a silent *thank you* to Jamie. Darcy was an amazing, resilient, joyous little girl. Even if the worst happened, and Lucy never came back, she was going to be okay. And for the first time in a very long time, Phoebe was starting to believe she might find a way to be okay too. But that could only happen for either of them if she cut her mother off completely. She was more ready to do that than she'd ever been before; she just needed to steel herself for the fight.

* * *

The rest of the party had gone like a dream. Scarlett and the others had asked Phoebe if she was okay, but no one else had even mentioned it. The other children had barely seemed to register what had happened, and had dismissed Janet as 'the shouty lady' and gone back to enjoying the party.

The cake was a hit too and Darcy had declared that she loved each and every one of her presents, from a simple, fluffy pink pencil case, to the Princess Elsa bike that Scarlett, Kate and Dolly had so generously bought between them. If there was the opposite of a narcissist, then Darcy was it. She was never going to end up like her grandmother.

Scarlett, Dolly and Kate had also offered to stay behind and tidy up, but Phoebe had told them she could cope, and that they needed to get their own children home. Despite her protests, Jamie insisted on being part of the clean-up crew and had made the point he had nothing to rush home for, especially as Fisher had accompanied him to the party.

It was late afternoon by the time Phoebe took the last bag of rubbish out to the bin. She hadn't had time to check the mail and had half-considered leaving it until Monday. It was only because she was walking past on her way back from taking the rubbish out that she decided to stop at the little post box outside Lucy's cottage and reach inside. When she pulled out a letter addressed to her, Phoebe's hands started to shake. The only post that had ever been sent to her direct to Lucy's address was the letter signed in her sister's name. Ripping the envelope open, she took out the single sheet. It was typed, just like before, with only Lucy's signature appearing to be in her distinctive handwriting.

My dearest Phoebe,

I know you'll have been hoping that I'd come home for Darcy's birthday, but when I made the decision to end the life I couldn't bear to live any more, I knew I was doing something that couldn't be undone and that I wouldn't be there today. That's why I wanted to make sure you got this letter.

I thought about what it would be like for both of you without me there, and I know it will be tough. But the thought of what life would be like for me if I didn't go through with my plan, was unbearable and I knew I couldn't stay, not even for you and Darcy.

I've wondered for a long time how to find a way to reach you, how to do something to repay all the kindness you showed me when we were young, before Janet drove a wedge between us, and we stopped being honest with each other.

I love Darcy with all my heart, but I can't be what she needs and, the truth is, she can't be what I need either. Nothing can fix what's broken inside me, not even my darling girl, and I didn't want to end up breaking her too. That's when I realised I only had one choice...

Some people might think I'm being selfish, maybe even immoral, by choosing to end my life. But they've never walked a mile in our shoes, have they?

I hope you don't think those things about me. But, in the end, it doesn't matter. As long as you and Darcy have each other, I know you'll be okay.

I'm sorry that I didn't get the chance to say goodbye to either of you properly, or tell you just how much I love you, but I know that deep down you both already know that.

So, miss me if you must, and grieve for what could have been. Just don't forget about all the good things you've got, most of all Darcy, and be happy about that. I need you to know that, as hard as my decision was, I'm happy too, because I'm leaving my two favourite people together.

All my love, until the next life, Lucy-Lu xx

The words were little more than a blur by the time Phoebe reached the end of the letter. She didn't need a handwriting analyst to tell her whether or not this letter really was from Lucy, because she could almost hear her sister saying the words as she read them. Despite the pain, a tiny spark of hope had ignited in her chest, too. For all Lucy's talk about ending her life, the letter turning up meant there was a chance she might still be alive. After all, she had to have been when she posted it. And maybe, just maybe, it still wasn't too late.

26

___

Dropping Darcy off for her first half-day at school in the second week of September, just two days after her fourth birthday, would probably have been impossible for Phoebe if Scarlett hadn't been there to take the little girl's hand. It wasn't that Darcy had struggled, but it was another huge milestone that Lucy should have been there to witness and Phoebe was grateful for all the support.

Darcy looked so tiny in the uniform her mother had bought her, which had clearly been purchased with the idea of growing room in mind. One of the other parents had a stack of envelopes she was handing out, to invite the children starting Reception to her son's birthday party later that week. He'd be turning five and was almost a whole year older, and half a head taller, than Darcy. It was all Phoebe could do not to pick her niece up and take her straight back home again, where surely she had to stay for at least a good while longer.

'I'm not ready for this.' Phoebe looked at Dolly, trying and failing to blink back tears as they walked away from the classroom, leaving their babies behind. She'd cried more in the past two months than the entire two decades before. Darcy had opened up the floodgates and now she had no idea how to close them again.

'You never will be. I've been a soggy mess with all of mine.' Dolly gave her a watery smile. 'The only known cure is tea and cake. Lots of it. Do you fancy coming back to mine, to drown our sorrows with Twinings and Victoria sponge?'

'Absolutely.' To her surprise, Phoebe genuinely couldn't think of anything she'd rather do. If anyone had told her a couple of months beforehand that she'd move back to Appleberry and form close friendships with the school-run mums, she'd never have believed them. But Darcy had changed her so much and, with Lucy still missing, she'd probably never go back to any aspect of the life she'd had before. And the truth was, she wouldn't have wanted to, even if her sister was waiting for her the moment she got home.

* * *

Phoebe had been back at the cottage for less than half an hour when Bradley's number flashed up on her phone.

'Have you found any of the people Lucy was in contact with from the forum? Or worked out where the letter came from?' Just like the last time he'd called, she didn't give Bradley a chance to waste any time on niceties. Every time her phone had pinged since she'd sent him a message about the second letter, she'd prayed for it to be news from him, and that they might finally be able to solve the mystery of Lucy's disappearance, even if they couldn't bring her home. She'd sent Bradley a copy of the letter and a photograph of the envelope. There was no discernible postmark this time, but because the postage was pre-paid there was a QR code. That had to make it traceable.

'Gerry went into her local station yesterday, and spoke to the duty sergeant there. Two of our officers are on the way up to Scotland now to interview her.'

'Gerry? Does she know where Lucy is? If she's that far north, it would be a great place for Lucy to hide out; no one would know her up there.' Hope surged through Phoebe's veins, her whole body seeming to pulse. She was scared too, about what the police wanting to interview Gerry might mean. She'd never really believed that someone had harmed Lucy; all the damage had been done to her sister long before she'd left Appleberry. But suddenly Phoebe wasn't so sure, and just the idea of it made her shudder.

'I really think it would be better if we could discuss all of this face to face, and I'll know a lot more once my colleagues have spoken to Gerry.' There was a false brightness in Bradley's voice, and if Phoebe had to channel the inner Janet Spencer, then that's what she'd do.

'Okay, I'm going to repeat myself slowly: does she know where Lucy is?'

'Look, it's early days, and my colleagues really need to verify what she told the officers at her local station.'

'Just tell me what she said. *Please*.' Phoebe clearly couldn't rival her mother's ability to demand what she wanted, but she could beg, and she'd do whatever it took to get any kind of answer.

'From everything Gerry has said so far, our original view remains the same.' Bradley did the throat-clearing thing he always seemed to do before bad news, and Phoebe held her breath. 'I'm so sorry, but it really does look as though Lucy had every intention of going through with the plan she'd made to take her own life.'

'No!' The force of her denial surprised even Phoebe, but she wasn't going to let the police just accept this woman's word and call off the search as a result. As much as she'd tried to process the prospect of Lucy never coming home, and accept she might really be dead, now Bradley was telling her that was what had happened, she couldn't believe it. Before it had been an almost abstract idea, one she thought she could come to terms with, but the reality was devastating. Her baby sister couldn't be gone, and Darcy couldn't really have lost her mother, not like this. She'd tried so hard to convince herself that the little girl would be okay whatever happened, but how could she be without Lucy? How could either of them ever be okay again?

'I'm so sorry, Phoebe, I know this is incredibly hard to hear.'

'Lucy *can't* be dead. She sent me the letter. You were looking into it; you were going to find her. She's not dead – she can't be.'

'We know how the letters got to you. I can't say any more right now, but there's an explanation for why you received them long after Lucy's disappearance. As soon as my colleagues have interviewed Gerry, and taken the necessary statements, I promise I'll tell you everything. But I shouldn't even have said this much. If there's a case for Gerry or anyone else involved to answer, me saying any more right now could jeopardise that.'

'None of that is going to bring Lucy back, though, is it? And what if she is still alive? If you keep delaying like this, we might have lost our last chance of bringing her home. For God's sake, help me! Why won't you help me find her?' The blood seemed to alternate between rushing to Phoebe's feet, then back up to her head, and bile was rising in her throat. She'd been trying to stay in control for so long, to hold it together for Darcy, but now she was spiralling. She was desperate for the police to do something, not to give up, but she felt completely powerless. Panic was making her breathe so hard she was in danger of hyperventilating. If she couldn't make them listen to her and keep searching for Lucy, she'd have let Darcy down in the worst possible way. Her heart was breaking for Lucy, for herself, and most of all for her niece. There had to be something she could do to turn this around. 'It's about money, isn't it? I'll find the money somehow, just please, don't give up.'

'It's got nothing to do with money; any decisions we make are based on the evidence. But I'm coming to see you right now. You're worrying the life out of me, Phoebe, and I was stupid to do this over the phone. I should have waited until after my colleagues had got the statement.' There was an obvious note of panic in Bradley's voice, but Phoebe didn't care how worried he was or if he'd risked his career just to try and keep her in the loop. She had to make him listen.

'Let me speak to Gerry; I need to hear what she has to say. And right now. Not after your officers have taken all day to get up to Scotland.'

'I'll be at your place within an hour, Phoebe. We can talk about it then. Just promise me you'll be there, and that you won't do anything stupid in the meantime.'

'Like kill myself?' Phoebe's tone was shrill enough for Norma take cover in the corner of the room, but she couldn't even slow her breathing down, let alone regain control of her voice.

'Please, Phoebe, don't talk like that. Is there someone who can come and sit with you? I'm really worried about you.'

'I'm going to talk to Jamie next door.' She was already halfway down the hallway, desperate to get to the one person who would understand her reaction.

'Lucy's friend? That's a good idea.' Bradley sounded relieved, but Phoebe hardly even recognised his description of Jamie. He might just have been a friend of Lucy's to her once upon a time, but he was so much more than that now. And he was the only person she wanted to see.

* * *

Jamie picked up the phone to message Phoebe to ask how Darcy had been when she'd dropped her off at school, but at that exact moment, a message came through.

> Hi Jamie. It's Gerry. I've been to the police this morning, as promised, and told them everything. The officers who've been working on Lucy's case are coming up to interview me later. You can tell Phoebe whatever she needs to know now. Thank you so much for not saying anything sooner. I don't think you'll ever know how much that meant to me, but me and my children are safe because of you.

He was still staring at the text, wondering whether or not to reply, when the frantic hammering on his front door started. Jamie had no idea exactly what Gerry had said to the police, but there was a good chance she'd told them just how much Jamie had known. So, he was half expecting to see a police officer as he opened the door, but when he realised it was Phoebe, his heart sank even further. The only reason she'd have come flying over to his place, the way she had, was if the police had passed on what Gerry had told them. She was going to hate him, and he deserved it.

'Phoebe, I'm so sorry, I—' Even if she hadn't pushed past him, cutting his apology off mid-flow, he wasn't sure how he'd have known how to finish the sentence. There was nothing he could say that would excuse what he'd done. But she'd already gone through to the kitchen, probably to find something to throw at his head, and all he could do was follow her.

'Gerry went to the police. To tell them she knew something about what's happened to Lucy.' Phoebe was pacing up and down. She hadn't even looked in his direction yet, and he was dreading the moment when she did, and he had to see the look of loathing in her eyes.

'Did they tell you anything?'

'They said all the evidence points to Lucy ending her own life. Can you believe that? They've taken the word of a woman who befriended my sister when she was at her most vulnerable. I can't bear it, Jamie, I can't.' Phoebe had finally stopped pacing, and her eyes were red and swollen when she looked towards him. 'Nobody cares about Lucy. They want the easy answer, and they want her to be dead, because then they can stop looking.'

'I care. About Lucy, and Darcy, and most of all about you.' He was still trying to work out why she hadn't come at him for not telling her about finding Gerry. But maybe she hadn't told the police that Jamie knew about the letter. She'd told him how grateful she was for his help, so there was a chance she'd decided to repay that by keeping a secret for him this time around.

'I know you do, but we're not going to be able to stop them ending the search if that's what they decide.' Phoebe finally walked towards him, but instead of lashing out, she dropped her head onto his chest. 'Bradley wouldn't even listen when I said that Lucy's latest letter might mean she's still alive. As far as he was concerned, what Gerry told the police about the letters explained it all. What the hell am I going to do?'

Jamie felt as though he'd been punched in the gut. The guilt had been killing him for weeks, but now it felt as if he was about to lose everything. He could have told Phoebe about Gerry's involvement in the letters, and stopped her clinging on to the hope that was going to make the reality all the more crushing once it was gone. He deserved all the pain that was coming his way, and losing Phoebe and Darcy was going to hurt more than anything else he could imagine. But he wanted to try and comfort her, while she still let him anywhere near her. 'As hard as it must be to believe, I really don't think the police would close the case without evidence to support Gerry's story.' He stroked her back, wishing he could find a way to take away some of her agony. 'The fact that Lucy gave Gerry her letters to pass on to you, suggests she wouldn't be around to do it herself. But I really wish I didn't think the police were right.'

'What do you mean, Lucy gave Gerry the letters to pass on to me?' Phoebe leapt away from him like she'd been burnt, her eyes so wide the whites were visible all the way around her irises. It was as if Jamie had been plunged underwater, and he couldn't unjumble his thoughts.

'You said Gerry explained to the police about the letters.' He was desperately trying to recall her exact words, but it had all gone fuzzy.

'All I said was that Gerry had explained the letters to the police. I didn't say anything about her posting them, because Bradley didn't tell me that.' Phoebe was visibly shaking now, her mouth in a grim line as she looked at him. 'So, the question is, why the hell would you say that? Unless you already knew about it? Did the police speak to you too, to try and get you to convince me to accept their conclusions?'

For a split second he considered telling her that they had. It would be a get-out-of-jail-free card, but it would only delay the inevitable. When she asked the police why they'd given more details to one of Lucy's neighbours than they'd given to her own family, Phoebe would discover the truth. And, if it was possible, she'd feel even more betrayed than she did already. He couldn't put it off any longer, but when he said what he needed to say, everything was going to change, and there'd be no going back. Every fibre in his body was screaming at him not to do it, just to keep quiet and hope for the best, but he loved Phoebe and lying to her had been the hardest thing he'd ever done. Until now. 'No, the reason I know is because Gerry told me.'

'After she spoke to the police?' It was as if Phoebe was almost as desperate as he was to come up with an explanation for how he knew about the letters. But he'd lied to her for far too long as it was.

'No, I tracked her down and she agreed to meet me.'

'You can't have done. You said you were still looking.' Phoebe's mouth dropped open. Her face and neck had gone red and she kept shaking her head, as if she couldn't even process what he'd said. 'Please don't tell me you've been lying to me.'

'I couldn't tell you. There were things going on in Gerry's life, the same things she spoke to me about in counselling, and she needed more time to make sure she and her children were safe. Telling you sooner wouldn't have made any difference to finding Lucy, but I still really wanted to tell you. I even texted you on the day I went to meet Gerry, asking you to come, but it didn't go through and I took it as a sign that keeping quiet, for just a bit longer, was the right thing to do.' It sounded like a pathetic excuse, even to Jamie, and Phoebe was still staring at him, her mouth opening and closing, without her making a sound.

'Even if I choose to believe that you tried to text me, or that you didn't want to tell me about Gerry to keep her safe, in what fucking universe do you think it was a good idea to keep that she was behind Lucy's letters from the police for so long?' Phoebe's face was so twisted by anger, she was almost unrecognisable. He'd never heard her swear like that before, and her anger was palpable.

'It's complicated and I can't tell you all of it, but we decided it was the best way to protect Gerry from—'

'Don't you fucking dare!' Phoebe's face was just inches from his when she screamed her response, but he couldn't blame her for any of it. 'You're going to stand there and tell me you were protecting an ex-client, when Lucy was missing, and Darcy was desperate to see her mum again? I trusted you, I told you everything, and you saw what getting Lucy's letters did to me. I bet you thought it was hilarious.'

'Oh God, Phoebe, you must know that isn't true. I'm so sorry, but I really was trying to do the right thing. I just made the worst mess of it that I possibly could.'

'I don't give a shit what excuses you want to try and make to me, or yourself. I don't even know who you are any more, but it's definitely not who you pretended to be. I let you in and you abused my trust, but I'm done with being abused; I've had it all my life. I should have known better than to trust anyone, because it always ends in me being taken for an idiot. But I never thought you'd do that; I thought you were different. So maybe I am an idiot after all. If you even *think* about coming near me or Darcy again, you'll be the one whose body they're looking for.'

The way Phoebe looked at him before she turned to leave left him in no doubt she meant every word. She looked capable of sticking a knife through his chest, and it would almost have been a relief if she had. He'd messed everything up and now there was no road back.

27

Phoebe had years of practice at suppressing rage. She'd lost count of the times she'd wanted to physically lash out at her mother, and sometimes herself, after they'd got into yet another argument. But the anger she currently felt towards Jamie was completely different; it was far more painful, for a start. She'd grown to accept that her mother lied like other people breathed in and out, and that she had no concept of empathy. As much as her behaviour frustrated and upset Phoebe, it was never unexpected. But she'd trusted Jamie, and truly believed he was the only one who really understood what Lucy's disappearance had done to her.

Only it turned out that Jamie knew far more about it than Phoebe had ever realised. He'd comforted her when she'd confided how hard it was not knowing what had happened, and when she'd told him how desperate she was for news of Gerry. He'd let Phoebe cry on his shoulder, and, worse than that, allowed her to get close to him in a way she hadn't been close to anyone in years, and it made her feel dirty.

He'd lied to her face about Gerry, and now she had no idea what else he'd lied about. Maybe he'd manipulated Lucy in the same way, and let her get close to him, before she too had discovered what he was really like. That could have been the thing that drove her over the edge in the end. Like Phoebe, Lucy's ability to trust new people had been severely impaired by their upbringing. It took a hell of a lot for either of them to let down their guard. If Lucy had discovered that the person she'd allowed into her life was every bit as manipulative and self-serving as their mother, it would have hurt like hell. Phoebe had no doubt a revelation like that would have devastated her sister, because it had done exactly the same to her.

By the time she got back to Lucy's place, and slammed the door so hard it made the windows rattle, she'd already thought of several ways to make him pay. The first thing she was going to do when Bradley showed up for their meeting was tell him exactly what Jamie had done, if he didn't know already. There had to be a case for wasting police time by not telling them Gerry had posted the letters, if nothing else.

He was a lying, manipulating piece of shit. They were the words she'd sent Jamie in reply when he'd texted begging for her forgiveness, almost the moment she was back inside Lucy's cottage. Thank God Scarlett was taking Darcy straight from school and bringing her home later, because Phoebe didn't think she could maintain the pretence of being okay, not even for her niece.

* * *

'Phoebe, it's good to see you again.' Bradley looked over her shoulder as she opened the door to him half an hour after she'd shot out of Jamie's place like his house was on fire. She'd already poured herself a large glass of wine and knocked it back in two swigs to steady her nerves, but it hadn't done anything to stop her shaking from a mixture of shock and anger. Solo daytime drinking, to obliterate reality, was yet another habit of her mother's she didn't want to get into. But just for today she needed to take off the edge, otherwise she might end up doing something really stupid. 'Are your parents here with you?'

'No. I told them you were coming, but they were too busy with other stuff, apparently.' Phoebe shrugged. It was a lie, but no doubt easy for Bradley to believe, based upon his knowledge of the Spencers.

'Well, I'm sure you'll do an excellent job of passing on the information, as always.' The young police constable smiled, but she didn't even try to mirror him. She'd laughed and smiled with Jamie, allowing time spent with him to lift her out of the misery of missing Lucy. But none of it had been real. 'Can I come in?'

'Sure.' She stood back and let him through, before turning to follow him down towards the kitchen. 'Do you want to sit down?'

'Thank you.' Bradley perched on the edge of the chair that Norma had only recently vacated. 'Before I say anything else, I just want to apologise again for the error of judgement I made in not coming straight round to tell you about the update on Gerry.'

'It doesn't matter and I'm not going to say anything to anyone that might cost you your job. As long as you do what needs to be done from now on.' Phoebe stood facing him. She had no intention of sitting down; for once she wanted to feel like the one with the power. And if she had to use blackmail to make sure Jamie got what was coming to him, she wasn't above doing it.

'I'm more worried about you than any trouble I might get into. You don't seem your usual self at all.' Bradley knitted his eyebrows together as he spoke. 'I thought Lucy's friend was going to come and sit with you?'

'Lucy's *friend*?' Phoebe roared the last word, sending Norma straight back to her bed in the corner of the kitchen, and making Bradley get to his feet. 'Jamie knew that Gerry was sending me the letters and where to find her, which means he's been aware, for all that time, that my sister is almost certainly dead. What I want to know is what the hell you're going to do about it?'

'He told you Gerry was behind the letters?' Bradley furrowed his brow as Phoebe nodded. 'I wanted to wait to tell you all of this until my colleagues had taken her statement, but I don't suppose it matters now. When Gerry spoke to the officers in Scotland, she told them Lucy had sent her an envelope, containing a note for her, and two letters to pass on to you. She wanted to come forward straight away, but she couldn't.'

'And you believe she's telling the truth, not just trying to save her own skin?' The white-hot anger was bubbling up again, and Phoebe had to ball her hands into fists to stop herself from punching something.

'Her own life and those of her children were in danger at the time she got Lucy's letters. The officers she spoke to were pretty confident there's compelling evidence of that.' Bradley grimaced. 'I shouldn't be telling you any of this, but I really need you to understand why we've approached this the way we have, and why Jamie did too. I think it's important you know the whole story. Gerry was in an abusive, coercive marriage, which she's only just got out of, and she begged Jamie not to say anything until the charity she was working with could get them to a place of safety. All of that was complicated by the fact that he was previously her counsellor, and there were things he couldn't tell you or anyone else about, because of that.'

'I thought none of that mattered if someone was in danger?' Phoebe spoke through gritted teeth; the last thing she wanted to hear was Bradley defending Jamie. There was no excuse on earth that would be enough to justify what he'd done. She was certain of it.

'It doesn't, and when that risk came to light, Jamie acted

entirely appropriately. Gerry said that she and Lucy originally met on an online forum and ended up making a suicide pact. According to her, it's only the fact that Jamie offered them so much support that she's still alive. He also did everything he could to help Lucy as well, and made her GP and the authorities aware of the fact that she'd been considering suicide. Gerry was convinced that Jamie had managed to turn things around for Lucy too, and Lucy promised she'd come off the forums. We know from our investigations that was true, but that for some reason she went back on them not long before she disappeared. But she kept up the pretence of being okay whenever Gerry spoke to her, and it sounds like she did the same thing with everyone else, including Jamie. Gerry had given Jamie fake contact details, but somehow he still managed to find her. He tried to persuade her to come forward, to us and to you, but she told him it could put her and her children at risk. So he agreed to wait until her husband was arrested and charged, and she was in a place of safety.'

'Are you going to arrest them too? Surely what they did has to constitute obstructing an enquiry, or something?' Some of the fire that had felt as if it might burst out of Phoebe already seemed to be fizzling out. If what Gerry had told the police so far was true, Jamie had been in an impossible position. Part of her desperately wanted to believe it, but there was another part that was more at home with the idea that Jamie had let her down. Almost everyone else in her life had, after all. Either way, she was certain she'd never be able to trust him again. Blaming him was also easier than listening to the other voice in her head that was clamouring to be heard, telling her that Jamie had done far more to support her sister than she ever had. But her guilt was so adept at twisting the knife, and if she didn't blame Jamie for the fact that it was almost certainly too late to save Lucy from the damage her mother had done, then she had nowhere to look but herself.

'We've got no plans to make any arrests in relation to Lucy's disappearance at this stage. My colleagues will be questioning Gerry further, and I'm sure we'll want to talk to Jamie again.'

'So that's it?'

'For now.' Bradley shot her a sympathetic look, but it didn't help. Nothing could. After he left, five minutes later, all Phoebe could do was curl up in the foetal position on the sofa, with Norma tucked into the gap between her chest and her legs. If everything Gerry had said was true, it wasn't her fault Lucy had chosen to take her own life, and it definitely wasn't Jamie's. But none of that did anything to change the fact that her sister was gone, and that she'd almost certainly never be coming back.

* * *

In the days that followed Gerry's revelations, Phoebe had thought about going to see Jamie a hundred times. She blocked and deleted his number so that she wasn't tempted to contact him in a moment of weakness. When Bradley had telephoned her two days after his visit to confirm that his colleagues' investigations had corroborated Gerry's statement, she'd got halfway to Jamie's house before she'd turned back. She couldn't imagine what it must have been like for him not to be able to say something, for fear of Gerry coming to harm. He must have felt torn in two. But it had still changed things between them. He'd deceived her and, even if that had been with the best of intentions, she had no choice but to cut him off.

The reason her relationship with Adam had lasted for so long was because everything was out in the open. They both knew where they stood and there was no need for deceit. It might look strange and undesirable from the outside, but absolute honesty was more important to Phoebe than anything else. She knew

Adam would never lie to her about where he was, or what he was doing, because there was no need. If he was with another woman, that was fine, as long as he didn't lie. But with Jamie, it had been different; she'd had feelings she hadn't allowed herself to experience since her ex-fiancé. When Eddie had cheated on her, in the worst way imaginable, she'd sworn never to be stupid enough to make herself that vulnerable again. But despite all that, the feelings she'd developed for Jamie had led to her taking a stupid risk by allowing herself to be part of a relationship that had the power to hurt her. But nothing Jamie could have said or done, no matter how painful, would have wounded her as much as his deceit. It didn't matter whether he'd lied for the right reasons; it had still proven what she'd always known – that trusting someone was a fool's game, and she'd been fooled far too many times already.

The worst part of it all was that the price of her mistake wasn't just hers to pay. Darcy had been so upset about not being able to go over to Jamie's to collect eggs from the chickens that she'd cried until she was sick. Even Norma was moping around, having missed out on her usual sessions at The Pines. Everyone was miserable, and it was all Phoebe's fault. Discovering what Jamie had been keeping from her, and the realisation that it meant her little sister was almost certainly dead, had left Phoebe with a kind of aching numbness. The dull pain had been constant, but when the full reality hit, catching her by surprise, it was excruciating. And Phoebe was certain no one could bear pain like that, if it was there all the time. Lucy couldn't be gone. A whole lifetime without her in it was impossible to imagine, and she didn't even want to try. That was why it was a relief when the numbness washed over her again, but the trouble was it never lasted long.

It wasn't helped by the fact that her mother had turned up at the cottage twice, steaming drunk and slurring her words. Phoebe had refused to let her in, so Janet had stood outside and ranted about everything instead, but the most shocking thing had been her claim that Phoebe's father was spending all his time at the allotments on the edge of the village. According to Janet, it must mean he had a 'fancy woman'. After all, she'd said, why else would he choose to spend every spare moment spreading horse shit over vegetables that probably wouldn't even grow? Phoebe could think of at least a thousand reasons her father might want to spend time away from his wife, but she didn't bother to open the door to speak to her. There was no point.

After what had happened with Jamie, all Phoebe's plans to retrain had been forgotten. She needed to get away from Apple-berry, and that meant having a stable, well-paid job to cover the running costs on her old flat, once Adam moved to New York. Phoebe hadn't told Darcy they'd be leaving; she hadn't even been able to face having the conversation with the little girl that she knew she needed to have. How was she supposed to tell her niece that her mother was never coming home? The person she most wanted to ask was Jamie, but with him out of the picture, there was only one other person she could turn to.

'You should have seen Ava and Darcy pretending to be butter-flies when I got to the community centre. They looked so sweet.' Scarlett took the cup of coffee that Phoebe had offered her when she'd come to drop Darcy off after dancing. The two girls had already disappeared to play with Darcy's dolls' house. With the children out of earshot, Phoebe seized her opportunity.

'I'm going back to London.'

Scarlett's mouth dropped open in response, and she set her coffee down on the kitchen counter. 'What do you mean you're going back to London? What about Darcy?'

'I'm taking her with me.'

'Why the hell would you want to do that?' Scarlett was the kindest, most even-tempered person Phoebe had ever met, but her face had flushed red and her tone was sharp. 'She loves it here, and so do you. Don't even try telling me that you don't, because I've seen Darcy and this place transform you since you came home.'

'It has been nice being back, especially having you around.' Phoebe reached out and touched her friend's arm, just for a moment. 'But, despite that, I can't be around Mum, not any more, not now I know Lucy isn't coming back. And this cottage... there are just too many memories of Lucy in every corner.'

'I can't even imagine what that's like. But if the police are right, it means you've already lost Lucy once.' Scarlett's voice caught on the words. Phoebe had told her about Gerry, but she hadn't mentioned Jamie's role in anything that had happened. 'Moving away and getting rid of Lucy's things won't change that, and it won't mean you can move on, because you never really move on from grieving for someone you love. You just gradually learn to live alongside that grief. Staying in Appleberry means you'll be surrounded by people who love you, and care about you. I know it's hard having your mother living just around the corner, but she's never going to change. It won't matter whether you're living a mile away, or ten thousand miles away. Don't let her take anything else away from you, Phebes, *please*, or from Darcy. She's taken far too much away from you both already.'

'You've got no idea how much.' Even as she spoke, Phoebe hadn't had any intention of elaborating, but somehow the words kept coming anyway. 'She slept with Eddie.'

'Your ex-fiancé, Eddie? You're joking.' Scarlett instantly clapped a hand over her mouth. 'Oh my God, I'm so sorry, of course you're not joking. No one would ever joke about something like that.'

'I only wish I was.' Phoebe felt nauseous at the memory. 'Or that I could convince myself it was all in my imagination. God knows my mother tried. I'd suspected something might be going on for a while, but then I caught them together.'

'Oh Phebes, why didn't you tell me?'

'Because it was too horrifying to admit to anyone. After it happened, my mother took her usual gaslighting to a whole new level. She claimed to have been comforting Eddie, because he was upset that I wasn't paying him enough attention. She'd already spent months denying that there was anything going on, when they were always sharing in-jokes together, or when she was blatantly flirting with him in front of me and Dad. She said I was jealous because they got on really well, and because men found her so attractive. After I caught them together, she still managed to convince Dad to talk to me and say it was my own insecurities making me imagine things.'

'How on earth did you stop yourself from killing her? Because I'd like to give it a go right now.' Scarlett was gripping her coffee cup so tightly her knuckles had turned white.

'At first I wanted to, but after all her manipulation, I just felt numb. I stopped feeling anything.' As painful as it was to recount now, Phoebe had begun to feel disconnected from the situation within weeks of it happening and it was a pattern she was beginning to recognise in herself. It was almost like she was watching herself in a movie. It had obviously been a coping mechanism, but she'd realised she was glad it had happened and allowed her to see Eddie for who really was. Although that didn't stop it leaving her completely unable to trust.

'I can't believe you had anything to do with her after that.'

'I know, but I think my new therapist has hit the nail on the head. She told me trauma can actually alter the wiring in the brain. It's the only reason I can come up with for why both me and Lucy continued giving Janet chances to prove she loved us, even after what she did with Eddie. And from some things Lucy told me, I think Janet tried it on with Callum too. But it's taken Lucy's disappearance to make me realise it's finally time to give up, and not just keep pretending to myself that I already have. Because there's no way I'm letting her anywhere near Darcy. I've lost my sister, and I'll never, ever stop missing her and wishing that she'd found a way to stay, but protecting her daughter is the one thing I can still do for her.'

'You've got no idea how amazing you are.' As Scarlett wrapped her arms around Phoebe, she didn't even try to pull away, because there were some situations when nothing else would do. 'Don't let Janet take away everything you've got here; there are so many people who love you and Darcy. Just promise me you won't make any rash decisions.'

'I promise.' Phoebe breathed in the perfume that had been Scarlett's favourite ever since they were at school. It was something else she'd always associate with Appleberry, and just one more thing she'd miss after she was gone.

28

Phoebe had read every article she could find online about how to break the news to Darcy that her mother had died. She still wished she could speak to Jamie, but she'd said such awful things to him, she was scared he'd tell her to get lost. Scarlett had begged her not to allow Janet to take away everything she had in Appleberry, but Phoebe had already wrecked one of the biggest things all by herself. She'd judged Jamie by the standards her mother had taught her to expect, and she'd thrown away the chance of something that might have been amazing, without Janet even having to lift a finger. So instead of speaking to Jamie, she was relying on advice from a website, to find a way of talking to Darcy that didn't scar the little girl for life.

She was in the middle of scrolling through the results of her latest search when an alert popped up with a notification from Facebook, and for some reason she clicked on it straight away.

Lucy Spencer tagged you in a post.

For a moment, Phoebe thought her heart might actually have

stopped. Her hand was shaking so much she could hardly click on the link. But when she did, it went straight to Lucy's Facebook page, and there was the post.

> Well, this is much harder to write than I thought, but it's time to say goodbye. The truth is, I'll have been gone for a long time by the time anyone sees this, and I scheduled it to appear once I knew the dust would have settled. I need the world to know that the reason I took my own life was because of my mother and she knows exactly why.

It was just a short paragraph, but by the time Phoebe had finished reading it, she felt as if every bit of air had been sucked out of her lungs. It was there, in black and white: Lucy was gone, and she'd been so determined to die that she'd meticulously planned every aspect of it, from her disappearance right through to the post that was now swimming in front of Phoebe's eyes.

For a moment, when the notification had come through, and her heart had leapt, Phoebe had allowed herself to hope that it meant Lucy was still alive. But now all hope was gone forever, and the pain was so powerful it doubled Phoebe over. The tears that were sliding down her cheeks had been inevitable, even though she'd have sworn just minutes before that she had none left to cry.

It was only when she finally managed to look at the post again, almost twenty minutes later, that Phoebe saw the responses popping up below it, from her sister's friends, recounting all the times Lucy had told them about things Janet had done. Her simple post had turned into something much bigger, a patchwork of stories spelling out just how awful a mother Janet Spencer had truly been. Seeing all the pain her sister had gone through reflected in those words made it hard to remember how to breathe. So many people had known and understood who Janet

Spencer really was, but neither she nor Lucy had ever believed anyone would.

It could all have been so different and she wished with every fibre of her being that Lucy had discovered another way to finally find her voice. They should have been sitting together now, reading all the comments, and raising a toast to the mask having been ripped away from Janet Spencer's face at last, and the whole world knowing who and what she was. But Lucy was gone, and none of the words on screen could bring her back. It was all such a terrible waste, and it was Phoebe who felt as if something had been ripped away from her, something that could never be replaced. Nothing would ever have been worth losing Lucy for, least of all their mother.

'You've got no idea how much I wish you were here.' Phoebe stared at her sister's profile picture as she spoke out loud, her eyes burning as she willed the message below it to say something different, or for a comment to pop up revealing that Lucy was coming back now everyone finally knew the truth. But it was never going to happen, and Phoebe had to face the fact that she'd lost someone she loved even more than she'd realised; someone who would leave a gap in her life for as long as she lived. She was going to have to find a way to help Darcy through that too, and she'd never stop wishing that it hadn't come to this.

29

What Jamie had done was unforgiveable, but he'd still wanted to try to explain. Not because he thought he deserved Phoebe's forgiveness, but because he couldn't bear the thought they might never speak again. He'd tried texting first, knowing she probably wasn't ready to speak to him. But by the time he'd decided to ring instead, in the hope she might pick up, if only to give him a piece of her mind, she'd blocked his number. If he'd gone rushing over to the cottage, trying to act like some kind of knight in shining armour, she'd almost certainly have told him where to go.

When Scarlett had rung to ask if he knew that Phoebe was planning to leave Appleberry, Jamie had been convinced he was ready for the possibility, but he wasn't. He understood that she probably couldn't stand the thought of spending another day in the cottage, waiting for Lucy to walk back through the door, and knowing she never would. Instead, there'd be someone else at the door eventually, probably in a police officer's uniform, delivering the news that her sister's body had finally been found. So he didn't blame Phoebe for wanting to leave Appleberry and never look back, but he still desperately wanted her to stay. Although if she did leave, he wanted to make sure her problems wouldn't just follow her. If Phoebe left Appleberry, and lost the support of Scarlett and her other friends, uprooting Darcy in the process, it might all be for nothing if Janet's harassment didn't stop too.

Jamie had spent the night after discovering that Phoebe was leaving, wide awake, going backwards and forwards about whether to try and speak to Roger or not. From what Jamie had seen of him, he was a stooped, servile-looking man – exactly as you might expect the husband of Janet Spencer to look. He probably couldn't stand up for himself if his life depended on it, let alone for his daughters. But by 4 a.m., Jamie had decided he had to try. Roger needed to hear that his wife's behaviour, and his own inaction, had driven one daughter to end her life, and the other to run back to London. It probably wouldn't make a scrap of difference, but at least Jamie would have said it. He'd had enough of keeping quiet, when he should have spoken up, to last him a lifetime. When he'd gone to knock at Roger's house, his neighbour had opened her door and for a moment Jamie had thought it was Janet, but then the woman's face had broken into a smile, and he'd realised she looked nothing like Phoebe's mother. Mrs Wolowitz, the Spencers' neighbour, had told Jamie that he'd almost certainly find Phoebe's dad down on his allotment.

The allotments on the edge of the village were adjacent to a disused railway line, from a route past the village that had closed back in the 1950s. For Jamie, that part of Appleberry had always had an eerie feel, as if echoes of the passengers who had passed through were somehow trapped there. He'd hung out near the railway line a couple of times with his friends, the summer before his parents had died, but the creepy atmosphere had put him off going back. This time his trepidation had nothing to do with imaginary spectres of the past, despite smoke from a dying bonfire swirling in the air around him. His apprehension was because there was a chance that speaking to Roger might make things worse, and he was determined not to let that happen. It was why he'd silently rehearsed what he was going to say to Phoebe's father all the way down to the allotments. But as soon as he saw Roger, all his careful planning seemed to be forgotten.

'I need to talk to you.' He was standing less than six feet away from Phoebe's father and, when the older man looked up, Jamie barely recognised him. Every other time he'd seen him, Roger's face had looked pinched and sallow, as if he barely saw any natural light. But now there was a golden tone to his skin and he looked almost relaxed, apart from the sadness in his eyes that no healthy glow could ever disguise.

'If you're from the parish council, the allotment association had a meeting last night and we're getting a skip to clear the debris from the sheds that blew down last winter. It would have been done by now, but no one would take any responsibility. I finally managed to persuade them that it'll only cost us thirty quid each, if we all club in, and we can get the allotments back to how they should look.'

'I'm not from the parish council.' Jamie could have cut him off sooner, but he'd been far too amazed by how passionate Roger was about the allotments. If only he'd channelled an ounce of that fervour into protecting his daughters. He clearly didn't recognise Jamie either, from the handful of times they'd met. Not even when he'd accompanied Janet to Jamie's place, just after Lucy had gone missing, and she'd tried to demand that he hand Darcy over to them. Admittedly, Roger had been looking at his shoes a lot of the time, but it wasn't the kind of incident that was easy to forget.

'Well, if you're looking to try and secure a vacant allotment, I'm afraid you're out of luck.' Roger smiled, looking for all the world like a normal man in his late middle-age. 'I had to wait years to get this one, and they won't get me off here until they carry me away in a wooden box.'

'Sounds like getting an allotment has made all of your dreams come true.' Part of Jamie wanted to take hold of Roger by the scruff of the neck and ask him how he could stand there, grinning like an idiot, when his younger daughter was dead, and his eldest was about to leave.

'Some might call it unambitious when it comes to dreams, but it's been a life-saver.' Roger smiled again, and something inside of Jamie snapped.

'It's a pity Lucy never got herself an allotment, then.' Every word was fired like a bullet, and Roger shrank towards the ground as if someone had actually fired a gun over his head.

'Who are you?' The older man's eyes darted left and right, as he asked the question. Jamie didn't know if he was looking for an escape route, or a witness, but he was out of luck on both counts.

'I'm Lucy's friend and neighbour, Jamie. We've met, actually, several times. I took care of Darcy when Lucy first disappeared. Do you remember her? Your granddaughter?' Jamie clenched his jaw so hard it ached.

In an instant, Roger's eyes had filled with tears, the sadness Jamie had seen magnified even further. 'We shouldn't have come to see you. I didn't want to, but excuses don't help, do they?'

'No, they don't.' It was like a bullet hitting him too, recognising a part of himself in Roger. They'd both made mistakes, but maybe the older man had felt every bit as trapped by the choices open to him as Jamie had done.

'When I said this place had saved my life, I meant it, because when Lucy disappeared and they told us she might be dead, I wanted to die too.' The pain was obvious in Roger's voice. 'I let the girls down, both of them, over and over again, but I didn't seem to be able to stop even after Lucy left. Janet has this hold over me that

I can't even explain, and I even started planning how to end my life, by going to Craggy Head, so that I could be with Lucy.'

'Why didn't you?' If Jamie's words sounded cruel, he didn't really care.

'Because then Phoebe would be left alone with Janet, and I'd have let her down again, too, and Darcy.' Roger pushed his glasses back up his nose. 'I finally got a letter telling me my name had reached the top of the list for an allotment, two weeks after Lucy disappeared, and coming here has been the only thing that's kept me going. She used to love being out in the garden with me when she was little, and she was always encouraging me to get an allotment. So I feel closer to her here than anywhere else. But when the police said last week that they're certain now Lucy went into the sea and never came out, I started questioning everything again. What right did I have to be alive, when my daughter wasn't? But I know Lucy would have wanted me to stick around for Phoebe and Darcy's sake. If my punishment had to be spending the rest of my life as Janet's whipping boy, no one could argue that I didn't deserve it. But I can live with anything as long as I've got the allotment to come to. What I couldn't live with was the thought of Phoebe having to take my place.'

'Phoebe's leaving. Moving back to London and taking Darcy with her.' The words sounded so matter of fact, almost as if Jamie were pleased she was leaving, when all he wanted was for Roger to say something that would make her want to stay.

'That might be a good thing, putting some distance between her and Janet. I know this is Darcy's home, but I wish to God I'd taken the girls away from their mother when they were that age.'

'Do you really think Janet will let Phoebe and Darcy have a quiet life, just because they've moved away?'

'The only way Phoebe will get that is if she cuts us off completely, and never tells us where she and Darcy are living.' The look in Roger's eyes reached a new level of sorrow, but he nodded as if to emphasise his words. 'When I realised that, it broke my heart, but how I feel doesn't matter, as long as they're okay. I can't let what happened to Lucy happen again.'

'Couldn't you just leave Janet?'

'If only it were that easy. It might be hell living with her, but I tried leaving once, just after Lucy left home. Janet was like a woman possessed; she wouldn't leave me alone, and she kept ringing the girls, and turning up at their places, all hours of the day and night, even though she was telling everyone – including them – that I was away on a training course. They never even knew I'd tried to leave, but I realised she wouldn't stop hounding all of us, and I knew it would have been even worse for the girls if I didn't go back. Janet's never going to stop, not until she's six feet under.' Roger straightened up. 'I'm glad Phoebe's getting out, while she's still got a chance. I only wish I'd pushed Lucy to do the same thing, and I won't ever be able to forgive myself for not having the strength to try. But she wouldn't want this life for Darcy, and I've got to get to Phoebe before Janet gets wind of her plans. I need to have the chance to say goodbye properly and tell her all the things I should have told her sister.'

'You're going now?' Jamie had planned to say so much to Roger, but in all the times he'd run through it in his head, he'd never once imagined Phoebe's father saying any of the things he'd said. The truth was, he'd expected the older man to want to fight to keep his daughter around, if only as a buffer for his wife's narcissism. Only it turned out that Roger wasn't the self-centred idiot Jamie had taken him for.

'I'm not going to miss my chance to say goodbye to a second daughter.' Roger grabbed the jacket that had been draped over the handle of a pitchfork, half sunk into the ground, shrugging it on and setting off in the direction of Kirkby Road, calling out behind him as he strode out, 'Thanks for letting me know about Phoebe's plans; you've been a really good friend to both my girls.'

'No, I haven't.' Jamie's response must have been lost on the breeze that suddenly seemed to be whipping the treetops into a frenzy, unexpectedly fast-forwarding the extended summer into autumn. He was walking in the same direction as Roger, without any real idea of where he wanted to go. Phoebe was going to be leaving, and cutting as many ties with Appleberry as she could. There was nothing he could do about it and, if he really loved her, he shouldn't even want to try.

Jamie could still see Roger up ahead of him as they turned in to Kirkby Road, but the older man's pace had continued to quicken, whereas Jamie felt as though he was wading through treacle. There had to be something he could do to change things, to bring about a different outcome, but the more desperate he was to come up with a solution, the more hopeless the situation seemed.

For a few seconds Roger disappeared from view, but then Jamie spotted him again, striding up the path towards his own front door. He wanted to call after him, to ask Roger to help him think of some way – any way – that Phoebe didn't need to leave Appleberry. If Jamie had believed there was any possibility she'd allow him to go with her, he'd have willingly left everything behind too. But the only chance he had of ever being allowed back in her life was if he had enough time to prove to her that he was the person she'd thought he was. Roger couldn't really want her to leave either; Jamie just needed to catch up with him.

Breaking into a run, he called out to Phoebe's father again, but Roger was already closing the front door behind him.

'It's not too late.' There was no one to hear Jamie speak, but for a split second he was sure he heard someone shout a response, and something deep down inside him was telling him not to give up.

Jamie carried on towards the house and, when he finally reached it, he started hammering on the door as if his life depended on. There was no response, but he wasn't giving up. He must have stood there for a least five minutes, knocking and calling Roger's name, and in the end it was Mrs Wolowitz who responded first, coming out of the neighbouring house.

'What on earth's going on?'

'I need to speak to Roger, urgently.'

'Like I told you before, I think he's down at the allotments and I think his wife's away on a—'

'Janet's gone; I've looked in every room in the house.' Roger suddenly yanked open the front door, shock written all over his face. 'She's taken everything out of the wardrobe and all the cash we had is gone too.'

'I saw her leaving first thing with a suitcase, but I thought she must be going on a trip.' Mrs Wolowitz widened her eyes. 'You didn't know?'

'No, I left for the allotments as soon as it got light. I wanted to get a head start on the clearance, before the skip arrived.' Roger still looked as though he'd seen a ghost, and he turned towards Jamie. 'You don't think Janet would do anything stupid, do you? After the message Lucy put online?'

'What message?' Jamie had no idea what the older man was talking about.

'It was yesterday.' Mrs Wolowitz shook her head. 'It was on some sort of timer, set up to post after she'd... after she was gone. Lucy blamed her death on her mother and I'm guessing Janet didn't take it well.'

'I've never seen her so angry; I was frightened about what she might do, but I didn't think there was a chance she'd harm herself.' Roger shook his head. 'I should never have gone to the allotment.'

'She took clothes and money, so maybe there's another explanation?' Jamie hadn't seen Lucy's message, but he could imagine Janet's reaction all too easily.

'Oh God.' Roger's legs seemed to give way, and he grabbed hold of the door frame to steady himself. 'She's had affairs in the past, but I always thought they didn't mean anything. I never thought she'd leave me. I put her before everyone, even when I shouldn't have. But I can't think of any other reason why she'd just leave and take so much money with her. She kept saying we couldn't trust banks any more, but now I think she must have been planning this for months, and Lucy's message was the catalyst.'

'Let's get you inside.' Mrs Wolowitz took hold of Roger's arm, and turned to look at Jamie. 'Do you know how to get hold of Phoebe? Her father's going to need her.'

Jamie nodded, not wanting to tell Roger's neighbour that Phoebe had blocked his calls. He could ring Scarlett and she'd be able to reach Phoebe. He doubted she'd want Jamie around when she got there, but he wasn't going anywhere until he'd seen her, because if there was even the slightest chance that she did, he wasn't going to miss it.

30

When Phoebe had got the call from Scarlett, telling her that her mother had walked out of her parents' home with a bag of clothes and close to three thousand pounds, but no indication of where she was going, she'd laughed. It was bound to be just another drama her mother had cooked up, no doubt in reaction to the message Lucy had put on Facebook. Janet needed to play the victim, and make sure her wellbeing was what stayed at the forefront of people's minds, so disappearing without a trace was almost textbook. People would immediately jump to the conclusion that 'poor Janet' was so distraught she had no choice but to leave, and some might think she was so devastated she'd be capable of doing what Lucy had done and ending her life. But Janet loved herself far too much for that.

It was only Scarlett's insistence that Roger was in a terrible state that persuaded Phoebe to go to the house at all, but she was fully expecting her mother to already have turned up again by the time she got there, or for her father to be following some kind of script he'd been put up to. Instead, she'd arrived to discover that Mrs Wolowitz had called the doctor, because she was so concerned about Roger. What had shocked her even more was finding Jamie sitting in her parents' front room.

'What on earth are you doing here?' Her voice sounded sharp, but it was shock rather than anger driving her response, because despite having no idea why in the world he was there, Phoebe couldn't deny she was glad he was.

'I went to the allotments to talk to your dad. After we spoke, I took the same route back through the village as him. When he went inside the house, I decided I needed to speak to him again, because I hadn't said all I needed to say.' Jamie searched her face, and he took a deep breath. 'I wanted to ask him to help me persuade you to stay. I know it's selfish, with everything that's gone on, but I promised myself I'd never keep anything from you again. I knocked on the door and there was no answer, but I wasn't going away until I'd spoken to him again. Eventually Mrs Wolowitz came out to see what was going on, and that's when your dad appeared and told us your mother had gone. Taking all their cash and most of her clothes.'

Phoebe looked at him for a long moment without saying anything, and it was Jamie who eventually broke the silence. 'Sorry, having me here is probably the last thing you want.'

'It's not that. I just need to try and get my head around what happened.' Phoebe took a step towards him, realising she'd had enough of hiding things too. 'I'm glad you're here.'

'You are?' Jamie's whole face seemed to light up. 'I was so worried about you and Darcy. I told myself I wanted to speak to your dad just to make sure he was finally going to step up, and be there for you. But the truth was that wasn't enough; the thought of you leaving was unbearable, because I'd miss you and Darcy more than I can say.'

'I'd miss you too. I *have* missed you, and so has Darcy.' Phoebe didn't know what it was about Jamie, but whenever she was around him, she seemed to completely lose the ability to filter what she was saying. 'Bradley came and saw me and told me the whole story about Gerry, and I know now that it put you in an unbearable position, and that you did what you had to in an impossible situation. I wanted to call you and say all of that, but after the way I spoke to you, I had no idea how you'd react. I couldn't face being rejected. Not again.'

'I could never reject you – you must know that?'

'After what you just said about going to see Dad, I do. And maybe now isn't the right time to leave Appleberry, because I've got no idea how he's going to handle this. Mrs Wolowitz insisted on going straight back up to check on him when I got here; she told me the doctor said he needs to rest.'

'Yes, and the doctor also gave your father some medication to help him sleep.'

'And has anyone tried to contact Janet?' After the incident at Darcy's party, she'd decided never to use the term 'mother' in relation to that woman again. Janet's own daughter wasn't here because of her terrible behaviour, and she didn't deserve to have the word applied to her. Lucy should have had an amazing life, and she could so easily have done if Janet had made a decision like this years before. Instead, there'd be an empty seat at every party Darcy ever had, and an empty space in the hearts of everyone who loved Lucy.

'Her number's just ringing out apparently, and Mrs Wolowitz offered to contact the police and report her missing. But they said it's too soon to start looking into it and everything points to her deciding to leave of her own free will. If she's not back in a few days, and no one's heard from her, then they'll investigate.'

'The police are clearly more aware of what my mother is capable of than I gave them credit for.'

'So you don't think she's really left for good?'

'I wouldn't get that lucky.' Phoebe shrugged. 'Sorry, you probably think I'm completely heartless.'

'I don't think I've ever met anyone with a heart as big as yours.' Jamie touched her hand, and it felt so good to be close to him again. 'Is it wrong of me to hope she's gone for good, if that means you can stay?'

'If it's wrong of you, then we're guilty of the same thing. What did my father say when you asked him to look out for me?'

'He said he'd let you and Lucy down, that he'd regret it forever, and that he'd take whatever Janet handed out as long as it meant you and Darcy were okay. He said he'd do anything not to let her hurt either of you.'

'And do you think he meant it?' So much hung on what Jamie said next and, when he nodded, her body sagged with relief.

'I know he did.'

'Then we'll stay, as long as I never think being here is wrong for Darcy.' She looked at him again. The only time things had gone wrong between them was when one of them wasn't being honest, so she had to take a risk on telling him the absolute truth. 'And right now, I think that staying in Appleberry, with you and the rest of our friends, is the best thing I could possibly do for both of us. We're already trying to find a way to get through each day without Lucy, and I can't help Darcy with that by myself. We are going to need a lot of support now and in the future.'

'I wish that wasn't the reason you were staying, but I'd be lying if I said I'm not happy that you are.'

'So am I. It's what Lucy wanted for Darcy, and I know now that it's where I'm supposed to be too.'

'You've got no idea how glad I am to hear you say that.' He was smiling, and Phoebe found herself following suit. She wasn't sure whether she'd ever stop feeling a stab of guilt when she smiled or laughed, and then remembered that Lucy was gone. But she never wanted Darcy to feel that way, and she knew Lucy wouldn't have wanted that for either of them. They both had to celebrate the moments of joy, whenever they came.

'I think I've got some idea.' As determined as she'd been to make the most of whatever pockets of happiness they could find, when she looked at him again she couldn't stop the smile from sliding off her face. 'There's something I need to ask you, something that's going to be really hard for both of us.'

'You can ask me anything.'

'I need to tell Darcy that Lucy won't ever be coming back and explain what happened in a way she can understand, before she hears it from somebody else.' Phoebe shivered; just picturing what that might do to the little girl brought tears to her eyes. She desperately wanted to protect Darcy from everything, but this was one thing she couldn't shield her beloved niece from.

'We can do it together.'

'Thank you.' This time, she took his hand and held it like she never wanted to let go. They were going to do it together and suddenly she felt like she could face anything with Jamie by her side.

31

_____

If Phoebe had expected the gradual realisation that Lucy was dead to soften the blow, once it became undeniable that she was, she'd been sadly mistaken. There were still times when the reality of it hit her like a hammer blow all over again. She'd take pictures of Darcy, like she had from the day she'd arrived, thinking she'd show them to Lucy when she finally came home. But then Phoebe would remember that she'd never get the chance to do that, and all she could do was allow the tears to keep coming. She'd always thought that crying was a sign of weakness, but now she saw it as a sign of strength: a symbol that she was carrying on, and somehow getting through another day, despite the agony of grief for the loss of her little sister.

She wasn't sure she'd have survived without Darcy and Jamie. They both gave her a reason to smile, every day, and it was because of them that she could picture a future without Lucy in it. It didn't stop her wishing that things were different and that her sister was still there with them, but she could spend her whole life wishing for something she'd never get, or she could focus on honouring

Lucy's last request. Her sister had trusted her to do the best for Darcy, and that drove her through the days when her grief threatened to overwhelm her. But there was something she'd been delaying, something she had to face, and today was the day. Jamie had been gentle but firm when he'd insisted they couldn't put off telling Darcy that Lucy was dead, and exactly a week after Janet's disappearance, they took the little girl for a walk by Lake Pippin.

For the first half an hour, they did what they always did, letting Darcy splash through the shallows with Norma and Fisher at her heels. Then Jamie reached for Phoebe's hand.

'Are you ready? Do you want me to start?'

'No, I need to do this.' She was already shaking, but they'd talked about this so many times, and Jamie was the only person she'd have wanted with her at that moment. He understood what it was like to lose a parent, and he cared for Darcy as though she was his own. Phoebe could see it in his face every time he looked at the little girl.

'Look, Auntie Phoebe, I found a red rock.' Darcy held out the rust-coloured pebble towards her aunt.

'That's brilliant, sweetheart. Do you want to take it home?'

'Yes, I can put it in a special collection to show Mummy when she comes back.' At first, whenever Darcy had spoken about her mother, she'd always get tearful, but now her words were matter of fact. She was as ready as she would ever be to hear the truth.

'Darcy, do you remember at your party, when I said that Mummy might not be able to come home?' Phoebe crouched down and took hold of her niece's hands as the little girl nodded solemnly. 'Well, I was still hoping then that she might come home one day, but now I know she won't.'

'Why not?' Tears were already welling up in Darcy's eyes, and the ever-present lump in Phoebe's throat felt ten times bigger.

'I'm sorry, sweetheart, but Mummy has died.' Every word felt like torture. The words sounded so harsh, and right up to the moment when she'd said the word 'died', Phoebe had almost backed out. But Jamie had told her to be honest with Darcy, and not to use words that might confuse her.

Four-year-olds didn't know what 'passed away' meant, but the little girl had some concept of death. Just a few days before, Betty, one of Jamie's chickens, had died, and he'd gently explained to Darcy that it meant she was never coming back. That they wouldn't be able to see the chicken again, because she was gone forever. Darcy had cried then too, but the three of them had talked about all the things they loved about Betty, and it had really seemed to help. It had been the catalyst they'd needed to decide whether it was now or never and, deep down, Phoebe had known that never wasn't an option, no matter how much she wished it was.

'Can I see Mummy? I saw Betty after she was dead.' A single tear fell from Darcy's eyes and plopped onto Phoebe's hand, and she wrapped her arms around her niece, suddenly having no idea what to say next.

'Do you want my help?' Jamie silently mouthed the words as Phoebe looked at him from over Darcy's shoulder, and she nodded slowly. She'd wanted to do this by herself, but she didn't need to be a hero; Jamie was there for her and leaning on him wasn't a sign of weakness, any more than tears were.

'Mummy went into the sea, darling.' Jamie crouched down beside them both. 'She was very, very sad, and nothing could make that better. So she went into the water and didn't come out. And that's why we can't see her like you saw Betty. But every time you feel like you want to see Mummy, me or Auntie Phoebe can show you pictures and videos, and you can hear her voice too. And we can talk about Mummy whenever you like.'

Darcy nodded, but the tears were coming much faster now, and Jamie's eyes were glassy too. 'I wish Mummy hadn't died.'

'Oh we all do, baby, we all do.' Phoebe's voice cracked on the words, and her throat was completely raw, as if she'd been screaming for hours. None of them could hide from the pain of Lucy's suicide; all they could do was keep clinging together. They stayed like that for what felt like forever, with Jamie's arms wrapped around Phoebe as she cradled Darcy on her lap. Norma and Fisher sat with them, too, not even getting up to move when the ducks came into view.

'Can we say goodbye to Mummy, like we did to Betty?' It was Darcy who eventually broke the silence, looking up at her aunt as her tears finally ebbed away.

'Of course we can, my darling. Any way you want to.' They might not be able to hold a funeral, in the traditional sense, but they'd find a way to honour everything that Lucy was. And Phoebe would never let her sister's little girl forget the mother who'd loved her more than life itself.

'I want to find some more stones, so we can put them round the flowers. Like we did for Betty.' Darcy had a look of determination on her face that her aunt had come to recognise, whenever her niece was on a mission. Jamie had buried Betty in one of the flower beds at the farm, and Darcy had collected stones to create a makeshift monument to her favourite chicken.

'All right, sweetheart. Do you want me to come with you?'

'It's okay, I can take Norma, she's really good at sniffing out the best stones.' Darcy smiled and it was like sunshine after the rain as she trotted off with the little dog in her wake.

'She is going to be okay, isn't she?' Phoebe leant against Jamie as she spoke.

'She's going to be more than okay, she's going to be brilliant, because she's just like her mother and her aunt.' Jamie pressed his lips against Phoebe's, kissing her gently before pulling away, and she let go of a long breath. He was right, Darcy was going to be brilliant, and the two of them would do everything they could to give her the best life possible. They'd never stop missing Lucy, but they owed it to her to be happy, and that was what they were going to do.

32

Two weeks after Janet's disappearance, she still hadn't come back. No one had heard from her and there'd been no cryptic messages or fingers of blame pointing at anyone on her Facebook page. She hadn't even responded to the post that Lucy had scheduled to tell the world who she blamed for her death. It was almost impossible for Phoebe to believe that her mother would have kept quiet in the face of Lucy's accusations, and every day she'd expected to see a message online from Janet protesting that she was the innocent victim. She'd never been the sort to run and hide; she'd brazen anything out, because she genuinely believed she was in the right. Always. And yet her silence spoke volumes. It was almost like Janet had been beamed up to another planet.

The police had eventually made some enquiries and the doorbell camera footage on the houses in her parents' street had shown footage of Phoebe's mother, in her favourite coat, hurrying down the road with her suitcase. It had been a windy morning, and she'd had her hood pulled up, probably being careful not to mess up her hair. Things like that had always been important to Janet, and it didn't surprise Phoebe to think of her worrying about something like that, even in the middle of walking out on her husband of more than thirty years. The police seemed to have concluded that there was nothing further to investigate, and Phoebe had begun to allow herself to hope that her mother might really never return.

When she'd gone to check on her father, as she did most days, she'd been shocked to find Mrs Wolowitz in her parents' kitchen. She'd told Phoebe she was still worried about Roger and that she'd been popping in to make sure he was eating properly, and she was making his dinner ready for when he got back from the allotment. Mrs Wolowitz had been widowed for at least ten years, and she was a similar age to Phoebe's dad, so maybe it shouldn't have come as a surprise that they seemed to have developed a close friendship in the wake of Janet's disappearance, but it did. Leaving Mrs Wolowitz to get on with the cottage pie, Phoebe had headed off to find her father.

'The allotment's looking good, Dad,' she called out as she approached him, and he stopped what he was doing and looked up. The lines he'd hoed into the dirt, in readiness for the next round of planting, were so precise, it was almost like someone had done them with a ruler. It was a stark contrast to some of the other plots, but her father probably needed to work within tight constraints. It was what he was used to, after all.

'I'm putting some broccoli and carrots in for next year. There'll be some garlic too; your mother never liked garlic.'

'I know she didn't, but you do, don't you?' Phoebe held a take-away cup towards him. 'I got you a latte from Maggie's café.'

'Your mother never liked coffee either. She couldn't even stand the smell of it on my breath.'

'Well, that's something else you don't need to worry about now.'

'Yes, but it's going to take some getting used to. All of this... you know, *choice*.' Roger raised his cup in the air. 'Here's to a whole new world of possibilities, I suppose.'

'You're going to be okay. In fact, once you get the hang of it, you'll love having so much freedom. And now that you've got it, you'll be able to come and see us whenever you like. Darcy's already asking when you're next coming over.' Phoebe had worried that her niece might be wary of the grandfather she barely knew, but Darcy had amazed her once again, and so had her father. He'd come over for dinner two nights after they'd told Darcy about Lucy's death, and she'd asked whether she could paint her grandfather's fingernails. He'd agreed, but only if he could paint Darcy's for her. Ten minutes later, the pair of them had been laughing together, co-conspirators, planning to give Norma a makeover by painting one of her toenails too. And Phoebe had started to see her father in a whole different light. It didn't make up for all the things he'd done, or didn't do, or for letting his daughters down. But she'd begun to realise that her father had been a victim in all of this too, and that some of his failings had been a misguided attempt to protect his daughters by constantly trying to placate their mother. Whatever his reasons, it was too late to change any of that now. All they could do was try and move forward.

'I don't want to stop you going back to London, if that's still what you want, but I'd really miss having you and Darcy around.' Even as he said the words, there was an undeniable sadness to his tone, and it was Phoebe's turn to shake her head.

'We're not going anywhere, not any more. Appleberry is Darcy's home, and it's mine now too.'

'I'm really glad to hear that, love.' Her father smiled and, despite the simplicity of the term of endearment, it meant the world to hear him call her 'love'. If he'd said anything like that before, it would have been enough to send her mother into a jealous rage. They'd all been robbed of so much that other people took for granted, but they were starting afresh and Darcy was leading the way. By the time they'd finished painting each other's nails, she'd already told her grandfather she loved him. They all needed to learn to be more like Darcy.

'We love having you around too.' Phoebe might not be able to tell him she loved him just yet, but they'd get there. They'd already come a long way in a very short time.

'I'm just so grateful you still want me in your life, and in Darcy's too. I should have been there for Lucy, and I'll never get the chance to make up for that. But I promise I'm not going to make the same mistake with you and Darcy ever again.' Her father's voice was gruff, and he had tears in his eyes that had nothing to do with the sharp autumnal breeze.

'I know you won't.' Taking a deep breath, she looked at her father again. There was something else she needed to say. 'When I was at the house, I couldn't see the rug that Lucy made, the one that used to be at the bottom of the stairs. You didn't throw it out, did you?'

The multi-coloured rag rug had been at the base of her parents' staircase for years. It was one of very few things made by either of her daughters that Janet had ever had on display. It had always made Phoebe jealous to see it there, but she hated the idea that it had been thrown away.

'Your mother took a knife to it, the day Lucy's message appeared on Facebook. We were upstairs on the landing, and she was screaming at me that I needed to go online and tell everyone it was someone's idea of a sick joke. But I'd seen what Lucy had written, and what her friends had said, and I knew every word was true. Your mother was angrier than I've ever seen her, and I just stood there while she carried on screaming. But then she spotted the rug and said that she was going to destroy everything in the

house that had anything to do with Lucy. I couldn't stop her, so...'
He hesitated for a moment and shook his head. 'Afterwards I
couldn't bear to see it lying there, ruined, so I brought it down
here and put in on the bonfire. I'm sorry, love, but you know what
she was like.'

'I do, Dad, I do.' For a moment, another question was on her
lips, and she very nearly asked it. She wouldn't have blamed her
father if he'd finally snapped, but she didn't want to know. In the
end she'd come to understand that some things really were best
left unsaid.

33

Over the years, the weather on Lucy's birthday had ranged from unseasonably warm, when hardy souls might risk going jacket-free, to bitterly cold, with hailstones big enough to dent the bonnet of Phoebe's car. That birthday must have been three years before Lucy's disappearance, when Phoebe had driven down to Appleberry to drop off a gift, but she'd been back on the road to London less than two hours later. There'd been so many missed opportunities to spend more time together, but Phoebe had meant it when she'd told Jamie she was done living with regrets. It was easier said than done, though and she wouldn't have known where to begin without the therapy she'd embarked upon. At every session, she still questioned whether there was anything she could have done differently to prevent Lucy from believing that taking her own life was the only option. Deep down she knew it wasn't that easy. Her sister's pain couldn't have been fixed by something Phoebe said or did. Lucy had been unable to reach out to anyone and, instead, she'd turned that pain on herself. It would never stop hurting that it had come to that, and, as Scarlett had told her, Phoebe wouldn't ever really move on from that loss. But she was finding ways to live alongside it, and to make life as happy as it possibly could be for her niece. So today was all about focusing on Darcy, and trying to mark Lucy's special day in a way that helped the little girl remember just how wonderful her mum had been.

This year, Lucy's birthday had dawned bright and crisp. It was mid-November and there was enough chill in the air to remind everyone that summer was long gone, but the sky was bright blue, and the light was what Lucy would have called perfect. She'd always wanted to be outside on days like this, even when they'd been young. Roger had bought them both mobiles one Christmas, fairly basic pay-as-you-go phones, which they'd had to keep a secret from their mother. But Lucy had been overjoyed to discover that her phone had a camera. She took pictures whenever she could and would try to recreate the light and shade of the images in her artwork. It had been her passion, and the weather on her birthday made it feel as though Lucy was sharing the day with them.

'She'd have loved this.' Phoebe took Jamie's hand as they walked along the beach at Craggy Head. The tide was out, and rock pools had formed in its wake, providing Darcy with an underwater world to discover that was suddenly at her fingertips. Norma and Fisher were following close behind, the two dogs having become almost her shadow over the past few months.

'It looks like Darcy takes after her mum.' Jamie smiled as Phoebe's niece popped another shell into her pocket. She'd told them she was collecting the prettiest shells she could find to put into the flowerbed at the cottage, which she called Mummy's Garden. They'd planted chrysanthemums, Lucy's birth flower, along with daffodil bulbs, daisies and a climbing rose for the fence, so that there'd always be colour. Darcy would often go straight out there after school and chatter away to her mum. What nobody knew was that her aunt often did the same thing.

When Phoebe had confided her worries to Jamie about Lucy's landlord one day asking them to leave, he'd finally confessed that the house belonged to him. It suddenly made sense why Lucy could afford the cottage, and why on earth the landlord would keep the rent so low when they could clearly be charging far more. It was just Jamie being Jamie, and doing a good deed for someone just because he could. Sometimes, Phoebe still found it hard to believe that someone could be willing to do so many kind things with no expectation of reward. Her mother had made her cynical, and it wasn't always easy allowing herself to be vulnerable by having such strong feelings for him, but she was getting there. Slowly.

'Darcy's like Lucy in so many ways, but she's her own person too and she's such a happy little girl.' Nothing brought Phoebe more joy than when her niece started to giggle about something and found it hard to stop; that morning it had been Norma's grunting as she gobbled up her breakfast. Darcy's laughter was a sound Phoebe would never get bored of; she just wished Lucy could hear it too. There were sad times as well, and, when she cried for her mother, all Phoebe could do was hold her and reassure her, as she had before, that it was okay for Darcy to miss her mum, because she did too. She'd found a therapist who specialised in bereavement support for very young children. Darcy had been along to a few sessions, and it gave her an outlet to express her grief, without her feeling she needed to protect her aunt from any of the difficult or conflicting emotions she must have been having. God knows Phoebe was struggling with those kinds of feelings, and she was a grown adult. But therapy had helped her understand it was okay to embrace the aspects of her life that she loved, without diminishing the grief she felt for her sister, or the gap that her loss had left behind. Darcy had to be feeling all of those things too, so she needed even more support than the adults around her. And Phoebe was just thankful every day that it seemed to be paying off.

'She is a really happy kid and that's down to you.'

'It's been a team effort.' Phoebe leant her head on his shoulder for a moment. 'The therapist is brilliant. But your farm was her safe place when Lucy first disappeared, and Darcy absolutely loves spending time with Dad now. I'm just worried she might start to forget Lucy. She asked me today what colour her mum's eyes were, and whether she was tall or small. There are pictures everywhere, but I don't think it's enough.'

'She won't forget Lucy, but Darcy's so young that eventually she won't have any real memories of her. What she remembers will be the things you've told her. Over time, the questions she has are going to change; they did for me, even though I was a lot older than Darcy when I lost my parents. What my grandmother did so brilliantly was to keep Mum and Dad alive for me by talking about them in an easy way, as if they were still around. She'd tell me that something we were having for dinner had been my dad's favourite. And when I was about to go to uni, she told me how my mum had nearly burnt down her halls of residence when she fell asleep with the chip pan on during her first week there. That's what you can do for Darcy. Just tell her little things all the time. It's like that saying, that a person dies twice – the first time is when they stop breathing, and the second is when their name stops being mentioned. We just have to make sure we keep Lucy's name alive.'

'She knew exactly what she was doing when she left Darcy with you for me to pick up, and she understood that I'd need to lean on you for support. I think she put us in each other's paths and I'd give anything to be able to tell her how grateful I am. But she should be here to see this, and I wish more than anything she was.' Phoebe's newly discovered tendency to cry didn't seem to be slowing down. Losing her sister had released a valve that had been shut off for years, but she'd realised over the last few months that she needed to stop trying to control difficult emotions.

'Me too and I don't know what I believe about all of that but, on some level, I think she does know. I'm so glad she thought I was good enough for you and Darcy, and as long as you let me, I'll keep trying to prove she was right.' Jamie kissed her and for a split second, she had the weirdest sensation they were being watched. But it wasn't a creepy feeling, it was as if the light had changed again, and it suddenly felt much warmer too. Even so, when Phoebe pulled away, she was surprised to find it was just the two of them, and Darcy and the dogs, on the otherwise deserted beach.

'You don't think it's strange that we come to the place where she died, do you?' Phoebe took hold of Jamie's hand again, as they continued down the beach.

'No, like you said before, she loved it here. She was always telling me she was off to Craggy Head to look for driftwood, or something else for her latest project.'

'That's why I wanted to make the birthday message for Lucy here, before we all meet Dad for lunch.'

'We'd better get started then.' Jamie bent down and picked up a smooth, flat pebble and then set it down on a clear stretch of sand in front of him. Forty-five minutes later the message to Lucy was complete; the words were spelt out in pebbles, driftwood and even some strands of seaweed. Darcy had also included the favourite shells she'd collected.

'Happy birthday, Mummy.' The little girl slid her hand into Phoebe's as she read the message aloud. 'I think she'll like that, don't you, Auntie Phoebe?'

'I know she will, and we can do this for her every birthday if you like.'

'And at Christmas?' Darcy gave her a hopeful look.

'And at Christmas, sweetheart.'

'Yay!' Darcy did a little skip and then a serious expression crossed her face. 'But we've *all* got to come. Every time.'

'Of course I'll come along if you want me to.' Jamie scooped her up into his arms and she grinned.

'Promise?'

'I promise.' He caught Phoebe's eye as he turned towards her, and she nodded. He'd already said he'd stick around for as long as she wanted him to. It was still early days, but she had a strong suspicion that might be forever.

'Come on then, let's go and meet Granddad for lunch.' Phoebe hung back slightly as Jamie started off down the beach, with Darcy riding piggy-back. Turning back towards the message, she breathed out.

'Happy birthday, Lucy-Lu. We'll take good care of Darcy, and I'll never let her forget her mummy. We love you.' Blowing a kiss into the crisp autumn air, Phoebe hurried after Jamie and Darcy, knowing that her father would be waiting to greet them all at the restaurant for lunch. They were a family now, the kind she'd always wanted, except there was still a huge part missing and there always would be. Lucy might not be by their sides, but they could keep her with them in their hearts, even though they'd never stop missing her. No one was ever really gone when there were people who still loved them, and Lucy was so very loved.

ACKNOWLEDGEMENTS

The Dear Reader letter at the front of this novel says a lot of what I might usually say here. So, I will focus on those who have helped me to shape Phoebe and Lucy's story into something I hope reflects the impact of their experiences. Primarily the thanks for this lies with my fantastic editors, Emily Ruston, Becca Allen and Candida Bradford, without whom this story would have been nothing like the final version.

Huge thanks to Danni Starley, the best social worker ever, who is sadly no longer with us, but whom I consulted in the very early stages of this story and who gave me her unfailingly brilliant input. I also need to give the lovely Lin West a big thank you, for her advice on therapy, and the procedures that are followed in taking on a client, or when a client may be at risk. To the team of therapists I've worked with on the impact of childhood trauma, and who it is sadly impossible to name here for reasons of confidentiality, thank you for everything you've taught me.

To my beautiful family and closest friends, including my writing tribe (The Write Romantics) for your unfailing support. Thank you in particular to the friends and family members who have had the generosity to share their stories about the impact of suicide, attempted suicide and mental health crises with me. This book is for L, who I know is loved and missed every single day.

My deep gratitude as always goes to all the reviewers who support the launch of my books and help get word out there, and to the entire team at Boldwood Books who are now too numerous to mention, but whose work I'm eternally thankful for.

And finally, to you, my readers. You have changed my life more than I can express, and allowed me to have a platform to tell stories like this which mean so much to me. Thank you all from the bottom of my heart.

ABOUT THE AUTHOR

Jo Bartlett is the bestselling author of over nineteen women's fiction titles. She fits her writing in between her two day jobs as an educational consultant and university lecturer and lives with her family and three dogs on the Kent coast. Her first title for Boldwood is The Cornish Midwife – part of a twelve-book deal.

Sign up to Jo Bartlett's mailing list for news, competitions and updates on future books.

Follow Jo on social media here:

ALSO BY JO BARTLETT

Second Changes at Cherry Tree Cottage

A Cornish Summer's Kiss

Meet Me in Central Park

The Girl She Left Behind

The Cornish Midwife Series

The Cornish Midwife

A Summer Wedding For The Cornish Midwife

A Winter's Wish For The Cornish Midwife

A Spring Surprise For The Cornish Midwife

A Leap of Faith For The Cornish Midwife

Mistletoe and Magic for the Cornish Midwife

A Change of Heart for the Cornish Midwife

Happy Ever After for the Cornish Midwife

The Midwife Series

The Midwife's Summer Wedding

The Midwife By The Sea

The Midwife's Winter Wish

The Midwife's Surprise Arrival

The Midwife's Leap of Faith

Mistletoe and Magic for the Midwife

The Midwife's Change of Heart

LOVE NOTES

LOVE IN EVERY CHAPTER

WHERE ALL YOUR ROMANCE
DREAMS COME TRUE!

THE HOME OF BESTSELLING
ROMANCE AND WOMEN'S
FICTION

 WARNING:
MAY CONTAIN SPICE

SIGN UP TO OUR
NEWSLETTER

https://bit.ly/Lovenotesnews

Boldw∞d

Boldwood Books is an award-winning fiction
publishing company seeking out the best
stories from around the world.

Find out more at www.boldwoodbooks.com

Join our reader community for brilliant books,
competitions and offers!

Follow us
@BoldwoodBooks
@TheBoldBookClub

**Sign up to our weekly
deals newsletter**

https://bit.ly/BoldwoodBNewsletter

Made in the USA
Monee, IL
29 January 2024

52274353R00184